I LEFT MY HAUNT IN SAN FRANCISCO

Praise for Mark Everett Stone

I Left My Haunt in San Francisco

"Another high impact, fast moving story from Mark Everett Stone. I am really enjoying seeing his growth as a writer reflected in the strength of his characters and am looking forward to seeing what the future holds for Kal."
—Michelle Herbert, Fantasy Book Review

"Kal Hakala is at his finest, throwing out one liners and sarcasm like candy at the local town parade. There's even some nifty new gadgets that would make Q green with envy. Stone concocts his tale with a generous helping of spells and weaponry, a dash of some familiar faces, a smidgen of new folks on the team, and tops it off with plenty of awesome battles with the Things That Go Bump in the Night .... A dish best read in one sitting because you won't be able to put this one down."
—Shay Fabro, award-winning author of the *Portal of Destiny* series

"The third episode of the Files of the BSI series is told with Mark Stone's trademark tongue in cheek humor. It keeps you wanting more with each turn of the page, to not only uncover the mysteries of the story, but also to enjoy Kal's quick but cynical wit."
—CP Bialois, author of *Call of Poseidon*, The Sword and the Flame series, and *Skeleton Key*

The Judas Line

★"This delightful Catholicism-infused quest fantasy stars a likable and original duo. Fr. Michael Engle, a pragmatic Catholic priest, and Jude, who has a considerably more uncertain relationship with God, are unlikely friends, but

when a blood-covered Jude runs into Mike's church asking for help, Mike listens to him, believes him, and joins him on a quest to find the Holy Grail, which Jude hopes will help him destroy a legendary and dangerous family heirloom. Along the way they encounter Cain, the Norse gods (drinking and watching *Bridge over the River Kwai*), and a Valkyrie with the requisite 'chainmail-covered pillowy breasts.' When Mephistopheles shows up, Jude manages to label him an Arch-Fiend of Hell without irony and without irritating the reader. Stone's depiction of magic is realistic and intelligent and his treatment of Catholicism refreshingly informed and three-dimensional. Even the obligatory near-apocalyptic ending is coherent, surprising, and exciting."
—Publishers Weekly Starred Review

"This evil mystery is a heavenly read! *The Judas Line* creates a believable mystery which links the ancient past to the present. By building on the ancient story of the betrayal of Jesus Christ by Judas, Market Everett Stone crafts a dark versus light drama which will keep readers hooked. I loved how Stone makes Jude an unwilling member of the darkest family threatening mankind. Simply brilliant!"
—Elizabeth Crowley, Fresh Fiction

"A fast-paced book which does not lack for history or adventure. The inclusion of death and destruction are a given and it is good that there is a lot of humour instilled throughout. I would say that if you're a fan of Jim Butcher's *Dresden Files*, you will enjoy Mark Everett Stone's work. Recommended."
—Michelle Herbert, Fantasy Book Review

"Evil does not die so easily. *The Judas Line* is a novel following Jude Oliver and the long family line that lies behind him, specializing in assassination, using the artifact known as the silver. Jude Oliver must find the origins and stories of his family to be able to end the Silver's legacy for good, with only a single Catholic priest by his side. Blending paranormal and biblical ideas, *The Judas Line* is a riveting thriller that should prove hard to put down."

—Midwest Book Review

"I have come to expect a lot from this remarkably talented writer, but Mark manages to please yet again by bringing new elements to his latest work. *The Judas Line* is, as anticipated, a lightning-paced thriller that is equal parts non-stop action and intelligent musing. This is, in fact, a surprisingly introspective book that delves into many interesting questions about the nature of good, evil, and faith. It's an enthralling read certain to delight and entertain, a well-crafted gem worthy of a place on any bookshelf."

—Michelle Izmaylov, author of *The Galacteran Legacy: Galaxy Watch*

"Mark Everett Stone takes the classic good versus evil plot line and puts his own unique spin on it. He effortlessly merges bible canon with the world and people he's created, adding off-the-wall humor to help break the tension. This book makes you laugh while making you think about the nature of evil and the power of faith."

—Jamie White, author of *The Life and Times of No One in Particular*

★ ★ ★ ★ ★ "A fast-paced read, with nail-biting moments and some humor thrown in. The characters were compelling, I often find myself picturing them in my head .... I can't recommend this book enough."

—Lisa McCourt Hollar, Jezri's Nightmares

"Once in a great while, a book comes along that challenges you to think outside the box. *The Judas Line* is one of those

books. I was absolutely amazed at the way Mark Everett Stone has taken religious stories and beliefs and intertwined his own tale of power, evil, friendship, sacrifice and redemption. The action is nonstop and the characters will stay with you long after you finish the last page."
—M.E. Franco, author *Where Will You Run?*

"The pacing is flawless in every respect .... Never before have I found a work of fiction to be so captivating. It picks you up, sits you down, and it does not let you even think about getting back up. A word of warning: Hide your pocketbooks, because once you read this, you will spend your next paycheck on every Mark Everett Stone book available."
—Grace Knight, author of *Sun And Moon* (2013)

What Happens in Vegas, Dies in Vegas

★ ★ ★ ★ ★ *"Things To Do In Denver When Your Un-Dead* was one of the most refreshing and original books I have read in a long time and the sequel is just as exciting as the first. In fact it may just be better than the first .... Exceptionally well-written and entertaining."
—Jerzri's Nightmares

"Vegas is non-stop action that will leave you with whiplash.... Stone leaves you gasping for breath by the end and of course, enjoys taunting the reader with the prospect of a third book in the series, which I will be waiting anxiously to read."
—Shay Fabbro, award-winning author

★ ★ ★ ★ ★ "A cracking good yarn from first to final page, no question .... Mark has cemented himself solidly into the position of Master in my self-created niche of Paranormal Suspense Thriller writing. His command of his art grows exponentially with each work of his that I read....Two very

enthusiastic thumbs up for a job well and properly done."
—Jeffrey Hollar, The Latinum Vault

"Don't expect a minute of down-time, for Stone is a zero tolerance taskmaster who brings a complicated plotline and well fleshed-out characters to heel and makes it look easy. What you *can* expect is for Stone to surprise you repeatedly, satisfy you completely and leave you wanting more."
—AJ Aalto, author of *Touched*

Things to Do in Denver When You're Un-Dead

★ ★ ★ ★ ★ "If you crave a really enjoyable Paranormal Suspense Thriller to read, THIS is your book. It grabs you from the very first page and drags you along (snarling for you to keep up) and dumps you at the feet of one of THE most unexpected plot twists of an ending that I have ever read."
—Jeffrey Hollar, The Latinum Vault

"If you like quick wit, sadistic charm, and bad-ass gadgets, then you will enjoy the hell out of this book."
—Shay Fabbro, award-winning author

★ ★ ★ ★ ★ "An absolute pleasure to read. It is witty, funny, dramatic and a well thought out paranormal with very fine storytelling. I couldn't put it down!"
—Clarrissa Lee Moon, author of the series, *The Nightwolves* and *Celeste Nites*

"I have really enjoyed reading this book .... The story could just be one of guns, blood and guts and magic, but ... Mark Everett Stone has made these characters seem real."
—Michele Herbert, Fantasy Book Review

"This is not a story for the faint of heart or stomach, nor for

those wanting a plot with any connection to reality. Personally, I'm really looking forward to the promised sequel."
—Gordon Long, TCM Reviews

"A fantastic read and very easy to follow. The way Mark combines magicians, zombies and super ghouls with a Bogart-style ultra sarcastic officer of the 'Bureau' makes you want to keep on reading. I highly recommend this for everyone—not just those into stories of the un-dead."
—G.R. Holton, author of *Soleri, Guardian's Alliance* and *Deep Screams*

"Five stars, two thumbs, fantastic! From the moment I began the first page to the final flip of the last, I was hooked .... The writing is sharp, fast and engaging."
—Patti Larsen, author of *Fresco, Wasteland, The Diamond City,* and *The Ghost Boy of MacKenzie House*

"The blending of dark twisted humor in this chilling tale is utterly perfect, written with a sure hand. Comedic timing is everything, and author Stone has perfected the classic one-liner .... Make no mistake folks, this isn't for the faint hearted ... the sarcasm is used as a brief respite in the fastest paced action horror that I have read in a very long time."
—Suzannah Burke, aka Stacey Danson, author of *Empty Chairs*

"In a first and quite brilliant novel, Stone proves himself equally adept at feverishly fast-paced action, edgy wit and banter, and the weaving of a richly satisfying and fresh world of mystery and intrigue. Write on, my friend."
—Michelle Izmaylov, author of *The Galacteran Legacy: Galaxy Watch*

I LEFT MY HAUNT IN SAN FRANCISCO

FROM THE FILES OF THE BSI
BOOK THREE

MARK EVERETT STONE

Seattle, WA

Published by Camel Press
PO Box 70515
Seattle, WA 98127

For more information, contact www.camelpress.com
www.markeverettstone.camelpress.com

Cover design by Sabrina Sun

I Left My Haunt in San Francisco
Copyright © 2013 by Mark Everett Stone

ISBN (Paper): 978-1-60381-927-5
ISBN (eBook): 978-1-60381-928-2

Library of Congress Control Number: 2012955538
10 9 8 7 6 5 4 3 2 1
Printed in the United States of America

To Brandie,

Thanks for keeping me sane

Also by Mark Everett Stone

The Judas Line

Things to Do in Denver When You're Un-Dead

What Happens in Vegas Dies in Vegas

Coming Soon:

Chicago, The Windigo City

Omaha Stakes

Contents

Prologue

San Francisco: 1890
On the corner of California and Dupont Streets

The graying man in the outlandish, threadbare soldier's uniform paused for a moment and stared at his palms, which were both sweaty and shaking. It wasn't the chill of the January evening that caused his limbs to tremble and twitch, but something deeper, beyond soft flesh, closer to the bone. He felt the frigid clutch of inevitability.

"Oh my good lord God," he breathed, lips blue and spittle dribbling into his full goatee, shot through with gray. A moment later his knees gave way and he collapsed.

Alice Mortimer, sometimes called Half-Penny Alice by the uncharitable, saw the man in the shabby uniform lying on the pavement and fell to her knees at his side, her cheap blue dress pooling around her knees.

"Oh, my Emperor," she moaned, cradling his head to her ample bosom after removing his large, feathered top hat and tossing it to one side. Sweat-soaked gray hair spilled out in a dirty halo around his head.

The man she called the Emperor opened his eyes a crack. Twin brown orbs, bloodshot and rheumy, stared up at the woman whose makeup did nothing to disguise her advancing years. In those eyes were a terrible clarity, and the woman fancied she could hear an eerie, yipping laughter. "Alice … what a fool I have been …" he began weakly, voice rough and choked with phlegm.

"Nonsense," she crooned while stroking his forehead. "You are the wisest man I know, my love."

He broke into a rattling cough. "I am … no Emperor. What have I become?"

Tears trickled down Alice's pudgy cheeks, streaking her thick makeup. "You are a symbol of hope and pride to this city, my love."

"An … idiot, more likely." There was more coughing and the sound of death in the old man's lungs. "So … much time … wasted."

She smoothed his hair and crooned, "No, my love, not wasted. You have done great things. Accomplished so much. You are loved."

"An … idiot, Alice. That's what I am."

A police officer, seeing that the downed man was being cared for, ran off to summon a carriage. Around the couple, a small crowd had begun to form. Several people recognized the prone man.

"Not an idiot, my Emperor," Alice insisted, "but a good man, which is to say only an idiot when it comes to matters of the heart."

The man sighed heavily. "Alice," he moaned. "You speak truly." The man shuddered as more coughs racked his frail body. "In front … of me the … whole time, but I … never saw …"

"Hush, my Emperor … Hush, my love."

But the man didn't hear her words; instead he gazed at the darkening sky. "Oh, how I love this city. It has been … so good to a … madman. Oh, how … cruel the fates are to now … grant me sanity."

"I know, my love," Alice whispered, laying her cheek against his. "I know."

They stayed huddled together long after his tired heart had stopped beating.

* * *

San Francisco: Present Day

The big man staggered up the stairwell, blood trailing behind him on the concrete steps.

He didn't know what building he was in. All he knew for sure was that it housed a bank on the first floor and that alarms had been tripped. Checking his watch, he reckoned he had about four more minutes before the cops arrived. Not enough time for much, except to die.

The wound in his belly hurt like a bastard. He had ripped free the bottom two buttons of his flannel shirt to clamp a hand over the wound. Although his large hand kept his guts from spilling out, it couldn't stem the inevitable drip, drip, drip of blood. His jeans were soaked in it and he fancied he could feel his shoes filling up.

Eighteenth floor … He'd made good time, but fatigue was taking its inexorable toll on his legs. The flyer wouldn't come for him in an enclosed space, but there were other things, terrible things, things that even a steel security door would not discourage. From below he heard the sound of rending metal.

Speak of the devil, he thought.

No more time to waste.

With a sigh of resignation, he began to climb again just as the first mournful howl drifted up the stairwell like a promise of pain.

Twenty-fifth floor … The man's legs were burning and shaking with fatigue.

Out of shape, he thought. *Should have worked out more, I've gotten soft.*

From below came baying, deep and shuddering. The man fancied he could feel the stairs vibrate.

Twenty-eighth floor … More blood escaped from between his fingers and a stream of it streaked the stairs. He knew he was dying, his time running out along with his blood. The hound would soon be upon him, ripping him apart as easily as a cat could rip apart a sparrow. It could shred a bull elephant without much effort, let alone a half-dead human.

"Keep moving, you bastard," he said aloud, his face distorted in a scowl of pain and self-disgust. As he climbed, he moved the fingers of his free hand—the one not holding in guts—along the blood streaming from his wound. At the twenty-ninth floor—the belling of the hound much closer, a sickening, deep, razor of sound that raised the hair along his forearms—he tore his blue flannel shirt open, spraying the remaining buttons everywhere, and drew the bloody finger along the torn t-shirt beneath. Three times more he ran his finger through blood and three times more he touched the shirt, drawing a word. One small word, that was all he needed. He could then die in peace, knowing he would set free something more terrible than the hound onto the creatures that had killed him.

Finally the word—simple, three-lettered—was finished. He leaned back against the exit to the roof and prayed that the flyer was not there, that he would be able to make it to the edge in time.

The roof alarm sounded as he pushed through the door, feet crunching on pea gravel pressed hard into tar. *There!* He cast weary eyes on the edge, only a couple dozen feet away.

Whoosh!

Cursing, the big man ducked as a massive, taloned paw tore through the air where his head had been. The paw collided with the stairwell door and ripped it from its hinges, tearing it from its steel frame as the creature passed overhead, giant wings beating hard, blowing gravel across the flat-topped roof.

It hurt so much, the wound in his belly. He was so tired … He needed to stop, to sit—needed to simply lie down and forget it all. Hadn't he done enough for his country, for his people?

No.

There was one more thing to do, one small thing. He had to die, and his death would unleash Hell upon the creatures that threatened San Francisco. Big-booted feet propelled him toward the edge as the flyer banked and started to come around for another pass. Behind the man, a large shape filled the stairwell, a misshapen form with glowing, cancerous red eyes.

"Goddamn you," the man rasped through blood-stained teeth. "Goddamn you all."

Less than a second later, barely a breath ahead of the shape that had leapt at him from the doorway, ahead of the flyer that had come so close, he was airborne.

As he fell, the man smiled in victory, a cruel, terrible smile—more a baring of red teeth than an expression of joy.

I wish I could be there, he thought, seconds before his death. *I wish I could be there at the end. When they all die.*

Chapter One

Bad News from Bay City

It had been two months since I'd been "recruited" back into the Bureau, back to Warehouse in D.C., and things really sucked the big one. BB (my boss, the director) had me training the Green Peas, new recruits to the Bureau of Supernatural Investigation and fresh meat for the grinder. Months ago a psychotic ex-agent/magician had murdered almost half of the Bureau's one hundred active agents, magicians and scientists, rendering it weaker than it had been since its inception in the late 1700s. From that moment the director had been scrambling to enlist the best and the brightest from the military, police and all the federal alphabet agencies in order to rebuild the ranks. A good agent was a one in a million individual, the elite of the elite and specially trained to hunt and kill those Supernaturals that preyed upon mankind. Even with special training, the average agent had the life expectancy of a mayfly.

The World Under (that strange dimension where Supernatural creatures come from) didn't care if we were understaffed; it still spat out the Things That Go Bump in the Night to harass the citizens of the U.S. of A. (the Straights). It was a tough job, keeping their existence a secret from the outside world, especially in this digital age where everyone had a cell phone with a built-in camera and recorder. Can you imagine the panic and religious hysteria if John Q. Public found out that vampires, werewolves and demons were *really* out to get them? It would make Superstorm Sandy look like a Spring shower.

Normally those recruited by the Bureau would be sent to Coronado, California, for a thirty-three week stint of SEAL training, to weed out the ones who couldn't hack the fast-and-furious pace the Bureau imposed on its agents. That training was the best available for covert operatives of an über-secret government organization.

Unfortunately for Mama Hakala's only boy Kal, BB had no time to turn such a large number of recruits into SEALS, so he cherry-picked the best and brightest and had me supply the requisite instruction so they could be up to the task of killing Supernaturals.

Oh, yippie.

BB knew I hated training the Green Peas because after surviving an unprecedented ten years in the Bureau, I'd seen a good many of them die or wash out in the first couple of months. Nothing like watching a Black Widow spider the size of a Buick sucking the juices out of a rookie agent to put a damper on your enthusiasm. I tried to pack my teams with veterans whenever I could, or at least with people who had survived their first year.

However, thanks to my vendetta against a legendary Finnish monster from the *Kalevala* (the Finnish national epic, sort of like Norse Mythology on Quaaludes), I had gone AWOL (by faking my own death) and broke the last six months of my contract with the BSI. Now, instead of burying me in a deep dark oubliette in the middle of the Antarctic, BB had consigned me to working with the Peas. I would have preferred a nice, cozy prison cell; it would have wreaked less havoc on my blood pressure.

And not just the Green Peas, but what I privately referred to as the Dried Peas—the older, tougher contingent of returnees. But I'll get to them in a moment.

I reflected upon all that had happened as I stood in the combat room, the huge space within Warehouse ("Warehouse" is what we call the BSI offices—an actual warehouse divided into several sections—that houses all our martial training facilities). Twelve men and women dressed in olive drab camo stood stiffly at attention while I paced back and forth in front of them. The three-inch thick wrestling mat under my boots made soft, irritating, squeaking noises as I considered the Peas, a sour taste in my mouth. Each sported contusions from hand-to-hand training, some more than others, and most tried unsuccessfully to hide signs of fatigue. That morning, before martial arts, I had them working archaic weapons training (you never know when a hand axe will come in handy) and knife fighting. I had, in my just and learned opinion, been easy on them. Had I been harsh, most would have been in Medical receiving the benefits of Healing magic.

"All right, Peas," I grated through the aftermath of a vodka hangover. The hazy headache had stubbornly resisted the vast quantities of ibuprofen and acetaminophen I'd taken earlier. "You haven't totally embarrassed my beloved Bureau today, thank the Good Lord Jesus Christ." I was well aware that two agnostics, four Jews, four Muslims, an Episcopalian and one atheist comprised my motley crew, but I still made them toe the Christian line just to get under their skin. Necessary? No, but I had to get my jollies where I could.

Looking at their battered faces, I felt the faint tug of sorrow that always hit me when I faced Green Peas. In the next two years, if they didn't wash out, six of these twelve would be buried in the cemetery of their choice, while the other six would cash out with a serious load of greenbacks, having been subjected to a spell called an Interdiction that would keep them from leaking any sort of information about the Bureau and/or the World Under. If the surviving six were smart, they would invest their money wisely, but most were barely in their mid-twenties, and I knew the money would most likely wind up in the safe of a Ferrari dealership rather than a bank.

In my opinion, most were punks who wouldn't cut the mustard, but a couple had serious potential. Only time would tell.

"Get yourselves back to your teams, get some chow and hit the rack," I barked. "Tomorrow will be more hand-to-hand because I don't trust you lot to kill a pixie with both hands and a grenade!"

All twelve double-timed out of there before I could change my mind and order them to run laps around Warehouse. I'd done that a few times, just for grins and partly because being a good agent requires an amazingly high threshold for frustration.

"Still hard on the Green Peas, I see," said a familiar, sardonic voice.

I bit back a grin and turned to Wilkes, Colorado native and an old football rival of mine. I'd become reacquainted with the man when on assignment in Denver. He'd been invaluable in the identification of a serial killer named the Organ Donor. Back then I figured he'd make a good agent and I'd been right. Older than most recruits (he was a spritely thirty-six, just like yours truly), he loomed over normal humans, a refrigerator-sized man with all the essential muscles to lift the big weights: Volvos, forklifts, etc.

"You've been an agent for what ... six months or thereabouts, if that?" I drawled, giving him the old stink-eye. "Come back and run that big mouth of yours off when you've seen a year or two."

Wilkes ran a huge thumb across a still red two-inch scar extending along his left cheek to the side of his nose, a memento of an encounter with a valraven (a malicious, Supernatural shape-shifting raven) that had been plaguing cattle ranchers in Wyoming. Wilkes, part of Team Delta, tracked the beast to Devil's Tower and took it out with automatic-weapons fire, but not before it attacked. The former detective from Denver took a swipe from a talon that laid open his cheek to the bone. He'd opted against a magical healing, stating that the scar would be a constant reminder to duck next time. In my opinion, he probably thought it gave him a rakish air.

"Well, I passed *your* training," he grumbled. "And I see you're still a hard-ass about it."

"I have to be." I shook my head as I moved toward the exit, waving goodbye to those agents who didn't merit my Remedial Training classes. Sadly, there were so few. Blood and gore were splattered across my mind's palette. "If these Peas die because I didn't train them hard enough, then it's on me. No one is going to be harder on them than me and if some live because of my training, then I've done my job."

"You sound like my DI, preparing me for war."

My hand paused on the doorknob and my voice became heavy while the vodka headache that pulsed my temples seemed to grind at my brain. "I've told you before, Wilkes—"

"We are at war," he finished softly.

"Exactly." Taking a deep breath, I opened the door and entered the long hallway that connected all the different rooms of Warehouse to each other. Fortunately for my hangover, the Dorms were located next to the Combat room. Unfortunately, Warehouse was large enough that I still had to endure a goodly walk down the hall.

"Aren't you supposed to be deployed with Kappa?" I asked the big man who followed me—the world's scariest ex-football player, ex-Army Ranger bodyguard.

He scratched his black crew cut. "BB had me replaced. Scuttlebutt is, he is rebuilding Zeta team and wants me to help choose the team members."

I raised an eyebrow. "He tell you this?"

Wilkes pulled his own eyebrow trick. "No, that's why I used the word 'scuttlebutt.' "

We reached the door to Dorms and I put my right hand on the black plastic plate on the wall next to the knob. It warmed momentarily as five different spells ascertained my identity. I didn't know what would happen to an unauthorized person attempting access and I didn't want to. Over the years I'd witnessed a lot of spell-related deaths. None were pretty and most required a bucket, mop and wet-vac for clean-up.

Every time I placed my hand on a scanner, I broke out in goose bumps. Sure, I'd been told time and time again that the damn things were foolproof, but it only took one time, one slip-up, to reduce the Bureau's best agent into steaming pile of lime Jell-O.

The lock gave a soft *click* and I let out a breath I didn't know I'd been holding. Wilkes must have heard it, though, because he said, "You do that every time. You're the most paranoid man I know."

"I'm also alive," I muttered, opening the door to the agents' living quarters.

Like firemen, we are required to sleep at work while on duty.

Unlike firemen, we are always on duty, so our spacious rooms in Warehouse are the closest things we have to a home. There is plenty of room to house all fifty agents and team magicians, plus the gaggle of scientists and research magicians, but at any given time at least one team is out in the field cleaning up the messes the World Under is kind enough to provide.

Our recent heavy losses always in mind, we experienced an empty feeling whenever we entered Dorms.

One wall, dedicated to an eight-by-fifteen-foot flat screen, was showing another episode of *Wipeout*, the current fave of our younger Green Peas. At first glance I thought it was a bunch of sophomoric crap, but almost immediately it sucked me in and I found myself sitting in one of the many leather recliners in front of the TV with all the other emotionally constipated agents, laughing my ass off.

Yeah, juvenile humor. Gets me every time.

Another long hallway arrowed straight through the common area, passing the closed doors of occupied and vacant living quarters. Each agent had his/her own bedroom, living room, toilet, washer/dryer and entertainment center with cable television. It was a lot like living at Embassy Suites, only without the chocolates on the pillow and complimentary breakfast buffet. Because we spent nearly every day together, privacy and alone time were more valuable than gold, so it wasn't unusual to see DO NOT DISTURB signs on doorknobs.

Recently, due to our manpower shortage, BB had taken my advice and re-hired those former agents who had become restless living among the Straights and craved to rejoin the dangerous world of covert ops. Outside the BSI, life was too banal and ordinary, devoid of dangerous purpose. Their experiences had made them larger than life; they no longer fit into the tiny niches the Straights wanted to force them into. They needed to be with others who understood how hazardous the world could be.

It all sounded great on paper, but I'd forgotten what cocky dickweeds most agents are (dare I lump myself into that category?). Now I had to deal with those who thought they knew it all and believed re-training was a waste of valuable time. I also had to take on the ones who had let themselves go physically and whip them into some other shape besides round. Those returnees are the "Dried Peas" I referred to earlier. More carbuncles on the butt of my existence.

The last two months had sucked huge.

Wilkes and I found ourselves in the kitchen and dining area, where we prepared our meals and generally ate like starving badgers. At any given time, even in the wee hours, Bureau members would sit at the tables in comfy chairs stuffing their faces. An agent's life involves killing Supernaturals, training, killing more Supernaturals, and more training. We burned a lot of calories, and if you're wondering why all the training, here is my answer: better to be a well-trained monster killer than a poorly trained and dead monster killer. Today's monster hunter could easily become tomorrow's monster crap.

I nodded to the few agents and magicians eating a late lunch and hunted down my private stash of Lucky Charms (the words "Property of Kal Hakala, do not touch for fear of a Painful, Very Permanent Death—Not Kidding" were written in bold black marker across the front), a bowl and some milk from a stainless steel industrial-sized refrigerator. Moments later I dove into marshmallow and whole grain heaven.

"You have something on your mind," I mumbled to Wilkes around a mouthful of cereal.

Wilkes shot me an ingenuous grin. He couldn't quite pull it off. "Everyone wants to know if you're going to re-hitch in four months." He stared me straight in the eye and didn't blink.

Crap. I knew it would come up eventually. Four months and my current contract would be complete and I could leave the Bureau a free man, walk my own path, no longer burdened by the icy need for revenge against the monster who killed my sister. I had slain that particular dragon. No longer would I have to tote that barge and lift that bale. I was rich, fat off of ten years of fantastic pay—I spend very little—so I could buy a Caribbean island and relax in the sun.

And do what?

Get fat? Grow old gracefully?

Not hardly.

"Don't know." More cereal went down the hatch. *Munch, munch.* I had a girlfriend now—Jeanie, a magician and a damned fine one. Found her in France in the year 1943 during a rescue mission turned sideways. She had decided to return with me to the twenty-first century, an era that was kinder to a black woman than England during WWII. She had brought a little emotional stability into my life, which was a dubious gift at best. As an agent, I was far more effective as a damaged, psychological misfit.

Jeanie's influence threatened to transform me from a half-crazed, elite soldier into one that was less effective. Could I live with that? Could I die with that? All I knew was that the thought of living or dying without her hurt me on a visceral level.

"Not sure yet," was my answer.

The big man snorted, his scar flushing a darker purple. "Figures. You get any more slippery and you'll slide right through the cracks in the universe."

I had a scathing retort ready, really I did, but at that moment a high-pitched *ping!* sounded in my head. A new bone-induction earpiece the size of a dime rested behind my ear, alerting me to an incoming call. Both earpiece and subvocal microphone (which looked a lot like a small circular bandage affixed to the throat) were to be worn at all times, even in Warehouse—an extra security measure since the attack a few months ago.

My finger lightly touched the mic. "*Go for Kal,*" I subvocaled.

The soft voice of Andrea, BB's Receptionist (executive assistant and personal bodyguard) slid into my skull. "*Kal, BB wants to see you, sharpish.*"

"*Got it. On my way.*" I slurped down the rest of the cereal (never, EVER, waste Lucky Charms) and waved goodbye to a bemused Wilkes.

Because my clothes smelled like BO and wet ass, I figured it was time for a change and ducked into my room. The bowl of milk resting on the floor next to a plastic toy Winnebago tucked into a corner had remained untouched since this morning. My Brownie friends must have been sleeping in. I had rescued the little guys from a Catholic church about a year ago and those tiny milk junkies could perform dry-cleaning that would blow your socks off. From my handmade oak armoire, I pulled out a U2 concert t-shirt and a fresh pair of jeans and made ready to see the man. Drifting from the Winnebago came an instrumental version of "The Devil Went Down To Georgia." Maybe the Brownies knew something I didn't.

I leaned over the toy vehicle and whispered through the music, "Dirty clothes in the hamper; the shirt has a rip. If everything is mended and clean by the morning, then the Mallomars are on me."

The music paused for a split second then resumed as if there had been no interruption. I had just guaranteed freshly laundered and mended clothes. Gotta love them Brownies.

Some Supernaturals deserve to live.

My long walk down the hallway to BB's section of Warehouse was not without its own peril. Spyeye spells and cameras watched my every move while ID spells buzzed underneath my feet as I stepped on silver spell Shapes lurking beneath neutral-colored cut pile carpeting. Security had been beefed up to the point that, if I were not the real Kal Hakala but some sort of doppelgänger, I would have been reduced to just so much ionized gas before I had walked ten steps.

Once I was past the door to the reception room, Andrea tossed me a carefully crafted dispassionate smile and had me place my hands on the Receptionist's Desk for further ID checks. Spell Shapes probed my palms with a warm tingle as she kept one of her hands underneath the desk, aiming a double-barreled shotgun loaded with silver spell Shaped deer slugs at my tender nether regions.

"You're clear, sir," Andrea beamed—a genuine grin—and waved me toward the door to BB's office.

Biting my lip on my usual retort to someone calling me "sir" (my Dad is a sir, not me), I pressed on through.

The first Director, the one who had hired me, had been a hell of an agent, but he liked his trappings of power: an office big enough to house a semi, a wet bar that cost more than the GNP of Mexico, and a desk that looked as if it had been dreamed up by Gene Roddenberry.

BB believed in a more Spartan working environment. Only half a semi could fit into the office and his desk was far subtler than a set piece from the original *Star Trek* series—black, sleek and ordinary-sized.

Before it would have been a hike to reach the director's desk, but now it was merely a pleasant stroll across hardwood and wool throw rugs. When I reached my destination, the director waved a hand toward a cushioned mahogany chair.

Benjamin Bauer had been one of the best agents in the Bureau's history and the longest serving—until I came along—but he made an even better administrator. Efficient, smart and incorruptible, he was the finest boss I'd ever worked for, not only because he could out-sneaky *me*, but because he knew what had to be done to get the job done. B.S. and BB never got along; there were several heads of the Federal alphabet agencies who found out the hard way that bullsquat didn't pay.

Everything regarding the BSI was classified TOP SECRET. Officially, we didn't exist. It was a shadow agency and we were its shadow people, moving in the twilight world of the Supernatural. Some might think it a lonely existence, but in the field we wielded awesome authority and BB was, in effect, one of the most powerful men in the world, answerable only to a handful of people plus the President. That power was yet another reason why there were so few of us. Hard to stage a coup on a large nation with only a hundred people.

The Joint Chiefs often complain about the power the BSI wields—that the organization is not required to produce flow charts or adhere to standards practiced by the other agencies. However, their rampant jealousy means there are enough eyes on the BSI that the abuse of our power brings a swift response. It is a form of control that has worked well for the last couple of centuries.

"Please sit, Kal," BB said in his usual terse fashion. Slim, trim, average height and weight, he was a dapper man you wouldn't look at twice, but if you ever landed on the wrong side of his temper, you would never forget him.

I felt a slight twinge of apprehension at his weary tone. "What's wrong, boss?" When BB fretted, nations collapsed.

Without a word, he tapped a complex rhythm on the desktop and the dark surface shimmered for a moment. Springing to life between us over the desk was a hologram—a shimmering, 3D representation of what looked to be a crime photo.

A dead man lay on the sidewalk. He had been a big man, with a massive chest and arms. He wore a wife-beater t-shirt under a torn blue flannel shirt, blue jeans and light brown Timberline boots. I took in all these details, but it was difficult to take my eyes off his head.

There wasn't much of it left. The dude must have fallen from a great height because when his skull was introduced to the sidewalk in a shining example of deceleration trauma, it was pumpkin on the pavement time.

The hologram was too good, with no smearing or jittering, and the image was displayed in bright, nauseating color. "Oh damn, boss," I gagged. "That's wrong on so many levels."

"Yes, it is, Kal," he replied, voice filled with a bucket load of sad.

Alarm bells went off in my head. "You knew him?"

BB's watery gray eyes speared me through his wire-rimmed glasses. A sheen of sweat slicked the area of his forehead where hair used to be. "You knew him, too, Kal. It's Thomas Mace."

Oh crap.

Chapter Two

New Tricks for Old Dogs

Thomas Mace, a blast from the past. I remembered him like it was yesterday. Big as a bus, strong as a bulldozer, and quietly competent, Mace had been one of the best martial artists I'd ever met. A few months after clearing out a nest of vampires in Texas—my first real mission with the Bureau—he had resigned. His four-year contract had run its course. That was ten years ago. Even among the elite, he'd been elite.

I stared closely at the grisly photo. The flesh of the face was stretched, bloated and covered with blood that ran from his ears, nose, mouth and eyes, but if I squinted, I could almost make out his homely features. All around the body was a butterfly spray pattern of blood, as if he'd fallen onto a giant, red, Rorschach test. It formed a macabre backdrop for his still form.

"What the devil happened, BB?" I asked, unable to tear my eyes away.

"He jumped."

I was aghast. "Suicide? Mace wouldn't do that." It was easier to believe that pigs could sprout wings and fly south for the winter than that Thomas Mace had killed himself.

BB tapped the desktop and another pic replaced the crime scene photo, a grislier one. It was a still from Mace's autopsy. The Y incision with its thick sutures stood out like an affront on the pale, waxy skin of his chest and abdomen. BB pointed to another series of sutures just below Mace's navel, running in a jagged, horizontal line, about eight inches long.

"I believe this is why," he said simply.

I studied the gash. "He was gutted … and whatever did it wasn't very sharp. The wound is too ragged for the blade of a knife. Some sort of garden tool?"

"Whatever it was ripped deep into his intestines and tore them to shreds." BB sighed and shook his head. Removing his glasses and rubbing his eyes, he added, "You want a drink, or is the hair of the dog too much for you today?"

Go figure that he would know about my hangover. He knew everything. While I was considering taking him up on the offer, my tired brain finally made a connection. I would have made it sooner, but the vodka headache had given me an ongoing case of brain-freeze. "This has to do with me, doesn't it?"

As he poured brandy into a snifter, he sighed. "Yes. Somewhat. Now, I suggest you have a drink. You will be glad you did." At my nod he poured me a shot of Liquid Ice Vodka and brought it over.

The smooth, organic alcohol burned a trail down to my stomach and settled in for the winter. *Damn, that was good.*

"Okay, boss … spill." I braced myself.

A few more taps to the desktop and another photo hung in the air between us. My breath caught in my throat and every nerve in my body screamed for me to *do* something.

It was the wife beater t-shirt from Mace's body, bloody and torn, but what had not been visible from the crime scene photo, what caught my eyes and held them with an irresistible power, was a word written in blood. Written in big, bold, red letters along the right side, running vertically from waist to armpit, was the word KAL.

"A message," I whispered, stomach flipping and flopping like a landed fish, "for me."

BB nodded. "I believe he knew he was dying and wanted to send a message, a message to have you come to San Francisco to investigate his death. I think he jumped because he was being pursued. It was a last-ditch effort to alert us."

"What makes you think he was being pursued?"

"The building he jumped from housed a bank, Trident National, on the first floor. Mace deliberately broke in through a window, setting off the alarm, and then accessed a secure stairwell, setting off more alarms, *then* made sure it was securely locked behind him." He called up another pic, this one of a steel fire door that had been twisted and torn from its frame. Gaping holes had been rent into the metal. "I guarantee you that, while Mr. Mace was indeed strong, he lacked the power to do *this*."

No, Mace had not done *that*. Whoever or whatever tore those holes in that door had claws like tungsten carbide steel and the strength of an elephant. The door must have lasted all of three seconds before it had broken.

BB continued, pulling up more photos to illustrate his narrative. "He climbed all thirty flights *in less than five minutes* while bleeding profusely. A heroic feat by anyone's standards. Once on the roof he leapt to his death, landing near two police officers who had come to investigate the alarm."

Here BB took a long pull from the snifter, swilling thousand-dollar-plus brandy like Budweiser. "Once his body was identified, it raised flags here and I had Ghost retrieve all the data."

Ghost was a friend and the Bureau's cybernetic specter that haunted the information superhighway. Once human, he had found his way into cyberspace—a point of no return. No encryption could resist his electronic advances, making him one of the most dangerous entities on the planet. If BB weren't so incorruptible, and Ghost rather divorced from human conceits, they could have carved out their own little Empire long ago. I thanked God every day that they were above such things.

"I want it, boss." My tone brooked no argument.

BB raised one slightly graying eyebrow.

"Please," I added.

He nodded.

Time to test the waters. "I want Canton."

"Thought you might."

Of course he did. "You want me to go," I accused.

A slight twitch of the lips was my only answer.

Bastard.

"And Winch."

Nod.

"Wilkes."

Another nod.

"Half-Life or Alex."

There he set the brakes. "Can't let Alex go, Kal, I need him to train our new magician Green Peas. We are still a good dozen short. Half-Life won't leave Malcom's team and I will not force the issue."

I understood. BB was in a full-court press to replenish the ranks and magicians were rarer than honest politicians. When I brought Jeanie back with me from 1943, my return was not as heralded as her willingness to join the Bureau instead of our British counterpart, MI-7. Alex, our best and brightest in all things magical, would probably be locked away in Special Branch (magical and technical R&D) for the next couple of years until we had a full roster again.

"Then I want Jeanie." *Boy, did I ever.*

"Jeanie, as you well know, is in Baton Rouge, Louisiana, with Team Alpha, taking care of their Loup Garou problem. She will be there for the foreseeable future." He crossed his arms. "I can give you Rat."

Rat? "I'd rather have the clap." The kid made perverts look Amish. I seriously believed he hadn't left a *Playboy* magazine in the whole place without its pages stuck together.

"Tweezer, then."

"He's half an idiot. And that's the good half."

"Then grace me with a compromise, Kal."

"I'll take Ilena." The little magician was more than competent.

BB normally grim face became grimmer. "Arye won't let her go, you know that."

"If you asked as a favor, he would. I don't think he'd pout."

"I could," he said meditatively. "But I won't. I need him like I need you, like I need every decent agent I can get my hands on. I don't need an angry Arye at this point."

"Have Team Gamma stand down until I get back." Arye could use the vacation and I could use the magic.

"That might work."

"It will. You've been working us to the bone because you've had to. Most of my Green Peas might live through their first mission, so borrow from that pool if something pops up."

BB finished off his cognac and took our glasses to the wet bar, pouring another shot each. "You can take one more. Who do you want?"

I shook my head. "No more. Five will be enough. Ilena can function as an agent. It's not the usual team the Bureau fields, but I want this thing to run lean and mean."

He nodded. "I see." Another long drink of brandy. "You realize that Thomas was a good friend of mine. This has to be handled and handled swiftly."

I stood and came to rigid attention. "Boss, someone or something killed one of ours and we have to respond. You know me; you know what I am capable of. If anyone can find Mace's killer, it will be my team and me. I promise you that."

"That's why I am letting you back into the field, Kal," BB said with a sigh. "That and the fact that Thomas asked for you, and I will not gainsay his last wish." More of the hideously expensive cognac passed his lips. I'd never seen him drink so much. "Go see Alex; he'll have some gear for you. I'll have him meet you in Combat."

Before I made it back, Alex's voice vibrated behind my ear, asking me to meet him on the firing range. That had my blood pumping because if anyone could create a fun and portable WMD, it would be Alex.

The little magician was a walking nerd stereotype in his usual birth-control glasses, plaid sweater vest, perfectly creased tan slacks and penny loafers. Despite all that, for some reason he'd been scoring quite a bit with the ladies lately. If I didn't trust his moral character, I would have said he was using magic.

"Whatcha got, Alex?" I inquired. The range comprised six firing alleys, each a hundred feet long. The place was conspicuously empty except for Alex and me and a shoebox laden trolley cart. The unusual conditions put a blip square on my radar. That and the Cheshire grin on the magician's face.

"I did it, Kal!" he cried, almost vibrating in place like a tuning fork.

Once again I remained heroically silent as a plethora of smart-aleck remarks tried to shove their way past my lips. Instead, I treated him to my patented stare, which he ignored. Maybe I needed a new patent.

With a flourish, he lifted a shoebox from the trolley and held it out.

"Gosh, Merrels," I drawled, grabbing the shoebox. Something *clunked* inside. "How'd you know my size?"

"Open it!"

"Relax, kid, you're going to burst a vessel." I tried to act all nonchalant, but his excitement was infectious. I popped the lid to see a matte-black pistol—a size 13 if the box was any indication—big enough to make a Desert Eagle look like a sparrow.

"What the f—"

He didn't give me a chance to finish. "I did it, Kal! It's the prototype, but it works!"

"Is this what I think it is?" I pulled the weapon from its cardboard case. It was surprisingly light for a pistol of its size, but the barrel was four inches too long and the rough-textured grip almost too wide. Big and bulky.

Alex's smile threatened to split his face in half. He nearly blinded me with a display of very white teeth. "Yes! It's a smart gun! The first of its kind."

"Okay," I said dubiously. Did I shoot it or use it to beat someone to death? "Give me the lowdown."

"It's made of shatter resistant ceramic and NewTanium. There are platinum spell Shapes worked into the grip that scan the user's aura along with a plate where your thumb rests." He pointed to a shiny obsidian patch the size of a quarter. "That's tech, and it scans your DNA from your skin cells. If someone besides you attempts to use the weapon, it will lock up. If they continue, it will deliver a charge of 50,000 volts."

I smiled. "Well, that's just too cool. What does it fire?"

His grin became even wider, which was almost humanly impossible. "That's the good part."

"*That's* the good part?"

"It's an auto-sizing pistol, which means that it fires any round up to 20mm."

Holy crap!

Yeah, I reckoned it was the closest thing to a WMD I'd get my hands on. As I admired the double handful of sleek lethality, Alex handed me a fat clip.

"Take a look."

So I did. The bullets in the clip looked like your standard 9mm Parabellum, but the jacket looked kind of funky, smooth and definitely non-metallic, grayish. I gave Alex a look he knew well.

"Caseless ammo," he explained proudly. "The jacket is a form of lightweight, thin and strong cellulose that burns when the weapon is fired. It is smokeless and leaves virtually no residue, so there is minimal cleaning. All your rounds will be like this; just specify the caliber and any special mods and you'll get 'em."

"Explosive rounds, too?"

"Kal, we can make anything, including armor piercing, flachettes, or needle rounds."

"Needle rounds?" I was amped. I wanted to find one of the great alligators in the sewers of New York and test it out.

Alex pulled out another fat clip and took the pistol from my hand, inserting the new clip into the fat grip. He then sighted down the firing range at a mannequin posed at the end, in front of the wall of sandbags. "I'd thought you'd never ask," he said, just before squeezing the trigger.

Bdda-bdda-bdda! The pistol made a soft stutter, much like the sound a wrench makes when removing lug nuts. A hole the size of my fist appeared in the mannequin as tiny bits of shredded plastic went flying. Four more stutters later and the mannequin was reduced to so much polymer confetti.

"Good shootin', Tex!" I whistled in appreciation. Alex was such a little squib of a geek that it was easy to forget he had had SEAL training as well.

"Thanks," he replied, ejecting the clip. "Thing about needle rounds, not quite as damaging as explosive rounds, but they leave a lot of metal inside the body and the clip holds five times the capacity. Perfect for the unarmored adversary."

"Damn, kid, you need a raise." I took the weapon gently from his hands and stared at it lovingly. "How does it adapt to the various rounds and how are the spells powered and what's the battery life of the tech components?"

"There are small diamonds embedded in the resin of the grip. They supply the energy for the spells and are recharged by heat. Any kind of heat, be it from your body or from a warm stovetop. The barrel and the inner chamber … well, that's technical."

I gave him a sidelong look. "Meaning I won't understand."

He nodded. "Best way to put it is that it has morphing internal components that allow for bullets of various caliber to be used."

Cool. My gun was a Transformer. Optimus KickAss Prime.

"Just remember to use the caseless rounds, Kal, because there is no ejection port. This is the most dangerous handgun in the world. It can go from semi-auto to fully automatic with a push of this slide here." He pointed out a small lever next to an odd looking little knob. "It is also the most expensive, well … at least this one is. R and D on the first of a kind is always the most costly."

"What's that?" I asked, caressing the little protrusion.

"Silencer. Left for 'on' and right for 'off.' "

"Magic?"

"Of course. As long as there is a charge, it will work well. You can fire about a hundred normal rounds silenced, perhaps four hundred of the needle rounds. One other thing, Kal, since this is the first of its kind, as the owner, you get to name it."

Damn. "Kid, you are too cool for school. I owe you big."

A chuckle. "Figure out a way to get me out of this nuthouse and that will be payback enough."

Oh, damn. "Aw, sorry Alex, no can do. It would be easier to take BB's cognac away than pry you loose from Special Branch."

The kid's face fell so far I think it might have bounced off of Hell.

In an effort to turn his frown upside down, I pointed to the trolley. "What's in the other boxes?"

His skinny face took on a little animation again as he began to open boxes. "These are the latest in armor." A white, button-down oxford shirt hit me in the chest.

I held up the shirt. "What? This couldn't stop a toothpick."

He grinned. "Look at the buttons."

Okay … shiny. Too shiny with a deep luster and a sparkle that caught the eye and wouldn't let go. "Crap … diamonds?"

The little magician grinned. "Artificial. Not quite as effective as the real thing, but we discovered a way to make them in quantity at a fraction of the usual cost."

"So what's the punch line? Cloth steel?"

He shook his head. "Nothing so obvious. The shirt absorbs kinetic energy, so if a bullet hits it, all that energy is absorbed into the bottom three buttons."

I whistled in admiration, but as I stared at the shiny buttons, something niggled at the back of my mind. "Bullets travel pretty fast, kid, how can the spell react so quickly?" I was still trying to wrap my brain around what was really troubling me.

"Bullets don't outrun magic, Kal. There is a two-meter field around the cloth that senses incoming projectiles, and that field is powered by the buttons on the cuffs. Anything faster than fifty miles per hour will have its kinetic energy bled from it as it travels through the field. Every test we have conducted has proven its efficacy."

My fingers played with the bottom three buttons. "You said that the kinetic energy absorbed is stored here, in these buttons?"

"Yes."

"How much energy can they store?"

"A lot."

"And what happens to that energy?" The thought that had been bothering me was swimming to the surface of my mind.

"Where are you going with this, Kal?" His tone held a note of caution. He knew me well.

"Trust me. What happens to the energy?"

"The buttons release it slowly over a period of time so as not to damage the wearer."

I scratched my head and slid the clip of depleted uranium rounds into the pistol. "How many in the clip, Alex?"

He narrowed his eyes at me, certain I was up to no good. He was right. "Forty."

I smiled. "Can you prep one more clip, please? I doubt I'll need it, but you never know." Alex nodded and opened another shoebox.

While he readied the clip, I took the shirt, walked the hundred feet to the sandbags at the end of the alley and draped it there—sleeves spread wide. By the time I returned, Alex had a total of two clips ready.

"What now, Kal?"

"Oh, now it's time to conduct a little experiment."

"Will we need to alert Security?" By that he meant everyone in Warehouse.

"Gosh, Alex, I sure hope not." Giving him a smile I know didn't do a thing to reassure him, I took aim at the shirt.

Usually I wore earmuffs to dampen sound, but I flicked the dial to the "on" position for the silencer and trusted the spell Shape to work … that, and the sound baffles along the ceiling and side walls. Shooting weapons indoors can produce sounds of over 140dB, which is louder than Led Zeppelin playing "Whole Lotta love."

Fire blossomed silently from the barrel of the great weapon with surprisingly little kick. My first bullet hit the shirt dead-on center and clattered to the ground, kinetic energy spent. The round was perfectly undamaged.

"Told you." Alex wore a crap-eating grin on his boyish face.

"I had no doubts about that, kid," I murmured.

"Then what?"

"Just watch." I continued to fire, and as the tenth round hit, the bottom three buttons began to emit a faint glow. At round twenty they were shining like mini-stars. Twenty-five and the shirt began to smoke. I flicked the slide with my thumb to full automatic for the last fifteen rounds.

It was a tribute to my training that I actually hit with at least twelve of my next shots. At least I think I did … it really didn't matter because somewhere in the middle of the rapid-fire burst the three man-made diamonds exploded with a roar that rattled my teeth.

A wall of scorching heat and dust accompanied the pressure wave that blew back my hair and tipped over the trolley. I leaned into the blast and managed to keep from being knocked ass over teakettle. Behind me Alex gave out a tiny squeak of alarm as he was taken for a ride.

I should have worn ear protection because even the sound baffles did little to lessen the noise that assaulted my ears.

Once the dust had settled and Alex crawled out of whatever hidey hole he'd found, I took note of the damage. Shirt … gone. Sloped bank of earth-filled sandbags … mostly gone. Good chunk of the floor, still there, but singed.

Spitting grit from my teeth, I said, "That is what I think they would call an Epic Fail."

Chapter Three

There's No "I" in Team, Unless You Spell It That Way

Later on, after answering a ton of questions and enduring a marathon session of butt-chewing from BB, the unnamed weapon of the apocalypse and I made our way to a new section of Warehouse, not as big as the others, but one I felt was vital nonetheless. I called it The Place.

Okay, not a creative name, but that didn't lessen its worth. In brief, The Place was a combination library, study hall, boardroom for meetings and testing facility for Peas. Located in a less-used section of Records, it was where the Bureau stored the largest library of Supernaturals in the known world. In the past studying up on the various Supernaturals had been optional, albeit strongly recommended, but over the years I had come to realize that in the field, lack of the most minute piece of information could kill. So, at my insistence and with BB's help, we created The Place for agents to get the skinny on the Things That Go Bump In The Night. All agents were required to spend at least four hours a week of study time, no exceptions. Many objected, but BB had given me *carte blanche* when it came to all training matters and his stick was the biggest around.

This did not make me popular.

Part of all good training is studying. Operatives aren't all about shooting and blowing things to hell and gone; there is also strategy, tactics, and up-to-date intelligence. While the senior agents were afforded the luxury of setting their own study hours, I made sure that the Green Peas studied every day and I tested their knowledge of Supernaturals and what was needed to kill them.

The meeting room was dominated by a long, dark oak table surrounded by ten plush leather chairs. In front of the chairs, each laying flat in their own niche, were ten RediPads, the most technologically advanced tablets in the world. Each niche was actually a RediPad recharge port and link to the Supernatural database housed on a Cray Jaguar VII supercomputer, a stand-alone system located ten feet directly beneath The Place, shielded by steel-reinforced concrete.

My new team (no designation yet) sat in stunned silence after my briefing on our mission. The bunched muscles at the corners of Canton's jaw and Winch's clasped hands, white with strain, were the only indication of their enormous anger and consternation at the death of a friend.

Canton, his face carved in copper-colored stone, had known Mace the longest. They had been on the same team for two years before I came along. It was clear that his Mescalero Apache stoicism was strained to the breaking point.

"We have to find out what happened," he stated flatly, obsidian eyes flashing in anger.

Winch, his girlfriend and one of the best snipers I'd ever met, nodded, eyes moist, her girlish features set in harsh lines. After a few seconds, Ilena nodded grimly. The magician hadn't known the former agent, but the details of his death obviously shocked her.

Wilkes held up a huge hand. "I'm sorry, Kal, but I have a couple of questions."

"Go ahead."

The former Homicide Detective nodded to Canton and Winch, who stared at him impassively. "All due respect to a fallen comrade, but does this fall into our purview?"

Canton's anger finally surfaced for others to see. "Wait a damn second—" he began.

"Hold it!" I snapped at my friend. "I understand how you feel, Canton, but let him speak."

As quickly as his anger flared, it died. He nodded and sat back, crossing his long arms, straining the thick cotton of his blue button down across his shoulders. The marine-style haircut he wore these days bristled with ire.

"Like I said," Wilkes continued as if the outburst had never occurred. "I have to wonder if the murder of a Bureau agent, even a friend, falls under our authority. Sounds like a case for SFPD."

"How do you explain the steel door?" Winch asked acidly. Two bright spots of color dotted her cheeks. She looked like Betty Boop with a bad attitude, curves in all the right places over hard muscle. "The one on the first floor with the big holes in it?"

The question didn't seem to bother the big man, who leaned back in his chair, tapping on his RediPad. The WallScreen behind me came to life, showing the battered door in question. "You have two tears," he began, as red dots appeared next to the foot-long rents. "While violent and impressive, these by themselves don't necessarily point to a Supernatural. Two or three men with axes could have torn the door from its hinges and made these holes."

Canton held his peace—a remarkable feat, considering the bright shade of terra cotta he was turning. Winch's mouth flattened to a thin, bloodless line.

"Good point, Wilkes," I conceded, picking up my RediPad and tapping a few keys. The image on the WallScreen changed to one of a gravel-coated rooftop—the distinctive buildings of the San Francisco skyline in the background. Lying on the gravel and tar composite was another steel door, this one also bent and torn off its hinges. It had a single rent on one of the short ends.

Wilkes shook his head. "So the man or men took an axe to the roof access door."

"Normally I would agree with you but that torn section is on the *top* of the door, and preliminary analysis shows that whoever or whatever tore the door out of the frame hit it from above and that the door was *open* at the time it was ripped away."

Canton was the first to see it. "Something flew over and tried to hit Mace, but nailed the door instead, causing that hole and tearing the door from the frame."

I nodded. "One other clue, Wilkes, was the message Mace left for me on his shirt. He clearly meant to tell me that Supernaturals were involved."

"Seems kind of thin," he muttered, eyeing the picture of the ruined door.

"Thin or not, we're going. This is big and bad. I feel it in my gut."

Winch smiled suddenly. "Well then, that's enough for me, boss."

Within moments after I'd been assigned the San Francisco mission, BB arranged for an empty building downtown to serve as a base and hired one of the many Bureau-sponsored construction companies to renovate a loft to my specifications.

When we arrived at the loft the next morning, we were lugging cases and cases of armaments, which we stowed away in a specially prepared secure room called, creatively enough, the Armory. Only I had access to the vast array of spell eggs, armor, weapons and other goodies inside. In case of my demise, BB would give Canton the codes to access the room.

One of our new practices was living where we worked. Normally we'd rent hotel rooms or apartments and travel to offices. That had worked well before the Bureau had been pared down by a few dozen agents, thanks to crazed former agents and evil Nazi bastards (long story, don't ask). There would have been a main lobby guarded by a shotgun-wielding Receptionist with an attitude problem and more training than most SWAT officers. Unfortunately, we would have to do without. My favorite Receptionist, Patricia, had been recruited into the Bureau as a field agent, as had all but two of the remaining Receptionists. So it was time to buckle down and hole up in a virtual fortress until the current situation could be resolved.

Fortunately, we each had our own rooms, although as a couple,

Canton and Winch would share. My only regret was not having Jeanie with me. Years of avoiding relationships then finally finding myself in one had my Loneliness-O-Meter pinging into the red. As much as I was starting to depend on Jeanie, my pining for her was really starting to piss me off. I didn't want to be that whiny, love-struck guy from formula romantic comedies.

The toy Winnebago (of course I brought the Brownies; who else was going to do my dry cleaning?) fit perfectly under the bed, and I placed a pint carton of whole milk next to it. "Sorry, forgot the bowl, guys. I'll pick one up today."

"Sympathy for the Devil" was the only reply.

Later, as I secured battle armor, fully automatic weapons and magical weapons of unbelievable lethality in the Armory, I heard soft footsteps coming up from behind. "What is it, Canton?"

"What's the play, Kal?" he asked, normally lighthearted voice heavy with concern. "There ain't no clues as to what really happened up on that roof."

I sighed. I'd been noodling on that thought during the whole flight out from D.C. (fell asleep on the private jet, a Challenger 601 … the seats were wicked comfy). So far I'd only come up with two options. "First we head to the scene of the crime."

"The bank?"

"The roof."

"Then what?"

"We go see an old friend."

Mission Street, a north-south thoroughfare, is one of San Francisco's longest and oldest streets. Our two black Suburbans (provided by a dealership owned by a former agent) parked illegally in front of the Palisades Building, our destination. Cars honked and people flipped us the bird, which we blithely ignored, snug in our warm black coats and cheap black suits—standard issue garments for the Fed On The Go. Leaving Wilkes with the vehicles to discourage police, the rest of the team and I trotted into the building where Mace had met his end.

Phony but authentic-looking FBI badges prompted the building manager to escort us to the 30th floor, where I firmly but politely told him to bugger off. From the 30th floor stairs we ascended to the roof. The entrance had been crisscrossed with yellow and black police tape, but someone had ripped it down with nothing to block the slightly chilly air. Compared to my home state of Minnesota, the weather was practically balmy, but a clammy fog was rolling in, obscuring the sun and raising goosebumps across my skin. Supernaturals I could handle, but fog creeped me the hell out.

Drawing my Lahti L35 (a WWII relic once used by my grandfather), I stepped onto the roof, followed by the others.

"Who the hell are you?"

I started, surprised that anyone would be up there. A thin, older man, tallish, with short, receding gray-shot black hair, a pinched face and an impressive honker of a nose, strode up to the lot of us from the edge of the building where he had been standing. By the worn look of his ankle-length light coat and shiny but cheap shoes, I knew him to be a member of the SFPD. A detective, if I wasn't mistaken.

Canton and Winch stood behind me to the left and right while Ilena remained in the stairwell, out of sight.

"And you are?" I asked, slowly holstering my Lahti.

The thin man's face twisted into a sour grimace. "I'm the one asking questions, damn it!"

" 'Dammit'? Interesting name, is it Swedish?"

Canton and Winch chuckled while the thin man, whose sense of humor had either never existed or not outlived his youth, paled in anger, turning his olive skin a pasty yellow. Before he could burst a blood vessel, I carefully reached into my inside coat pocket and removed my badge and shield.

"Special Agent Dumont, FBI."

That brought him up quick and, surprisingly, his face became even more sour, as if he had reached the bitter limit. "Goddamn it!" he barked. "Just what I frickin' need, the Feebs coming in to mess up my investigation!"

"Well, so damn sorry, hoss." Canton sounded anything but. "However, if we mess up any investigation, it will be *ours*."

And here I thought the detective's face had already reached the peak of acerbic apoplexy. Good to know that I could still be surprised.

"I'll be damned if I give up this investigation." He bit off every word with carefully calculated force while he stared at my badge with sullen intensity.

I decided to toss him a bone. "The victim, Thomas Mace, was one of ours. So you *will not* balk at handing over this investigation to the Bureau." I leaned in close, just to test the intimidation factor. He didn't budge. Score one point to Mr. SFPD.

Slowly, as if he'd developed a leak, his antagonism drained away. He gave a terse nod; every police agency knows the value of resolving the death of one of theirs—no ifs, ands or buts. "You better keep me in the loop, wise guy," he ground out, showing his teeth in a feral smile. But he'd conceded enough for me to relax a tad. There was no time for a pissing contest.

Frowning, I put the badge away. "Not going to keep anyone who doesn't show me their ID in the know."

It must have hurt, having to show me his badge. Eric Sarkasian. Gold shield, big attitude and no waiting.

I liked him.

"Okay, Sarkasian. I'll keep you up to date, and I may need to coordinate with you."

He spat to the side. "I want in on the collar. I want to know where this leads."

From behind I could *feel* Canton and Winch tense. Sarkasian must have felt it, too, because he tensed as well, one hand moving unobtrusively toward his shoulder holster. This guy was wound tighter than a two-dollar watch.

"Ease off, you three. Don't need everyone getting all nervy," I said, letting some exasperation show.

Canton, who had been touchy ever since the news of Mace's death, was the last to retract his claws, but he finally did. "Sorry, boss," he whispered so only I could hear.

I took a deep breath, staring at the blue sky peaking through the clouds, and let the breeze cool my own jets. My friend wasn't the only one with nerves all a-jitter. It felt as if I had been scraping my nails along a chalkboard and the sound, plus the shivery vibrations, were twittering my flesh something awful. I wanted to leap out of my skin and scream.

Deep breaths. "Listen, Detective, I will keep you informed. I promise." My hand came up, forestalling his next comment, which I reckoned to be a beaut. "Please, just let my team and I have the scene for a while; then we'll be on our way." My hand fished around in my pocket for a few moments before producing a card.

Give credit where credit is due; he took it without a word and left. And yet somehow I had the feeling that Sarkasian was one of those cops who never let anything go. It was a trait all good cops developed.

Wonderful.

"Okay, folks," I said, not taking my eyes from the edge of the building. Heights and me didn't get along much. "Look around and hope we find something worthwhile."

Twenty-five minutes of staring at the rooftop and eyeballing tar-stained pea gravel finally yielded results.

"Kal, look here," Ilena called, staring at the gravel near the edge of the building. As I neared the edge, my legs became all jangly/wobbly as vertigo slipped through my flesh.

The vertigo lasted for only a few moments as I stared out over the city. The fog was fully in, blanketing San Francisco well enough that only the taller buildings such as ours peeked through the cottony vapor. Leviathans through the mists, obelisks through the haze, the buildings were the rocks rising up from obscurity.

It was surreal and I could almost imagine that if I jumped, the fluffy mass would cushion my plummeting body instead of allowing me to terminally face-plant onto concrete. The pull toward the fog was seductive, and it was with a grunt and a snarl that I tore my eyes from the view.

"What is it?" *Crunch, crunch* went the gravel under my rubber-soled loafers.

The slender magician pointed at the gravel. Long, dark hair had come unbound and was whipping around her head like a crazed black halo.

I stared where her finger pointed. "Don't see any—wait-a-minute." For a brief moment I caught a glimpse of something, then the vision was lost. Closing my eyes, I relaxed, took two deep breaths, then looked again.

There. Barely visible, a pattern in the gravel as if it had been pushed deeper into the tar. Whatever had pushed gravel that deep into cold roofing tar had to be as heavy as a Honda.

"Canton!" I hollered over the wind. "Come see this!"

When he arrived, his eyes spotted what mine had trouble focusing on. "A footprint," he said in disbelief. His fingers hovered over the print, fluttering slightly. "A dog or a wolf."

"Yeah. A big one." My splayed fingers covered the print. It was larger. "What kind of dog has a foot bigger than my hand?"

It was Winch who answered. "Black Shuck."

I stood there quietly for a minute or two staring down fifty feet into the chill winter fog that moved like a flow of living cotton through city. Black Shuck. I'd heard of that particular Supernatural before, but had been lucky enough not to encounter it. It had the reputation of being nasty to the *nth* degree.

Why did I always have to be drawn to the nasty ones? Just once I wouldn't have minded a cushy case, like "The Sex-Starved Nymphs of New York," or something like that.

Bzzz!

The drone hit my ears a split second after I found myself on the receiving end of a tackle of heroic proportions. As my butt slammed down behind the line of scrimmage, I caught a glimpse of a big, glossy black *something* pass through the space I had occupied a second before.

It was a hornet—one the size of a Cadillac and sporting a stinger like a rhino's horn sticking from its swollen abdomen. Thick, clear fluid dripped from the stinger to land with a smoking hiss on the roof, melting both tar and pea gravel.

Note to self, stay away from the stinger.

The tackler was Canton, who had body-checked me better than any Vikings lineman to remove me from the path of the overgrown pest.

And me without a can of RAID.

"Dude, you gotta learn how to duck," Canton said, drawing a Browning from his shoulder holster.

That awful buzzing—a bone-vibrating hum that was a cross between a chainsaw and a dentist's drill—speared my eardrums, and I had to resist the urge to scratch them out.

Multi-faceted eyes shone with gemmy malevolence as its triangular head cocked to the side, keeping me centered in its vision while bullets bounced off its iron-hard chiton. Its wings, thin as a politician's promise, blurred as it swooped at me, abdomen curling under its black thorax, ready to plunge that poison-coated stinger into my gut.

My reaction time was as good as ever ... The stinger missed me by a fraction. I could feel the wind of its passage against my cheek, full of the promise of a painful death.

Just another day at work.

As it flew upwards at astounding speed, a mere blur barely perceived by my retinas, I chased it with a few rounds from the Lahti.

It was no use.

Again the bug came at me in a divebombing run that once again I barely avoided. That thing was *fast*.

"It doesn't like you!" yelled Wilkes, trying for a clean shot at the beast. "Is that normal?"

"It's a wasp the size of a Buick," I yelled. "What's normal about that? Just kill the damn thing."

Once again I ducked to the side and that terrible, hard stinger gouged a furrow in the tar, sending gravel flying. My ankle turned as the sole of my shoe slid on the roof and a sickening wave of pain shot up my calf. Butt met tarred gravel with a *thump* and my heart plummeted. That thing was too quick; I wouldn't be able to dodge when it came back for me.

Damn, I hate being right all the time ... The thing was on me before the pain of slamming a butt cheek onto gravel had a chance to register. In my head I heard the final *tick-tock* of my life's clock because my Lahti was moving far too slow; I couldn't bring it around in time and that stinger was too close.

It was almost on me. *Jeanie,* I thought, the only word that came to mind, as the wasp suddenly hit the roof with a crash, twisting and flipping end over end, abdomen slapping uselessly against hardened tar.

It was Wilkes. He had his arms wrapped around the thing's thorax and was riding it like it was a bucking bronco. Its thin wings, each twenty feet long, buzzed and blurred with frantic speed, but no matter how hard it tried, it couldn't achieve flight. It seemed that 200-plus pounds of angry agent was too much for the irate insect. Its bulbous abdoman, chiton pocked with bullet scars, swept back and forth to no avail, poison droplets flying.

I scrambled to my feet, but Canton was faster, jamming the muzzle of his Browning past the creature's mouth parts and pulling the trigger until the slide racked open.

Gore spewed from the multi-faceted eyes, spraying thick green/yellow fluid in high arcs across the roof. The beast shuddered and flailed for a few seconds before flipping onto its back and curling its black, chitonous legs in death.

A muffled voice came from beneath the monster. "Get this damn thing offa me!"

Wilkes. *Right.*

"Let's get this thing off," I growled, standing shakily. Adrenaline began to bleed from my system, rendering me dizzy and weak.

It took all of us, but we managed to lift the corpse off of a slightly flattened Wilkes, who needed help to stand.

"You okay, big man?" I asked. He looked relatively whole, considering that a five-hundred-pound bug had done the Watusi on his bod.

"Yeah." He nodded. "But that thing looked plenty pissed at you. Why is that?"

Canton toed the body. "Kal, I've never seen a bug focus on just one person before. This thing wanted you bad."

I nodded. "So it seems, but that's not important now. We have to dispose of the body." Fourteen inches of razor sharp blade emerged from within my long coat. My Bowie, a gift from Dad. Harsh ridges lined the flat of the blade, the remnants of its previous existence as an industrial file.

Ilena stared at the Bowie. "What the heck?"

"The body is too long by about five feet," I said, pointing to the wasp's abdomen. "I need it to fit in a ten-foot diameter circle."

Canton gave me a nod and produced the twin to my Bowie, a gift from me. We both went to work on the wasp, cutting through the foot thick cable of flesh connecting the abdomen to the thorax.

The details are boring. Suffice to say that there was a plethora of pus-colored blood. Ilena gagged, Wilkes puked, and even I nearly barfed, but we finally had a nice little stack of wasp parts. The wings were the last, quartered and stacked neatly atop the carcass.

"Kal, working with you is always a thrill," Canton said, looking a little green around the gills.

I smiled and pulled a small silvery vial from a concealed pocket in my coat. "The fun has just begun, buddy. But now's the time we dispose of the body and there's nothing like these disintegrators for getting the job done."

Ilena sneered. "I hate those things, too unstable."

"Nah. It's like plastic explosive: hideously stable until the detonator is attached. This thing is fine until you unscrew the cap." I did just that and my heartrate escalated. "Like this." I grinned. "I would run if I were you."

They accepted my invitation and seconds later I was alone on the rooftop. I placed the vial center mass on the corpse and beat feet to the stairwell. From the doorway came an actinic white flash that lit the stairwell in harsh, razor-edged light and shadow.

"What now, Kal?" asked Canton as he inserted a new clip for the Browning.

I stretched. "We call BB and tell him there might be some structural damage to the roof of this building, and then we find out who the hell sent that wasp. That was *not* an accident."

Chapter Four

Time and Punishment

"Good job on the tackle," I told Wilkes from the driver's seat of the black Surburban we shared. "You saved my butt."

He smiled, twisting the scar on his cheek. "I just imagined tackling you during the big game back in '95. Came natural."

That was a reference to the first time we met, during the game between the Colorado Buffaloes and the Nebraska Cornhuskers. Back then he was a feared tackle and I was lickety-split wide receiver. In the fourth quarter at Folsum Field, I got on the wrong end of one mean tackle that broke my arm. He finished the season a hero while I finished it on the couch watching the last three games on my television.

"Well, good job. Glad you still have your college football instincts."

"You think it was the Supernatural that ripped the roof door off its hinges?"

I gave that a good think or two before replying. "No. The wasp wasn't strong enough to fly with you on its back, so I doubt it had the muscle to rip through steel hinges and screws on a fly-by."

"What is a Black Shuck?" he asked in a swift change of subject.

I decided to roll with the conversational rollercoaster. "Sort of a ghostly black dog that was said to have roamed the Essex, Norfolk and Suffolk countryside in England. Demon dog would be another description, huge and terrible. Also called a Grim."

"So a big dog chased Mace off a building?"

I shook my head. "Not hardly. He jumped; he wanted his body to be found with my name written on it. He needed to get away from the Shuck so it *could* be found. That mutt would've torn the evidence to shreds." I licked my lips; Black Shuck might have *eaten* the evidence. Gross. I shared that thought with Wilkes. "What else do you think a dog the size of a prize Angus steer would do with a corpse?" Things much worse than what a ginormous wasp would do, that's for sure.

Wilkes turned a little green as he thought about that. "Where to now, boss?" he asked in an attempt to steer the conversation onto safer ground.

"Think like a cop. Where would you go?"

"Mace's house."

"Then that's where we are going."

I already had the location entered in the Suburban's voice-activated nav system. We were on our way.

Hillsborough Heights is the fancy-schmancy, rich residential area located between the 101 and the 280, next to the San Francisco State Fish and Game Refuge. It was the garden spot of San Mateo and saw more money than most European nations. That's where Mace had hung his hat after leaving the Bureau. Hopefully my team would find some conveniently placed clues so we could wrap this thing up quick.

Yeah, right.

Thomas Mace had been an agent for four years and had spent his money wisely, purchasing a house after the real estate collapse in the early 2000s for almost half its original value. And when I say *house*, I mean a small mansion surrounded by an eight-foot-tall brick fence, an electronic wrought-iron gate in front, and a swimming pool in the back that could double as a whale habitat. The whole setup was nestled behind a thick growth of trees and tall hedges that provided plenty of privacy.

Wilkes had his RediPad scroll through various frequencies as we approached the gates and by the time I'd nosed the Suburban up close, it had locked onto the correct one. The gates rolled back behind the fence and both SUVs motored up the long driveway.

Wow. And I mean *Double Wow.*

I've been to rich places, but the understated elegance of Mace's home screamed WEALTH more than gold-plated double doors or hand-painted murals. Cream-colored brick with white trim, nine bedrooms, six bathrooms, etc., etc., etc. Last reports indicated Mace was single, which begged the question: why such a big house?

However, such concerns had to be put on the back burner as I spotted a black Crown Victoria parked in the circular drive. Cop car, standard issue.

And look who was stepping out of the driver's side? My new friend Sarkasian.

Wonderful.

"Who *are* you people?" he asked with a hint of exasperation as the two Suburbans parked and we emerged.

I scrubbed my face with my hands. "What do you mean, Detective? And what the hell are *you* doing here?"

"I came to check out the home of one Thomas Mace, curious as to how he could afford such a grand place in such an affluent neighborhood." It was his turn to lean in close and invade my personal territory. "And I was listening in at the stairwell."

What the—? I resisted the impulse to plant a size 11 in someone's backside. Such security breaches shouldn't be possible. Precautions should have been taken. From the stricken look on Ilena's face, I could see they hadn't been. I jotted down a mental note to threaten lots and lots of death when we returned to the loft. Whole bunches, reams, of hot death.

But that had to wait. I needed to know if he had heard about our fight with the big, bad bug. "You listened to our conversation?"

"I heard the words 'Black Shuck' before being called away. Why do you ask? You talk about other things I should know about?"

Wonderful. At least he hadn't heard us fighting with the bug. I guessed he had been far enough down the building to be out of hearing range of the gunfire.

But sometimes the Universe just loves to crap in my Wheaties.

"Ilena," I said softly.

"On it, boss."

Sarkasian, "What?"

Ilena, "Look at me, sir."

He did. Canton caught the body before the driveway could do any damage.

Me, "Ilena." Nice grim tones.

Ilena, "Yeah, boss?" Frightened. Good. It was time for some fear.

Me again, "You were supposed to secure the stairwell, right? By hook or by crook?"

A brief moment of silence. "Yeah, boss."

"You did your training in Coronado, right?"

Canton and Winch were smiling. It wasn't pleasant; sharks would have feared those grins.

"Yeah, boss." Oh, she was catching the drift and did *not* like where the current was taking her.

"Remember when you screwed up, what the instructors would do?" My tone suggested perilous seas.

"Yeah, boss." Was that a quaver in her voice?

"This is going to be worse. Much, *much* worse."

Perilous seas, indeed.

Deciding to start her punishment early, I left Ilena with the car and Sarkasian's unconscious form, which was stuffed into the back seat of his Crown Vic. She could deal with anyone else who appeared and maybe put the mojo on them as well.

A sophisticated security system, the best that money could buy, was bypassed after a couple of minutes on the RediPad and we were in. Our first glance took in the sight of crystal chandeliers, teak flooring and hand-carved crown molding.

Nothing else. Empty. What the hell?

"Canton?"

"Don't know, Kal. This is listed as his official residence."

"Winch."

"Yeah?"

"You and Wilkes check the rooms upstairs." I drew my new pistol and watched eyes widen in shock. "Canton and I will take this floor."

"What the hell is that?" the Apache blurted, eyes locked fast to the huge weapon.

"New toy from Alex," I replied with a smirk.

The three cried in unison, "I want one!"

I snorted. "What are you guys? Twelve? This damn thing might not work that well."

Six eyes stared at me in disbelief.

No faith in their fearless leader, I tell you. Impatiently, I waved them on and we scoured the house from top to bottom. Nada. If Mace had lived here, he'd moved out long ago and taken everything with him, down to the last follicle. The place felt like the world's largest dollhouse, slightly sterile and unreal. The longer we stayed inside, the more jittery I became.

Outside, Ilena sat glumly on the hood of the Vic, waiting for us or for Sarkasian to wake up. "How much longer?" I asked her, shooting her another glare to let her know she was nowhere near out of the doghouse.

"About another hour. What do you want to do?"

Buggering off was probably not the wisest course of action, so I had her lift the sleep spell and smiled while the Detective snorted and snarled his way into wakefulness.

"[CENSORED][EXPLETIVE][CENSORED] happened here!" he yelled as he stumbled out of the Vic, barely saving himself from a heroic face plant.

Ears burning from the profusion of cussing—if I ever talked like that, my mother would somehow know and fly in from Grand Rapids, Minnesota, just to kick my butt until the crack ran horizontal—I helped the Detective to his feet.

"Careful there, Sarkasian, you took quite a turn," I said, brushing imaginary dust from his shoulders. "You have a medical condition I should know about? You fainted dead away."

More cussing, inventive and detailed, the gist of which was, *You've got to be kidding me!*

"Sorry, Detective." I motioned for the others to mount up. "But you gave us a scare there. You want me to call an ambulance?"

He told me what I could do with and where I could put that ambulance, an anatomical impossibility. I nodded, hopped into the lead Suburban and fired it up.

"Hey!" yelled the Detective. "You didn't answer my question about that 'Shuck' you all were talking about."

I gritted my teeth and smiled. "No, I didn't," was my reply as I hit the gas, leaving a very angry police detective in my wake.

Back at the loft, I had Ilena prepare the daily report to send back to Warehouse while the rest of us made short work of a couple buckets of KFC. I told Ilena she could eat what she hunted and killed for herself. She scowled, but kept her peace, knowing her punishment was only beginning.

Back in my room I set a soda cup I'd cut down to size under the bed, pouring what remained of the whole milk from the pint carton inside. "Hungry Like The Wolf" drifted from the toy RV. My Brownie tenants, it seemed, were not without a sense of humor.

"Kal?"

Turning around, I saw both Canton and Winch at the doorway. They looked uneasy.

"Come in," I said. "Close the door behind you."

Once inside, Canton licked his lips and launched into what was eating him. "I'm wondering about … well, your sister." He almost flinched, as if afraid I would deck him.

It came to me then exactly how ferocious my rep must be if my best friend and the most courageous man I'd ever met could actually be afraid of me. That thought was almost enough to break my heart.

Wonderful.

"What do you mean?" I kept my voice pleasant as I sat, brushing imaginary lint from my thighs.

"She's still with you, isn't she?"

Oh. He was worried about the rage.

Ever since I was fifteen, since the death of my sister at the monster

Iku-Turso's tentacles, it had been there, hiding. When under the rage's influence, my speed and strength were vastly increased, sort of a controlled version of Berserker/Blind Rage syndrome. Any minor damage taken by said feats of strength and speed were healed almost instantly. It struck me again how ironic it was that the serial killer Margaret Whitcombe had been trying to duplicate those exact effects, to no avail. She had created a spell Shape for enhanced physical capabilities, but had been unable to heal ruptured and torn tissues. Her solution? To cast the spell on the undead. No need for healing when you're already a corpse.

Two months ago, a group that included these two, my parents and my new love Jeanie had pushed Iku-Turso back into the World Under (where much stronger, and meaner, things awaited it). It was then I had made a discovery.

Leena, my sister, whose soul I thought had been eaten by that vile monster, was actually the rage that had been fueling me. The power of her love, her protective instincts toward me, had been the catalyst for my enormous strength and speed. Like a remora, she had latched her soul to mine since her physical death and had been my secret tenant ever since, slumbering until danger woke her, woke the rage.

I treated Canton to an intimidating stare and was happy to see him take it without flinching. "She's there. I can ... almost feel her, like the ghost memory of a limb that's been amputated."

"What we want to know, boss," Winch asked, taking the bull by the horns. "Since that time in San Diego ... can you still call on that anger of yours? Have you felt it?"

Had I? Training Green Peas surely pissed me off, but I hadn't felt the white-hot power of the rage. Not since I discovered her inside of me. "No. I mean, I haven't felt it or tried to summon it."

Now Canton grabbed the horns. "Will you be able to, Kal? I mean, you've had some closure back there on that sub where we fought that Class Five monster of yours. Is she at peace and leaving you alone, or can you still call on her?"

Damn. Double damn.

I had been avoiding the issue at every turn. Canton was right, I'd had some closure, and my revenge was complete, served nice and cold in the traditional Klingon fashion. But did that mean Leena would forever slumber, quietly attached to my psyche like a mental barnacle, or would she come back when needed?

Hell if I knew.

They both saw the answer in my face and traded a look that only couples in a committed relationship could interpret.

God, I miss Jeanie so.

"Look," I said irritably. "Are you worried that I won't be able call the rage anymore, or are you afraid I still can?"

Canton looked at Winch then the door, and she took the hint, exiting quietly. "Listen, Kal," he said when she had gone. "I'm your friend and what I really want to know is … are you all right? For years you stayed at the top of your game because of the rage and the emotional damage you'd received because of that Class Five." He took a long breath. "I'm just worried about you, pard. If you've lost your edge, you could get taken down big-time because you bit off more than you could chew. Getting down to brass tacks, can you still summon your rage?"

Damn, I hate it when others make so much sense; it messes with my reality. Taking a deep breath, I carefully considered my answer. "I know myself, Canton, and I know what I can do. I'm a tough guy, like always, and I know I can still make the hard decisions if necessary."

A second, then two before he visibly relaxed. "Well, shoot, that's a load off my mind. Thought you might be losing it a little when you recycled that old Agent Dumont ID today."

Big, *huge*, alarm bells jangled through my cerebral cortex, shaking loose the cobwebs and dust that had been gathering in the halls of my mind. It was common practice to never use the same ID twice unless absolutely necessary; however, my mistake gave me an idea. "Damn!" I swore, angry at myself. "You may be right … I might be losing my touch." I stood abruptly, towering over the shorter man. Smiling, I grabbed him by either side of his skull and planted a smack on his forehead. "Thanks for the idea, Canton, you're brilliant!" Smiling, I opened the door. From behind I heard my friend mention "picking out curtains."

"ILENA!" I screamed into the loft at the top of my lungs. It might have been a flight of fancy, but I could have sworn the bulletproof windows rattled slightly.

The team's magician bolted out of her room as if rocket-propelled, while Winch and Wilkes, sitting around the dining table in the middle of the large, open space talking and drinking, jumped to their feet in alarm, hands moving to weapons.

Ilena rushed over and came to a very smart attention, almost quivering in place. "Boss!" she yelled, face dead white.

I took a deep breath. "I need you to contact Warehouse and find out all the aliases Mace has used over the years; then I want you to cross-reference those aliases against all real estate leases, purchases, and rentals since he left the Bureau. That's about ten years' worth, so there's going to be a hell of a lot of records. If there are matches, check those against age, height and weight, if possible. If it's not possible, make it happen anyway." My eyes found those of the rest of the team. "I have no idea why he bought that mansion, but it wasn't to live there—maybe as a long-term investment. What I know for sure is, he lived somewhere else in the city." Back to the magician. "Find out where he rested his head, and do it before daylight."

She looked daunted at the prospect. Even with the advanced tech of the RediPads, it was a whole grip of work. "What about Ghost?" she asked "He can do it quicker than anyone."

I crossed my arms. "Ghost is currently busy investigating the disappearance of a trio of ships gone missing from the L.A. Harbor, so we're out of luck on the cyberspook front." BB wanted to know if those ships vanished due to magic or thievery before committing any more assets in the field.

She knew better than to stamp her foot, but I could see she wanted to. "Boss that will take *forever!*"

No pity, not during a time of punishment. That may sound cruel, but strict discipline and unstinting retribution keep an ops team functioning well. We all believed it, expected it, and it had been drilled into our bones before ever taking an assignment with the Bureau. If I showed leniency, it would be the end of my authority. A team leader had to be a terrible, awesome thing.

"Yeah," I said in a flat voice, my expression pitiless, "then you better get going."

I tramped back into my lair to brood about the day's events.

Just when I thought I would have some peace and quiet ... *knockity-knock!*

Wonderful.

"Come in."

Wilkes entered, brow furrowed. "Sorry, Kal, do you mind?"

Actually, I did, but the team came before my need for comfort, more's the pity. "Sure. What's up?"

The former police detective from Denver shut the door softly. "That was a good idea, you know—Mace's former aliases."

I rubbed my cheeks. "Would have been more clever if I'd thought of it a few hours ago. Have to work the rust out of my brain."

"That's not what I'm worried about, boss."

My eyebrow crawled toward my hairline. Not *another* inquiry into my state of mental health?

"Is that our only play, hacking into databases to find out if Mace had another place to hole up?"

I relaxed and shook my head. "No."

His features scrunched. "You're not going to tell me, are you? You've got another iron in the fire and you're keeping it to yourself."

My tired baby blues stared into his fierce gaze and met no resistance. Fact was, I was the boss and he wasn't. He knew it, but still wanted to be kept in the loop. Wilkes was a little arrogant, self-assured, cocky, and diamond hard. All the makings of a great agent.

It never hurt to toss a bone or two, though. "Listen, the reason I'm keeping this close to my chest is because it involves potentially ... harming another person as well as putting yours truly in the line of fire. That is a last-resort for me, so let's leave off for now and see if Ilena finds a result."

Wilkes's eyes thawed slightly and he nodded. "Fair enough, boss," he conceded and with that, saluted and found the exit.

I sat on the bed and slowly stripped off my rubber-soled black loafers. I was already starting to feel tired and worn out and it was only the first day of what, so far, had been a frustrating mission. For the first time ever, I was starting to feel my age and that sucked more than I thought it would.

If Ilena couldn't find Mace's hidey-hole, I would have to seek out a person who just wanted to be left alone and rub salt in some wounds. I was responsible for a bit of that hurt and the present task would involve a type of torture, one I'd witnessed before and hadn't enjoyed at all. A cruelty, for sure, but the only consolation was that the person was already dead.

From under the bed came "Unchained Melody."

Friggin' Brownies.

Chapter Five

A Ghost of a Chance

Morning came like it usually did, way too early for my comfort. My room had no windows, no alarm clocks, but I still needed to rise at 6 a.m., so I'd left instructions for a wake-up call, which Canton took to with a vengeance.

"Get up, you lazy bastard!" he screamed from the other side of the door, pounding mercilessly. The sound hammered through one ear and out the other in painful, thrumming waves that chased out pleasant dreams of me, Angelina Jolie, and a slice of New York-style cheesecake.

Bastard.

"I'm up," I mumbled through lips thick with sleep and drool. *Come back to me, Angelina.*

Pound, pound, pound. My EX-friend was doing quite a number on the door. *Note to self: kill him when convenient.*

"C'mon, Kal, wake your lazy ass up!"

My pillow hit the door at Warp Speed. "I'm up, you friggin' jackass!"

Laughter. More than one person.

Bastards.

From under the bed, "Taking Care Of Business."

"I get the message, guys," I muttered sleepily. Actually managed to make it to a sitting position with only minimal *creaks* and *pops* of aging joints. Every year the symphony of noises from my body became louder and louder. I also had started to produce natural gas in prodigious quantities as well as sprouting excess amounts of ear and nose hair.

Later, once I'd shrugged into a 49ers sweat shirt and jeans, I gathered the team around the kitchen table and started to dig into a massive bowl of Lucky Charms. Someone had thoughtfully provided me with a cup of coffee, aka Liquid Love. "Ilena, report."

Her voice emerged small and timid and I knew she'd made no progress. "So far, nothing, but I've only managed to hack into and search half of the databases out there." Dark circles under her eyes attested to an all-nighter.

I nodded. "Then get to work. I want that information."

Ilena sighed and wobbled on unsteady legs to her room.

"Why so hard on her, boss?" Wilkes sounded concerned.

My mouth quirked into a smile that was taken up by both Canton and Winch. "You think I'm too tough?" He nodded and I pursed my lips, examining the other three carefully. Each of them had come to me worried about some aspect of my leadership, if only in a minute way. Perhaps it was time to loosen things up a little.

I turned to our sniper. "Winch, you remember the Everglades, don't you?"

Her Betty Boop face brightened instantly and she nodded eagerly.

"Then you do the honors."

Canton groaned. "I wanted to tell the story!" he complained.

She elbowed him in the ribs. "What are you, six?"

Wilkes treated them to his own eyebrow trick and the Apache grumbled, a sour look on his coppery face, but signaled her to continue. "Did you know that Mace became the team leader after BB became Director?" she asked, a look of subdued glee on her round, impish face.

The big man shook his head.

Winch continued, "About three months after BB took the job, we were joined by Mouth."

Wilkes had heard about Mouth—former agent, a hand-to-hand specialist, famously foul-mouthed. A few months previously she'd been lost to us, taken back to 1943 where she'd decided to stay while Jeanie decided to join the 21st century. Mouth wanted to be with the dashing Richard Fleming, a legend in MI-7. She had chosen love and I really couldn't blame her, although thinking about her sometimes brought suspicious moisture to my eyes.

"Anyway, we were called away to a bug hunt—"

"Another insect?" Wilkes interrupted. "Like the wasp?"

I grinned. "Giant insects are one of the most common Supernaturals there are, hence the term 'bug hunt.' Try to keep up."

Before he could flense me to the bone with his rapier wit, Winch continued, "There was a problem in the Florida Everglades, a Praying Mantis the size of a Greyhound bus was clearing the swamp of wildlife, including the local residents. If you know anything about those things, they don't just kill their prey, they eat them alive, so it was a totally gross situation."

Everyone winced at the thought of being devoured alive by a big bug. Although not a pleasant way to go, it was still one of the least painful considering the other horrors the World Under offered. A scratch from a harpy could dissolve a grown man in half an hour. The pain was so excruciating that most agents ate a bullet rather than suffer.

"Most big bugs are vicious and quick, but not intelligent, so taking them out is not the hardest job for a team. Usually we throw a boatload of ordnance at the creepy-crawly and it shreds apart just fine, festooning the area with gooey green guts.

"When we arrived at the 'Glades, the only we could do was take a couple of fan boats out and commence hunting, but we weren't out to take trophies." She took a deep breath. "Strange thing, even though the bug was humongous, the 'Glades are sixty miles wide and a hundred long with thousands of tiny islands, providing a ton of hiding places. For three days we hunted, preparing fortified camps at night and starting out again at the break of day. It was mid-afternoon of the third day when we caught up to the damn thing.

"Canton thought he saw movement on a medium-sized tree-covered island, so we maneuvered our two fan boats over to the spit of land and Mace told Kal to secure them, to tie them off on a tree half-sunk in water, but Kal spotted the bug and instantly everyone readied their weapons. Of course, Kal completely forgot to secure the boats.

"You should have seen that bug, at least sixty feet from tip to top and lightning-quick for all its size. We unloaded everything we had at it, but it seemed to dodge everything, even RPGs and a LAW. It scuttled forward, bullets from M16s bouncing off its carapace, and we had to retreat, but the boats had drifted away in the gentle current."

"Wait a sec." Wilkes held up his hands. "You said that thing was sixty-feet long, right?"

Winch nodded.

"Then how could it exist? Insects can't grow to that size. It, like, violates the laws of physics and such."

"The Cube Root Law," I noted.

He nodded. "Yeah. Wouldn't its carapace weigh so much that it wouldn't be able to move?"

"You haven't quite caught on to the whole *magic* thing, have you?" Canton's voice was drier than the Gobi and Wilkes's face turned a bright shade of crimson, but he shut up and motioned for Winch to continue.

My stomach churned at the memory. The bug had moved like liquid death, with speed that a creature that size should never had been able to attain, but like Canton said … magic.

When, as we retreated from the skittering horror, our boots had hit water instead of encountering the fan boats, I'd felt a wave of sickness well up from deep within. Both boats had floated at least thirty feet away and it was my fault we couldn't retreat any farther. If anyone died, that would be my fault, too. Shame replaced the feeling of sickness.

Then the rage had hit, rushing through my blood like a tide of bubbling acid. My skin pebbled and my muscles swelled, ready for battle. If anyone was going to die, it would be me, but first I had a mantis to kill. The creature, its dangling claws flashing at us from less than twenty feet away, became my entire focus as my body reacted before my mind had a chance to catch up to the action. Time became encased in sepia-toned treacle as I streaked forward.

From behind I heard Canton scream "No!" as I raced between those two saber-like appendages, under the triangular head the size of a big-block V8 with its faceted green eyes sparkling in the noonday sun like malefic emeralds.

Its mandibles *clacked* together behind my neck as it missed by the merest fraction, but I didn't really notice, didn't pay attention. I was too caught up in the rage, drawing my fourteen-inch Bowie knife. Legs pumping, I sped under its bloated abdomen and thrust upward into the tender flesh protected by a much thinner belly carapace. The knife entered with the slightest resistance as the razor-sharp steel blade sought the beast's tender internals.

My face was tight with a grin of hate as pale insect ichor spattered my skin and scalp, but I pushed on, running and dragging the knife with me, opening the mantis like a sack of wheat. As I neared the end of its abdomen, I could hear *things* fall out to land on the wet earth with a *splat!* and I exulted, the rage carrying me past the insect.

Fifty feet behind the monster, I came to an abrupt stop, thanks to a convenient southern live oak. I turned to see the fallout of my attack, the Bowie dripping filthy whitish fluid onto the dirt.

The mantis had also halted its progress and stood there, not even dodging the bullets that peppered it. Abruptly, with a wet squelch, it seemed to unzip and a flood of unidentifiable parts erupted from its abdomen and rained down upon the hummocky ground.

A split second later, Canton nailed its head with a LAW and blew it apart, festooning the rest of the team with mantis brain, ichor and bits of carapace.

The memory of that burning insect body—the smell was beyond nasty, like the flaming corpse of some long dead creature already rotten to the core mixed with burning insulation—crashing to the ground in a heap brought me back to reality as Winch finished the story.

"So you could imagine how pissed Mace was," she said, relishing the memory, her wiry body thrumming with enjoyment. "He cornered Kal and dressed him down for ten minutes while this big lug hung his head in shame."

Oh, yeah … *memories*.

"Not only did Mace put Kal on Big Bug Corpse Disposal Duty, he also had him do every crap job that came along for the next few weeks and ran him absolutely ragged. We had us our very own valet." She gave me an affectionate but painful punch in the arm, her curvy bod packing a serious amount of muscle. "Good times."

"Wonderful," I growled, inciting more gales of laughter. Their appreciation of her story lasted well into my second bowl of Lucky Charms, but if you can't take it, don't dish it out. I admit, the memory of the mantis bonfire I created to dispose of the corpse and the smell it made was certainly gag-worthy. Mace could've used three or four disintegration vials to devaporate the beast, but had wanted me on serious crap detail. Memories of cutting that huge insect into smaller, more burnable bits hit me hard and my stomach gave a little flop. I knew right then that breakfast was over. I pushed the half-eaten bowl of cereal away.

I took stock of the faces before me. Canton and Winch wore smiles I hadn't seen in quite a while, relaxed … happy. Wilkes radiated eagerness and confidence, a sight better than when he'd come to see me earlier.

Good. I'd take humiliations galore if it would boost the team's morale, no matter the cost to my vast and fragile ego.

Once the hilarity died down, I had them gather their gear and FBI IDs and we loaded into the Suburbans located at an indoor parking garage next to the loft. We had places to go and people to see.

San Francisco, like most large cities, is not composed of just one metropolis, but several. Briarlawn Memorial Park, a very swanky cemetery for those who can afford it, lies in the middle of the city of Colma, directly south of, and connected to, San Fran. Taking the 280 allowed us to avoid the major, traffic-clogged side roads and arrive before 8 a.m.

I had to give it up for the people of Briarlawn; they had the whole "Death with Dignity" schtick down pat. Seeing our IDs, we were granted entry by a bemused and tired caretaker at the grandiose entrance called The Castle Gate, a long, light-gray gatehouse fashioned like a fairytale castle wall with two arched openings, an entrance and exit. I felt as if we were entering a Renaissance Faire for the Dead.

The caretaker offered to escort us, but that wasn't going to happen. I had a dead guy to grill.

"Where are we going, boss?" asked Wilkes, cool and calm behind a pair of Oakleys, working the Fashionable Fed angle.

The Suburban cruised slowly across the paved drive that looped and whorled around the cemetery. I zipped to our destination and parked. "Here we are, Wilkes," I said.

Canton and Winch hopped out of their SUVs, along with Ilena, who looked more than a little exhausted. The Apache and The Sniper had pensive looks on their faces; they knew exactly what I had in mind and didn't like it one bit. I didn't blame them. What I was contemplating was cruel, but I honestly felt there was no alternative.

I made my way to a large, rust-colored headstone flanked by two small evergreens. Someone had left a toy panda on top of the marker and recent rains had left it a bedraggled, sad, black and white ball of polyfibers. It looked like the loneliest statement in the world.

"Ilena, put a 'Notice Me Not' around the area," I said, staring at the looming gray clouds. *No fog so far, thank God.* "And get back to looking for those aliases."

The "Notice Me Not" spell was a stationary effect that worked on the visual cortex of the brain, creating a blind spot around those within the area. It had less impact on those with strong wills, but every little bit helps when summoning the dead.

After our magician placed the spell and trudged away back to the vehicles, I reached into my inside coat pocket and pulled out a thin, hard, transparent plastic envelope containing a yellowing, rectangular sheet of paper almost as big as my hand.

"Jesus, Kal," Winch whispered, standing at my elbow. "Where the hell did you get that?"

I grinned. "My personal collection. Bought it six years ago for more money than I really cared to part with."

She trailed a finger over the plastic. "Seems a shame."

"Yeah, but the Bureau will re-reimburse me." I opened the envelope and shook out the rectangle. One side read: THE IMPERIAL GOVERNMENT OF NORTON 1.

The wind tried to tear the paper from my fingers, but I held on tight to one of the few remaining ten-dollar bills printed by Joshua Norton, self styled Emperor of the United States and Defender of Mexico.

Wilkes was staring at the headstone as if it had the power to cure cancer. "I've heard of this guy," he breathed, kneeling and reverently tracing a finger across the letters of Joshua Norton's name. "I read his story in one of Gaiman's *Sandman* graphic novels." He shook his head. "I thought it was all bull. A clever story written to amuse."

I shook my head. "No, Norton was a real man. A real madman."

He looked up, eyes bright. "We're going to talk to him."

"Wilkes," Canon said in a warning growl.

"He doesn't know," I told my friend. "He doesn't know."

"Know what?" Now Wilkes was pissed at his ignorance and I didn't blame him. Very few people knew the unique circumstances of Emperor Norton and his particular attachment to San Francisco.

I knelt down before the headstone and placed the bill on the ground in front, weighing it down with a few quarters. "There are so few of these left," I said softly. "Norton had them printed up to be his very own Imperial Currency and they are real collector's items. What I'm about to do is a real shame."

A lump formed in my throat and I coughed to cover up a sudden thickening of my voice. "You see, Joshua Norton, despite his rampant madness, really loved this city, and I mean with a deep, abiding passion that was untarnished by his madness. And that love created a bond, a mystical connection to the city. When he died in 1880, his body failed, but not his spirit. It … lingered. He was buried in the Masonic Cemetery, courtesy of the Pacific Club, and his spirit stayed there until 1934, when his remains were moved here, to Briarwood."

"And the spirit, it moved with the remains?"

Good, Wilkes was starting to suss out how things worked in the magical, mystical world. "Yes, but that's not all."

Wilkes narrowed his eyes at me, not buying any of this.

Canton stepped forward. "Legend has it that when Norton died, the Ohlone people—the natives to this area—sent a shaman to bind his spirit to his remains and give it the power to protect the city. In effect that darn shaman gave the spook real power, power enough to watch over the city and influence events. No one knows why the Ohlone would do such a thing—they don't have any more love for the white man than my people—but they did and ol' Josh Norton has remained here. He is the Protector of San Francisco and Ohlone lore states that as long as his spirit remains within the city, it will never fall."

The Apache barked out a laugh that sounded almost like a sob. "But the shaman invoked Coyote and when you do that, even if you are a mighty shaman, you take risks. Coyote is a canny Trickster and loves throwing a monkey wrench in the works. He don't ever play fair. He gave Norton the power to become a mighty Spirit Protector of San Francisco, but also granted the man his sanity, so instead of a mad haunt with no emotional baggage, he actually became what the Ohlone didn't want—a dude with a gutful of angst."

"So, the madman became sane and became what? Bipolar?" asked the former detective. "How is a sane ghost a bad thing?"

I fielded that one. "Whatever ritual or spell the Ohlone performed kept Norton from moving on, preventing him from going to …" I snorted. "To wherever spirits go when the body dies. But it comes with a price, you see … the need to move on, to move past this world, tears at him like fishhooks. If he had remained the Mad Emperor of the United States, he wouldn't have that inner conflict because the insanity he had lived with for over twenty years would have been his shield. Sane, every day is agony, every moment a reminder that he may not leave and find true peace. It is an ongoing torture."

"Holy crap."

"Exactly right. In the past few years he's found a semblance of peace, a sleep mode if you will, that allows him to pass the time with minimal discomfort."

Wilkes sighed. "And we're going to wake him up."

"Yeah."

"Let me guess, going back to that 'sleep mode' isn't easy."

"Ghosts don't have 'off' switches, pard." Canton shook his head. "They ain't computers. It'll take a little time before this unquiet ghost settles." He turned to me, features contorted by anger and frustration. "White boy, do we really have to do this? Really?"

My fists were clenched so tight that the knuckles were white. "You know the drill, buddy. We started on this case late and we are running out of time. If it's a simple murder—which I don't believe it is—our forty-eight hours are up, and if a Supernatural killed Mace, time is of the essence because it *will* kill again and we can't let that happen."

No way in hell, not on my watch.

"So what now?" asked Wilkes.

Canton turned away, jaw muscles bunching and unbunching, while Winch rubbed her eyes, not really wanting to see what was going to happen next.

"Go wait by the cars, you three." I didn't want them to witness my crime.

Winch's hands moved from her eyes. "Just do it already!" she snarled, two spots of red high on her cheeks. Her breathing was ragged, as if she'd run a few hundred yards.

Wonderful.

"You know, Wilkes, the surest way to get the Emperor's attention is to shock him and the only way to shock him is to destroy something that was connected to him, something that he touched or had great sentimental value. For him it's like the ringing of a telephone." I gestured to the bill fluttering in the wind. "Norton printed his own money and people thought it was hilarious. Tourists exchanged their own money for his and that helped keep him warm in the winter, paying for whatever flophouse he could afford at the time. These bills are so rare, not many left, and if I set fire to it just so ..." My other hand emerged from my jacket pocket, revealing a silver Zippo lighter. One, two, three flicks of the wheel and the wick caught, burning steadily, despite the breeze. "If he comes, be quiet. Trust me when I say that you don't want his attention upon you."

Sighing, I lit the paper and watched the edge of the bill turn black and begin to curl and smoke, turning into flickering yellow fire that began to eat its way toward the center. Before the flame reached the quarters weighing the bill down, I felt the hair on the back of my neck begin to rise and my skin began to crinkle with goose pimples. I had his attention.

"Come forth, Joshua Norton," I whispered. "Your people, your city, has need of you."

By the pricking of my thumbs ...

Winter in San Fran is relatively mild compared to, say Nebraska, but the cold that brushed through my soul felt as if it could freeze the juice in my eyeballs. My lungs crackled with frost and a voice touched my mind before it hit my ears.

"Hakala." He had spoken my name with such anger and spite. My stomach clenched in apprehension.

Something wicked this way comes.

I didn't bother to look up. "Hello, Joshua."

"Why have I returned? Why have you shaken me from my sleep? Is it to bring torment into my existence eternal? Does my pain quicken your blood? Was it not said that I desired never to see you again?" The ghost's voice was an echo of distant sorrows.

Winch gave a hiccoughing little sob while Canton swore an oath under his breath. From the corner of my eye, I saw Wilkes stiffen and grow pale.

"What I do, I don't do lightly, Joshua. I do these things because they are necessary."

"The organization so charitably dubbed 'The Bureau' has done much under the flimsy guise of necessity and always to some ill effect. It falls, invariably, to the common man to bear the brunt of your incompetence."

"The last time you were woken, Joshua, you didn't feel it was for an 'ill effect.'"

Heat like a black blast from the depths of Hell burst around me and singed my toes through my shoes. *"The last time your scurrilous Bureau deigned to lift a finger, that which was most precious to me was lost!"* The haunt's screech pierced my insides with blades of fury. *"You, Kalevi Hakala, are a plague upon this fair city, a plague upon the innocents who dwell within her bosom and I wish you to absent yourself forthwith!"*

Somewhere in the middle of that tirade, I'd had enough. I lifted my head so I could fully visualize the specter that confronted me.

What met my eyes went from his torso on up. The rest was obstructed by the headstone I knelt before. I could see clear through him to the trees beyond. The ghost was of perhaps average height, dressed in a uniform similar to a Union army officer's, circa 1860. But instead of a low-fitting cap, he wore a top hat with a large feather glued to the front.

Unlike in the movies, where the ghost is all cute and adorable and you find it quaint, the pressure of Norton's presence was enough to have the lizard portion of my hindbrain scurry under the nearest mental rock to gibber madly before passing out.

His eyes—those terrible, terrible dark eyes—were filled with anguish and unrelenting, jagged sanity. The anguish and anger that flowed from him buffeted my senses, and it took every ounce of will I had to rise on shaky legs. The desire to rage, to fling my own anger at his fury like a gauntlet boiled within my gut, but I tamped down on the urge. Here was a spirit so poisoned by pain and loss that its agony was almost a physical blow to my gut; it was all I could do not to surrender to despair.

"Joshua," I finally ground out after an eternity of weathering his regard. "What happened last time wasn't my fault, but that of a madman."

Joshua's scream ripped at my skin. *"You did not save her!"*

A warm liquid trickled from my nose into my mouth … blood. From behind me I heard a high-pitched sob as Winch collapsed to her knees, hands over her ears.

Damn it! I was willing to put up with a certain amount of flagellation from the spook, but when a member of my team gets hurt … *oh hell, NO!*

"Joshua!" I shouted back at the ghost, letting it feel the full measure of my anger. "That's enough!"

And just like that, Norton collapsed in on himself, reverting to a sad little movie special-effects ghost, sobbing incoherently.

Great, I had made the spook cry. Feeling like a total dickweed, I strode through the mud to stand next to the sobbing specter, rubbing life back into my hands. I should have remembered how mercurial the former madman could be.

"Joshua," I murmured gently, "a good man, a man who fought for this country to keep people safe, was murdered a couple days ago. His name was Thomas Mace and he was a citizen of this city. You remember him, don't you?" My words slowly sunk in and Norton's sobs abated. After a few moments, he lifted his ravaged face and met my eyes with his ghostly black orbs. "I think he was killed by a Supernatural and I need you to see if you can sense anything."

"The city has become a different beast since the time of my roaming, Hakala. It has become a warren of glass and steel." His voice had become whispery and thin, while retaining its sadness and despair. "Time and tides have changed much, as have I."

"What do you mean, Joshua?"

"When the Ohlone shaman performed his ritual of binding upon my spirit, my power was at its apex due to the good people of this fair city. Their love and respect flowed into my spectral being, filling me like the finest of wines. Too much time has passed since those days and I have become much reduced. The people have slowly forgotten me over the past century, rendering me but a dim reflection of what I once was. I no longer have their belief to bolster my essence."

"How can that be, Joshua? The magic of Coyote fills you, drives you to be the Guardian of the City."

"Hakala, spells are not perpetual engines that drive forever, as you well know. Coyote was powerful in his time, but the belief of his people has diminished, and with it his power. Even in the few short years since we last met, I have grown weaker and am not what I once was. However, the magic that holds me here is still strong and will be for quite some time. I doubt I hold the power to accomplish what you need."

Wonderful.

Still, we had to make some sort of move, make the effort. "Try, Joshua. For the sake of a fallen comrade, a former soldier in the United States Army Rangers. He was a good man who deserved a better death."

Joshua stared into my eyes, as if gauging my resolve; I could feel hate and anger for me radiating from him. Only a couple of feet separated us and I could see every ghostly hair of his wild, black goatee and thick moustache as if they were tangible. A minute, then two passed before he tipped me a fraction of a nod and relief flooded my veins. I let out a breath I hadn't known I was holding.

No ceremony, no mystic gobbledygook. Joshua stood there for a good ten seconds, head tilted slightly to the left and became … unfocused. The lines of his transparent form blurred and seemed to vibrate at a frequency unknown to the physical world. Seconds later he became a grayish smear hanging in the frigid air.

When Norton spoke next, it was with a voice that sounded like the howl of lost things and damned souls. *"It is … difficult."*

"What is, Joshua?" I licked my lips.

"I am … the way is … there is an obstruction, a clouding of my sight. My city, my beloved city is threatened and I cannot see the peril that rushes toward it like a locomotive! It is as if a cloud of nacreous magic floats over all and renders me impotent."

Oh crap.

"A cloud? Of magic?" Canton and I traded puzzled looks. How was that possible? Before I could ponder that, Joshua screamed, a sound like the world's most horrendous traffic accident, a rending tear that sent a jagged spike of pain through both ears. The team and I shrieked our agony into the gray sky as we fell to our knees. A coppery taste flooded my mouth and I dimly realized that I'd bitten my tongue.

"I am not strong enough! There is not enough of ME left to pierce this dread veil! It has a strength that is beyond my ken. Oh, my city, what will become of you? I do not believe I can save you! I have betrayed my sacred oath, my sacred watch."

Sacred oath? I shook my head, flinging shards of pain from my skull as Joshua's voice receded and all thoughts of sacred oaths fled.

There came a period of silence where we began to recover from that awful scream; then Joshua Norton spoke again, his voice carrying even more sorrow than before. The brunt of it nearly broke my heart.

"I know only this, Hakala … danger comes from the West, a power dire, a power unlike anything I have ever beheld and its puissance is vast, terrible. It obscures the setting sun and tears at reality with claws of bone and hate. That power brought the beast that killed your friend and summoned a hound to devil his steps. This is a power unlike anything you've ever faced, Hakala, and you will die if you and yours confront it alone. The Bureau will be of no use; it is a weak and febrile thing compared to what comes. I, who am the Guardian, do not have the power to face this thing. My people no longer believe in me. They do not remember and so I am diminished."

With a sigh and a groan, Joshua Norton faded from sight, leaving behind the stink of anguish and regret.

Chapter Six

Things That Work and Things That Don't

It was a grim scene in the Suburbans as we motored north. A pall clouded the cabins of both vehicles. I had no clue as to what Joshua had rambled on about, but that didn't mean he was wrong. In fact, he was *never* wrong, which means that the Bureau would not, *could* not, defeat this "power dire" and that any attempts would only end in disaster.

Prophesy sucks. Never really cared for it, even when it came from an impeccable source such as Joshua. The horns of this particular dilemma were gouging my tender nether regions: should I call the Bureau for re-enforcements, discounting Joshua's prediction that they would be of no use, or go it alone with the team—hoping to outthink the bad guys and most likely getting us all killed in the process? Did I really have a choice?

Wonderful.

A buzz came from behind my ear and I felt Ilena's voice come through the induction pad. *"Boss, I have the info you needed on the aliases, and you ain't gonna believe what I found!"*

From her tone of voice I knew the answer already. *"It was under the name of Joshua Norton,"* I subvocaled. Beside me, Wilkes looked over in surprise.

"How the hell do you do that?!" She sounded genuinely outraged.

"Because he used it last time we came here, back in 2000." I felt like slapping my forehead. Sometimes I'm thick as a brick and twice as quick. *"My fault, Ilena. I should have known. Good job."*

"Does that mean I'm off crap detail?"

I grinned. *"You wish, kid."*

"Hey, boss!" Canton sent. *"She should clean the bathroom. Looks like the aftermath of a Black Eyed Peas concert."*

"Boss, permission to turn the Indian into a sheepmonger tree frog."

"White boy, permission to spank our magician."

Winch, *"You spank her, you die."*

"How about all of you shut up?" I snapped.

"Shutting up."

"Yep, me, too, white boy."

"I know when to keep it shut, boss."

"Gonna close my trap any second now, Kal."

I let them babble on and on about shutting up as we entered the heart of the city. According to the files Ilena sent to my RediPad, Joshua Norton, AKA Thomas Kevin Mace, had rented an upscale apartment not too far from the loft. This was no great surprise for me because my life tends to be much like a game of Scrabble where I'm blindfolded and missing half the tiles.

"Boss," Wilkes began. *"What happened last time you were here? What was taken from Norton that he prized so much?"*

Blood, black in the bright light of the full moon, splashed across the landscape of my memory. Last time in San Fran had been a dubious victory at best; we killed the bad guy and saved lives, but at the same time lost the heart of Joshua Norton.

"I'll tell you later," I muttered, the foul taste of the memory coating my tongue. Off to the right, out of the corner of my eye, I saw a young kid—perhaps thirteen, with long, stringy blond hair and a gray hoodie—pointing a stick. I saw a flash of mirrored sunglasses before the world went all jiggery.

Heat burned up my arm and the roof of the Suburban hit me in the face and torqued my head at a nearly impossible angle while the steering wheel hit me in the Misters. The cramping, grinding pain that shot through my crotch was a blunt message that my sex life would be curtailed for a while. A tail of yellow briefly flickered across my vision, accompanied by a strange crackling sound. Burnt pork assailed my nose. For some reason, everything was topsy-turvy and it slowly came to me that I hung upside down by my seat belt, which was odd but I couldn't quite figure out why.

I tasted blood and burning plastic. A square of glass had invaded my mouth and spitting it out hurt like hell, but not as much as my left arm. What …? A body blocked my sight to the right, a big one. More blood filled my mouth and the universe spun on its axis. I felt the sudden urge to throw up. I wiped my eyes and realized that my left sleeve was on fire and the burning pork was ME! I smelled almost delicious but I couldn't hear much because everything seemed to be muffled in a pad of cotton and when that cotton was suddenly ripped away, I could hear *everything*, a cacophony of harsh sounds—the blare of horns, the crackle and whoosh of fire, the jagged raw sound of metal slowly scraping asphalt. It all overwhelmed me and I could feel my eyes crossing in consternation.

Crunch, crunch, crunch …

The noise was close enough to draw my attention because for some reason the fire eating my arm didn't hurt any more, but what was crunching my way with such slow, deliberate steps?

White high tops, Air Jordans, were all I could see of the person who calmly walked around the black SUV, rubber soles crackling the tiny bits of safety glass that were sprayed around the vehicle like a silicate web.

It hurt like a mother to twist my head around as the shoes made it to the driver's side window and halted, the toes pointing straight at me. A black, bulky object lay next to my temple and I fumbled for it, driven by panic. Cool metal greeted my palm just as a face fronted by a pair of mirrored lenses peered in.

It was the kid, the kid with the stick, wearing gray sweatpants to match his/her gray hoodie. I couldn't tell if the kid was male or female; its features were perfectly androgynous. Long blond hair that

I had thought was stringy was instead silk-fine, hanging to an inch above the asphalt before fading into invisibility. The sight of that hair, the ends dangling into nothingness, sent a worm of fear gnawing at my gut and it wasn't just the heat of my burning flesh that popped sweat on my forehead.

"A ghlacadh mé aon áthas seo," he/she said in a high, fluting voice, full of music and chiming notes that brought a tingle to my ears. For some reason I thought of forest meadows and the taste of honey nectar. In contrast to the music of the kid's voice, the face behind the mirrored shades was dispassionate, hard as mountain gutrock. "Ní hé seo an pearsanta, tá sé gnó." That said, the kid raised his/her stick.

Something about that foot-long piece of wood struck me as the most terrifying thing I'd ever seen, not that it actually radiated menace or evil or had "One Stick to Rule Them All" inscribed on it in fiery runes. Terror seemed to be part of the reality that surrounded it and I did the only thing I could under the circumstances, I aimed Alex's new invention (the object that had landed next to my skull) and pulled the trigger.

Clack.

Oh crap. Again, I pulled the trigger.

Clack. Nothing.

The kid smiled, revealing slightly oversized and very white teeth, and aimed that damn stick at my face. I knew I was dead, that whatever magic that piece of wood held would blow my head apart like a melon hitting the highway. I closed my eyes, hoping it wouldn't hurt.

Crack!

Crack!

Gunshots? Why would a stick sound like a gun?

"Kal!" Canton screamed, voice filled with panic. How very unlike him to be panicked and, for a moment I grew concerned, but it didn't last.

I considered opening my eyes, but the darkness was so comforting that I decided to stay there for a while. As I darted down the rabbithole, the image of Jeanie's face was the only thing I took with me.

Darkness still. Comfortable and deep. No dreams, only a sense of well-being.

"Oh, man, this is so messed up." Deep voice. Male.

"Shhhh ... let her work." Not a deep voice. Pleasant. Female.

"She's done already."

"Then let him rest."

"We need him awake."

"That's not your call."

"Actually, it is."

"Canton," the female warned.

That was it, Canton. I knew that voice was familiar.

"No," said Canton firmly. He sounded pissed. Why was that?

"But—" Winch ... yes, it was Winch.

The dark haze surrounding me began to fray, shredding like fog in a wind, and the light resolved into a picture of Canton, Winch and Ilena hovering over me.

"He's awake," Ilena smiled, relief etching her face. She really was quite pretty when she smiled, reminding me of a buff version of Audrey Hepburn.

Over me? Awake? Of course I was awake! My head moved creakily from side to side, noting the hospital bed and an IV drip loading fluids into the back of my right hand. My left was swathed in bandages. Winch brought a straw to my lips and I took a long drink of tepid water, which lubricated my throat nicely. The smell of every disinfectant in the world assaulted my nose and left an arsenic tang on the back of my tongue. I didn't care because I was happy to be alive.

Speaking of which ... quick head count and a look at the faces of those surrounding me. Canton—grim and somewhat impassive. All business. Winch—dark circles under her eyes, normally tan face drawn and sallow. Ilena—exhausted, cheeks hollow with sorrow that pulled at her skin. She looked much older than her twenty-six years.

The evidence allowed only one conclusion. "Wilkes?" My voice was a rattly rasp, thick with apprehension.

No one met my eyes.

Oh crap.

I closed my eyes, but the reality, the enormity, of the situation refused to fade. Another one gone. "Canton, report."

In a dry monotone, the Apache laid it all out. "Saw your SUV flip over and catch fire and something, some force, hammered into ours. Our vehicle was thrown back a couple dozen feet and the doors locked on their own. We used our weapons to break the windows and crawl out, but by that time some kid in gray sweat pants and hoodie was at your car." He took a long breath and his darker than dark eyes grew troubled. "I regret to inform you, sir, that I fired on a civilian. I don't know why, but something about the kid felt wrong. I fired without thinking." Another long breath and a quick glance at Winch. "After I fired, the kid disappeared, ran faster than I thought humanly possible, heading west. I missed the kid, Kal, and I don't know how. I had that kid dead bang, but I missed him. When I arrived at your vehicle, both you and it were on fire. I pulled you free and doused the flames on your arm. It looked pretty damn burnt. The SUV is a total loss. I called for an ambulance and alerted Warehouse that we would be in the Hospital under the aegis of the FBI. Currently, you are listed as a victim of a traffic mishap." Two, then three heartbeats passed. "I will formally put myself on report for firing on a civilian and submit myself to a review by both the director and IA."

Facing Internal Affairs means submitting to an in-depth interrogation by a Bureau magician using the latest in invasive, truth-sensing spells. The process can cause pain, insomnia, involuntary muscle spasms and diarrhea. Pretty much all the worst side effects of any prescription drug on the market ... except for death and depression. There are other truth spells out there, but they rely on the co-operation of the person under scrutiny. The spells the Bureau uses for these situations are a bit more ... drastic and one of the reasons so few agents cross ethical boundaries. For Canton to volunteer for such examination meant he felt he'd really screwed the pooch on this one, which was wrong on all counts. Fortunately, I was in a position to disabuse my friend.

I held up my free hand, the one swathed in bandages. "No need, Canton. That kid *was* the bad guy."

The news both surprised and relieved him. Winch snagged one of his large hands in both of hers. They shared a look that spoke volumes.

"Tell me about Wilkes."

That put a damper on any happy-happy joy-joy feelings anyone might have been experiencing. "He was dead already, boss." Ilena sounded as exhausted as she looked. Her lips barely moved, as if the words had no substance and could easily be launched. "His neck was broken when the vehicle landed upside-down. There was nothing to be done."

Nothing to be done. How many times had I heard those words in conjunction with a death of a colleague? Far too many and far too often. I would rail against unjust fate later. It was time to man-up and carry on with the op. "My injuries?"

A little animation entered her face, as if taking her mind off Wilkes lent her energy. "Massive burns on your left arm. I was able to heal your wounds, except for the one on the back of your left hand. Bone and muscle tissue are just fine, but I had no reserves of energy to complete the job."

"So there will be a scar?" One more among the many already collected serving my country.

"Yes, boss, about the size of a silver dollar. And I have to say, compared to the ones on your torso, it's nothing special."

That almost earned a chuckle. Once I had wrapped silver wire around myself before confronting a magician. Silver, like most precious metals, is quite good at absorbing magical energy, however, when it absorbs too much, it tends to overheat. By the time I'd killed that magician, I was cooked medium well and ready to be served. Magic had healed me, but the scars remained.

To Canton, "How long was I out."

"Three hours, Kal."

"Try to get in touch with BB?"

"Negative."

I nodded, relieved. "Good. Get me a RediPad. The rules of this game have changed." Winch, still dressed in her black FBI-issue no-nonsense outfit, pulled one of the powerful tablets from her purse and handed it over.

While I powered up the mini computer, Ilena withdrew her own RediPad and performed a standard scan—checking for bugs, both tech and magical. When finished, she gave me a thumbs-up.

Under my fingers, the screen came to life and I pressed the phone app. A number pad popped into life and I dialed. Two rings later and Andrea's solemn face appeared. "March Hare Services, how may I direct your call?" Her tone was clipped and perfectly professional.

"Agent Ident Kilowatt 22, Lima Zulu 3." On the other end, her computer confirmed the Agent Code and voice recognition identified me as Kalevi Hakala.

"Ident confirmed. How can I help you?"

"Max encrypt my authority, eyes and ears Director only." Bureau-speak for an Emergency call.

"Roger that." Without delay, BB came online and a red dot appeared on the upper left corner of the tablet confirming the line was encrypted with the best tech and magic money could buy.

"Go, Kal." BB's normally serious demeanor was downright funereal.

My hands pressed an icon and a virtual keyboard appeared. If whoever was behind Mace's death could break the encryption and decipher what I was about to do, we were already done for. *Assume comms compromised,* I typed. Verbally, we carried out another conversation entirely. "Just called to give you a sitrep. I am in the hospital, but I will be fine. However we can't go back to the loft."

BB's eyes bored into mine. A single word flashed across the screen: *Report.* "How long will you be in hospital?"

"Oh, about a day or two." Meanwhile I tried to stay detached as I typed a quick summary of the day's events, starting with the conversation with Joshua and ending with me waking up in the hospital.

That elicited a reaction, a large one for BB: his eyes widened slightly. The Director knew full well the efficacy of Joshua Norton's clairvoyance. "What about the situation there? Mace's suicide." *Understood. Situation almost sounds untenable. What do you need?*

"Not clear yet. I will investigate further." *Requesting that the BSI stay out of San Fran. Too dangerous. As for right now, send no one else. If my guess is correct, later on tonight I will have more to report.* If Norton was right (and he had never been wrong yet as far as the Bureau knew), then more agents would likely result in more bodies.

BB's eyes narrowed. "Understood." *Necessary?*

"Boss, I will contact you later if there is anything else to report. As for now, we are keeping our heads down." *Believe so. Major magical attack on us and I bet it didn't register or you would have been all over this city. Our merlin sensors here most likely compromised. Give me time, please, to regroup and to gather more intel. I will report later on the disposition of Wilkes's body, but in the meantime, download his will to this RediPad.*

Direct hit. We'd been hit with major mojo and the Bureau had heard nothing. From the tightening around his eyes, I could see that BB was more than a little pissed. The bad guys had slipped on past him. "All right, you take good care of yourself. Get well." *Get me a result, Kal. You have seventy-two hours before I intervene.*

Three days to figure out what the hell was going on or the boss would send in the cavalry, which might result in said cavalry dying in horrible, unique ways. "Thanks, BB. I appreciate it." *Got it.*

My message delivered, I terminated the call. If anyone had been looking in, all they would have seen and heard was a standard report.

Canton and Winch stared at me. They'd been reading the messages and knew we weren't going to receive back-up. Their faces were open and expectant, absolutely trusting in my judgment despite getting our asses kicked by a kid with a pointy stick. These two friends, agents forged in the crucible that is the Bureau, were placing their lives in my hands, absolutely positive that I could figure out a way to win.

I needed a drink.

"Ilena, am I okay? I feel all right, maybe a bit tired."

"Should be fine, boss."

Nodding, I stripped the bandages from my left hand and Ileana made to protest, but shut her mouth with a *snap* at my sharp look. The last layer of gauze came free, sticky with anti-burn cream and my injury was revealed. Like she said, a roundish, silver-dollar-sized wound comprised of pink and red melted skin shiny in the sickly fluorescent lights. Oddly smooth and hairless, it looked like Tyler Durden had given me a chemical burn kiss that signaled my initiation into Project Mayhem. Bureau members turned up their noses at *Fight Club*, preferring instead *Fight Dirty and Win Club*. Playing nice wasn't in the vocabulary. Marquis of Queensbury would have been torn limb from limb.

After a heroic effort to become vertical (involving some huffing-puffing and a moment of dizziness), I gathered the remainder of my clothes—pants, socks and underwear. Thanks to the fire, I had no shirt or jacket and had to do without. Not even a San Francisco winter was something I wanted to experience in the raw, so I sent Ilena out on a search for something to wear and Winch for a cup of coffee or three. When I had my pants and shoes on, Ilena came back with a navy blue Tigger t-shirt.

"It was the only one in Lost and Found that would fit you," she said. *That wasn't a twinkle in her eye. She wouldn't dare. Would she?* I stared at the shirt, slightly rumpled, the figure of the bouncing feline was faded and frayed from many, many washings. However, it was clean and it fit, albeit a bit snugly.

After a stretch to work the knots out–my muscles had more kinks than an S&M club—I turned to Canton. "Wilkes?"

"Morgue," he ground out. The Native American hadn't known Wilkes long, but the dead detective had been such a congenial sort that I had no doubt Canton had come to like the big lug.

"Police?"

He shook his head. "Homeland Security and FBI. I called both Directors and they pulled strings. As far as the Straights are concerned, there was no accident leading to fatality involving a black Suburban. All records have been erased."

Good. Despite some friction between the directors of the Alphabet Agencies and the Bureau, they were secretly glad it existed. Not only were we protecting the good ol' U.S. of A. from all goons Supernatural, we were also a dumping ground for agents they considered sackworthy. Given the choice between termination and Bureau service, a surprisingly large number chose the Bureau. Considering our attrition rate, we were happy to have them. Because of the brutality of the training, very few made it past Coronado. All in all, it was a twisted symbiotic relationship that worked and rendered the Bigwigs of various agencies extremely cooperative.

"Ilena."

"Yeah, boss?"

A deep breath steadied my nerves. What I was about to request kind of creeped my socks off, but it was something I couldn't avoid. "I need a memory-enhance spell. Do you know that Shape?"

Her pixie face became troubled. "Sure."

My index finger stabbed an icon on the RediPad. "Do it."

Nodding uncertainly, she stared into my eyes before a protesting Canton and Winch could stop her.

Those two blue orbs became my world as I concentrated on the accident. Everything else faded at the edges and a bright thread of pulsing magic connected us, running from my forehead to hers. It didn't hurt. In fact it was quite pleasant, feeling like the soft tingle of spring sunlight on skin. A sort of lassitude spread through my limbs and, as if from a distance, I heard what I had so desperately wanted to remember.

"A ghlacadh mé aon áthas seo," I spoke tonelessly, the words tripping off my tongue easily, as if I had just heard them. "Ní hé seo an pearsanta, tá sé gnó." The words of the kid in the gray hoodie with the pointy stick.

And the world came back to me in a sudden rush, harshing my mellow.

"White boy," Canton uttered angrily. "What the hell are you

doing?" He served up a good glare to Ilena, who shrugged it off.

I held up a finger. "Wait." My finger touched the TRANSLATE icon on the RediPad. A soft chime came from the device and an asexual voice announced, "Translation complete. Gaelic to English. Quote, 'To this I take no pleasure. This is not personal, it is business.' End quote."

Interesting.

Before either Winch or Canton could explode on me, I clued them in. "It was something the kid said to me after flipping the Suburban like a pancake. He or she sounded kind of raw about the situation, so I figured it was important."

Winch wasn't buying. "So you risk brain damage from a mind spell to remember what the little dork said? Have you lost what little wits you once had, you ginormous dickweed?"

Okay, so maybe I had that coming. Any sort of mind altering or enhancement spells had risks of hurting said mind. And before you ask, the Interdiction spell was created by one of the greatest magicians ever and honed and perfected over hundreds of years so it was virtually risk free.

Virtually.

"Be that as it may, Winch, I had to know what the little skink was saying." To Ilena, "Find the nearest cell tower and pull the sensor. I want to know why—when we faced a magical attack—our RediPads weren't warbling loud enough to deafen us." Those sensors, when detecting magic, piggybacked the signals from the cell towers. Our RediPads were set to receive those signals and sound an alarm if sufficient magic was used. Flipping that Suburban would have activated nearly every sensor in San Fran.

I looked up to find the little magician staring at me in surprise. Obviously, during all the hubbub, she hadn't thought of that angle. "Well, what are you waiting for? Applause? Git!"

She got gone.

"Winch, you're our resident gear head. How much does a Chevy Suburban weigh?"

Her Betty-Boop face scrunched up in concentration. "Uh, a little more than two tons," she finally said. That sounded about right.

I nodded to Canton. "Weapons?"

He nodded back and produced the Lahti, my Bowie and that enormous monstrosity of Alex's. I examined the weapon. Didn't look broken; all the sliding bits still slid, all the ratcheting bits still ratcheted. Ejecting the clip showed me nothing.

"You know, kids," I muttered as I examined the weapon, "I wonder how much magical energy it takes to flip a four-thousand-plus pound SUV and shove an identical vehicle twenty-plus feet like it's nothing." Barrel was clear. Didn't see any warping or odd bits of broken metal here and there.

Canton was the first to speculate. "Jesus, white boy, at least ten gigamerlins, probably more!"

Winch nodded, face tight.

Ten gigamerlins. A merlin is a unit of magical energy and ten gigamerlins is enough to seriously stir-fry the population of the Astrodome and hold the sauce. I twirled the pistol like a Wild West gunslinger. Anyone who owns a pistol has tried it, and those who say they haven't are lying. "I can't think of anything that produces that much power except for a magical Tesla coil, but the kid sure wasn't lugging one around. That begs the question of how the little rat bastard did it because no magician I know of has that kind of raw juice."

Frowning, I thumbed the dial to SILENCER and pressed the barrel to the pillow, pulling the trigger.

Clack! "Piece of junk," I muttered.

Sighing, I tossed the weapon to Winch who tucked it away while I strapped the Bowie to my leg. At least my trusty knife would never suffer a mechanical failure. "You two head on to Mace's place, check it out. I'll catch a cab and be there shortly." I kept the RediPad, leaving only one for the pair.

"White boy, what are we gonna do?" Canton sounded worried, but his expression remained inscrutable as ever while Winch stared, stone-faced. "Joshua said we would die if we tried to face this thing head on and the Bureau would be no help."

That dilemma had been on my mind every second since Joshua Norton spoke the words. The truth was that I had no idea what to do. I didn't even know what enemy I was facing, but I sure wasn't going to clue my team in on that little detail. "Don't worry," I said with my best hundred-dollar smile. I have … an angle."

They looked unconvinced.

I sighed. "Do you trust me?"

Canton nodded. "Of course."

"Then head out to Mace's and don't worry too much."

"What are you going to do, boss?" Winch asked, adjusting her black, no-nonsense suit jacket.

Bile teased the back of my throat and I had to swallow heavily before replying. "Go buy a shirt and jacket that doesn't make me look fat. Then I have to go see a friend. I made a promise and I mean to keep it."

After they left the room, I dialed a number on the RediPad. A few moments later, Jeanie's sweet face appeared on the screen.

"Hi, babe." My heart lurched with a very familiar, sweet sensation.

Very white, even teeth flashed at me. "Hello yourself. You look like hell." She, on the other hand, was the same, lovely Jeanie who haunted my dreams in a good way. Smooth, milk-chocolate skin, big deep-brown eyes you could swim in.

"I'm in the hospital. Got beaten up by a midget with delusions of grandeur. How was your day?"

Jeanie's face crinkled with worry for a half-second, but then the lines smoothed out. If I was well enough to crack lame jokes, I couldn't be too bad off. "Fine. We are still in Louisiana. I love the food here, but should be back home soon, just waiting for the second encounter."

Ahhh, "the second encounter." Every time there was one Supernatural outbreak, another was sure to follow. It was the one constant of the job.

We exchanged pleasantries, communicating more with our expressions and tone of voice rather than words. By the time we were done, I was ready for the crap part of my day.

Chapter Seven

San Francisco Story, Part One

The pathologist was more than willing to assist when I showed him my badge. It's amazing what you can do with one. Like a skeleton key, it opens doors everywhere. Made me realize again how easy it is to abuse.

It was a big room, that morgue, with two walls of slide-out refrigerated drawers and six tables with sheet-draped corpses, bare toe-tagged feet sticking out like pale sticks. Fluorescent lighting, harsh and painful to the eyes, lit the place, recreating the set of a mainstream horror movie where the filmmaker tries to evoke an "authentic" atmosphere of cold metal and dead, waxy flesh. Unlike the rest of the hospital, that place didn't reek of disinfectant and other harsh chemicals. No, what assailed my nostrils was something more hideous and unnerving.

It smelled like dead things and emptiness.

"Will you please give me a few minutes alone with my friend, Doc?" I asked the pathologist who bore a marked resemblance to a young Denzel Washington, except a little shorter and a whole lot chubbier.

He smiled, which created fine lines around his kind eyes. It was a good smile, a smile you could trust. "Of course, Agent Dumont."

His tone was smooth as warm honey, a singer's voice. "Your friend is in drawer eighteen." That said, he walked away without a backward glance.

Right. Drawer eighteen, his penultimate home. The thought of actually touching the silvery steel latch raised my hackles, but I did it anyway. Wilkes deserved better from me than squeamishness.

A puff of cold air. It smelled like … nothing. No corpse smell, no disinfectant. It smelled sterile and bereft of hope. Inside, a shiny black body bag. I pulled at the cold metal tray and it rolled out with a faint rumble, as if reluctant to disgorge its contents.

Three feet of steel tray and three feet of black bag with a shiny zipper running down the middle lay exposed to the harsh fluorescents. My hand refused to touch the tiny tongue of the zipper and I cursed myself for a fool. I'd seen plenty of dead bodies in my time, more than I really cared to recall. This one should have been no different. The Bureau always produced plenty of fodder for the Reaper and deaths on the job were rarely clean. Usually the corpses were in various stages of disassembly. How sick and wrong is it that I was more used to torn and mangled bodies than whole ones?

Time to take the bull by the horns … or the zipper by the tab.

Ziiiiiip.

Oh damn …

Dead flesh, gray, blue in places. The tissue of Wilkes's face had settled, spread a bit across the skull, giving him a fierce, scowling countenance. His eyes, under waxy lids, seemed sunken and lost. He didn't appear to be asleep or resting. No, he looked dead.

A lump the size of a Volvo hit my throat and a familiar burning sensation started behind my eyes. It took one, two, then three seconds for me to gain a modicum of control, but not before a stray tear fell from my eye and *plopped* onto my friend's cheek.

"Aw hell, man," I husked, barely able to force the words out. "Out of all the Green Peas, I thought you would be the one to last, the one to actually grow old."

In life, Wilkes had been a big man—I mean the kind of big that makes a large room seem small—but lying there all pallid and drained of vitality, he seemed to be half the man he used to be. The clay of his flesh no longer swelled with his personal energy and that realization brought more tears. Sorrow clutched at the bones of my chest with cold fingers.

I reached into my pants pocket and pulled out a shiny black rectangle the size of a domino. A matte-black button adorned one side and I gave it a push and set the little device next to Wilkes's head. Of all the new toys from Special Branch's R&D, it was one of my favorites—a sonic scrambler. Any sound within three feet of the device would be knotted so those persons outside the range would hear only so much gibberish. The Bureau had a magical equivalent, but tech is usually easier to account for and batteries are cheap.

"You know, Wilkes, I promised you a story. I promised I would tell you about Joshua Norton and the first time I met him."

I started to settle into a groove, to create a comfy camaraderie with the slab of dead meat that used to be my friend. If I squinted just so, I could almost pretend he was sleeping, albeit on a very cold bed.

"It all started a month or so after we came back from that Florida bug hunt and Mace was still pretty pissed about the whole boat thing..."

After killing the mantis, we helped some selkies (sort of were-seals, normally very nice and polite Supernaturals, most of them female) find their way back to the Florida Keys. Apparently a tropical storm had blown the poor ladies off course and they wound up frantically dodging 'gators and poachers. Being an agent isn't *all* about killing Supernaturals, thank goodness. The Bureau doesn't mind sharing the world with them, as long as they behave. It's a Rodney King "Why can't we all just get along" type of attitude. Unfortunately, the most Supernaturals haven't heard of Rodney King.

Warehouse in those days was located just south of Alexandria, Virginia, which is a pretty cool town to chill in and enjoy. When off work, most of the agents went to a little dive bar called The Hazmat Club, the kind of place where they had live music and the bar staff swept up digits at the end of the night along with the peanut shells.

But the drinks were reasonable and not watered down and the owner was ex-Bureau, so she never called the cops when an agent got all frisky-like and sent a few drunken loudmouth douchebags to the hospital.

Unfortunately for Mama Hakala's baby boy, I was stuck back at Warehouse while the rest of the team boogied the night away at the club. Mace had me filling out AARs (After Action Reports) and double-checking the RODI (Returned Offensive/Defensive Inventory) for returning teams. They were more than happy for me to help with the scut work, which usually involved hours upon hours of mind-numbing tedium. More fun than human-beings should be allowed to have.

After counting off the shelved spell eggs and a grip of carefully hung Faraday coats (think of a black duster or trench coat that runs from throat to ankle), I checked them against the list on my Slate (a slightly smaller precursor to the RediPad). I was ready for a little downtime. It was a hair before midnight and I knew my team wouldn't be back from the nocturnal activities until the wee hours. Of course, it was then that a chime came from my earwig.

"Hakala," I said, racking the Slate into its cradle before locking up the Armory. Biggs, a two-year vet, motioned for me to hurry up. Ceiling cameras, spell Spy Eyes, and a Shape buried in the concrete of the floor to prevent theft, didn't stop the director from making doubly sure that items were housed in the Armory *stayed* in the armory. Biggs had kept his beady little eyes focused on me the entire time, as if I were planning to pull a Houdini with a couple million worth of spell gems.

"Agent, the director wishes to see you in the meeting room." It was the voice of Sylvia, BB's new Receptionist, coming through my earwig. Latin-American, slim, and with shoulders a boxer would envy, she was five sticks of dynamite in a small package.

I closed the door to the Armory with a *thunk* and deep, clanging noises came from within. Locked, not even a thermal lance could breach the warded entrance. "Did he say what for?"

"Agent Hakala, the director has his reasons." She might have been addressing a particularly dim-witted child. *"It is not for us to wonder what they are."*

I resisted the urge to argue and affirmed that I would be there posthaste. At that point in time I still didn't quite understand the total bad-assness of Receptionists, but back then I was young and clueless.

The meeting room was a large rectangular affair with a long table and a dozen or so soft leather chairs. BB was waiting, sitting at the head of the table, hands clasped in front of his face, fingers steepled.

Alone.

Oh crap.

"What can I do for you, boss?" I asked, taking a seat on the opposite end. Was I fired? Or in trouble? Or both?

My former team leader and new Director stared at me like I was his next meal. "You're not in trouble, Kal," he intoned with all the gravitas of a mortician.

Thanks to more training than I'd ever wanted, the relief that flooded me didn't reach my face. Instead, I gave the director an impassive nod.

BB must have been impressed because he actually smiled. Oh, not a big one—a mere twitch, a millimeter or two—but enough for me to see. "Your team is not available. I believe they are at the club."

"That is correct, sir."

His watery eyes grew sharp behind his glasses. I could see no reason why he wore them when contacts would have been simpler, or even Lasik. Perhaps he liked the look. "Call me sir again and I'll toss you out faster than you can blink."

I was pretty sure he was kidding. Well, mostly.

"Okay, boss."

"Better." He lifted a Slate and held it up. "Here is all the available information on your team's next assignment."

Wait-a-minute. "Hey, boss, the whole damn team has been drinking like fish for the past few hours, except for me. Don't you want a team that is, well, *sober* to tackle a mission?"

He shook his head. "You will have to trust me on this on, Kal." He slid the slate across the table where it came to rest a foot from my hand. "Read it, memorize it, brief you team and delete it. The clock starts at six a.m."

Wonderful.

Once again a smile so minute it might not have been there. "Think about it, Kal."

I thought about it and felt my own smile blossom. BB graced me with a small chuckle and left me to my reading.

"God, white boy, you're more annoying than a junkyard dog!" complained Canton, holding his head as if afraid his skull would burst apart. A light sheen of sweat slicked his head.

The entire team sat in the meeting room and I stood in front of the DisplayWall, an eight-by-ten-foot monitor that filled the entire surface of the wall behind me. Manufactured out of super-cool nano polymer that did some technogeekbabbleblahblahblah thing that turned a wall into a giant flat screen television ... All I know is that it worked and the sound and fury issuing from it had the rest of the team cringing and whimpering as they writhed in the grip of ferocious hangovers.

Yeah. I was having a great time.

"You want me to turn it up?" I shouted over the din from hidden speakers. Currently, "Ride of the Valkyries" blared while a satellite shot of San Francisco covered the monitor.

"We get it, Kal," Mace rumbled dangerously from deep within his wide chest while the rest glared hot death at me with bloodshot eyes.

I touched an icon on the Slate and the volume of the music dropped a few decibels. I could almost *feel* the relief that flooded the room. "All right, kids." My voice thundered only slightly less than Wagner's famous music and it seemed as if Canton's eyeballs were about to bleed. "Two bodies, both found in the Central West district of San Francisco, both dumped by the Sunset Reservoir. Both victims were viciously beaten and raped." With that I shut Wagner down and let the room stew in the sudden, shocking stillness.

It was Canton who shattered the silence. "What the hell does this have to do with the Bureau, white boy?" His voice had a whiny, scratchy quality I'd never heard before. Of course, I'd never seen him so hung-over.

I touched the Slate and a fifty-six red dots appeared, all scattered throughout the district. "Because at the times of the attack, all these sensors lit up. Two separate attacks, two one-thirty-six-point-four-four megamerlin energy expenditures, then two bodies. Coincidence? I think not, and neither does BB."

Mouth, a one-year veteran who looked like she could kick a hole in an Ogre, spoke up. "You saying that the rapist killed them with *magic?*"

I nodded. "According to the Special Branch, one-thirty-six megamerlins can easily kill a person. Hell, it can practically sauté your entire nervous system, which is what happened to our two victims."

Mace's eyes cleared a little. "So we have a rapist slash murderer slash magician on our hands," he stated in his deep-as-a-well baritone.

My fingers ran across the Slate, and behind me two life-sized color photos appeared. Two women, both dead, both on autopsy tables, both naked, but leached of anything that resembled humanity. Plastic-looking flesh, waxy and gray, coupled with large Y incisions on their torsos gave the two an air of unreality, as if the images had been cobbled together in a rather poor special-effects lab. Unfortunately for the women, that wasn't the case. Their faces had been beaten to a pulp and their breasts had been slashed to the bone with a very sharp knife or razor. The exposed flesh was a washed out pink with hints of gray. Whoever the murderer was, he qualified as sick on a whole other level than most Supernaturals.

At times like these I think humans are worse than the monsters we hunt.

I highlighted the girl on the left in blue—a shortish blonde who some might call "pleasantly plump." Now she just looked unpleasantly dead. "April Tennant, nineteen, coffeehouse clerk, snatched from a mall. No camera footage, no witnesses. No nothing. The girl simply disappeared."

More blue circled the head of the second girl, who could kindly be called "big-boned." Very attractive, very plump, not fat, but very dead. The resemblance to the first girl was striking. "Samantha Weringer, seventeen, snatched when walking home from her friend's house."

"Why didn't her friend drive her home?" asked Winch, her round face pale and drawn.

"Because they lived less than a block from each other."

Mouth leaned forward, eyes glued to the pictures and a hand on her queasy stomach. "This guy ... two kills in one night. These can't be his first victims, can they?" She shook her head. "Normal excitation rapists start slow. This is practically a spree in and of itself."

"Good point and one the director already noted," I remarked dryly and once again displayed the satellite photo of San Francisco. Four green dots were scattered in the Central West district. "Here are the locations of four previous rape victims, all within an eleven month period of time. All beaten bloody and cut with a knife, but in each case with one remarkable difference: they all survived ... brutalized, but alive. Unfortunately, they could not identify their assailant; he wore a mask and black rubber raincoat. We know he is extremely strong, because all the victims were easily subdued. If he is a secretor, he wears a condom. Zero DNA, not even a pubic hair. Local law enforcement has dubbed him 'The Magic Man,' because he simply disappears. No witnesses, no evidence."

For a split second it looked as if the entire team had forgotten how miserable and hung over they were. In that brief moment, you could hear a pin drop.

"Same guy," Winch observed.

I nodded. "We believe so. A serial rapist." I tapped the Slate and the pictures of the four victims replaced San Francisco.

Mace grunted. "Damn, seems like our boy has a type."

He certainly did. All the victims were plus-size girls, and all were under the age of twenty. Those seemed to be the only criteria because our sick puppy didn't care if his victims were blond or brunette. One girl, Twila Shelton, had streaks of pink in her punk purple haircut. All that seemed to matter was that the girls were young and obviously part of the Fast Food culture.

Mouth. "This means … he popped his magical cherry and killed the girls because he's getting off on using magic for murder? He's discovered a new toy and he's trying it out?"

I nodded.

She shook her head. "Damn sonofawhore."

Canton spoke up. "White boy, was this peckerwood stalking the girls?"

"Not enough data at this time, but it seems likely. All we know is, he attacked two women in one night, savagely raped them, beat them, cut them, and then killed them both using magic." My finger traced the surface of the Slate, replacing the photos of the four previous victims with the two autopsy photos. A glowing blue dot appeared on the pics. Using the dot, I created a circle of blue around each girl's head. "The inside of each skull was turned into mush, as if the perp scrambled their brains with an ethereal mixer. Every artery and vein popped like a balloon and the gray matter was the consistency of tapioca pudding. Death was virtually instantaneous."

That took a few moments to sink though alcohol-soaked bone and when it did, Winch's already pale face turned a shade of pale I'd never seen on a living person. She booked out of that room as fast as her long legs could take her. Meeting over.

Time for fun.

"Wonderful," I said. "Now that the image of a splattery mess inside human skulls has made Winch puke up her guts—" Mouth, green around the gills, chose that moment to exit.

"White boy, you suck," Canton burbled, trying to deny the consequences of a night of drinking.

"Sorry, man. Just because their brains look like chunky strawberry oatmeal …"

And that was when I lost the Apache.

"That," Mace rumbled. "Was a totally dick thing to do."

My smile was the only answer I offered.

"Hmph. When do we get a magician? We've been doing without for far too long." He scratched his head with one massive hand. "Not that Mouth hasn't been a fine member of the team."

"We don't. Not enough magicians to go around since Torrance got himself extra killed by that Type Four demon last month. BB also said you're from San Francisco and would be perfect to take the case… that you have a special contact there."

He grimaced. "I was afraid of that. We go soon?"

I nodded. "Today. We downloaded a profile of the killer for everyone to study en route. Consensus is that the perp is a white male between the ages of twenty-five and thirty-five. However, considering that he just popped his magical cherry, we can assume he's a few years younger." The majority of magicians discovered their power while in their teens. In a very few, it manifested in their early twenties.

Thomas Mace grunted and stood, towering over my own 6'4". "You know, they won't forget this any time soon," he said blearily.

"What would you have done?"

He rubbed his chin. "Same thing, but nobody messes with the team leader. They are going to make you *pay*."

"I know." A heavy sigh. "But totally worth it."

His pained laughter shook the room.

"By the way, boss," I said when he was silent and poised to wobble back to the Dorms for a cup of coffee. "Who is this Joshua Norton fella, and what is the your relationship to him?"

My voice was hoarse and cracked, so I checked my watch and found that I'd been talking to Wilkes for about an hour. Time flies when you loiter among the dead.

Some people might think it callous that I had used the victims' gruesome deaths to cause the other team members to barf buckets, but one of the very first things the Bureau teaches you (besides how to kill bad guys) is professional distance. Those girls' remains weren't the worst I'd viewed at the time and it had only been eleven months since I had arrived at Warehouse. By then I'd seen vampire young try to eat its way out of its mother's womb, Preying Mantis guts and so much more.

If agents couldn't step back and grow calluses on their souls, then they would wake at night, screaming for mama and wetting the bed right before nice men in white coats administered Thorazine.

In other words, we had to be right bastards.

I zipped Wilkes up in his polymer cocoon and slid the drawer back into the wall.

"Where do you want to body sent?" asked the pathologist as I exited through the stainless steel double doors, "after the autopsy, of course."

My level stare stopped him before he could step any closer, his mahogany face paling to gray. "No autopsy," I said gravely and with finality. "He stays here for at least another three days."

He sputtered. "This is most irregular, Agent Dumont!"

I turned away. "I'm not done yet." Before I reached the door to the outer hallway, I turned back to find the man staring at me, mouth open.

"There are promises to keep, sir," I said evenly.

And miles to go before I sleep.

Chapter Eight

Home Less

Thanks to our connection at the dealership, another vehicle—a dark blue Honda Odyssey—waited for me in the hospital parking garage. Ilena sat in the driver's seat with the engine running and the heater on.

"Why a freaking minivan, boss?" she asked as I climbed in.

"Would you suspect members of an ultra-secret government agency to be driving a minivan?" I gave her an extra pointy look, hoping that she appreciated my savvy choice.

She seemed unimpressed. Maybe I was losing my touch.

After a quick trip to the nearest clothing store, it took us all of ten minutes to arrive at Mace's apartment, located in a downtown high rise on the fifteenth floor, a penthouse with a commanding view of the city. Entering was a temporary hassle, due to the security personnel and the fact that a keycard was needed to access the elevator. Even though I looked exhausted to the bone, my ID did the trick.

"Joining your other two agents?" asked the security officer in a blue blazer and tan slacks. He was large enough to have played for the 49ers.

"Yes, yes we are."

His darker than dark eyes bored into mine. "Mr. Norton was a nice man, always had a good word for us working stiffs." Brown skin from the top of his shaved head to his goatee-covered chin flushed with anger. I got the feeling that most people would regret landing on his wrong side.

"You think he's dead?" My tone was neutral, noncommittal.

"The FBI don't come around asking to check out a fella's apartment because they think nothing is wrong." He crossed his arms, which caused his blazer to stretch almost to the ripping point across his broad back. "Mr. Norton was the type of cat who was on the up and up. You could tell just by lookin' at him he was a good man. Only way a good man's place gets a visit by the Feds is if he's dead or missing."

I couldn't fault his logic … much. "You see anything strange in the last few weeks?" His name tag read: Anthony. "Anthony, did you? Even the smallest thing could be important."

He shook his round head slowly, eyes fixed on a faraway place. "No, sir. Nothing that I can think of."

Shot in the dark, anyway. I thanked the man and pushed the "up" button for the elevator after sliding a master keycard in an access slot.

From behind. "There was that strange little kid."

Cold things began to squirm in my guts. "Little kid?" I asked, turning slowly.

Anthony shrugged, a tectonic movement. "Some kid in a gray hoodie was hanging outside a week ago at all hours. Had to shoo him off. Ran like a little bit of lightning."

Those chilly things playing with my insides decided to do the Macarena. "Thank you," I said absently.

As the elevator door closed, he added, "Hope I was helpful, sir!"

He had no idea.

Up top, private apartments were connected only by a plush, carpeted hallway. There were only two and Mace had one of them. Two doors, both faced with stainless steel, one to the left and one to the right. Canton waited at the right hand door, his normally broad face drawn long in anger.

"What?"

"Come inside, white boy, you gotta see this."

Yep, the cold squirmies were back. Canton and Ilena followed me in where Winch was examining what looked to be cured white maple flooring. Glass littered the blond wood, a good deal of which had come from a window. Or at least, from where a window and its frame *had* been sandwiched between two other windows of the same size. A ragged hole marred the wall instead, letting in the chill air. Bits of wood from the frame, shattered brick and lathe littered the floor, along with the glass.

"Holy crap," I breathed, more than a little surprised. "What the hell came through that window, a truck?"

Winch didn't bother to look up. "Something big."

I restrained my murderous impulse and simply waited. It helped that I thought of her tied on an anthill covered in honey.

Before I could count to ten she spoke, "Something strong, too."

"You having the anthill fantasy again?" asked Canton under his breath.

I nodded.

"Yeah, she has that effect sometimes."

"You two done?" Winch cut in, not looking up from the debris.

"And she has ears like a bat."

"I heard that."

"See?"

Enough. Anymore and *my* ears would start to bleed. "What did you find?" I snapped. At her reproachful look, I muttered a contrite, "Sorry."

Her snooty little sniff was enough to re-ignite the ant fantasy. "Out of all this crap, the only thing that stands out, the only thing that doesn't belong is this."

An object the size of my thumb flashed through the air and I caught it mostly by reflex before it could bonk me on the nose. It turned out to be a small chunk of stone. No geologist, I handed it over to Canton, who at least had a passing knowledge of minerals.

Whatever it was, he didn't seem impressed. "Basalt," was all he said.

Strange. "Basalt?" I asked. Winch looked up from where she knelt, an expectant look on her face.

Canton clarified. "It's a common extrusive volcanic rock. Fine grained and heavy as hell. Used in construction for building blocks or in groundwork. Also used to make statues."

"So, boyfriend-o-mine," drawled Winch. "What the heck is a piece of common extrusive volcanic rock doing one hundred fifty feet above the street, inside an apartment?"

Good question. I retrieved the bit of stone from Canton and examined it closely. Triangular, slightly curved, the fat end ragged as if broken. The rest was smooth, almost polished. "This broke off whatever came through that window," I mused, "and was big enough to tear out not only the window, but a good bit of the surrounding wall." From far below the sound of a car horn blasted in the still evening air.

"What I find strange," I said, "is that no one heard whatever the hell it was that broke through the wall. And why hasn't anyone noticed that big damn hole? If it's our mysterious critter that ripped the door from the roof access where Mace died—and I think it is—he didn't encounter it here."

Canton rubbed his lower lip. "Why is that?"

"Because security would have told us if Mace left the building wounded, or running like hell." I shook my head. "No, whatever it was broke through the wall ..." My voice trailed off as a notion burbled to the surface of my mind.

"What's that look on your face, white boy?"

"Somebody has a clever idea," Winch answered, rising to her feet.

I smiled slightly and shook my head. "Find anything? Any personal effects, names of the guilty conveniently written in a ledger?"

The Apache shook his head. "Not really. Some clothes, some pictures, toiletries. It's like this place is a hotel room. Pretty, but sterile. He did leave a cell, but it's been crushed into dust."

I tapped my fingers together as I thought. "You said pics ... Show me."

Canton reached into his jacket pocket and retrieved a couple dozen five by three inch glossy photos.

"What the hell," I grumbled. Wildlife shots. Sea Lions on ragged, jagged, dark rock, various sea birds, and an underwater shot of a great white shark. That was about it. "Where did you find these?"

"Under his mattress."

Interesting. There was something there, but I couldn't quite put my finger on it, so I slipped the photos into a trouser pocket and turned to the gang. "I suggest we get back to the loft."

Winch and Ilena tossed me incredulous looks that bounced off my air of superiority while Canton gave me a good long squint.

"You have something up your metaphorical sleeve, white boy," he accused.

"Currently, just my metaphorical arm, but I'm hoping to change that."

Later at the loft, after a dinner of Chinese take-out, I got down to business. "Ilena, report on the sensors."

A silvery disk the size of a quarter but twice as thick landed on the table next to my Kung Pao Pork and rolled in a circle for a few seconds before clattering to a stop. Both sides were plain, nothing to indicate who manufactured the object. It was one of the almost-never-seen sensors designed to pick up magical emanations of one hundred megamerlins or more. Although I suspected it might be far more sensitive than that.

"That, boss," she said, "is an inactive sensor. I pulled it off a cell tower five blocks from here and performed a basic diagnostic spell. It hasn't been fried, as far as I can tell, but it doesn't work."

"Can you perform a tech diagnostic?"

She shrugged. "It will take a few hours and a RediPad, but sure."

I nodded. "At this point, we have time. Do it."

Winch and Canton stared at me while Ilena went off to do something tech-savvy and geeky to the sensor. Finally I couldn't take all the eyeball action anymore.

"Stop looking at me!" I snapped in mock anger. "You got them bug eyes!"

They kept staring. It was starting to become unnerving.

"What?"

More eyeballing.

"You want to know the plan, right?"

If looks could kill and all that. They knew I was enjoying the hell out of the moment and intensified their glaring, which made it all the more precious, a moment to savor like fine wine. Before Canton could draw his Bowie and slice off a few of my more delicate parts, I relented.

"All right, all right. Don't get your tighty whiteys in a knot. All I really have to go on is a hunch ..."

* * *

The assassin slipped down from the roof, wand in pocket. The exterior of the building was faced in brick, offering the diminutive killer more than enough purchase to climb down. The way he moved across the façade—swift and silent in the cool night air like a spider— any passerby who might have looked up would have been amazed at his speed and grace.

The climber did not think of himself as an assassin, but as a servant who had been given an order—a directive—he could not refuse. In fact, refusal was as alien a concept to his world as an apple falling upwards from a tree is to the human world. Not a glimmer of doubt entered his facile mind. He was a tool for his people and the one who commanded and that was all right with him. It was how it should be, how it had always been.

What he did consider, however, was the danger of the Big Man and the Female Magicker. The other two, the Native and the Woman, were of no concern and could be handled at his convenience. They posed the lesser threat, despite their facility with weapons. Magickers had the ability to channel the Source, albeit in a vastly inferior manner. The assassin had learned the hard way, long ago, never to underestimate the animal cunning of a human who wielded magic.

The Big Man, the one with the sleeping spirit attached to his essence, he was another matter entirely. When the assassin faced the Big Man, who seemed so helpless, blocked in that black metal contraption, he'd assumed killing him would be simple; the spirit inside the Big Man was quiescent, so it posed no threat. The wand had come up, the Word to tear the human in half was on his lips when he found the giant weapon called a "pistool" suddenly pointed between his eyes. That was when the assassin knew he was dead. The Big Man, despite his injuries, had cold, cold eyes like glacier ice that marked the assassin for annihilation. For the first time in centuries the assassin was afraid, deathly afraid.

When the pistool made that strange clacking noise (he knew from watching those odd *Lethal Weapon* movies that it signified a malfunction or that the weapon was empty) he felt a sense of triumph like nothing he'd felt since the Old Days, the Days of Dominance and Blood.

Then the Native shot him in the ass.

The projectile, made of soft lead, caused no great damage (his ability to Heal was second to none), but it stung worse than iron. The assassin almost wept with pain, but discretion was the better part of valor and he ran as if the Hunt were chasing him.

Fingers and toes, slightly elongated, immune to the clammy chill of the foggy air, probed cracks and crevices, finding holds where almost none existed. Fifty feet below, the sidewalk lay ready to flatten the assassin if he faltered on the way to his destination, a large window.

One small hand detached from the wall and fished inside the pocket of the assassin's gray sweatpants as he hung upside down like an insect over the deserted street below.

Gently, feather light, he touched the glass and one of the four great panes began to shimmer and tremble like lightly disturbed water. Soundlessly, he slipped through the glass as if it were an illusory membrane and landed gently inside the darkened loft.

* * *

Right into my grasp.

I had expected trouble at the loft ever since the ambush and my expectations were confirmed by Anthony the Security Guard's description of the kid hanging around Mace's apartment building. The kid knew where to find Mace and that ambush right outside the loft told me he knew where to find us.

It was time to catch me a magic-wielding midget.

All of us were awake, jamming on stay-awakes (seriously strong pharmaceutical-grade uppers unknown to non-Bureau pharmacists with all the awake time with none of the jitters) and in full gear.

The kid had lobbed a spell that flipped an SUV like an omelet, so I had everyone ready for war: Faraday coats, nightvision contact lenses, silver capture nets and more spell eggs and guns than you could shake a stick at. Microcams the size of pinheads had been spread on the roof, glued to the exterior, seeded in the elevator and shaft as well as the hallway. A RediPad monitored the signals from the hundreds of tiny cameras and processed all the information, ignoring all irrelevant data (rats, insects, etc.) and focusing on movement within one meter of each camera.

When the rooftop cams picked up movement from something larger than a pigeon, the Pad emitted a small *beep*. Instantly everyone hidden around the loft tensed and I checked the tablet. Sure enough, the kid was on the roof. Momentarily confused at his appearance above us, I realized that he must have dropped or climbed down from the adjoining, taller building. Imagine my surprise when micro-Spiderman began to climb down the exterior wall *headfirst*. The kid had mad free-climbing skills.

"Get ready," I subvocaled and moved carefully, silently toward the window, staying out of the beam of the streetlight.

When he approached the right-hand window, I expected a blast of magic to shatter the bulletproof glass into a gajillion pieces. Instead the kid tapped the thick glass softly with his little stick—the stick surely had more magic in it than all the spell eggs in my possession— and oozed through as if the barrier was made of jelly.

The second his bare feet hit the carpeted floor, I was all over him like a politician on a donation. A ridge hand strike sent his stick flying, followed by a massive bear hug. The little twerp was mine.

Or so I thought.

The nasty little skink slid out of my arms like a greased monkey and flipped over my head to land behind me in an attempt to recover his stick. Fortunately, Winch had my six. Keeping one foot on the stick, she aimed the pistol at the kid's head. Without warning, the, lights flashed on and illuminated the scene.

The loft, a large space even with added rooms and armory, stretched around us. The team formed a semi-circle around the kid who, still wearing his mirrored shades, crouched before us, cool as a cucumber. Not a spark of panic or any other emotion at the sight of five normal-sized people in black, full-length Faraday coats (leather, very swanky) over charcoal-gray chitonous body armor encasing them from neck to feet. That armor, which could stop anything from knife thrusts to a 20mm round, looked like it belonged on the set of a *Batman* movie.

The kid smiled, revealing incredibly white teeth, and vaulted into the air, feet connecting soundlessly with the sheetrock ceiling. Then he ran upside down, hair flailing madly, toward the door.

While the other three gaped, their Weird-Crap-o-Meter Detectors chattering like squirrels, I took off after him. Years and years of witnessing the most bizarre events imaginable had long since dulled my sense of incredulity.

Still, it was a pretty cool trick. Right up to the time my Pazer took him in the ass.

Sometimes you don't want to kill a Supernatural. Sometimes they are scared and lonely after entering our world from the World Under and mean you no harm. In those cases—referred to as Tag & Bags— we resort to the latest in subduing tech. Hence the Pazer (Pistol/ Tazer).

It looks like your common variety 9mm pistol, except with a flattened, slot-like barrel that fires a disk the size of a dime, with seven quarter-inch long barbs along the edges. Inside that disk is the most powerful battery known to man. The device works like a normal Taser, but no wire is needed to connect the disc to the weapon. Instead, when the disk hits the subject, the barbs hook into flesh and enough electricity flows into the bad guy to have him/her do the jelly dance for a moment before collapsing. The ultra-cool part of the weapon is that it has a nineteen-disc capacity and a firing rate of one-per-second. Unfortunately for law enforcement, each Pazer costs more than the GNP of Bolivia.

One disc hit the kid smack dead center in the left butt cheek; however, the little sucker kept on booking, pausing only long enough to shudder. The second disc hit him in the thigh, with roughly the same effect. By the time the third disc hit his lower back, he was almost to the door. That one actually gave him pause for the cause and he performed a little stutter-step before falling to the floor, landing on his feet like a cat. Except that no earthly cat had such grace and balance.

It was the fourth disc that dropped him.

Taking no chances, I tackled him while Canton and the rest backed me up, each grabbing hold of an appendage. I wasn't worried about any leftover electrical charge; our body armor would protect us from that.

When I flipped the kid over, his mirrored shades went flying and I saw what kind of Supernatural twisted like a crazed python in my grip.

His eyes were as green as summer moss, as Emerald Butterflies and malachite seen in the fading light of day—an intense green that nearly stunned me as I was caught in his stare.

Cat's eyes, slitted and feral, spoke of wild things and places no human had ever trod upon. Those eyes were ageless and wise, sorrowful and regal, filled with a degree of spite and fury I couldn't have imagined until now. Those eyes speared through mine, their gaze cold and relentless and I was powerless against their might, their ageless magic.

The realization of the identity of the childlike form pinned beneath me flashed through my mind as swiftly as the electricity that had dropped the creature.

It was *no* kid.

"Púca," I whispered as it hissed and spat. Everything made sense. Everything made too much sense. But I couldn't move, couldn't speak further because my mind was being extruded from my body like toothpaste from a tube and I wondered how it could do such a thing while I wore my spell-absorbing Faraday coat.

I felt Leena stir along the edges of my soul as the púca pushed through the windows of my mind and into my body, my gross flesh no barrier to its ancient magic. Briefly Leena roiled the fires of my rage, but it was too late... The creature was in while my essence was slowly exiting, making way for the púca.

Its mind scraped across mine as our spirits passed each other and its memories slid into me with the force of a mack truck hitting a 'possum on the highway. Through its eyes I saw me, the Big Man, snag him after he had landed on the floor, felt his contempt of Canton and Winch, then the memories began to scroll backward like a film projector in reverse … out the window, swiftly up the wall and a jump from the adjacent building. Each memory carved pieces out of my soul and laced the wounds with sulphuric acid. Somewhere along the way I must have screamed—it felt like I did—but there was no sound, only the pain that tore chunks from my sanity and left me soul riven and tormented. I was dying, the Supernatural's spirit/energy/magic was tearing me apart as it pulled me from my body and not even Leena could help because I could hear *her* scream and I could hear the púca scream because this was a murder/suicide. It would die killing me, shredding its very essence to kill me because that's what it had been ordered to do by—

Wrench.

Back to myself, back to the real world, no longer assaulted by the Supernatural because it was dead, a larger than life Bowie stuck through its throat. Its blood bubbled and steamed as its flesh began to liquefy around the knife and I was covered in sweat and fear-stink. I felt like puking right there and somewhere in the back of my mind there was screaming, loud and mournful, as Leena, my sister—my soul-mate if you will—had been hurt, I mean really *hurt*, for the first time in over twenty years and it sounded like the echoes of damnation.

Her ghostly sobbing tore at me with knives of glass, but that wasn't what shot the adrenaline through my system. It wasn't Canton's worried look or Ilena'a quiet strength as she probed me with healing magic. It wasn't even Winch's swearing like a sailor in a brothel that jerked at the cords of my sanity with talons of steel.

No, it was what I felt in the púca's mind, a bit of information that had my heart trip-hammering in fear and more terror sweat slicking my brow.

The púca had not come alone.

Wonderful.

Chapter Nine

The Hardest Monster

No time to shout a warning, or to move, before the window the púca had climbed through exploded inward, along with several feet of wall. Dust, broken glass, wood and shattered brick flooded the loft in a choking cloud. Debris pitter-pattered all round us, stinging exposed skin and raising welts.

We did the only thing we could do: we scattered in different directions, leaving the slowly liquefying corpse of the púca where it lay pinned to the floor by Canton's Bowie. The entire loft was enshrouded in a fog of dust and debris, making it hard for me to spot the others.

Then the roar hit.

How can I describe it? A deep, visceral wall of sound that plowed into my skin, more an explosion than a roar. It nearly knocked me off my feet, forcing me backwards and sending dust flying. Off to my right, I heard Canton moan in pain.

The dust eventually settled around a dark form looming in the middle of the loft, standing on the shattered remains of the dining table. With a creak and groan, it spread enormous wings.

Yeah, I said *wings*. Over thirty feet in total span. The monster had to crouch to keep from punching through the ceiling. Its huge head swung this way and that, the tips of its horns gouging chunks out of the ceiling, raining sheetrock dust and debris on its head. That huge head stopped suddenly as the creature's alligator maw gaped and slathered in my direction.

We both froze as if mesmerized by each other. I'm not sure what it saw in me, but what I saw had my insides racing to be my outsides. I dimly noted that the tip of one of its horns had broken off and my hand reflexively went to the outside pocket of my Faraday coat to touch the basalt remnant found in Mace's apartment.

Imagine a bat. A big freaking bite-your-head-off-man bat. Take that evil looking sucker and throw in some Rottweiler and an alligator or two for some extra flavor and you have what stood there, tall, terrible. It stared at me the same way a great white stares at a plump little seal and my bladder suddenly felt uncomfortably full and hot.

Oh yeah, make the monster out of basalt. Dark, thick grained stone, black as sin and so heavy the hardwood floor splintered and cracked with the creature's every movement. I could hear the creak and grinding of twisting and flexing stone, which did nothing to alleviate my current state of freakoutness. The monster tensed with a soft rumble of stressed stone.

"What the hell, white boy?" Canton called from my right.

I didn't want to say the word because if I did, then what stood in the loft would become really real, but some things have to be said. "Gargoyle." There. I was right. It had become more real and fear was going to town on my insides.

My three teammates sucked in panicked breaths. Not that I could blame them. Of all the Supernaturals we didn't want to face, a gargoyle is in the top five, but that didn't stop us from springing into action almost as one.

Roaring back at the monster, I reached to an outside thigh pocket and drew forth an extendable, titanium baton. I took a few swings in an effort to distract the beast. Unfortunately the baton bounced off its stone hide and sent a numbing shock up my fingers to my elbow without even chipping the damn thing. Four hard swings later and the baton was starting to look a little worse for wear.

Two loud blasts came from the left and a pair of deer slugs hit the monster in the wing, peppering me with basalt shrapnel. It roared again and my ears took an awful beating as the pressure wave hurled me back five feet into the kitchenette. The armor on my back absorbed the brunt of the damage as I slammed into the fridge. I straightened just in time for a big claw to take me hard in the stomach.

Airborne … for a second, then I hit the floor hard enough to jelly my insides, a raw jangling agony that knocked the wind out of my sails. The pain of the gargoyle's strike started as a gut-bomb and spread its cramping way all through my body, momentarily paralyzing muscle and causing every nerve ending to feel like it had been tap-danced on.

There was shouting and the sound of wood splintering and tearing, but I didn't pay attention; my insides were caterwauling something terrible. I looked down to see the armor, tightly woven Kevlar and NewTanium, torn asunder along my gut. The skin of my stomach was bleeding. The wound wasn't deep, but that wasn't what was grabbing my attention; the big sucker was looming over me, foot raised, ready to stamp me into creamed Finn, and there was nothing I could do about it. My abused muscles couldn't respond fast enough. I watched the claw begin its descent and hoped my death would be quick.

Blamblamblam!

Three shots close together and large chunks, as well as stony grit, flew from its towering form. It gave a rending cry like the sound of tearing rock as one of its huge wings shattered into three large pieces and fell. One piece pierced hardwood and stuck upright. The gargoyle, suddenly off balance with one talon in the air, toppled over backwards and crashed so hard that it embedded itself in the floor. The force of its impact nearly launched me to my feet.

Canton reloaded while Ilena and Winch took turns with their shotguns. By the damage they were inflicting, they had to be using armor-piercing shells made from depleted uranium. Expensive as hell, but always a plus to have in stock.

I managed to get my legs under me, albeit shakily, and take quick stock of the situation. The loft reverberated with the sound of rapid-fire shotgun blasts, but even though my three teammates continued to pour on the pain, the gargoyle, rock chips flying from its torso, slowly began to rise, digging into the wood with its horrid claws to pull itself out of the floor. Within seconds it would be in a sitting position and poised to strike again.

Another blast tore through its remaining wing, tearing it loose and leaving a foot-long stub. The loss of such enormous weight helped it come to an upright position.

Oh, crap.

Looking at the shattered flooring, an idea began to form. "Shoot its damn legs!" I screamed.

I guess they heard me because while Winch reloaded her shotgun, Canton and Ilena shot at its legs, just enough to keep it flailing at the floor and buckling under the strain. More floorboards splintered as its claws continued to seek purchase, but there its great weight worked to its disadvantage. It roared again and my teammates staggered back, momentarily buffeted by the pressure wave, but I had braced myself against the concussive force and flipped a small gem between the monster's legs.

"Only three armor-piercing rounds left!" screamed Winch, firing two in as many seconds.

"Doesn't matter. Run! Fire in the hole!" I hollered in my best Command Voice. "My room, NOW!"

Less than three seconds later, all three ran the twenty feet to my room with me hot on their heels. An instant before I slammed the door shut behind me, I yelled, "CHOWDERNOSE!"

Spell gems are activated by words, a sort of "if/then" statement for magical effects. All Bureau authorized spell gems come in polystyrene containers the size of eggs with an icon stamped on the outside, indicating their use. Glued to the underside is a one-inch paper ribbon where the activation word is typed so that it can be easily seen when peeled from the casing. In preparation for the ambush (something I had thought likely), I had three spell gems out of their casings and ready for use. It would have been bad news for the home team if I'd tossed the wrong gem and activated one of those in my pockets, which is why I rarely took such a risk.

A small concussive force ripped through the loft, not as intense as the gargoyle's roar, but unnerving just the same. From my position next to the door I felt as well as heard the splatter against drywall and wood and quickly backed away. From beyond the door came a splintering of wood and a huge crash, followed by another, and then another. More roaring—faint and with notes of pain and despair, like a mournful avalanche.

"What was that, white boy?" Canton asked.

"Acid bomb," I replied, naming one of the most feared spells in the Bureau arsenal. Invented in the 70s, it creates a beach ball-sized globe of thick, gelatinous acid that bursts like a grenade, coating everything in a twenty-foot radius with the dense, corrosive gunk. I've seen one eat through three floors of a parking garage. Any tissue caught in the spray is dissolved almost instantly. Being indoors while detonating one is not conducive to longevity.

Almost before the words left my mouth, we heard sizzling as the acid started eating through the drywall and door. "Back up," I commanded.

Soon enough large holes began to appear in the wall, dark gelid globs steaming and hissing through insulation and drywall. I glanced to Ilena as a foul stench hit us. "Got a wind spell or something?"

She nodded, sweat and grit smeared across her pale skin. "I think I can cobble something together."

"Then cobble! We have to keep those vapors out of this room!"

For a couple of minutes we choked on disgusting fumes that reeked like a cross between burning insulation and pig farts; then the little magician concocted a breeze that blew the odor out of the room. We all smiled as sweet clean air filled our lungs.

We moved out into the loft, or what was left of it. Holes of every size and shape decorated every possible surface and it took some acrobatic high-stepping across the Swiss cheese floor to cross to the largest one, where the gargoyle had lain. Roughly circular, the hole it had left was the size of large sedan, the wooden edges burned and scored. Corroded edges of the PVC piping that had lain beneath the hardwood still bubbled. Ilena's fresh air spell still pushed the stink away, sending it out the gaping hole in the outside wall, which had just accumulated a bevy of much smaller holes.

I looked down … and down some more. And some more after that. The loft occupied the top floor, five stories above ground. The acid had eaten through all four floors beneath, taking the now liquefied black glob of gargoyle with it, to land on the ground floor, a smoking ruin of a Supernatural. I thought I saw some weak movement from the shapeless glob of goo—perhaps the melted stub of an arm or leg—but couldn't be sure.

"That's for you, Mace," I whispered, tossing the basalt tip down into the goopy mess. It landed with a *plop* and a *hiss*. Two down and one doggie to go. A big doggie.

Good thing we used unoccupied buildings. Imagine what the neighbors would think.

"Damn, white boy! Sometimes I just get plumb lucky," Canon shouted in glee. I started, nearly losing my balance and turned my body to see him pulling his Bowie out of the floor.

"Jesus, dude," I barked. "You scared the crap outta me."

He waved the Bowie. "Look, white boy! The acid missed this completely." A puzzled expression crossed his wide coppery face. "Where that little twerp's body, Kal?"

I raised my voice so everyone could hear. "That kid was a púca, the inspiration for Shakespeare's Puck, or Robin Goodfellow. It was a type of Supernatural called a Faë, also known as Sidhe and Tuatha Dé Danann. Iron is poison to them, so when you stabbed it through the neck, it dissolved, melted, or whatever."

I noticed that everyone was staring. "What?"

"How the hell do you know all that?" Ilena asked from where she knelt by the whomping great hole in the exterior wall.

It was Winch who answered. "He's been reading and memorizing the archives for the last ten years, honey. Almost the entire list of Supernaturals is stuffed into that big skull of his."

Ilena shrugged. "Why?"

Canton carefully wended his way toward me across the pitted floor, testing each acid-splattered plank and maneuvering with surprising grace. "That's why Kal is the apex predator of the Bureau," he drawled, eyes never leaving the floor.

"Yeah. The best killer is an informed one." I began to search for more solid footing. "The last known Sidhe incursion was on Roanoke Island in 1589. The colony that lived there disappeared, pulled to the World Under by the Faë."

"Wasn't that the whole Croatoan thing?" Ilena asked, her eyes fixed on the floor.

"Yeah. That was a blind. John White, one of the colonists, instructed his people to carve their destination on a tree if they had to evacuate in case of Spanish hostilities. Croatoan was the name of an island to the south, now called Hatteras Island. England's Supernatural Services found traces of the Faë on Roanoke—a broken dagger made of rose glass. All Faë weapons are made of glass or crystal." Deep breath, taken in an effort to calm myself. I knew more about the Faë than I was sharing and what I knew scared me spitless, but they didn't need to know, not yet. If they did, they might insist on bringing in the whole Bureau in spite of Joshua's prediction, and I wasn't going to let that happen. The BSI was still far too weak to take the Faë head on. No, the best way to take on the Faë was to go with subtlety and a whole pile of sneaky.

Winch must have seen something in my face as my foot probed acid-eaten floorboards. "What's wrong boss?"

I looked up into her darker than dark eyes. "How did they know we were here? From the ambush this morning right outside I reckoned somebody had found us out and learned where we laid our heads, but how?"

"Do the Faë have any special scrying or clairvoyant magics?"

I shook my head. "Their magic has always been pretty straightforward—harsh, brutal and efficient, never subtle. Although they are said to use magics that no human can perform. Not much in the Archives deals with their innate abilities, except that some can shape change and all can sense other Faë, but noth—"

Oh, yeah ... The penny dropped, straight onto my pointy head. "Oh crap," I breathed as I shot into my bedroom, heart thudding wildly in my chest.

Canton and Winch followed, faces set in stone. They knew I'd figured *something* out.

Praying I was wrong, I knelt by my bed and the faint strains of "Somebody's Watching Me" from the Winnebago only confirmed my worst suspicions.

"God dammit!" I swore and the music abruptly cut off. "Sorry guys," I whispered, my heart sinking. "Didn't mean to startle you."

Sad, mournful music wafted from the toy and I felt a lump form in my throat. It wasn't their fault and they knew it, but that didn't stop them from feeling bad about the whole sorry mess. I had completely forgotten that Brownies were a species of Faë, albeit a kindly one.

"Oh, damn." Canton sounded as sorry as I felt.

"Yeah," I muttered, staring at the Winnebago. " 'Oh, damn' is right."

A strong, feminine hand landed on my shoulder. "It's not your fault, boss."

"I know, but I still feel like a big stinking load of refried crap."

Ilena chose that moment to join us. "This isn't going to make you feel any better."

"I know." My eyes closed of their own accord and I stood, hefting the Winnebago in my arms. Reluctantly, I parted my lids in time to see her hold up the kid's stick.

Wonderful.

I noticed she carried it as if it were a pint of nitroglycerine, the stick carefully balanced on the palms of her combat gloves. "Bad mojo?" I inquired.

"Bad mojo," she agreed. "Look closely, but don't touch, that would be ... unfortunate."

"Define 'bad.'"

"Well, imagine your skin touching it and then your body slowly melting into a puddle of guacamole."

Right, that was a very good definition of bad. I carefully leaned forward and took a gander at the pointy little stick. Beige wood, perhaps pine, loosely grained, about nine inches long, it seemed pretty unremarkable … *whoa!*

Tiny black lines, thinner than a hair, ran through the wood, twisting and whirling round and around in a bizarre conglomeration of a Celtic knot and an M. Escher nightmare. The lines twisted around themselves like snakes in a mating ball, curving in impossible directions that seemed to warp into right angles to reality.

"What the flying cow-flop is that?" asked a wide-eyed Canton.

"You are looking at, I believe—one of the most dangerous devices I have ever encountered," said the magician, a tremor in her voice. "One of the simplest spells in any magician's arsenal is a diagnostic, which gives us purpose and magnitude of power." She stared at the stick in her gauntleted hands. "This registered as a storage device, but the magnitude could not be calculated. It was beyond the boundaries of the diagnostic spell. Boss, we're not talking gigamerlins here, we're talking teramerlins! Nothing holds teramerlins, boss, *nothing.* This … *thing* is impossible; it doesn't even have *any* precious metal in which to store energy!"

I would have told her about the Tesla coil, but BB had instructed me to reveal its existence to no one on pain of Very Bad Things happening to my favorite Kalevi Hakala. "Can we break it?"

She paled. "Boss, you try to break this, it might release all its energy at once. It could take out this building. Hell, this *block.*"

I nodded. "Right, don't break the stick. Good safety tip. What do you recommend?"

"I recommend we encase it in a ton of lead and drop it into the deepest part of the ocean."

"Right, give it to the Bureau. What a wonderful idea."

"I didn't say that at all."

"Sure you did, you just didn't realize that was what you were saying."

Winch pointed to my midsection. "Jesus, Boss, you're bleeding!"

Right, my stomach. Funny how adrenaline can temporarily cut you off from pain. The wound was a long ragged cut. Though shallow, it bled something terrible. I knew down to my bones that what had caused my wound had also gutted Mace. Damn, the fact that the big guy managed to climb thirty stories with such a long and deep slash to the gut was a freaking miracle. From the looks the other three tossed my way, they had the same thought.

"I'm okay—it's nothing Ilena can't heal later—but first there is something more serious to address."

Canton and Winch gave me the eyebrow treatment while Ilena just stared, so I continued. "When the púca tried its mind mojo on me, just before Canton stabbed it, I received some of its memories. It was told to kill us, me first, Ilena second, saving Winch and Canton for last. It was a lackey, not the major player, and that major player is still out there."

"Bloody wonderful," the magician groused. Canton used a few choice words I will refrain from repeating.

Before I could continue, Ilena's smart phone beeped twice and she took off without explanation but returned shortly with her RediPad.

"Boss, I have the results of the deep diagnostic on the sensor," she began, holding up the quarter-sized disk. A few taps on the tablet later and she grunted. "The damn thing isn't broken after all; it just appears that way on the surface. It still senses magic and still sends a signal through the cell tower."

My stomach did one of those flip-floppity things that compounded the pain from the wound. "But?"

"But … it doesn't send the signal originally programmed. The signal goes somewhere else."

Oh, my head hurt.

"Gonna take a wild stab in the dark here: the signal uses an encryption we don't have the key to and you have no idea where the signals go to, right?"

She nodded. "When the Acid Bomb spell detonated, it tried to send the signal, but with no cell tower, it went nowhere. We now have the data, but it is using some weird encryption I've never seen."

"Let me guess, we would have to attach it to a cell tower and then cast a strong enough spell to try to track the signal."

"Yep. And that's if we *can* track it. I get the feeling we won't be able to."

Wonderful.

Time to get things in gear. To Canton, "Get on your RediPad and keep the police from coming because with our luck, they'll be here any second."

To Ilena, "Coordinate with Warehouse, find us another place to hole up, preferably with no neighbors. I want to be moved in there yesterday. Oh, and send BB a sitrep and then keep sending reports every two hours until this mission is complete. Then you can try to track the signal, but keep that experiment far away from our new digs." She nodded.

I grabbed my own RediPad and started typing on the virtual keyboard. "Here is a list of some of the more experimental tech Special Branch has been working on. I want it here, all of it. If Alex has any new stuff he hasn't told me about, have him send that, too."

Canton scratched his head. "What's going on, white boy? What's the play?"

I didn't bother looking up from the tablet. "The Faë, or I assume it's them, are tracking our use of magic with the help of our own sensor system, which means that right now, we go dark as far as magic is concerned. Tech-only unless it's an emergency."

All three seasoned vets of the Bureau went expressionless as years of training took over, brutally quashing the fear I know they were feeling. I felt it as well. It had been a long time since a Bureau team had gone against Supernaturals without magical backup.

"From now on we wear our Faraday coats, our armor, and load up on ammo. I want us to clank when we walk. I'll pass out some spell gems, but, like I said, they're emergency-use items. Hopefully Special Branch can help us even the odds a bit, but for now, all magic is off the table, including hybrid devices like nightvision contact lenses."

There were a couple of groans, but no real protests.

To Winch, "There, I've sent my request to BB and the items will be here in a few hours. Get to the airport and pick them up and take the Brownies, see they get back to my apartment at Warehouse." I swallowed past the lump in my throat. I was going to miss my dry-cleaning service.

Don't judge me.

Chapter Ten

A Shot in the Dark

Two rounds. High powered rifle. It was a brick that saved my life. The second round took me in the chest, hitting the Kevlar/ NewTanium armor at what felt like cometary speeds, the bullet tearing through the Kevlar before the NewTanium plate stopped it.

NewTanium (Titanium aluminide combined with niobium) was a fairly new alloy of titanium. Years ago, astronauts had found that in Zero-g new alloys could be created because the lack of gravity didn't allow normally incompatible metals to separate. Of course, various companies had tried to create new alloys en masse by using airplanes flying in a parabola to simulate Zero-g, but that didn't work; they couldn't maintain weightlessness for a long enough time to get the metals to mix then cool.

Of course the government launched an incredibly expensive shuttle mission, placing a large metalworking facility in geosynchronous orbit over the United States. *Of course* they made several thousand pounds of NewTanium and *of course* the Bureau managed to obtain several hundred pounds of the stuff. Job number one with the new material: armor. Job number two: anything else they could think of. And *of course* the American taxpayer footed the bill.

Alex wanted to call the new alloy Unobtainium. I manfully resisted the urge to suck his brains out with a wet-vac and steal his *Avatar* DVD.

The NewTanium actually bent around the bullet as it struck, but it didn't fail. Instead, the residual energy was transferred to me, causing muscle, bone and organs to wobble like Jell-O in an earthquake.

I had been concentrating on packing the Armory away into several coffin-sized containers for the move when I took a break for a stretch and a breath of fresh air. The loft still smelled of acid-eaten wood, wiring and pvc pipe and I carefully threaded around the various holes and made it to the shattered wall where a cool breeze refreshed my lungs.

Every mission I'd been on brought with it a measure of uncertainty and fear that gnawed at the insides. Normally I could contain the worry. I leaned against the wall looking out at the San Francisco business district, the glow of neon and the halogens doing nothing to alleviate the harsh, bitter fear that continued to erode my confidence. For all my success at the Bureau, all the Supernaturals I'd killed over the years, the Faë were out of my league. Way out.

It was thought that the Faë left this world because of mankind's ability to use iron—Sidhe kryptonite. Because we breed like rabbits and iron is abundant, the Faë had to quit this world or be destroyed. Until now they had been content to make small surgical strikes. The fact that they were coming at the Bureau head-on meant that they had an advantage I didn't know about. A big one.

I could have called for more back-up, but without proper intelligence it would be no good. The Faë were a force of nature and you can't wrestle a tornado with an army. All you get are a lot of dead soldiers as the tornado passes blithely by, unaware it had been opposed.

No, I had to approach the crap storm obliquely instead of directly and without a plethora of Bureau agents underfoot; the BSI didn't need another crippling blow. All I required was a little more information and a cunning plan.

I had nothing. Hard to admit that my gray matter was devoid of anything that resembled an idea. It made me feel helpless and at sea.

Craptastic.

An inch above and to the left of my skull a brick blew apart and showered me with terra-cotta colored fragments and dust. Before my brain could react, my body was already in motion, jinking to the right when the second bullet hit me in the chest and took the wind out of my sails.

I bounced off the edge of a hole and fell through, my chest screaming at me to give up the ghost while my lungs decided to shut down for a while. In desperation I flung out an arm and snagged something smooth and hard. A pvc pipe that creaked and groaned as it took my weight. My shoulder shrieked as 210 pounds of Finn stretched muscles to the breaking point. Red and white stars exploded behind my eyes and blood thudded in my ears.

"Kal!" Canton yelled from above. I had no air to answer. The bullet had stolen it all.

"Where did he go?"

"I don't know!"

As I hung there, shoulder on fire, I had an epiphany, or at least adrenaline kick-started my brain. Closing my eyes, I let go of the pipe … and fell a few short feet to the floor below. Figuring that I might be heading toward another hole, I spread my legs wide, hoping that I wouldn't be plummeting through a weakened floor to discover deceleration trauma on the floor beneath that one. Luck was with me. Although there was another hole, it was smaller, not quite as wide as my shoulders. I managed a precarious balancing act with feet on either side. The fourth floor had suffered less damage than the loft.

Lungs pumped, and sweet, sweet air rushed back into my body. I drew great, heaping breaths while warding off a crippling dizziness. It took only a few seconds for me to regain some equilibrium and steady my jangled nerves. From above I heard a grunt and a thud.

Tapping my throat mic, I went subvocal. *"Report,"* I gasped.

Winch answered immediately. *"Kal! You okay?"*

"Fine, I'm on the floor below."

"Canton was coming for you, but I think he got shot! He's moving,

but he's in pain. Whoever the sniper is, he or she is either far away or using a suppressor. I couldn't hear a thing."

Wonderful.

Looking up, I could see Canton's armored shoulder through one of the holes and knew the Native American could hear us. *"Canton, I'm almost directly below you. Don't stand unless you want to die. Roll through the hole and I'll catch you, buddy."*

He didn't bother to answer, but I did hear some grunting and what sounded like a groan before he wiggled his way to the hole and fell through. In the movies the hero almost effortlessly catches the body as it falls a scant few feet into waiting arms. I was lucky not to break my ass on the floor as 185 pounds of rock-solid Apache forced me off my feet.

"God, buddy, you have to go on a diet."

"Very funny, white boy," he puffed as air leaked back into his chest.

Winch's subvocal voice carried a tinge of worry. *"You okay, babe?"*

"Just feel like I've been kicked in the chest by a mule. Give me a minute and I'll show you how okay I am."

"Hubba hubba, big boy."

Pretty sure I threw up in my mouth just a little bit. *"Knock it off, you two."*

I don't know how they were able to laugh subvocally, but they pulled it off. *"What's the play, white boy? We're pinned down."*

Fortunately, my smart phone proved to be undamaged. I showed Canton my full set of pearly whites as I dialed. *"We do what all good citizens should do. We call the cops."*

"What? Are clothes cheaper in *The Matrix*?" Sarkasian asked, eyeing our body armor and Faraday jackets. One corner of his mouth quirked upward.

A joke. Sarkasian had made a joke. I almost fell over backwards in shock. What next? Honest politicians?

The ghost light of false dawn was coloring the sky and the SFPD had long since rolled out after answering the call of an officer in distress, driving up with lights a-blazing and sirens a-blaring. Seeing that they hadn't been shot to pieces by the sniper, I figured it was safe enough to make an appearance. The usual round of question-and-answer took place while the uniformed police stared at four people wearing shiny, black leather trench coats and flashing FBI badges.

Shortly after I thanked the officers and sent them on their way, Sarkasian rolled up in his black Crown Vic. By that time, the rest of the team had buggered off to take care of their individual assignments.

"What the hell are you doing here?" I had asked, slightly surprised.

"When your name came over the wire, Dumont, I *had* to come down to see what this was about." It was then that he made his sarky *Matrix* remark. Like I hadn't heard that dozens of times before.

"They're terribly comfortable," I replied. "I suspect that everyone will be wearing them soon."

The detective looked us up and down, not hiding his amusement as he turned his attention to the building. "What's with the hole?" he asked, pointing to the chasm in the wall. The sour lemon expression returned to his face.

"What hole?" I asked, innocent as a four-year-old.

His eyes grew liquid nitrogen cold as he stared at me. "Don't be cute."

I couldn't help it, I was born irretrievably cute, but enough was enough. "What do you want, Detective?" I let a hint of impatience creep into my voice.

The force of his frigid glare nearly rocked me back on my heels. Sarkasian was *pissed.* "I want you to answer my god-damned question, Dumont."

"And what question would that be, Sarkasian? It's hard to keep track."

He took a step forward and leaned in, an attempt to intimidate with body language and personal space. Problem was, he had to look up at me and I've been intimidated by the best. "You didn't tell me about that Shuck character."

Oh. *That* question.

"Detective, why are you so interested in my case?" Once again, the response was not what I was looking for.

"Because it was *my* case before you showed up!" He stabbed a finger in my chest with every other word and didn't seem to notice the armor under the Faraday coat. "And I don't like my cases being yanked out from under me."

"Stop that, Detective."

"Stop what?" *Poke, poke.*

My annoyance tolerance was at full capacity. I took a deep breath (hard to do in full armor) in an effort to keep calm. There. A sense of equilibrium achieved. "That poking, Detective."

Poke, poke.

"Detective," I said, a thread of anger in my voice.

He ignored the warning. *Pokity, poke, poke.*

Time for a poke back. In the throat. With stiffened fingers.

Not *too* hard.

There was gagging and other interesting noises as Sarkasian fell to his knees on the cold concrete, trying to regain his breath. Okay, poking his throat with stiffened fingers was a bit childish and mean; I was at least twenty years younger and in much better shape. If BB had been there he would have dressed me down no matter who was watching.

But, boy, did it *feel* good.

"You okay, Sarkasian?"

More gagging noises. He sounded like he was trying to throw up a cat.

I held up my hands. "Take your time. I'll wait."

"Need help, boss?" Canton appeared out of the dark of the building, both eyebrows raised as he stared at the coughing and gagging detective. "He don't look so good."

"He ran into my fingers. Give him a second. If he doesn't start breathing, we'll give him an emergency tracheotomy."

As if the words were a magic spell, Sarkasian stood and took a swing at me. I didn't bother to block it because Canton caught his arm and twisted it into a wrist lock. With a grunt, he forced the detective to his knees. "Don't be an ass," the Apache grunted. To me, "What do you want me to do with him, boss?"

"Don't break him."

Sarkasian looked up at me, his head cocked up at an uncomfortable angle from his bent position. The rage and hate that flashed through his features nearly scorched my skin. What chewed at his insides and caused such intense emotions? My desire to get to the root of his animosity was limited by my complete and utter apathy to the whole situation.

I had bigger fish to fry.

Squatting down, I put my baby blues on the level of his fiery brown orbs. "Listen, Sarkasian, attacking a Fed is not too bright. You get zero bonus points for bravery." He bared his teeth, and it wasn't a smile. "Like I told you, the murder falls under my jurisdiction, not yours, and I will keep my answers to whatever questions you may have to myself. Is that understood?"

"[EXPLETIVE][CENSORED] [BLEEP][EXPLETIVE]!"

"Boss," grunted Canton, holding the detective's wrist tight. "He sure sounds like he might be a little raw with you some."

I kept up the staring contest with Sarkasian. "You think?"

"Maybe he needs more fiber."

What he needed was a few CCs of Thorazine, but there was none to be had and his heated gaze hadn't cooled one degree. "Last time, Sarkasian: do you get what I've been telling you? You stay away from *my* case or I'm going to have my partner here do very bad things to your shoulder and wrist." Two heartbeats. "Permanent things."

Growl, grumble, grumble.

"What's that?"

"I said, 'okay'!" he grated through clenched teeth. Sweat beaded on his upper lip.

Hmmm. Didn't trust him as far as I could bowl him, but I had little choice unless I allowed Canton to break his arm just to keep him out of my hair. Tempting. By the look in Canton's eyes he was sorely tempted as well.

"Let him go."

The Apache grunted and stepped back, wary that the detective might try something. Sarkasian straightened slowly, rubbing his wrist and giving us both the ol' stink eye. "This is my town, Dumont." His voice sounded like grinding glass. "*My* town and I know what happens when the Feds investigate in *my* town. It's the locals who have to clean up the mess, so go do what you have to do, but do it quickly and *go away*."

"What is your major malfunction, dipstick?" Canton yelled, teeth shining bright in the glow of the halogen street lamps.

Maybe the detective realized he'd pushed too hard, or said too much, because his jaw closed with a *snap*. He jumped into his Crown Vic and tore off, leaving a trail of smoke and rubber in his wake.

"What is his problem, white boy?"

I stared after the Vic, sure that there was more to Sarkasian's hatred than met the eye. I had that funny feeling you get when you brush against a spider's web, kind of goose-pimply and creepy/horrible. The detective wasn't done sticking his big nose in our business. Of course, it wouldn't be a BSI mission if there weren't a problem or two in the wings waiting to muck things up, but I didn't have time to keep an eye on the local law enforcement types.

"You're almost vibrating in place, buddy, what is it?" To the untrained eye the slight tremor in my friend's hands would be attributed to post-adrenaline edginess, but I could tell he was busting at the seams with news.

He shoved a RediPad into my hands. On the screen was a satellite image of what looked to be an island. Actually several. "What is this?"

"Satellite imagery of the Farallon Islands."

Strike one. "Sorry, no clue what you're talking about."

Canton laid one of the photographs we found in Mace's apartment on the pad. Sea lions stared mournfully at the camera amidst rocks strewn with bird crap. "Get it?"

Okay, I was feeling particularly slow ... still didn't see what the big deal was. "Let me guess, same place?"

"Kal, Kal, Kal," he *tsked*. "You never studied."

I slowly counted to ten, resisting the urge to pull his spine out through his mouth. "Please, Canton."

"The Farallon Islands are twenty-seven miles *west* of the Golden Gate Bridge."

"Did you say 'west'?"

"I said 'west.' "

West. Where Joshua said the peril would come from. I didn't think he meant Japan. That feeling of aimless helplessness began to fray at the edges as my lips stretched wide.

"So what now, white boy?"

I stared at the dimly lit fat clouds above; their bellies seemingly close enough to touch. "Buddy, I have an idea forming in my brain."

"Oh, lord. *That* never bodes well."

My grin was liquid nasty. "Ferb, I know what we're going to do today."

Chapter Eleven

Farallon Island Holiday

The boat was called *Gettin' Jiggy*. Really. I'm not making that up. When Winch told me she'd secured a little thirty-foot cutter we could use to bebop over to Southeast Farallon Island—the largest in the chain and the only inhabited one—I was ecstatic. Then, when I saw the name writ large in cursive letters on the ass end … well, my ecstasy wilted around the edges. A lot.

"You couldn't find a different boat?" I yelled, cold air scrubbing tears from my eyes. The moisture in the air inflicted a biting chill, and clipping along at thirty knots made it worse. I can tolerate cold with the best of them, but that didn't mean I had to like it.

Winch, her hair done up in a brand new bottle-red dye job, smirked. "Only one I could find. We were lucky it had been seized as part of a drug raid, or we would be rowing."

Actually, she'd done a bang-up job, making sure the Brownies made it on the plane, receiving our new payload from Special Branch and bringing it to our new place.

That new place was one of those small houses built way back in the day, which eventually the city just grew up all around, surrounding a slice of humble Americana with glass and steel. It had gone through several hands as different businesses but now was empty. Not the perfect base of operations, but time wasn't on our side and the renovators did the best they could in a short amount of time.

When we arrived, I already had my plan, such as it was. We began phase one: disguises. Most people try for an elaborate latex job, but in my book, the simpler the better. The creative use of make-up, dyed or false hair and false teeth worked better for us spy-types on the go. Although, if we could perfect a *Mission Impossible* style mask, I'd be pretty stoked.

So Winch's pageboy haircut was bottle-red and my blond locks were black as sin, while Canton wore a knit touk and a false set of ugly, brown teeth. Ilena had cut her hair short and decided on platinum blonde. She looked like—ironically enough—a pixie.

Our cover story was that we were PETA loving sightseers who wanted to check out the local marine and avian life around the islands. We would dock at Southeast Farallon Island for a quick, impromptu tour. We hoped that the Point Reyes Bird Observatory (PRBO) Conservation Science staff would be accommodating. A non-profit organization studying wildlife around the island, they maintained a facility there. If luck was with us, they would be chatty with those who shared their passion.

The boat with the despicable name surged under my feet, an eager beast, and I cursed the drug runner with the bad taste in nomenclature. "How much longer," I hollered.

"About twenty minutes at this pace."

I nodded and continued staring into the bleak, gray west, my mind drifting to points east to a certain English lady love who was occupying my mind more and more. Who knew that love could be so annoying?

"How can you stand this clammy cold, white boy?"

Not bothering to remove my eyes from the horizon, I said, "How is it that you cannot?"

"Really? *Kung Fu* lines at eight-ten a.m.?"

"Yes, Grasshopper. It is wise to laugh in the face of adversity."

"Hmph." A few seconds of relative silence as we both stared into the distance. "Who do you expect to find on the islands, Kal? What did Mace find?"

I shook my head. "Not sure what Mace found. All I know is that what he found got him killed. We just have to act like your ordinary conservation types on a tour and keep our eyes open."

"Got a bad feeling, white boy. This ain't gonna end well."

Yeah. I had the same feeling, but I couldn't let the others know that. Being the leader means never revealing your fear, your uncertainty, because that could destroy the team faster than an AK-47. So I got to be the big, bad dude with the 'tude and act like I knew what I was doing, even though I wanted to tell the others I was just winging it.

Soon Southeast Farallon Island came into view, a humpy, rocky gray mass that looked more inhospitable up close and personal than in the photos.

"The Islands are outcroppings of the Salinian Block," Winch commented, moving up to stand with us. "A vast geologic province of granitic continental crust sharing its origins with the core of the Sierra Nevada Mountains. The block was torn off far to the south of its present position and rifted north by the movement of the Pacific Plate on which the islands stand."

That earned her a look or two.

"I thought you were an Art History major at Columbia, darlin'," Canton mused, his brown false teeth turning his normally radiant smile into a horrifying spectacle.

Winch held up her RediPad. "Wikipedia."

We shared a rare laugh as we drew closer to the bleak island, the double humps of its rocky profile dominating the view. I felt a strange, nagging fear. There was something wrong with the calm island surroundings. Something I couldn't put a finger on.

Fortunately Winch was more observant. "There are no birds," she said over the splash of the water slapping the hull.

"What?"

She pointed. "Look. The islands are a refuge for over a quarter million birds and there aren't even any gulls." Her generous mouth was pulled into a frown. "When's the last time you didn't see a seagull near the ocean?"

Holy crap, she was right. Plenty of dung-splattered rock, but no splatterers in sight, and instead of the raucous cries of birds there was an eerie stillness.

"No seals, either, white boy," breathed Canton. "There should be seals, sea lions, all sorts of marine mammals decorating those whomping big rocks along the shoreline. Where the hell did they go?"

Damn, he was right. Closer still and we noticed several small, white houses at the base of Lighthouse hill and Little Lighthouse hill. The homes of the PRBO researchers.

Soon enough we came to the dock—a ratty looking affair that hadn't been maintained for quite a while—where Canton made another observation.

"No boats," he said. "Where did they go? Who would live out here with no way to evacuate in case of emergency? White boy, this is starting to give me the willies something fierce."

The cutter's hull *thudded* against the tires lining the dock, causing the dung-covered wooden structure to groan alarmingly. The short hairs on the back of my neck prickled in fear. Gingerly, I stepped onto the dock and tied the boat fast, grateful that the water slick boards beneath my boots didn't give away and splash me into frigid waters.

"Boss," Ilena whispered, pointing inland. "Someone's coming."

I looked up to see a short, bearded guy with curly brown hair making his way along the trail from one of the houses, head down, hands stuffed into a large, expensive-looking Patagonia coat. Big Timberline boots stomped down the dock as he marched grimly toward us. Up close, the man looked to be in his early thirties with sharp lines bracketing his nose and mouth, giving him both a stern and pensive look. Brows furrowed, he seemed to be working on a good case of angry.

"Hey there," I said, extending a hand. "You must be Daniel McFadden." We had researched the PRBO members, so I knew all about the island's inhabitants. McFadden was the nominal leader of the research group, an environmental engineer and ornithologist who had joined the PRBO five years ago. Through diligence and careful butt-kissing, he'd risen quickly through the ranks to his highest level of incompetence.

McFadden ignored my hand and gave me a "Kiss off and die" look. I lowered my hand as I felt the other team members *thonk* onto the dock behind me. The wooden structure swayed slightly beneath our combined weight.

"You are not welcome here."

McFadden's voice emerged hoarse, gruff and strained, as if he hadn't had a drop of water for days.

The worm of unease that nestled in my gut turned. "Not your island to bar us entrance, Mr. McFadden." There was a time to be polite and that wasn't it.

"You are not welcome here."

"You said that already."

"Please go." McFadden's face became pained, almost tortured, as if he were wrestling with conflicting emotions that tugged the flesh of his features every which way. It was creepy as hell.

I shook my head. "Sorry, Mr. McFadden, that's not going to happen. We came here for the birds and the sea lions and we're not going to leave until we've seen them."

"The birds and the seals are gone. Nothing to see here. You must go."

"Uh, boss, there's something you should know." Canton sounded like he was ready to draw his Bowie and go to work.

"What?"

"Look."

I looked. And swore.

A lot.

Boiling out of the houses were dozens of people of all stripes. Young, old, fat and thin, men, women, boys and girls, a seemingly endless tide of humanity vomiting forth from a confined space like a macabre version of a clown car at the circus.

Wonderful.

"You must leave," McFadden urged, his face a wreck of twisted flesh and naked agony. "Please! I don't want to fail—" Those last words were cut off by a gut-wrenching scream that spiraled up and up until I thought his throat would burst.

Before anyone could react, McFadden was at my throat, hands grasping and clutching, tightening with a frightfully powerful grip. He managed to do a credible job of crushing my windpipe and I began to gag as I landed ferocious combinations of strikes to his midsection.

I might as well have been punching a tree for all the good it did. My knee connected with his groin and all the man did was squeeze harder. I brought my hands up between his arms to break the lock, but that maneuver didn't work. His arms felt like steel cables and his fingers were steel springs, choking the life out of me. Another punch broke ribs, but his grip remained firm.

Black spots swam before my eyes and it came to me that I could actually *die*. There was no film-school flashings of my life, no light in the tunnel to lead me to my ancestors, only an intense anger that I was going to get my precious self killed by a dude half my size.

A flat *crack* and a dime-sized hole appeared in McFadden's forehead. Blood, bone and brains showered out of the back of his skull in a pink spray. The researcher's hazel eyes rolled back until only the whites were exposed before his fingers loosened from my throat and he fell to the dock in a heap.

Air! That blessed oxygen/nitrogen mix filled my lungs with life and I decided on several lungfuls, while McFadden lay on half-rotted wood and bled all over my boots.

Canton's warm breath touched my face. "You okay, white boy?"

What came out of my mouth were dry, crackly, gagging sounds like a cat choking on a hairball, and I had to settle on a nod.

"Uh, boss, Canton," Winch and Ilena chorused.

We both looked up to see the flowing stream of humanity beating feet our way. It would have been almost comical if that rushing mass hadn't been so quiet. Not a word, no screams or catcalls. Without hesitation I drew my Bowie and hacked at the line holding the cutter fast to the dock. The nylon parted easily to the razor's edge of the knife and we all were aboard within five seconds.

Fifty feet away the quiet horde ran on, legs pumping furiously to catch the cutter as the engine sputtered to life.

Thirty feet away they were close enough for me to tell them apart. Every person had a blank-eyed intensity that scared me out of my undies. They looked like fresh zombies given a purpose and the will to carry it out. The dock emitted the harsh, cracking sound of splitting wood.

"Must go faster," I croaked. My hands gripped the rails until the knuckles shone white. The cutter began to move with some speed along the dock. Canton raised his Glock, but I put a hand on his arm and forced it down.

Toward the end of the pack of quietly rushing humanity, the dock emitted a deep, crackling groan and gave way, a ten-foot section collapsing into the frigid water of the pacific. At least ten people fell in without uttering a sound.

I felt bile splash the back of my throat.

We roared past the end of the dock and the leading edge of the crowd jumped for the boat, arms outstretched to catch the rail. I could see a scary blankness in their eyes, as if shiny stones had replaced those dispassionate orbs.

They missed, and the cold ocean swallowed them as it had the others, without pity.

As we pulled away, I noticed they didn't surface.

"What the hell, white boy?" Canton yelled over the scream of the engine. "It's like they were possessed!"

Possessed? "Get me Ilena," I managed through my mangled throat.

"One sec, Kal."

Winch took the helm and Ilena joined me at the rail as I watched the island slowly grow smaller. "Whatcha need, boss?"

Damn, but my throat hurt something awful. "Have you heard of a Supernatural that can mind-control a mass of people?"

She shook her head.

Damn. If it was the Faë that controlled those people, how come nobody had ever heard of them performing such a feat before? "How come that man had been so strong, much stronger than he should have been?"

Ilena considered a moment. "Well, it could be that all his pain centers had been disabled. We are limited by the pain we want to endure. If something hurts when we squeeze or punch, we stop. Take pain away, take away inhibition and we can apply more strength. Enough to break our own bones, if necessary."

Canton joined us at the rail, legs wobbling as he tried to adjust for the chop. "Why aren't they following us?"

Good question. Very good. So good, in fact, that I had the screaming willies. I settled for shaking my head and shrugging.

Th-thump! The whole boat shook and listed to port.

"What was that?" yelled the Apache.

Tha-thump, thump, thumpity-thump. The cutter juddered and shuddered with each impact, wallowing in the ocean's heavy chop. All three of us worked our way hand over hand along the rail. Frantically trying to steer away from whatever was hitting us, Winch had to cut the speed down by half.

"We're taking on water!" she screamed as we passed by, pale face flushed with worry. "I've got the bilge pumps working! What's going on, boss?"

Two more steps and I found out.

Seals. Dozens of them, all committing seal suicide by flinging themselves in front of the cutter. Blood and fur stained the water as the boat battered the animals to death. A big bull sea lion leapt half out of the water directly in front of the cutter and the prow took it in the belly with a liquid *squelch*. The poor animal flopped bonelessly back into the ocean while the boat shook like an epileptic.

"White boy." Canton sounded uneasy, as if he had been tiptoeing around graves.

"What?" I couldn't tear my eyes from the dying seals. *Thumpity, thumpity, thump.* It was one of the most disturbing things I'd ever seen and like the people on the island, the seals carried out their mission in silence.

"Uh … I know where the birds went."

From Ilena, "Oh, damn…"

Canton's hand landed on the top of my head and directed my gaze toward the sky.

Oh damn was right. "Winch," I screamed. "Go faster! Must go faster!"

She looked up in horror. "We could wreck the damn boat!"

"If you don't, we're all dead!"

Winch followed my gaze and her eyes flew open wide. Without another word she hit the juice and the cutter surged forward.

Thunkity, thunk.

Above and behind the boat a black cloud followed, a swirling whorl of feathery bodies beating wings our way. It wasn't the total birdie population of the Farallon Islands, but it was close; there had to be at least a hundred thousand winged assassins blotting out the sky. Death by pecking wasn't the way I wanted to exit, stage right, and the image of that great big whopper of a wasp came to mind. It had concentrated on me and me alone. It must have been controlled by the same beings that controlled the seals and the birds.

From the cloud of swirling birds, barely heard over the roar of the engine and the thud-splat of the suicide seals, came a sudden raucous caw. Every other bird cried out in unison. It was the sound of lost and damned souls crying out to an uncaring god. The cloud of birds began to funnel downward toward the boat. They formed a cloud of winged death.

Oh crap.

"Faster, must go faster!" I yelled.

Winch's voice rose an octave. "I canna go any faster, Cap'n, she's giving it all she's got!"

Wonderful.

Then the bottom dropped out of my world and my sanity nearly took a walk off the map as we noticed a trio of extremely large triangular shapes cutting through the boat's wake about twenty feet behind. Following each of the blade-like projections were smaller triangles a third of the size. All six dorsal fins sliced through the water with the ease of millions of years of lethal evolution.

Craptastic.

"Are those *sharks*?" Ilena sounded like a frightened six-year-old.

Canton shook his head. "Don't ask me, I'm from New Mexico." He didn't *quite* sound like a six-year-old.

As for me, I had the incredibly logical, quite natural, extreme terror of all things shark, shark-like and all shark-related products ever since I watched *Jaws* on cable TV when I was eight. While my hindbrain was drooling and babbling in horror, my cerebral cortex went into overdrive. I estimated by the distance between greater and lesser dorsals that each shark was at least twenty feet long if not longer. My insides decided to take a bath in liquid nitrogen.

Thump!

Shouting over the seal impacts and the whine of a stressed engine—my throat on fire from my recent throttling—I yelled to Canton, "Get the grenades! Throw them off to the front and sides." He nodded and went below.

To Ilena, "Shotgun, explosive rounds." I pointed to the trio of long bullet shapes. "Blow those things to hell." She followed Canton below deck.

Which left me staring at the swirling funnel cloud of beaky death heading our way.

Thump!

"Kal," Winch cried, mouth stretched in a rictus of excitement or fear. "She canna take much more o' this!" Her Scottish accent was atrocious.

I made a mental note to shoot her later. Keeping an eye on the swelling mass of birdie rage above and behind, I estimated we had a minute, maybe two before the feathery assassins swarmed us.

Canton and Ilena arrived as another seal bit the hull and the cutter jinked to the right (or starboard, whatever). All of us held on for dear life, knowing we were at imminent risk of becoming a shark's entree.

Ilena carried one of the new Mark VII Hinkler fully automatic shotguns with a fifteen-round box clip. Matte-black with hard edges and a boxy design, it looked like hard-core death waiting to happen.

Meanwhile, Canton had secured a bandolier from left shoulder to right hip with silvery shotgun shells in the black leather loops. Those shells were actually powerful concussion grenades, much more portable than their military cousins. They were a mainstay of any Bureau operation, rarely used except when things went pear-shaped.

Like now.

THUMP!

The cutter lifted slightly and the engine gave an asthmatic groan. "Hurry up!" Winch yelled. "We're talking on more water than the pumps can handle!"

"I got this," Canton growled and carefully made his way forward, knees flexing with every seal-bump against the boat.

Standing at the bow, the Apache removed a couple of grenades, twisted the ends and threw them far outward. Just before the boat reached the impact points, great gouts of water and blood shot into the air, raining down on the deck. A small glob of seal blubber and fur landed at my feet with a wet *splat*. Canton let out a victorious whoop and tossed two more ahead, to the left and right with almost identical results. The hammering against the boat lessened. Three more grenades and it stopped altogether, although the cutter's speed didn't improve. The look on Winch's face told me it wouldn't.

"Your turn, white boy!" he thundered, a crazy smile on his wide face.

I gestured toward the sharks that were slowly gaining on us. "Do you mind?" I asked Ilena.

She nodded and starting firing. Four shots, four hits, four explosions of blood and flesh. After a clip, one of the dorsal fins sank out of sight while the other two soldiered on, undeterred by gaping holes leaking blood into the water.

"Sonofabitch!" swore the magician as she changed the clip. "Whoever is controlling those sharks can override the ability to feel pain or react to it, just like the people at the dock."

That wasn't news. "Hurry up," I urged. The birds were only a couple hundred yards away and closing fast—eerily silent gulls, cormorants and petrels aiming to deliver an unpleasant pecking.

"Pushy, pushy," she snarled and fired. A fountain of blood and seawater shot four feet into the air as the round exploded in front of the dorsal fin of the shark to the right. Chunks of meat spun lazily off and the creature sank out of sight.

One more shark down, one to go.

Ilena's face became gleefully savage as she emptied the clip at the last shark, sending more tissue spraying as the explosive slugs tore it to shreds. The creature rolled, exposing a pale belly before disappearing.

"Get down below!" I hollered, reaching into my heavy coat.

"What are you going to do, white boy?" hollered Canton, features stretched into a grim war mask.

I looked at the descending birds. Fifty yards, closing fast. "No time. Get below!"

Canton nodded, dragging the protesting Ilena with him.

From my pocket I drew forth a thick black disk, five inches in diameter with a horseshoe handle on one side. At the base of the handle, where one of the ends connected to the disk, was a smooth black button. I swallowed and backed into the wheelhouse.

"Keep piloting the boat," I told Winch, my throat strangling my words. "Don't stop for anything."

Her eyes grew wide. "What is *that*?"

"Something new. One of the toys Special Branch has been working on."

She blanched, hunched her shoulders and ducked her ahead.

The new gadget we had received from the Bureau had been in development for quite some time: a sonic weapon. Alex had attached a note to it that read: Disk Of Death, Handle With Care.

Trust the Bureau R&D to turn a non-lethal crowd-control weapon into a miniaturized, extraordinarily lethal version of what the police use. Most sonic weapons damage the eardrums and can vibrate the eyeballs, distorting vision. Other effects can include epileptic seizures and cavitation of the gas nuclei in tissue, which can heat flesh to the point of damaging organs.

Now amp that up by a factor of ten. That's what I held in my hands.

It was a prototype and had not been tested thoroughly.

Wonderful. I blamed Alex.

But what choice did I have?

The leading gulls and cormorants were almost upon us; their wings arched back as they dove. Praying that the scientists at the Bureau were more successful with beta testing than most software companies, I gripped the handle of the sonic disk, pointed it at the oncoming wave of birds and pressed the shiny button.

The handle jumped and wriggled in my grip, vibrating with an intensity that rattled the bones of my hand, as if a zillion volts of electricity were shooting through it. My arm wanted to wave crazily back and forth, so I gripped my wrist with my other hand. My teeth felt as if they would crawl out of my skull as a high-pitched whine delivered a sharp, stabbing pain to my eardrums. Through the eerie scream of the weapon I heard Winch cry out.

Its effect on us humans was disconcerting enough, but what it did to the birds would have delighted fans of slasher flicks worldwide.

Fifty or so birds vanished in red mist and feathers that were blown back in a crimson cloud, staining the surface of the water. Bits of bone and meat that hadn't been pulverized by the enormous pressure waves emanating from the disc streaked through the spray. Some ended up in the water, but a lot landed in the boat.

More birds vanished into that blender, pushing steadily forward as the bodies of the slain provided a buffer against the tearing waves of sound. One foot, two, closer and closer as the red spray rose wider and higher—more blood and microscopic particles of tissue wafting into the air before floating down upon the ocean.

To the left and right and above, the three-sided Plexiglas canopy comprising the wheelhouse disintegrated, the aluminum framework twisting out of true. Plastic dust joined the red fog created by the sonic weapon.

Arms cramping from the strain, I held the disk steady, pointed at the center mass of diving birds, my eyeballs crossing and watering. Soon, I knew, my grip would fail and I'd drop the weapon. When that happened my organs would either burst from sonic pummeling or the birds would peck me to death.

Closer and closer, more birds flying into the death storm and more pieces of flesh, bone and blood making it through the barrier of sound. I shouted my frustration to the indifferent clouds as red droplets began to rain all about.

Then it was over.

No more birds. The remainder flew off, scattering to the winds and squawking in terror. I thumbed the shiny button with a numb finger and the weapon stilled and fell from my trembling hands.

As the swiftly fading cries of birds spiraled to silence, a relative quiet gripped the boat in a soft embrace.

"What just happened?" asked Winch, her voice a harsh grate against the eerie stillness.

"I think … I think we won." My lungs strained to pull in every molecule of oxygen they could.

Then I noticed the red. All over me, the wheelhouse, Winch … everywhere. A thick, gelatinous slurry that clung to everything. I wiped at my face, removing a layer of sticky red sludge. God, it was everywhere, even in my nostrils, bringing the scent of blood and crap to the party. Then I saw the back of the boat.

And right then and there I lost it. Yeah, me, Mr. Big Tough Guy blew chunks all over the wheelhouse as adrenaline aftershock punished my body with the shakes. Behind me I heard a splatter and a guttural *hurk* as Winch joined me in the barf fest.

From the wheelhouse on back lay at least two feet of thick red mush that had been hundreds, if not thousands of birds. It coated the seats, the deck, everything. Slow moving rivers of muck plopped down the stairs to the cabin in a turgid flow with every jolt of the boat. I'd rendered thousands of birds into so much crimson mush in less than two minutes.

Winch wiped her mouth, staring daggers at me. "Don't look at me, boss. I ain't cleaning this up."

Wonderful.

Chapter Twelve
San Francisco Story—Part Two

"**A**nd so we sailed on into the docks with a load of blended bird bits. Damn, you should have seen the stares, the goggling as we tied off."

I took a sip of my soda and stared down at Wilkes's slack face. Lips still bluish, still dead, still cold. Once again sorrow tugged at my soul.

"Turns out the boat had taken some serious damage from those seals; we barely made it back. The damn thing was wallowing like a hippo. I expect calls will be made. People are going to bitch and moan about the condition of the thing, but nothing will come of it, you know that."

Wilkes's had no comment and probably wouldn't for … ever, but I stood there and pretended he was in that middle place between sleeping and waking where everything is just right and you feel so good. It comforted me to think he was aware of my presence, that I was keeping him entertained with my stories.

I couldn't figure out if my little self-delusion was sad, pathetic or maudlin. Maybe a combination of all three. Another sip of soda washed the lump from my throat. I wondered if this was how Audie Murphy felt at the end of WWII, alone amidst the sorrowful ghosts of his fallen comrades.

"Okay, big man, that's been our day so far. Of course the Faë can control people and animals; they knew exactly how to screw up the reconnaissance. Just my luck, huh? But don't you worry." I tapped his cold shoulder. "Even now I am forming a cunning plan." My grin had nothing of humor in it.

Another sip of the soda. "I know, I know. You don't want to hear any more of that boring Faë crap. You're just happy Canton speared the sonofabitch who killed you to the floor. Shoulda seen that sucker melt around that steel blade. All those stories about fairies and their aversion to iron are true.

"You know that little puća bastard tried to mind-rape me, too? Can you believe that noise? It hurt like the blazes and there was nothing I could do about it but share some of its memories. I owe Canton my life. Again.

"But you don't want to hear all about that, you want me to continue my story, so continue it I will."

The Bureau installed us in a defunct auto parts store in the very district where the rape/murders had taken place. Allied Infosystems was in business ... at least on paper. We had a profile of the killer from the FBI and were cross-referencing all the data we had (which was zilch) in an attempt to find the killer, but we all knew we would have to catch the perp in the act.

"Okay, who put liniment in my toothpaste?" I shrieked, mouth on fire. Every little molecule of air that touched my tongue felt like another drop of acid on my sensitive tissues. Tears streamed unbidden down my cheeks

Laughter was my only answer.

Wonderful. We'd been on the ground for less than three hours and the payback had already begun. Was that an extra glint of gleeful malice in Canton's eyes?

Bastard.

Mace laughed just as loud as the others, a glob of cream cheese from his bagel decorating the corner of his mouth. "I told you, kid, they will get revenge."

I stared at the assembled agents gathered around the circular faux-wood table in the lounge, their faces registering from amused to triumphant at my oral agony. Fortunately the fridge was fully stocked. I grabbed some milk and drank straight from the carton, eliciting groans from the rest of team.

"Serves you right, you bastards," I said between large, messy gulps.

I didn't bother to dodge the napkins and the bagel remnants that flew my way.

After my mouth was reasonably less volcanic, I sat down. "Got a question, boss," I announced while snagging a cinnamon-raisin bagel from the box in the middle of table. Some raspberry cream cheese later, I was munching contentedly, albeit gingerly.

"Shoot, kid," he replied, leaning back and crossing his massive arms over his broad chest.

"I know we're supposed to be all super-secret and clandestine, but why don't we just keep the same offices in all the major cities and use them when we arrive for business?" Damn, those bagels were *delicious*!

Mace nodded as the rest of the team smiled knowingly. "How up to date are you on the Soviet version of the Bureau?"

I scratched my head. "The Призрачные убийцы?" Pretty sure I butchered the Russian, but roughly translated, it meant "Ghost Killers." I heard they were a surly bunch until the booze started flowing; then you couldn't get them to stop dancing on the tables. The agents from Japan were the same way, except that their penchant was for karaoke bars, where they belted out mangled versions of "Tie a Yellow Ribbon 'Round the Ole Oak Tree."

"Nope, the *Soviet* version, before the Wall came a tumblin' down."

"Don't know a lot, only that they were a right bunch of assbags."

Canton snorted into his cola. "White boy, you've been learning about the VGG, those Nazi Bureau assholes who worked for Hitler?"

He knew I was; it was required study for all the new guys. "Sure."

"Well, these guys were worse. Not because they used Necromancy like the VGG, but because they were so damn efficient. And their primary goal, after protecting the CCCP from Supernaturals, was to destabilize the BSI."

Mace nodded while my jaw did some dropping. "That's right." He leaned forward, steepling his fingers. "You see, a country with an effective defense against the Supernaturals is a country that could withstand the Soviet expansionist plans of the '50s and '60s." He took a deep breath. "So what do you think they tried to do?"

That was easy. "Kill or recruit BSI agents."

One big finger stabbed the table three times. "Ex-act-ly. For years they tried to kill, steal from, or subvert every Bureau agent they could locate." Mace took a deep breath. "In early September of '62, a Bureau station in Charlotte, NC, took out a dragon."

"A dragon?"

"A real, live, classic, fire-breathing, scaly horror of a dragon, about forty feet long. The team used a bazooka to kill it, or so the record says, and took its heart. They stayed around because, as you know, where—"

"—there's one Supernatural, there's going to be others," chorused the entire group, myself included, finishing Bureau Rule #1. No one knows why Supernatural occurrences happen in pairs in the same general vicinity, but for as long as mankind has been fighting those Things That Go Bump In The Night, that rule has never been proven wrong.

"So what happened?"

"A day later the office was attacked by the Soviet Bureau. Back then it was referred to as the KGB's Unit D. Anyway, Unit D had an agenda: obtain the dragon's heart, which is believed to carry magical powers. They killed all but one member of the team, a man named Orson who the Soviets assumed was dead, having shot him in the head."

"Did we have the dragon's heart?"

"We did."

Okay, gross. "They blew the dragon out of the sky and were tasked to retrieve the heart for the Bureau?"

"Abso-damn-lutely."

"So the heart did have magical properties?"

Mace nodded.

"How did Unit D know we had the heart?"

"It's unclear, but best guess is, they had the team under surveillance for a while because back then, we *did* have specific offices in every major city. Once Unit D located an office, all they had to do was wait."

I shook my head. This was almost too weird, even for the Bureau. "What kind of powers was the heart supposed to give?"

Mace's dark eyes glittered like gems. "Invincibility, strength, command of languages, and even invisibility … to name a few."

My mind made like a pachinko ball, pinging around the data he'd just fed me, trying to come to some sort of coherence. A little voice in the back of my head told me I was missing the bigger picture. Bigger picture. What was the bigger picture, some thirteen years before I was born? Another bite of bagel, followed by a hefty swallow of milk (I knew I'd be tasting that awful *camphor* of the liniment for days) brought me no joy.

"So," I mumbled around a glob of cream cheese. "In 1962, Unit D ambushes and kills a Bureau team and steals a dragon's heart. One man lives to tell the tale, but Unit D makes off with the heart … back to the Soviet Union?"

Mace shook his head. Everyone was staring intently at me. I had a feeling I was being tested, which is a common occurrence in the Bureau.

"Where?"

"Guess."

Where would the Soviets go in 196-… my thoughts trailed away to dark places as my high school history lessons came back with a rush.

Oh crap.

Canton grinned, his teeth very white against copper skin. "Mace, I think the penny has dropped."

"The Cuban missile crisis?" Naw, it couldn't be.

Mace put paid to my doubts. "It was thought that the dragon's heart would give the Soviets an edge. Unfortunately for them, we managed to insert a team into Cuba composed of Spanish-speaking agents. In mid-October, they located the Unit D team and neutralized them, along with the dragon's heart."

That was Bureau-speak for "They killed them all and the heart was destroyed somehow." My world teetered about, a sensation I was to become familiar with during my career. "How the heck did they think a dragon's heart would help them with the American blockade?"

"I don't know, but the moment Unit D was taken care of and the heart eliminated as a threat, the Soviet Union began back-channel talks with our government to halt the upcoming crisis." Mace took a large swig from his glass of juice and sighed. "To this day we have no clue as to what they were trying to do with the heart, or what powers they thought it would give them. How it was supposed to help the Soviet navy pierce the American blockade. All we do know is that when the heart was destroyed, a possible world war was averted." He rubbed his face, looking more tired than a big twenty-eight-year-old man had a right to. "It was also the last time that a Bureau team functioned like a hit squad."

"Why was that?" I noticed that everyone was staring at Mace now, entranced. Apparently he was the expert on cold-war Bureau activities.

"The Director at the time threatened to quit. He felt that the duty of policing Supernaturals was hard enough without having to kill Straights."

"Who was the director?"

"Man by the name of Audie Murphy."

My jaw nearly clattered off the table.

"What did you bring me?" asked Brenda the Receptionist once my identity had been confirmed and she took her hand off the shotgun that lay hidden under her cheap Formica desk. She was a second-generation Japanese with hair cut so short it almost wasn't there; somehow that made her even more attractive. She could also punch a hole through a cinder block without breaking a sweat. A well-manicured finger pressed a button and a concealed door behind her swung open.

I handed her one of the two paper bags I was carrying. Grease had started to discolor the bottom. "Take out from Ming's."

She took the bag as if it contained a plague virus. That was highly doubtful, although I was willing to put my money on a bacillus or two.

"We make all this money and you managed to find the nastiest dive in Frisco to order from?" Her lip curled in distaste as she slowly opened the bag.

"Not that bad, really. I got you sweet-and-sour pork." I considered the bag in my hand. "Might even be real pork."

She dropped her bag. "You. Are. So. Gross."

I treated her to a hundred-watt smile. "My work here is done." With that said, I passed through the hidden door into our current sanctum sanctorum.

Canton sat in the lounge, big old hiking boots perched on the table, reading *Car and Driver* and drinking a Pepsi. "What did you get us this time?" he asked, eyes never leaving the magazine while he absently stroked his lower lip. "Not Ming's, I hope. That place sucks."

"God, no!" I said. "The new burger joint down the street." I planted my butt and opened the bag, removing several wax-paper bundles. "I gave Brenda Ming's."

Canton looked up. "Oh, she'll do you for that, white boy."

"I'm pretty sure she's the one who poured Rice Krispies in my bed."

"Heh. That was a good one. Laughed my ass off."

"Yeah, heard you all the way down the hall."

Smiling, the Apache unwrapped one of the packages and took a huge bite from a third-pound of beef stuffed in a sesame seed bun and topped with enough condiments and vegetation to choke a goat.

After I had joined the Bureau, the rangy Native American had almost immediately taken me under his wing and had steadfastly supported my every play, from the vampire nest in Texas to a giant bug in Florida. He always had my back and we clicked together like pieces of a puzzle—so very strange for two men from such different backgrounds.

With a start I realized that he was the best friend I'd ever had. How bizarre was that? I usually got along famously with everyone I met, but for some reason never formed real friendships. Canton Alsate was the first person outside my family and my ex-fiancée Carol who I ever let into my odd little world.

The thought made me sad. There I was at age twenty-five, finally realizing how isolated I had become.

Enough of that, I mused. Too much introspection gave me gas.

I realized that I hadn't seen anyone else. "Where is everyone?"

Canton took a sip from his Pepsi and said, "They are out and about, policing the neighborhood, being all cop-like and stuff."

"Huh?"

"Mouth went to talk to the first victim to see if there was anything she might have remembered. Mace and Winch are getting a feel for the area, learning the lay of the land."

Because of the lack of data, the plan had been to wait until the rapist cast another spell strong enough to trip a sensor. A mite callous, but when dealing with magic, it was better to err on the side of caution. Thomas Mace absent from our hidey hole like that could only mean one thing. "They were bored out of their tree and wanted to get out."

The Apache's finger shot in the air. "Got it in one, white boy."

Whoop, whoop, whoop!

We both beat feet to Comms while the alarm blared loud enough to hurt. Someone had cast a powerful spell and tripped a sensor. Looked like Mace and the ladies wouldn't be bored for much longer.

"Where did it come from?" Mace demanded, staring straight into the camera of his slate. The second we hit Comms, our fearless leader had called in—notified by his tablet that the alarm had been tripped—and his face appeared on the DisplayWall.

"Triangulating now, boss," Canton replied, typing furiously on the virtual keyboard that appeared at the head of the eight-foot black table that dominated the center of the room. Mace's face was stony, but I sensed a strange undercurrent I hadn't seen before. He looked ... agitated.

"Got it, boss." The Apache tapped a couple more keys and the image of Mace shrank and moved to the right, while a satellite map of San Francisco took the left. Overlaying the photo were blue lines forming a grid over the Central West District. A green pinpoint of light blinked. "The spell was cast at Golden Gate Heights Park." He scowled. "That's less than a mile away."

"Suit up. We'll meet you two there." The left side of the DisplayWall blanked as Mace hung up.

Canton and I snagged our Faraday coats, and we headed out of the offices. "Time for a shutdown," Canton barked at Brenda as we raced out the door. The Receptionist would close up shop after us and help coordinate local backup on the off chance we would need it.

On the way, Mace phoned to say that he and the ladies would meet us on Rockridge Drive, the street hugging the park to the north. Less than two minutes later we pulled up next to Mace's Vic. The cool night air caressed my face as I exited the vehicle. For some reason, to me San Francisco smelled of wet grass and flowers. If it wasn't for all that creepy-looking fog, I'd have considered retiring there.

Mace, Mouth and Winch exited the Vic, all dolled up in their black leather Faraday coats and nightvision sunglasses. All together we looked like a gang of trendy mobsters with a love for Gucci. Or a group of hackers attempting to rescue Neo.

Golden Gate Heights Park sat on a hill overlooking a good chunk of the city and contained enough trees to hide all manner of sins. Usually abandoned after sundown, there was always someone walking around, taking the air. The trick was to find the bad guy without being seen by a Straight.

A sick feeling entered the pit of my stomach as I stared up the hill to the trees decorating the crown. We were alerted by the sensors, which meant the rapist had already struck, so we were too late to save the girl. From their mouths twisted in disgust, I could see that the rest of the team was thinking the same thing.

"Canton, you take Kal, Winch go with Mouth. Spread out, keep your mics on and be careful. Stay subvocal from now on. If you find our perp, call for backup. Check?" Mace's voice had an acid edge that bubbled across the nerves. He was *pissed*.

Everyone nodded, inserting earwigs and muttering, *"Check."*

Canton leaned over. *"White boy, I'll take point. Watch my six."*

"You got it, buddy."

We ghosted up the hill, separating to find one sick twist of a magician, our nightvision glasses rendering the night into stark shades of black and white.

Grass smell, leaf mulch, flowers, and a whiff of fryer grease slid through my nostrils. With the hunt on, the city no longer smelled familiar, comforting; instead it smelled of potential violence and the violation of innocents. A slow burble of hatred started deep inside as I realized the rapist would still be in the park, perhaps gloating over the body of his victim.

Trees enfolded us as we ran in silent half-crouches, me with my Lahti in my right hand, Canton with his Ruger. This wasn't a mission to capture a Supernatural; we aimed to kill a psychotic magician by any means necessary. Some things have to be put down for the protection of others. Or so I kept telling myself. What prison could hold a magician? Who would we trust to guard that magician? It wasn't U.S. policy to put a hit on one of its citizens, but we could no longer classify the rapist as human. Instead, we had to consider it a Supernatural and mentally divorce him from humanity.

I'd killed a human before, just a kid, actually. He was a Renfield, a vampire's human assistant and all around valet to the whole filthy nest. The Renfield had been sneaking up on me in an attempt to stab me from behind, but I'd been too sharp and had plunged my Bowie into his gut, venting life from his shuddering body. I'd stood over that young kid—his long, lank and greasy hair spread out around him on the floor of the Cascade Caverns—and felt like utter crap.

It was the most horrible feeling, killing another human being, even though SEAL training had given me the skills to do so. That night, as I walked up the hill toward the dense protection of trees, I prepared myself to do it again, to gut or shoot another person, to steal from them the rest of their natural days. To become the ultimate thief.

It didn't matter that the raping, murdering magician was also a thief of lives, that he caused these women terror and pain before frying them with his magic. He was still human and therefore entitled to some sort of consideration, wasn't he? All this burned through my mind and boiled the acid in my stomach enough that I would have paid a hundred bucks for a Tums at that moment.

This was all before I had come face-to-face with the *real* human monsters, the ones who killed women and children with no thought or remorse. It was before I learned that people could become monsters inside the shell of human skin. It was before I killed Nazis without hesitation because of the pure evil they not only radiated, but also the evil they represented.

Back then, among those trees on top of a hill in suburban San Francisco, I hadn't learned that hard lesson and still felt aching regret over killing human monsters.

"*Kal, you hear that?*" Canton subvocaled, stopping suddenly. I saw his gray and black man-shape through my nightvision glasses.

I stopped, cursing myself silently for not paying attention and listened. Nothing. "*Negative.*"

"*Wait for it.*"

Closing my eyes helped me focus on listening … Canton's breathing … the slight crunch of dead grass as he shifted his weight minutely … and "*Was that a moan?*"

"*Think so. Mace, we may have something, keep an eye on our signal, we are going to check it out.*"

"*Check that, Canton.*" Mace sounded cool and calm, which was not at all what I was feeling.

Canton ghosted forward, a stealthy shadow blending into the night. While not silent (it's impossible to keep completely quiet in the forest), his every footstep, every rustle as he stepped on leaves and twigs seemed to blend into the sounds of the night. I could only envy his skill as I tramped on behind him. Moving slow, I could be liquid death, unnoticeable, but at jogging speeds I was a shambling, racket-making mess.

As if to confirm my lack of forestry skills, Canton said, "*Damn, white boy, you sound like a herd of water buffalo. I gotta train you up some.*"

I gritted my teeth and remained silent, following as quietly as I could.

Then, "Miss, are you okay?" from up ahead, not too far. A male voice, concerned, kind.

We emerged into a small, three-sided clearing, the west end opening to a sharpish slope and a magnificent view of the city lights and deep, dark ocean. Standing in the middle was a chunky teenage girl, perhaps fifteen, maybe younger, in a torn and stained peasant dress. She stood stiffly, with her head cocked to one side, staring at us, eyes almost unnaturally wide and face curiously blank. In my black and white world, her mouth looked discolored, as if she'd worn heavy lipstick and had been kissed violently, smearing it across her lips.

A man, perhaps in his twenties wearing a long-sleeved henley shirt and jeans, approached slowly, his Vans dragging softly on the grass. He had one arm half raised. "Miss, are you okay?" he asked again, as if the girl were some skittish animal.

"Sir," Canton barked, raising his weapon. "Step away from the girl."

The man jumped, startled by the Native American's deep voice and sudden appearance. He squinted, trying to see in the dim light of the half-moon.

"What? Who's there?" he asked, his voice shaky.

Before anyone could react, the girl turned her twisted head and vomited.

Fluid, black as sin, spurted from between her lips, traveling an incredible ten feet, and hit the man dead in the mouth. Incredibly, the liquid didn't splatter, fall, or drip down his chin. Instead, it seemed to flow into the man's orifice *under its own power.*

"Grk ... hkk!" he gagged as a violent trembling seized his body, every muscle standing out in stark relief like wires under his skin. Inhuman gurgling noises filled the night as his eyes rolled to the back of his head and that dark fluid, that hideously mobile liquid, stained his mouth black, black as the pits of hell.

"Please tell me I'm seeing things, Canton," I breathed, terror plowing through me like a bullet.

The Apache's voice emerged, strained and harsh, through the earwig as the girl's head ratcheted toward us, dead eyes staring. *"Mace, we have zombies."*

Chapter Thirteen

San Francisco Story—Part Three

"You remember those zombies in the stairwell of that parking garage in Denver, don't you?" I took another drink of my soda to soothe my throat. All that storytelling dried the pipes something fierce. "That was the second time you saved my life. I knew then you had what it takes to be an agent."

Wilkes remained silent.

"So this is the zombie part of the story. Remember in my trashed apartment what I told you about zombies? That they are the malevolent spirits of mass murderers possessing the dead, driving them to create more of their own kind? They seem like such innocuous shamblers, slow and uncoordinated, but they are strong as all get out and their puke … well, I already told you what happens to those who get hit by Zombie Puke." Their sputum was actually liquid magic, a fluid-bound spell that, upon entering a host body, kills and instills a malevolent spirit. Forget about those stories where zombies ate brains; zombie puke was far worse. Another sip of soda and I continued my tale …

"Zombies?" I asked, stomach dropping like an express elevator.

"Everyone on Canton's position!" Mace barked through the earwig.

"*Check!*"

"*Check!*"

Winch and Mouth were on the way.

"*Canton?*" I subvocaled. "*What's the play?*"

"*Stay back, white boy. That little lady can puke up to twenty-five feet. Let's wait for the others to arrive.*"

I took a step back, even though I was at least forty feet away. The girl continued to stare at me, eyes lifeless and glazed. Then my gaze turned to the young man, who was gagging and gurgling.

His skin had become even whiter in my black and white vision, a harsh and uncompromising shade that turned my stomach with its absence of life. As he gagged, chunks of something flew from between his lips to land at his feet. A strange undulating motion took over his torso, rocking it in waves. Faster and faster those waves ripped through his abdomen, rippling up and down as though his muscles had liquefied.

"*What the hell, Canton?*" I sent. "*What's wrong with him?*"

"*He's turning into a zombie, white boy. His organs are becoming Zombie Puke, liquid evil magic that transforms those it touches into zombies.*"

That was about the grossest thing I'd ever heard.

"*Why aren't we shooting them … lots?*"

Even through the earwig he sounded disdainful. "*White boy, we didn't pack explosive rounds, and any others might piss them off. So let's wait until the rest of the team arrives.*"

By that time wild undulations of the man's torso had ceased and he stood there, head cocked slightly to the side, staring at us. He was a mirror image of the girl, who also stared, unblinking.

"*Then, buddy, I think you better tell those two to cool their jets, because I don't think they're going to wait for Mace.*"

Canton swore under his breath because the two zombies were already lumbering toward us, moving as if their joints had been connected incorrectly. "*Shoot the knees!*" He sent.

I didn't have to be told twice. Both of our guns quietly spat bullets at the knees of the zombies. (Without a magician in the group, we had to settle for suppressors rather than temporary silence spells to dampen the barking of our weapons. It was like settling for grilled cheese when you were used to filet mignon.) Bone and flesh tore free from their bodies and they fell to the grass, their legs almost severed, held together only by strings of meat.

"Elbows and shoulders," snarled the Apache.

Not bothering to ask why, I drew my .45 ACP and fired. When that ran dry, I reloaded the Lahti and set back to work. Soon the zombies were reduced to wriggling trunks on the ground. *"We couldn't do this earlier?"* I managed to say subvocally. I wanted to barf right then and there, but with some difficulty kept my stomach contents in check.

"Okay, so I was wrong."

Three familiar shadows ghosted in from the surrounding trees. *"You couldn't wait?"*

Canton snorted. *"They started to come for us."*

"Damn, I hate cleaning up after zombies. So gross," Mouth groused.

Mace shook his head, eyes focused on the gagging, gurgling zombies trying to move shredded limbs to propel themselves to us. He held up a small cube the size of a thumb drive and pressed a button. Seemingly satisfied with whatever results the device revealed, he turned to us. *"No worries, people. No clean up. Thanks to magic we have something that just might save us a lot of elbow grease."*

Everyone except Mace and myself groaned. At my look he quirked his lips into something that almost resembled a smile. *"Sometimes Special Branch makes devices that do not quite work as intended. If I were you folks, I'd seriously consider moving farther back. Much farther. We had a test run in Texas and it worked fine, but you never know."* With that he reached into one of the many pockets on his belt (we all had them—called them Bat Belts) and drew out a silvery vial. *"This should be interesting."*

Canton grabbed my arm. *"White boy, when he says that, we better be far away."* The rest of us moved fifty feet back into the trees.

"Does anyone but Mace know what's going on?" Mouth sent. *"Sometimes those Special Branch guys can really fu—"*

"*Enough!*" Mace sounded like a chiding father. "*Wait for it. I will be right there.*"

Canton's teeth gleamed in the dim moonlight filtering through the trees. "*I love this stuff.*"

Less than ten seconds later an intense white light flashed from the direction of the clearing, a vivid bright backdrop to the stark blackness of the trees. Fortunately, the nightvision glasses were constructed to counteract the painful glare from sudden light. As suddenly as the flash appeared, it was gone, once again leaving us among the shadowy pillars of the trees.

"*Well, that was remarkable,*" Winch said dryly.

"*Come on back, team. You should see this.*"

We all exchanged looks of wonder and ambled back to the clearing. Mace stood at the edge of a circular patch of earth cut right through the grass. In nightvision, the earth looked dry and crumbly, as if it had been damaged. I knelt down to examine the circle of dirt. Some ten feet in diameter, the line of demarcation between dirt and grass was razor sharp and flawless. It was as if someone had used a giant cookie cutter to remove the section of sod. Gingerly, I trailed my gloved fingers through the soil. It was as crumbly as it looked, and curiously dry. Not too far away I noticed several small objects, so I snagged one and held it up for examination.

"*You ladies care to guess?*" asked Mace.

Winch stepped forward. "*A disintegration spell?*"

"*Almost.*"

"*What the hell do you mean by that?*"

"*Organic,*" I cut in. "*Whatever disintegrated the bodies only disintegrated organic material.*" I held up the object I had found—a zipper. "*Look to where the bodies are. Some plastic buttons, some wire—probably from a bra—and the soil is crumbly and dead with no roots running through it.*" We had used the same magic to dispose of the vampires we had killed in Texas, but I had been too freaked out at the time to really pay attention. That can happen when fanged folk are trying to rip your arms off.

"*Score one for Kal,*" Mace sent.

A quick flash from the corner of my glasses—a small something moving faster than the laws of physics should have allowed. My hand flew to the Lahti, but before I could complete the draw, the thing hit Mace at high speed. The big man grunted and was swept off his feet and hurled several feet away to land at the base of a tree.

Mace roared like wounded bull. He was flailing his arms at a small animal that was almost too quick to see. Repeatedly it lunged at his throat, only to be foiled by an armored arm, which the lightning-fast creature savaged with jaws almost as big as its body.

One claw, at the end of a twisty, double-jointed arm, swiped out and drew a line of blood down Mace's cheek to his jaw. The big man gritted his teeth and flailed his arm, flinging the creature fifteen feet into the clearing, where it landed gracefully and paused long enough for me to get a good look.

I wish it hadn't.

Skinny, barely five inches thick, the thing had six appendages—like an insect's, only scaled like a snake's—each ending in a four-toed claw with half-inch talons. The head was shaped like a shark's, bullet lean and pointed. Its huge slash of a mouth brimmed with oversized triangular teeth. It was black, even the eyes, the kind of light-absorbing darkness of matte-black paint that hides all manner of detail and sin. Before it could move, I had the Lahti in my hands and its bullets were quietly streaking toward the creature. To her credit, Winch matched me for draw and firing, her big HK Mark 23 .45 ACP bucking in her hands.

We missed, both of us. Moving as if time was its plaything, the creature twisted and juked out of the path of each bullet. More rounds were fired as Canton and Mouth joined in, filling the air with almost-silent death.

Five rounds fired out of the Lahti and I began to see how the creature moved. The sixth bullet failed as well. I watched the thing spin across the grass, a whirlwind of spiky limbs. I took a deep breath as the others poured on the lead, focusing on where the creature would most likely spin to avoid my teammates' fire. Dimly, I was aware of Winch changing clips while Canton drew another weapon, a 9mm. Off to the right and behind, Mace surged to his feet, big fist filled with his own 9mm.

The seventh round struck close to the monster's head, sending up a spray of grass and soil. *Almost*, I thought grimly. And then, as if God himself whispered in my ear, I knew where the creature would move next and I adjusted my aim, exhaling slowly.

I fired.

The round almost missed. The diminutive Supernatural seemed to sense the danger at the last moment and began to twist in a way no creature with bones could. Not fast enough. Its left rear leg separated in the middle in a shower of fragments and gore, the claw end falling to the grass.

I felt its scream like a screwdriver to the brain—sharp, brutal and paralyzing. All of us clapped hands over our ears in an effort to drown it out. From the bottom of the hill, houselights came on as people were roused from slumber by that chainsaw squeal.

Then the Supernatural leapt at me. All earthly creatures when they jump do so in a parabola, an arc describing the launching and landing point. Not that little wiggler. No, it leapt in a straight line, aiming unerringly for my throat at blurring speed.

Reflexively I brought my arms up and caught it in my armored hands, where it hung there, staring at me, disbelief in its beady, dead, black eyes.

Then it turned into the blender from hell. The damn thing seemed to move in every direction at once, its body becoming eerily plastic. Its shark mouth bit down on my wrist, serrated teeth blunted against the titanium greaves. While the teeth didn't penetrate, the strength of its jaws built up a terrible pressure against the bones of my wrist and I had to chew back a scream.

Even with its teeth in my wrist, it writhed and shook like a runaway rotary engine trying to tear my arms out of their sockets. I shook so bad that it began to really piss me off, and that must have activated the dreaded Stubborn Finn Gene. Snarling, I took a wide stance, bunched my shoulders and flexed my muscles. It wasn't my legendary rage, it was plain old human anger and I used my considerable strength to *squeeze*.

My arms were iron bars, my fingers steel and my body the rock that weathered the violent thrashings of the crazed Supernatural, which coughed and growled in pain. Harder and harder I squeezed, pressing my hands closer and closer together, ignoring the strangled howl that raked my ears. I grunted against the pain, concentrating all my will on my arms and hands to hold and crush the vile piece of filth contained in the cage of my fingers.

Blam!

Its head disappeared into a black mist that settled upon the grass, and it stopped its manic thrashing. Like candle wax, the body started to melt until the only thing I held was a foul black ooze that dripped from my fingers.

"Well, that's just gross," I heard myself say.

"You okay, white boy?"

Was I? All the relevant parts seemed to be working, although my wrist throbbed from where the little Supernatural chewed on it. "I'm okay, I think."

A hand the size of a country ham slapped me on the back hard enough to take the wind out of my sails. As I struggled for breath, Mace said, "Good job there, Kal." He turned to the others, face flinty with the force of his anger. "That magician is probably long gone, but let's perform a thorough search before we head out."

Mouth sauntered up and whispered in my ear. "High praise from the boss man. You did good, big boy." Her hand lingered on my arm, sending warmth rushing up to my shoulder.

Interesting. Was Mouth hitting on me? A part of me hoped so, but the iron part said it wouldn't be a good idea. Who knew how long any of us had on this job?

"Whoever this magician/rapist is, he has a metric crap-ton of power," Mace mused, taking a long swig from a glass of apple juice. "He was able to create a zombie out of his victim, not to mention summon a Type Two demon. I have no idea how he accomplished *that*."

Almost 11 p.m. and we were gathered in Comms, eating leftovers. BB's face stared impassively from the DisplayWall, eyes disturbingly bright behind his wire rims. Even though it was after two on the east coast, he still looked dapper and wide-awake, and for the umpteenth time I wondered why he didn't opt for Lasik.

Mace had briefed the director on the night's events. During the report he had remained stoic, only raising his eyebrows a fraction at the mention of the Type Two.

"He created a zombie and summoned a demon on the fly without the use of a magical battery or learning the proper spell Shapes," BB mused. "Raw power and a greater than normal facility for magic. We are either dealing with a genius or a savant." He removed his glasses and rubbed his eyes, fatigue marring his face.

"Do you think he's playing around?" I asked. "Testing what he can and can't do? I imagine the excitement he feels about his new abilities matches his urge for rape and murder."

"I should think so," BB said. "He will most likely continue to escalate his timeline so he can 'play' some more with his magical ability. Mace, do you have IDs on those two bodies?"

Mace pulled the little rectangle that looked like a thumb drive from his pocket and set it carefully on the table. A rectangle of light appeared beneath the small device. "Downloading images now, and checking against police files, although I doubt we'll get a hit on the girl. I suspect once a missing person report is filed we'll have an answer."

At that moment there came a ding and a window appeared on the DisplayWall. It was a picture of the young man who had been zombiefied right in front of us. It was obviously a mug shot.

"The male was one Parker Jenks, arrested twice for solicitation."

"What's a male prostitute doing in the park in the middle of the night?" I blurted.

A wall of eyes fixed on me in incredulous stares.

Oh.

My cheeks flamed and the ladies laughed at my discomfort.

"You are so innocent, white boy," Canton whispered. "You grow up in a nunnery or something?"

"Be that as it may," continued Mace, shaking his head in resignation. "We will have to wait on an ID for the girl."

"Well, Thomas," BB sighed. "I suggest you try extraordinary measures."

Mace's normally granite-like face creased in a frown. I half-expected to hear the grinding of tectonic plates. "Sir, he's been asleep for over twenty years. It will cause him great pain."

"Understood, Thomas, but we have to consider that a rogue magician not only created a zombie, but summoned a Type Two demon without killing himself or falling unconscious." His eyes became diamond hard. "I am afraid drastic action is required. Do what needs to be done, Thomas, as soon as possible." He severed the connection and the wall resumed its glossy gray color.

I cleared my throat. "Ever since Texas I've been studying the Greater and Lesser undead, as well as vampire lore, so I haven't gotten to demons. What is a Type Two?"

"Lesser demon," Winch replied, devouring a burger. "Non-sentient. More of the Pit's version of an attack dog than anything else."

"So I just tangled ass with a demonic Rottweiler? Is that what you're saying?"

"What you just tangled with, white boy," Canton drawled, "was a wood chipper with six legs. It may be one of the lesser demons, but I ain't *never* read of an agent actually grabbing a hold of one like you did. Not even in those old Templar records."

My brain spasmed for a moment. "The Templars?"

He nodded.

"The Knights Templar?"

Another nod.

"*The* Knights Templar?"

"Enough, you two," growled Mace. "I swear it's like having Abbott and Costello on my team."

Mouth's lips twitched. "But better looking."

Winch. "And not fat. Or skinny."

Mace closed his eyes and counted to ten with heroic patience while the rest of us shut up. I'd faced Mace in unarmed combat my very first day on the job (a test of sorts) and that was an experience I didn't want to repeat. Pushing him past his limits was a good way to get pummeled or fired.

Mouth stared at our team leader until he quit his counting. "What is the 'drastic action' BB was talking about?"

For the first time since we returned to the office, Canton's jovial attitude evaporated. "You can't seriously be considering this, boss?"

"Would someone care to clue us in?" Winch asked.

Mace paid her no heed. "Sorry, Canton," he said. "But the boss man is right; this sick twist is going to escalate his timeline. He can't control himself. We have to find this perp *now* before he kills another Straight and maybe does something worse with the body."

I raised an eyebrow. "Worse?"

Mace's face was grim. "Believe me, you don't want to know about worse."

"Would somebody please answer my [CENSORED] question?" Mouth cried.

A moment of silence that stretched. And stretched. Finally she blew an exasperated breath from between her lips. "Okay … sorry about that," she muttered.

When Mace was sure everyone was paying attention, he said, "We are going to wake the ghost of Joshua Norton."

All but Canton gave him blank looks, so he spent the next half hour telling us about Emperor Norton and his eternal mission to safeguard San Francisco from Supernatural threats.

"So you see, waking him up would cause him severe emotional distress, but if anyone or anything could give us the information we need to catch this magician, it would be Joshua Norton."

Canton sighed. "Boss, is there any real chance old Joshua can help us, or are we barkin' up the wrong tree?"

Mace rose to his full height, towering over the four of us. "The thing you have to ask yourself, people, is can we afford *not* to take the chance?"

None of us spoke.

My voice wound down as I stared at my empty beverage container. Wilkes still lay there being dead and extremely quiet about it.

I had a plan, but I also had a ton of doubts. A little bird told me this wouldn't be the usual life-and-death mission that Bureau agents faced in the field.

It would be much worse.

Chapter Fourteen

Which Witch Where?

In the largest office space in the small house in the middle of the city, I finished outlining my plan to the others.

They were not enthused.

"What's the probability of survival, boss?" Winch's voice was all sandpaper and oil, a mixture she achieved when scared out of her wits. She gripped Canton's hand tightly.

I took a deep breath and scrutinized the two of them. Canton was his usual stoic self, calm on the outside, but I knew that inside his emotions were roiling and boiling. Surprisingly, Ilena looked nonchalant, almost bored. "I'd say about twenty percent," I murmured.

"Twenty percent!" she whispered.

"If we're lucky."

Winch closed her eyes.

I leaned forward, resting my elbows on the six-foot oak table that separated us. Behind me, the DisplayWall flickered and another satellite photo appeared. "Something bad is coming and the Bureau can't help, Joshua told us that. This plan is the best shot we have at stopping the Faë." Deep breath and a slow five count pause. "But I know it's a near suicide mission, so I won't force anyone to play. It's a decision you each have to make. I will respect your judgment."

There. A way out if they wanted it.

"What about you, white boy?" Canton asked quietly.

"I'm going for it no matter what." My voice was calm, even.

He took a deep breath and shook his head slightly. "I done fought Nazis with you, vampires, demons, magicians and even a Class Five Supernatural and I ain't gonna stop now. I'm there." As the words tumbled from his mouth, Winch nodded, her eyes glued to the Apache's face. She knew the mission might be the last thing they ever did together.

Ilena piped up from the depths of her comfy chair, seemingly boneless and totally relaxed, "Hell, boss, I don't have anything better to do. Besides, if we don't do this, there's a one-hundred-percent chance of tons of Straights dying. Plus the Bureau will step in with both feet and get its ass kicked again. Can't have that."

No we couldn't. I stared at my team and felt a swell of both sadness and pride. Once more into the breach and all that and they were willing to follow me in the entire way.

Before I could say anything else, Ilena continued. "How are we going to recruit this 'help' that you've mentioned, boss? I think she's not going to be cooperative."

Canton grinned. "I think the white boy already figured out a way." *Yeah.*

About ten times a year a magician trips a sensor somewhere in the United States (yes the gene for magic is *that* rare) and agents come a-running. Not to kill, but to assess. The Bureau is not out to eradicate all things magical, but to use them. That includes magicians. Surprisingly enough, many of them turn down the ridiculous salary the Bureau offers, opting to live quiet lives and raise families. That's all well and good, but we do inform them that they will not be allowed to cast any spells that even approach 100 megamerlins (enough power to kill). We also inform them that they *will* be watched and if the Bureau learns of any magical abuse, they *will* suffer the full wrath of the federal government. That's not an idle threat. There needs to be a balance to everything, and we are on the other side of the scale from those magicians who could pose a serious threat to the Straights.

Most of the magicians stay on the straight and narrow, but every now and then one steps over the line. Usually said line is only stepped over once before the Bureau jumps all over the situation like a crazed jackrabbit.

Thanks to my link to the Bureau database via RediPad, I knew of someone nearby who could possibly help us. In Balboa Terrace, the Twin Peaks West District, near Commodore Sloat Elementary School, was a smallish ranch-style house that contained a semi-lucrative business: Madame Trisol's All Natural Tinctures and Potions.

Cute.

It was midday, foggy and damp as heck when I pulled up in front of the yellow house with the well-kempt lawn, white picket fence and red door. It looked perfect, a quaint little place where you'd expect to find a little old lady who served tea and sewed quilts. There was even a garden gnome near the front steps, its ceramic face a picture of elfin jocularity.

It was way too perfect.

My knuckles drummed a tattoo on the red door, the paint slick and shiny against my skin. No one answered. I knocked again and still nothing. Maybe Madame Trisol wasn't home. Clacking and rattling from within put the lie to that assumption.

The door opened a crack and a dark brown eye, highlighted by aqua eye shadow and thick liner, came into view. The eye also had longer-than-normal lashes, at least an inch-and-a-half long, and it occurred to me that they were fake.

"What do you wan' from Madame Trisol?" asked a somewhat melodic female voice with a slightly raspy undertone. "You ain' got no appointment."

I tried out a thousand-watt smile. The lady behind the eye didn't open the door. Must've been losing my touch. "Ma'am, I just need a moment of your time."

"You don' have no appointment an' you dress funny. I don' wan' anything to do with you." The red door closed.

"I can pay!" I hollered. "A thousand bucks."

Like a magic spell, the mention of money opened the door a crack. "Let's see your money," demanded the eye in disbelief.

I cast a greed spell, pulling out a fat roll of twenties from my inside coat pocket and holding it up so the eye could get a good look. The spell worked because the portal to the house opened all the way and I took a tentative step inside.

My eyes didn't have to adjust; it wasn't dark inside the house. Plenty of open windows to let in the gloom of the typical San Francisco day. The living room might have graced the cover of *Better Homes and Gardens*, with crisp white walls and cream-colored carpeting. A dainty white settee occupied the long end, and a mahogany coffee table in front was strewn with magazines. The room screamed "quaint" in such loud and strident tones that it actually wasn't. However, it was the woman who dominated the room.

Hands on her hips and treating me to a world-class scowl, she was almost as wide as she was tall. To call her shapely would be generous, because the only shape she conformed to was round. A heavy bosom was barely contained in a low-cut white bodice set over a multicolored pleated skirt that dropped to her ankles. Gold hoops jangled on said ankles and clashed with a pair of no-nonsense flats that strained to contain her bulk. Gluttony wasn't her only sin; the sharp, funky smell of cigarettes assaulted my nose. Menthols, if I wasn't mistaken.

If Madame Trisol had hair, I didn't see any evidence of it because of a voluminous brown rhinestone studded scarf. It was wrapped tightly around her noggin so that not a follicle was visible. Under that glittering mass of fabric was an apple-cheeked and almost perfectly round face with olive skin, pug nose, and a generous mouth. Big hoop earrings tortured her lobes and jangled every time she moved her head. At an outside guess, I would've placed her age at early thirties, but the Bureau said she was forty-three.

"Okay, Mr. Man, wha' you wan' me to do for a thousand dollars?"

she asked, eyes glued to the roll of twenties. "You better not be expectin' any sex stuff."

I looked at her circumference and realized that, had I wanted any "sex stuff," I wouldn't know how to go about it. "No, Ma'am, but please, drop the bad Mexican accent. You're a Sicilian girl from Long Island."

Her heavily made-up eyes narrowed dangerously.

"And don't try a spell," I growled, all trace of good humor gone. "It won't work on me."

Her olive skin became ashen. "Oh no! You're one of them."

I nodded.

Trisol (who, according to the database was born Nina Scarpelli) held up her hand and *tears* sprang from her eyes. "Oh please don't kill me, Mister!" she wailed in a voice that sounded like a nail file in a blender. I guessed that years of smoking had calcified her vocal chords.

"Oh, shush!" I snapped. "No one is getting killed here. Simmer down, now."

"Really?" A faint spark of hope.

"Really, Miss Scarpelli, I just came here to offer a business proposition."

The panic disappeared in an instant. "What are you doin' then?" she blasted at the top of her lungs. Someone must have pushed the volume to eleven. "Tryin' ta give me a freaking heart attack?" Fat, ring-laden fingers pressed themselves to her heaving bosom. Gone was the phony accent, replaced by the pure rounded vowels that screamed Long Island.

Once again I held up the bundle of twenties and her mouth shut with a snap. I moved the wad back and forth, her eyes tracking its every motion. "Now, do I have your attention?"

She nodded and thankfully kept her mouth shut.

"Good. I wish to conduct some business." I pointed to the dainty white settee that in no way could have sustained her weight, then to the white corduroy recliner. "Perhaps here?"

Nina shook her head. "No, this is the waiting room. You come with me. We'll go into the back where I have my shop."

Shop? Oh well.

Without ceremony, the roly-poly magician led me down the only hallway to a plain white door. I stepped into someplace ... very strange.

Now, I've seen some weird stuff in my time, but that "shop" really took the taco. The large space must have once been several rooms, but the walls had been removed, creating one chamber where Madam Trisol conducted her business. Bookshelves lined the walls and stood in rows in the middle of the room. Every available shelf, every space, was stacked with strange odds and ends. Jars of amber liquid where things better left unsaid floated. Coke bottles filled with strange fluid and test tubes in racks, all with a different colored powder. There were stuffed animals, parts of animals, and parts of parts of animals on display. Mason jars of herbs, small wooden boxes that contained God only knows, and even Tupperware containers lined the shelves. Everything was meticulously labeled, but I didn't bother to look, unsure that I really wanted to know what lay within the various containers.

On the ceiling were hundreds of bundles of plants hung out to dry, like leafy stalactites reaching toward the floor. There were so many bundles that the ceiling was totally obscured, lowering the height of the room by nearly two feet. I was reminded of *Where the Wild Things Are*, where Max's room becomes a forest for the world all around. I half expected to see an ocean tumble by with a boat just for me.

Along the far wall was a counter that ran the entire length. Smack in the center was an old-fashioned cash register that looked like it was made of brass, gleaming in the pale green light filtered through all the plants.

And the smell ...

Imagine lush, tropical forests, wet earth and an herb garden, rich and verdant. Then mix it with the best restaurant smell you ever laid nose on and that might come close to the succulent odor issuing from that room. It caused the small hairs on the back of my neck to stand on end.

"My next appointment will be here in ten minutes," the big woman said matter-of-factly. "Will this take long?" She ended the last word with a hard "g." *Lawng.*

I stood among the bookshelves and moved in a languid circle, taking it all in, drinking in the smell. "No, but will we be interrupted?"

"No, Mister. My customers know to come on in and wait. That's how come I knew you weren't no customer of mine. You knocked."

Made sense. My eye was caught by one of the creatures mounted on the wall. "Really? A stuffed alligator?"

She shrugged. "My customers expect it."

I shook my head in wonder. "So why try to sound like a Mexican *bruja*? You, a nice Italian girl."

"Most of my customers think that only the 'ethnic' types have magic," she snorted, removing the mass of cloth that surrounded her head. It came off in one piece, revealing night-black hair cut close to the scalp. "My next appointment is Mrs. Alba, and she wouldn't come here if I wasn't a *bruja*. For others, I play a good gypsy woman." She spoke the last in a thick Eastern European accent while scratching her itchy scalp with both hands.

Things went clickety clackety in my head. "You're an alchemist, aren't you?"

"Gee, what gave it away, Mister? The potions? The herbs or any of the other zillion bits of arcane crap I have hanging around here?"

Okay, not my best moment, I admit. Face flaming, I ran my fingertips along the hanging vegetation. It felt strange, like fall leaves and parchment paper. Herb dust floated down and tickled my nose, bringing on a thick, musty scent. "Why potions?" I asked.

"People want to see something concrete, Mister," Nina said, reaching into one of the shelves and pulling down a thick vial. A silvery powder coated the inside of the glass. "Something they can hold in their hands. If I just cast a small spell, they usually don't feel it. But if I cast a spell that removes the pain of arthritis for a few days and give them a potion to mix with tea that has the same effect as aspirin, then they think *that's* the real magic."

Made sense. "So you cast a light healing—"

"Because it's the only kind I can cast," she interrupted with a snarl. "Anything stronger and your kind will be after me like *that*." She snapped her fingers for emphasis.

The Interdiction she wore like an invisible cloak kept her from elaborating, but we both knew what she meant by *your kind*. I didn't feel sorry for her at all. My face must have told her the same thing because she seemed to collapse in on herself slightly, biting her lower lip.

"Listen, I have a job for you, one that will let you use all the magic you are capable of without getting you into trouble. Plus, you'll make some good scratch. Interested?"

The fire in her eyes answered my question and I had to hold the wad of bills away from her greedy, chubby hands.

"Okay, Nina. Looks like you're in," I drawled, reaching into the back pocket of my jeans and pulling forth a crumpled envelope. "Read this and tell me if it's impossible. You get a hundred bucks just for looking." I placed the envelope in her hands.

Self-preservation warred with greed and greed won, hands down. Bits of paper went flying and in a moment she was scanning the envelope's contents. As she read, her face went from olive to dishwater gray and her eyes grew wide.

"Are you *crazy*? I don't know no spell Shapes for what you want done!" Her face was full of anguish; the thought of a thousand dollars flying away must have stung.

I produced another envelope and handed it over. "In here you will find the Shape needed."

If the thought of a thousand bucks pushed her greed button, the mere mention of a new spell Shape pushed all her other buttons, plus a few she didn't know she had. A hail of confetti landed on the floor as she tore the envelope to bits, revealing a simple piece of lined notebook paper.

To me, a spell Shape looks like an eye-watering assortment of squiggly lines, loops and whorls, a pattern I could never hope to draw once my eye left the page. However, to a magician it is more than a mere conglomeration of random marks on paper, it is *power*.

For reasons unknown to me, magicians can look at that Shape and divine a purpose, a meaning; to them the Shape is a blueprint to a spell, magical DNA. That doesn't mean they can hold the Shape in their minds and cast the spell immediately upon looking at it. Some Shapes are so complex that casting those spells would be like reciting *Romeo and Juliet* in its entirety while juggling chainsaws.

Those complex Shapes require study. The more complex the Shape, the more it has to be studied to master the spell. For example, if magicians wish to cast spells with more than one effect (such as silence and flash suppression), they need extremely complex Shapes; whereas single spell effects *usually* have simple Shapes (depending on the effect desired).

What I gave Madam Trisol was a simple spell Shape for a simple spell, one that used less than the 100 megamerlins it took to trip the magic sensors. It was simple enough that just about any magician could master it.

"Oh, yes," the round woman moaned. "Oh yes, ohyesohyesohyes!"

"I take it you are satisfied with the Shape?" I asked. The woman was practically drooling.

Her beady brown eyes, almost lost in folds of fat, found mine. "I get this Shape, Mister… Mister…"

"Pike. Christopher Pike."

"Mr. Pike." She ran a hand through her centimeter-long ruffle of black hair. "I can cast this spell, I can *feel* it. The Shape is not hard to imagine, but you want so many castings in so many different locations…" Nina's voice trailed off.

I crossed my arms. "What?"

"Mr. Pike, it's too many spells. I don't think I can cast them all," she said, sounding as if her soul was ripping in two. "It will take more power than I've got."

My heart sank.

"But," she purred, eyes glistening with greed. "I have a solution. If you're willing to pay."

"What do you mean?"

"All you need is a little help from some witches."

Witches?

Wonderful.

Oh yeah. When Nina pitched her proposal, I felt equal parts elation and dread. The elation part came from the fact that the team *might* have some serious magical backup. The dread part came from the source of the backup. Witches.

I'm not talking pointy hats, brooms and cauldrons at midnight. No cat familiars or long noses with warts at the end. When Nina said "witches" I knew immediately what she meant.

Wiccans.

Okay, *Reader's Digest* version: Wicca, or Pagan Witchcraft, or Crafters or whatever moniker you want to paste on it, is a Pagan religion first practiced in England in the early 20th century. A dude name Gerald Gardner gave the movement a boost in the 1950s and '60s, claiming it was the surviving remnant of a pre-Christian religion.

Gardner went on to create his own version of Wicca, a mixture of traditional Wiccan beliefs, ceremonial magic, grimoires, Freemasonry and some of the writings of the occultist Aleister Crowley, like he took all the really nifty ideas, put them in a blender and hit *frappe*. It should come as no surprise that both Gardner and Crowley were former members of His Majesty's Supernatural Services, or MI-7.

Whether a Wiccan follows the Gardnerian Wicca, or the more traditional Crafts, most worship a pair of deities, generally referred to as the Goddess and the Horned God. They're believed to be balancing forces in the universe, like yin and yang, Democrats and Republicans, forces that work in harmony and complement each other. Most Wiccans believe in magic, whether it be a law of nature provided by the god or goddess, or change produced by willpower and ceremony.

These were the people she suggested I call upon for help. People with magical talent who had yet to be discovered by the Bureau. It seemed like a long shot, but what choice did I have?

Witches it was.

Chapter Fifteen

Dead of Night Drop

Looking down, I prayed for warmth, but I knew it would be a while yet before my flesh felt heat because when you're at fifteen thousand feet above sea level it is cold, cold, cold. In the middle of a mild San Francisco winter it's freeze-your-ass-off time.

The DeHavilland DHC-6 Super Twin Otter held the whole team, plus the mid-size duffels we sported, and still had room to spare. Light and fast, it was the best plane for drop we could get on such short notice and proof of the uniquely American concept of "throw enough money at it and it will get done." The owner of the San Francisco Skydiving Club had named a price for the use of his plane and pilot and nearly had a heart attack when I put the check in his hand.

Money may be the root of all evil, but it is a good root to have when you fight Supernaturals.

Every member of the team had jumped out of a perfectly good aircraft at one point or another during training. Some, like Winch, did it for fun, which only proved the theory that she had a death wish. I got enough adrenaline just being on a mission without acting like a damn fool who sought danger for the fun of it all in my off hours—which, come to think of it, were nonexistent. Of course, doing what I do for a living would give most adrenaline junkies the screaming fits. Forever.

Two minutes to the Farallons and we silently readied our parachute-like packs, checking the distribution of weight along our bodies. The big difference from a normal looking parachute was the two-foot-long, cloth-covered cylinder running lengthwise down the middle. Six inches wide, the cylinder gave the pack a humped, deformed look. Rolling my shoulders to check the weight, I gave the team a thumbs-up and received four in return. Good to go.

"You think these things are gonna work, white boy?" Canton screamed over the roar of the wind and the prop. One hand thumped the pack on my back.

"They have a great track record!" I hollered back. "Tested and retested, just never been used on a mission until now."

Winch and Ilena smiled, while Canton still looked slightly dubious. The pale overhead light of the cabin gave his ruddy face beneath the helmet and goggles a demonic cast.

"Besides, it's not the packs that worry me!" I shouted, kneeling at the opening in the side of the plane. Darkness greeted my eyes. Grinning, I patted the cylinder running down the length of Canton's pack. "It's these things. I just hope they don't explode!" That said, I left the agog Apache and team behind, jumping out into the night.

The cold air bit my cheeks, lips and chin with teeth of ice and I was glad for the thick plastic goggles protecting my eyes. Somewhere down below, unseen and relentless, was the Pacific, rushing toward me at 120 miles-per-hour. I checked my glow-in-the-dark wrist altimeter. Ten thousand feet.

I knew that Canton and the rest were behind and above, freefalling through freezing air. Before another thousand feet passed by, I touched the side of my goggles and the world resolved itself below me into shades of green. Nightvision, the best tech could create. No magic allowed.

Seven thousand feet and my skin felt flayed. It was almost time. The first real thread of fear tugged at me.

Five thousand ... reaching the failure point if the rig didn't work. I reached up and tugged at a small plastic ring on my harness.

The pack exploded, ripping itself apart at the seams. A slim NewTanium bar unfolded and appeared in front of my chest and I grabbed hold. The wind in my ears prevented me from hearing the snapping of fabric, the twanging of cables or the rip of velcro. Behind and around me, NewTanium rods telescoped out, dragging lightweight carbon fiber cloth to catch the wind. There was a surge as my descent slowed and my harness grabbed at my belly and shoulders. Then came a sudden jerk at my midsection, and I was flying, the wind no longer deafening me. I wanted to shout my exultation as an ocean of air buoyed me up.

Billowing out behind and around, black as a raven's wings, was the delta shape of a glider that had unfolded from the parachute-like pack on my back. Developed in Special Branch over a year ago, the device had never actually been used on a mission. No opportunities.

Until now.

Lightweight NewTanium rods provided the frame while the tightly woven carbon cloth caught the air. The rig—incredibly durable, designed to unfold in an instant—included the L-shaped steering bar. It was a wonder of Bureau technology and engineering and probably would have earned a gajillion dollars in the private sector. All very impressive, but as I hung in the air, gliding toward Southeast Farallon Island, I was just happy the damn thing worked.

From above I heard a war-whoop, a triumphant cry. I guessed that Canton's glider was working, too, and the fact that no bodies were falling past me seemed to indicate we were all in the clear.

"Damn, Kal," Winch subvocaled. *"Wasn't sure these things would work! I'm sure glad they did."*

Me, too. Alex had assured me the gliders had been tested thoroughly, but no one wants to be a guinea pig for first mission-use items. You were never sure if they would perform as planned or blow up. Literally.

With a few nudges of the steering bar, I made my way toward Southeast Farallon Island, a humpy dark mass perched atop the void of the Pacific. A shining spear of illumination came from the Farallon

Island Light, a small lighthouse on the hill above Marine Terrace, the home of the researchers.

One thousand feet and softly descending, I began to circle the island right below. Thanks to the lighthouse, we had a spot to aim for. Our only spot actually; the houses on the terrace were all dark, and even though there were no trees to crash into, the island itself was stony and ragged enough to cause serious damage.

"Avoid being hit by the light, team," I sent. *"I don't know if there is anyone in there, but let's not take the risk of being seen."*

All three responded with, *"Check."*

Five hundred feet and my nightvision started to fill in the details, transforming Lighthouse Hill and the surrounding craggy terrain into a hellish green nightmare landscape. At three hundred feet, I began to time the circling of the light.

Two hundred feet and my heart was firmly cemented in my throat. The rotating light looked like an accusation waiting to find a miscreant, and despite the cold, a thin film of sweat formed in my armpits and around my goggles.

I made it past the top, missing the light by a few feet as I spiraled around the lighthouse, moving far too quickly for my own good. On the last turn I pushed the bar forward in an effort to stall, but not soon enough. My booted feet hit the ground and I tumbled head over heels, coming to a halt upside down on top of the glider. The various hinges and connections of the NewTanium frame dug into my back, even through my armor and Faraday coat. For a brief moment my lungs refused to function. When they came back on line, I felt a dull, hot throb pulsing in my left ankle and I knew I'd sprained it. *Damn.* No magical healing until the mission objective had been met.

I stood, favoring my left leg, and lifted the lightweight glider over my head, giving the plastic ring on the harness shoulder strap a sharp tug. The contraption gave a soft *whirr,* and the glider folded in on itself. Seconds later, it was again a normal-looking pack with a two foot cylinder running down the middle.

Standing, rubbing sore muscles through my armor, I reckoned my landing was a serious fail in the stealth department. I prayed that no one was awake to hear the fiasco. From a pocket, I pulled out a small vial of painkillers. Not quite Percocet, but strong enough to take the edge off the pain in my leg.

Thump. Thud. Thud.

Like a flock of ravens, the rest of the team landed almost in unison, embarrassing me with their skill and grace. Bastards.

"Kal, that was the funniest thing I ever saw," Winch sent with a wide grin on her pale face.

Ilena piped in, *"Yeah, do it again, boss!"*

Canton didn't say anything, but his crap-eating smile spoke volumes.

"Yeah, yeah, yuck it up." I managed to put a wry tone in my subvocals. *"Ilena, check the door. Make sure no one is inside. Canton, take care of the gliders."*

A trio of *whirrs* later and Canton took all four packs into the darkness while the rest of us ghosted to the front door, a heavy-looking affair constructed of thick planks. It looked like it had been taken from the set of a Robin Hood movie—solid planks of oak banded with iron. Ilena stood before the door and tapped a button on her goggles, switching them from nightvision to thermal, scanning the room behind the door for body heat. After a few seconds, she gave me the "all clear" signal.

The doorknob didn't budge. Winch's turn. Smiling, she took a set of picks from her Bat Belt and began to work on the lock, which surrendered after a few seconds. The door swung inward.

Canton joined us as we drew our Pazers and entered quickly. While suppressed pistols might be more expedient, we had no desire to kill unfortunate Straights who happened to be mind-controlled by the Faë. There was no such thing as "acceptable collateral damage" in my book.

The first floor of the lighthouse was one big room with rough wooden floors and metal stairs running up along the inside wall. The whole place had an air of desolation, as if even the memory of humanity had long been scrubbed away, leaving a slightly dusty, yet antiseptic, interior.

"Don't think anyone is here, white boy," Canton said, looking up the stairs. *"What makes you think they are?"*

"I think they are somewhere below us, in the rock. The Sidhe were the people of the mounds, the Dwellers Below. This is where I would put an access point—on the biggest island with the best view all around. But let's not take any chances."

Winch scanned the walls. *"Why would they even turn on the light?"*

"Ships that go aground tend to bring unwanted publicity," I replied. *"Canton, check upstairs."*

He nodded and got gone, slipping up the metal steps without so much as a telltale creak. We waited, Pazers at the ready until Canton came back down, shaking his head. *"No one, boss. There are stairs going up in to where the lamp is located, but everything looks deserted."*

Okay, that wasn't creepy, much.

"Kal," Ilena sent. *"Look at this."*

I stepped over to where the slim magician knelt, running a gauntleted hand over the floorboards in front of her. *"What is it?"*

"Look at floor right here. Wood looks new."

I squinted hard at where she was pointing. The floor was constructed of what looked to be six-by-twos, sturdy and strong; however, a large section—perhaps ten feet by ten feet—seemed less ... worn, and was pale. *"Strange,"* I commented. *"New wood on an old floor, but the boards all around look fine."*

"Wet rot?" Canton asked.

"Then why only this section of floor? No, something doesn't feel right." I stood. *"Everyone ... check the floor, new wood only."*

I stood by, keeping watch while the others spread out along the edges of the fresher planks, gently running their gauntleted hands over sanded wood. A few minutes later Winch stopped suddenly in the middle of the fresh patch.

"Boss, you gotta look at this." Winch hopped to her feet and took a step back. I stepped forward, concerned she'd hurt herself, but Canton beat me to the punch. Winch grabbed his free hand in hers and pointed with the other. *"Right there. There's something strange."*

Nodding, I bent, ignoring the creak from my aging knees, and ran my hands over the spot. At first nothing—just smooth wood under my thin gauntlets—but after a second I thought I felt something, a slight irregularity, a brief resistance.

What the hell?

I felt an imperfection where none was visible, at least not in the green light of nightvision. I ran the fingertips of my gauntlet over the supposed imperfection again.

And there it was. Even through the tough polymer of the form-fitting gauntlet I could feel a smooth sort of irregularity. I traced it with a fingertip. A circle. A hard circle the size of a silver dollar. A ring.

Poking around, I sensed movement, as if part of the ring somehow *gave* and my finger pushed into the floor a quarter inch or so.

"Invisible," I sent, incredulous. *"There is an invisible ring here. A pull ring for a trap door. An invisible trap door."*

"That's not possible!" Ilena said, crab-walking to where my fingers caressed the unseen ring. *"Magicians have been trying to create an invisibility spell for centuries."*

I grabbed her hand and guided it to the ring, where her fingers grasped the metal circle. "Damn," she whispered, forgetting to keep the conversation subvocal.

From behind, Canton whispered a thick curse and crept past us, dropping to all fours where the old wood joined the new directly opposite to the ring. Hands brushing the floor, he grinned.

"They are so sly," he sent, barely audible through the bone induction pads, *"but so am I."* A few moments later his face lit up. *"Bingo, white boy."* Each hand rested on unseen somethings, placed about two feet apart. *"I've got hinges here. Am I good or what?"*

"I'll reserve judgment for now," I countered. Shedding both my gauntlets, I reached into my Bat Belt and extracted what looked like a small roll of thin wire.

"Somebody find the edges. There has got to be a gap somewhere," I said. *"Ilena, keep watch."*

We found the edges quickly, a gap of perhaps an eighth of an inch. I clipped one end of the wire into my smart phone's USB port and fed the other into the gap. Slowly, carefully, I fed the wire into the opening, inch by inch, while keeping an eye on the cell's display, which gave me a good view of the other side of the trap door.

"*There's weak illumination,*" I observed, the thin boroscope drinking up the ambient light. "*Ladder going down, looks like wood.*" Re-angling the 'scope, I caught sight of my quarry. "*Found a bolt and the damn thing looks to be about two inches thick. Bronze or brass, I can't tell.*"

One eye on the bolt, I removed a three-inch cylinder from my belt and gently set the cell on the floor. "*Canton, good buddy, I need your can, too.*"

"*What is that?*" Winch asked as the Apache knelt next to me, an almost identical cylinder in his hand—except that his was red where mine was blue.

"*Something ... wonderful. If it works,*" I answered with a smile. "*Brand new from the technogeeknerds. It's a binary acid, two liquids that are inert when separate but when combined form a powerful corrosive. Been wanting to test this one for a while.*"

"*Yeah, but be careful, boss,*" Ilena said wryly. "*With our luck that stuff will cause a thermonuclear detonation or something.*"

"*Well, at least it will be quick.*" I popped the endcap off the cylinder, revealing a pointed plastic applicator. Using the 'scope as a guide, I gently squirted some of the colorless liquid into the invisible gap between the trap door and floor then placed the cylinder back in the Bat Belt.

"*Let me do this, white boy,*" Canton sent, a thread of excitement in his voice. "*I never get to test these things.*"

"*Really? You see a new toy and you get all excited?*" Winch sounded more than a little exasperated.

I disengaged the cell and 'scope, pulling it free from the unseen gap, and stepped away from the two. I gestured for the Apache to proceed. It took only a few seconds for him to apply the liquid from the red cylinder. Almost immediately there came a loud *hiss-pop* as the liquids mixed. We all beat feet outside to wait.

"*How bad could it be?*" Ilena asked as we knelt against the wall on either side of the door. Winch punched Canton in the arm, but he looked far from apologetic.

"*Remind me to tell you about Alex's bulletproof shirt.*"

At that moment a foul and acrid odor wafted out the door, a miasma that cut right into the nasal membranes like a burning knife. The four of us stumbled away, wheezing and gasping.

"*How much of that crap did you use?*" I sent, trying not to gag.

"*The same amount as you, a few drops!*" the Apache said, rubbing his nose. "*Man, that stuff smells like sh—*"

I didn't bother to listen to his griping. If Canton wasn't belly-aching, he was in real trouble. It took a few minutes for the bitter vapors to clear, and what we found on the inside was a bit anticlimactic.

"*I expected something … grand.*" Ilena sounded a touch let down.

We stared at a softball-sized hole on one end of the trap door, which exposed the dimly lit shaft below. "*I dunno, the damn thing looks pretty big for the small amount of acid we used,*" Canton said. "*At least the invisibility spell wore off when we made that hole.*"

I grabbed what was left of the ring, a brass semicircle with a tongue that swiveled in a frame inset into a plank, and heaved. The trap door opened easily, exposing the melted stub of the thick brass bolt. "*I think the hole is unusually large because the acid was so reactive, boiling the brass and wood with enough speed that the vapors spit acid everywhere. Gotta give it to the boys in Special Branch: when they do it right, they really do it right.*"

Winch grabbed my arm. "*Hey boss, I've been wanting to ask you something.*"

"*What?*"

"*I have tickets to* Les Miserables *at the National Theater in D.C. How about you and Jeanie join Canton and me?*"

"*Really, babe? Now?*" Canton said incredulously.

"*I gave you plenty of time to ask, you dork, and you didn't. Now it's my turn.*"

Les Miserables. Swell. Just what I wanted, musical theater. I was about to give her a firm, but polite, "no" when I caught sight of Canton's face. He tossed me a look of such desperation that I knew he wanted to go as much as he wanted a nitroglycerine enema and he needed a friend to share les misery.

I had no doubt that Jeanie would love the show, she was a big fan of *Grease*, but for me it would be a night of slow torture. As I gazed at Canton's unhappy mug, I realized that sometimes you have to do for friends. *"Okay, that will be cool,"* I lied.

Winch was more than a little pleased. *"Thanks, boss!"*

Behind her back I mouthed the words, *You owe me* to the relieved Apache. He nodded gratefully and we got back to business.

Beneath my feet was the wooden ladder, descending into the twilight world below. I wasn't a hundred percent sure of what we would find, but I had a good idea.

By the pricking of my thumbs ...

Girding my loins, I started my descent, my .45 ACP tucked underneath my Faraday coat. It was all I could do not to draw the damn thing. My palm itched for the familiar weight of the weapon. I'd left the Lahti back at the office, not really believing that I'd get out of this mission alive and that the pistol—the same one used by my grandfather in the Continuation War against the Soviet Union—was too valuable a piece of history to risk on such an adventure.

Fifty feet down and the shaft still plunged into semi-darkness, lit only by what looked like some sort of phosphorescent fungi or lichen. My knowledge of botany didn't extend much beyond the difference between Romaine and Iceberg lettuce.

After another hundred feet or so, I passed a barrier, unseen, but felt. It was a portal from cold and wet to warm and humid. I stopped for a moment and pulled off a gauntlet, raising and lowering my hand to feel the difference, to determine if the transition had been abrupt or gradual. A couple feet over my head ... cold. Chest level ... warm, sultry. The line of demarcation appeared to be six inches from the top of my head. I glanced around through the nightvision goggles, but saw nothing. I powered them down, but the dim light of the shaft offered no clues to my too-human eyes.

The ladder continued, held fast to the wall by bronze or brass clamps pounded deep into granite. Two hundred feet and I was sweating freely, listening to the subvocal bitching coming from the other three as they slowly poached in their armor. We had to be below the level of the researchers' terrace, but still there was no end in sight and the shaft was as quiet as the space between the stars, the quiet disturbed only by the scuffling of our descent. Not even noise from the Pacific penetrated the millions of tons of rock around and above us. I wasn't a claustrophobe, but an awful itch began at the back of my neck and ran down between my shoulder blades. It was a pregnant, oppressive sensation that raised the short hairs on my arms and crawled across my skin like the memory of maggots.

The floor appeared almost out of nowhere. One second I was descending, arms burning with the strain and legs beginning to quiver, then my foot *thunked* down upon hard-packed dirt.

Dirt? In the heart of a granite island?

Oh, crap.

Chapter Sixteen

Faë Day

"Uh, guys, we ain't in Kansas anymore."

"Whatcha mean, white boy?"

I looked around carefully and ran my hands along the walls. It felt like hard-packed earth or clay. Strange. The ladder led to a hallway, perfectly level as far as I could see. About six-feet wide and nine tall, it arched over our heads in flawless symmetry, as if it had been machined.

My three other teammates arrived a few seconds later and, judging from their gasps, caught on to the difference right away. Winch's jaw was set and Ilena was biting her lower lip. Canton remained inscrutable as ever, but I knew my friend's tells, and the way he gripped his weapon so tight that his knuckles bled white broadcasted his apprehension better than a shout.

"No firing unless necessary and for Pete's sake, let's stay silent from now on." I knew they could hear the anxiety in my voice, but no matter how hard I tried, nonchalant wouldn't come.

Sighing, I took point and headed down the hall. Our rubber-soled boots barely scuffed against the packed earth, and from behind I heard the telltale whisper of both women readying their Mac-10As—the latest generation of highly compact machine pistols with a 50-round clip of .45 ACP ammo and a suppressor half the length of their more commonly known cousin. While Canton and I each had handguns and some other goodies, I had wanted a greater rate of fire to back us up. Winch and Ilena didn't seem to mind; they handled the weapons with the fervor of desperate lovers.

I just hoped they wouldn't shoot me in the ass.

Sixty steps later, the hall turned to the right, revealing an archway a few yards away that led into what looked like a large room or cavern. Bright red light shone through the archway, the red of rose petals. It was oddly warm and welcoming.

"*Winch,*" I sent.

"On it, boss."

One tap of an icon on my cell and the screen resolved into a bug's-eye view of Winch's face. She held in her hand another cool toy I'd requisitioned from Special Branch. Those crazy, wonderful technogeeknerds had cobbled together the ultimate in spy devices: the spiderbot.

With a body the size of a dime and eight long legs, it looked like a common wolf spider, all the way down to the black, spiky hair on its little metallic body. Its eight tiny eyes were mini-cams with an 180-degree field of regard. Hell, the damn thing could actually climb walls. The device's only downfall was the general distaste for spiders. I smiled at the thought of a bunch of people in a desperate fit of arachnophobia trying to stomp something that cost more than a Porsche.

Winch placed the little creature on the ground and I used the joystick icon on the phone to move it forward into the room.

The spiderbot scuttled off to the right along the edge of the room for a few feet before I stopped the little machine and had it turn about and scan the room with the wide angle of its eight eyes.

Rose light from the ceiling shone from a half-dozen quartz crystals the size of basketballs. From spider-perspective, the room was as big as a football field, but pressing the DISPLAY icon caused the little 'bot to measure the space, revealing its true dimensions—a mere fifteen-by-fifteen feet. The basket ball-sized rose quartz was the size of my thumb.

To the right was another archway and I scuttled the spiderbot over for a look. Another hallway, this one lit by more rose-quartz imbedded in the ceiling. The readout showed the length to be longer than thirty feet: "30+ft." So there was a limit to what the 'bot could measure.

I gave the others the signal to continue and once again took point, weapon at the ready and one eye fixed on the cell. Rose light bathed our eyes, but it wasn't harsh. Pleasant, in fact. We took a few cautious steps into the room, eyes peeled for trouble.

Then the world came apart around us.

One second we were under soft scarlet light in a medium-sized room and the next, a circular cavern of dark stone the size of a soccer field surrounded by a surrealistic nightmare scenario. What looked to be a couple dozen giant insect-shapes circled us, red crystal swords pointed our way. It took a moment for my eyes to adjust because the rose light had been replaced by actinic blue. When they did, I realized the insect shapes were actually tall, thin men and women in black, glass-like armor studded with fantastic protrusions. Some had bat-winged helmets, some had spikes like a forest of razors sprouting from every surface. Some bore runes that glowed with a silver crystal purity that hurt the eyes. All were no more than fifteen feet away, and all had their swords ready to render my entire team into Bureau cutlets.

Wonderful.

"Uh, white boy, is this part of the plan?"

Not quite ... *"On my mark, guys, get ready..."*

"I would not give that order, Kalevi Hakala," a rich, deep voice like silk brushing rough wood purred in our ears. A bored, male voice.

Oh crap.

Two of the black-glass knights parted to reveal another tall figure, slender yet well-muscled and wearing what appeared to be brown and gold leggings tucked into calf-high doeskin boots, softer than eiderdown. The leggings themselves had swirling patterns that were constantly in motion and the cloth emitted a soft light, as if the fibers themselves had been spun from twilight. A belt of gold and silver wrapped around the slim waist while the man's bare torso seemed to be chiseled from alabaster, every muscle clearly defined. Michelangelo would have killed his grandmother to carve a likeness of those defined abs, powerful pecs and arms. Long blond hair, with ends that disappeared into nothingness, hung a good eight inches below his wide shoulders, providing an interesting contrast to the paler than pale skin. Pointed tips of ears poked out through the gossamer hair. A narrow, ascetic face with a long thin nose over even thinner lips topped the vision off and a circlet made of hair-thin strands of platinum or silver rested over his long, slender eyebrows.

Next to him, like a gremlin, stood another púca, twin to the one Canton had nailed to the floor of the loft. Instead of a hoodie and sweats, this one wore multi-colored skins of a rabbit-like creature.

And this púca also sported a wand. My stomach hit temperatures below absolute zero.

"We can take them, boss," Ilena sent, a trace of excitement or panic in her subvocal voice. *"Shoot the leader and the rest will crumble. Let me pop Mr. Male Model there ..."*

"Chill out and do it now."

"You really should listen to your leader," the bare-chested man said to Ilena.

"He can hear us?"

I spared the small magician a glance and said out loud, "Obviously."

"Lower your weapons," the man said in his silk and wood voice. His yellow eyes, like dog piss shining in the snow, glittered with malice. "Now."

Looking around, I gave the team a nod and we pointed our weapons at the floor. All except Ilena, who hesitated.

The man looked almost bored. "Geógh," he said casually.

Before I could react, the púca pointed his wand and squinted.

Faraday coats absorb magic because of the silver mesh that is threaded beneath the fortified leather exterior. Most spells—hell, even *multiple* spells—can be absorbed by the silver mesh, but the more spell energy absorbed, the hotter the mesh becomes. Ninety-nine out of a hundred times a magician will never be able to cast a second spell because the shielded agent introduces the magician to several bullets at speed. The best Faraday coats use platinum mesh because platinum can absorb up to three times the energy than silver can without heating to a danger point.

We all wore the best Faraday coats.

The spell hit Ilena and within a second the platinum mesh beneath the leather absorbed so much magical energy it became a superheated gas that burst through the leather and seams as if they were not even there. The incandescent platinum gas began to burn outward and inward, launching Ilena into the air an instant before it could burn its way to the rest of the team. Even so, the intense heat wash blistered our exposed skin, and I could smell my hair burning.

Up, up, up went the magician, who was dead an instant after the platinum overheated, flesh flash-burned from her bones. Half way to the rocky ceiling of the cavern some fifty feet overhead, her scalding hot bones began to fall. The only part of her corpse to reach the ceiling was the skull, which burst into ashy flinders against the hard rock.

Warm fragments and bone dust settled gently on our upturned faces like regret. The whole sick charade had taken less than five seconds and we just stared, shocked to the core by the abruptness of Ilena's brutal death. Even our vaunted hardness, our iron souls, couldn't cope with what we had beheld. Our gazes remained fixed to the spot where the little magician had collided with the ceiling, the pain of our burned skin not registering.

Four weapons clattered to the cavern floor from nerveless fingers and I closed my stinging eyes, heart-heavy with defeat and sorrow.

"You cannot win," murmured the half-dressed Faë, his near lipless mouth curled in a half smile. "I know all about you and have anticipated your every move."

Tears blurred my vision as I met his amber eyes with my baby blues. "I am going to kill you." The words tumbled flat and heavy from my lips.

The Faë took a step closer. His wide eyes and open mouth expressed childlike wonder. "You actually believe that, don't you?" he breathed. "Even after I have killed your magicker. Even though I could order your death without blinking, you actually believe that I will die at *your* hands." Joy filled his features. "How wonderful!"

His death was a fraction away and I knew that the price would be the lives of my entire team. Was I willing to make that kind of sacrifice for the death of one Faë? Judging from his demeanor and dress, I believed him to be a leader, perhaps *the* leader of the Sidhe, but that wasn't enough. I doubted we could complete the mission by killing just one lousy Faë.

But I could avenge Ilena's death.

A twitch of the muscles on my right forearm sprung a knife into my palm and I immediately pushed a switch on the handle. Four inches of double-bladed death sprung forward and plunged through rabbit skin into the chest of the wand-wielding púca, who moaned slightly and toppled lifelessly to the floor.

I dropped the handle of the ballistic knife and stared straight into the piss-yellow eyes of the head Faë, a humorless smile on my lips. "Yeah, I believe it."

As anger replaced the shock on the Faë leader's face, I heard Canton mutter from behind, "Uh-oh, Kal, now you done it."

Yeah.

You don't need thick manacles or a pick-proof door to construct a good prison cell; all you need is a hole in the ground. The French have a word for it, *oubliette*, which means "forgotten place," a form of dungeon accessible only from a hatch in the ceiling. Now, I'd always believed the Sidhe Celtic in origin, but from the looks of the place they stuck us in, stripped to our underwear, they had learned plenty from the French.

After the púca's death, I expected to be killed on the spot. Instead, a few of the black-glass wearing dickweeds gave me a serious pummeling, not enough to break bones, but enough to render me black and blue. Now the pain from my sprained ankle had lots of company, enough that it hurt to blink.

After I was unceremoniously hauled to my feet, the black-glass knights surrounded us, and we were bound, blindfolded, and herded through a dizzying array of corridors and stairs—all lit with that same irritating blue light—to a small room with a heavy trapdoor. Stripped of our armor and outerwear, we were lowered by a slickened rope through the doorway at least twenty feet down. The walls of our circular prison wept moisture and were slick with slime, offering no purchase.

We were well and truly corralled. Fortunately, a fist-sized crystal attached to the underside of the trapdoor provided some, albeit harsh, illumination. The pit looked as if it had been machined into a solid block of basalt, black and pitiless. I ran a finger along the stone and it came away with a coating of slimy green algae.

"Okay, white boy," Canton muttered, the great muscles at the corners of his jaws bunching. "What now?"

Good question. Obviously our chances of success had dropped quicker than the Dow Jones during a Presidential election. I felt the familiar tightening of fear around my chest that had nothing to do with impressive array of bruises the knights had put there. My two friends bristled with righteous anger. They had seen people die before—we all had—but the sheer, sudden brutality of Ilena's demise touched us all on a visceral level.

"We wait, guys," I growled. "We wait for our moment."

Winch looked like she wanted to chew her way out of our hole. "And that would be …?"

"Oh, a few hours."

"Yeah?"

"Oh yeah. That pointy-eared, yellow-eyed son-of-a-bitch wants us to stew. We'll wait here until he's good and ready to haul us out."

"What makes you think that it'll be hours, rather than days?"

"He didn't strike me as the overly patient type." I took a deep breath. "No, he'll wait just long enough for us to get tired, but not to get some sleep."

"Thrills."

"Ain't it just?"

Canton took her hands and they sat facing each other, carrying on a hushed conversation. After a few minutes Winch gave the Apache a hug and a stray tear landed on his shoulder.

I ran a hand down my chest, feeling the jersey cotton of my Stafford t-shirt tug against my rough calluses. With a sigh and a groan, I sat in a cross-legged position and proceeded to wait.

We had time.

A little more than two hours later the trap door above opened and a basket was lowered by rope. A voice, sweet like springtime and thick with an accent that sounded vaguely European, came through the hole: "Empty the basket, sharply now."

When the basket came within reach, I tipped it over and emptied the contents. Silky clothing and soft leather tumbled into my arms. Divvying up the clothing, we took a look at what we had.

Canton and I had shimmery, soft white tunics that fell to our knees, and plain brown leather belts with wooden buckles. For our feet we had leather moccasins. Winch's tunic was a creamy yellow with a thin brown belt. Her sandals laced over the top.

Not the most complex wardrobe assembly ever—just slip the tunic on over the head like a t-shirt and let fall to the knees. Tie belt around the waist to complete the effect and *voilà*! Instant toga party.

I looked like an idiot.

From Canton's expression, he felt the same way. At least his legs were better than mine. It was Winch who really took our breath away.

Va-va-voom!

Okay, that was a little over the top, but Winch was a whole lot of woman in one stunning package. Gone was the cute Betty Boop look. Instead we had a brunette with legs for days, her calves and thighs perfectly proportioned. The neckline of the tunic was low enough to showcase ample cleavage—enough sun-bronzed skin, in fact, to cause a traffic accident.

I may have been giving her the hubba-hubba eyes, but Canton was practically drooling all over his new duds. For a split-second I felt a small stab of jealousy; then Jeanie's face flashed before my eyes and I realized that I was one lucky sonofabitch to have her in my life. That is, if I had a life after this mission. The jury was still out.

"Damn, hon'," Canton smiled. "You should take that thing home with you, wear it for me every now and again."

She struck a provocative pose and tossed him a come-hither look. "Ya think?"

"Enough, kids," I said, loosening my belt so it didn't rub my side. "You keep doing that, Winch, and this old Injun is gonna spray testosterone everywhere."

Before they could hand me a sarky reply, the springtime voice said from above, "You will climb the rope now and be quick. Know that failure to comply will mean death." Funny how someone who sounded so wholesome and fresh could convey such menace.

Up we went into the dinky room, where we were met by a Faë woman and a mess of knights in their twisty, spiky black armor, all with drawn swords that fractured the harsh overhead lights. The woman, tall and lithe with hair that drank the light and gave nothing back, stared at me; her iridescent purple eyes and arched brows showed no hint of compassion or any real emotion at all. Those eyes gave her beauty a callous frigidity. She looked like she ate her young.

Without a word she led us into the hallway, the knights following, absolutely silent except for the soft scuff of their armored boots against stone—no creak, no groan of glass plates rubbing together. It was as if the sound their armor would have made had been edited from reality.

Once again we were led through a dizzying array of passages. This time the walls were studded with crystals of every color, glittering in the overhead lights. Those bitter blue crystals were partially obscured by what looked to be a chaos growth of spider webs that sparkled like diamonds.

"What is that?" I breathed in wonder, gazing through a particularly thick bundle of hair-thin fibers at the diffuse blue light.

"Your kind calls that 'Fairy Glass,' " the woman said, sounding bored. "For us it is a way to soften the light. They are used only in this portion of the Sidhe mound."

I filed that away under "useless tidbits."

Before long the thick crystal deposits disappeared. The new section of passageway was made of dressed stone, carefully fitted blocks of masonry. The work was so fine that I couldn't see any mortar. The stone shimmered with small particles of crystal so that the blue light, no longer covered by Fairy Glass, was refracted millions of times, making my eyes water. The hallway became so brilliant, in fact, that I could barely keep my eyes open; visibility was limited to only a few feet. If the female Faë felt any discomfort, she didn't show it. Canton's strong hand landed on my shoulder and I knew that his eyes hurt as much as mine.

"Kal ..." Winch said, pain lining her voice. "What's going on here?"

"Dunno. This whole place looks like it's been designed by gay Rastafarian pastry chefs on Quaaludes."

Then, with no sense of transition, we were in a meadow. An honest-to-God meadow with lush green grass and wildflowers and laurels and oak trees reaching for the sky with woody fingers. Butterflies, dragonflies, grasshoppers and hummingbirds flitted around in abundance and total harmony. The sun, at high noon, burned overhead in a cloudless sky, instantly bringing a light sheen of sweat to my skin.

We stood at the top of a small hill and at the bottom, in a small valley the shape of a bowl, was a gathering of Faë. Dozens of them were seated in a large circle on a variety of cushions, taking their ease, drinking from blue-glass goblets and eating fruit and meat from blue glass-plates. All the Faë wore clothing made of the same luminescent material as their leader's—robes of carmine and indigo, tunics of cobalt belted in gold and silver and soft trousers in every shade of tan and russet. Only the Faë leader, lounging on the largest cushion, left his torso bare. Perhaps it was a sign of power, or the fact that he liked showing off his finely sculpted abs. Didn't matter, he was still the douchebag I planned on killing once I quit freaking out.

"White boy, there's no hallway behind us. It's gone."

Wonderful.

"Maybe they teleported us here ... wherever this is." If they had, they'd also teleported our guards with us; a solid wall of black glass and crimson swords stood behind us, along with the Faë woman.

"Then mankind is gonna lose, boss," Winch murmured. Her slender but strong hand gripped Canton's. "If they can teleport, we can't stop them. You remember the last time we saw someone teleport, don't you?"

Oh yeah, I remembered.

"It is an illusion," whispered the Faë woman quietly, her springtime voice sounding almost … sad. "Merely smoke and mirrors for the idle who have nothing but eternity to look forward to."

Well, bowl me over with a feather, the Faë woman sounded almost … civil, although she expressed a bucketload of contempt for the other Faë. Something strange was going on, a strange undercurrent I couldn't make heads or tails of, but I resolved to dig deeper and find out. I spared a look for the black knights.

"Do not fear," the woman said. "They are mine."

Right. Of course they were. Just a bunch of friendly puppies … in hideous black-glass armor with huge, pointy swords. Cuddly, really.

Friggin' wonderful.

Down the gentle slope … If this was indeed the Faë version of a holodeck, I couldn't distinguish it from reality. It sure felt like I was ambling downhill. The grass flowing against my moccasins didn't feel illusory and neither did the rich smell of wildflowers.

As we approached, the Faë parted, moving a few stingy inches to provide access to the interior of the circle. The Faë leader smiled, revealing slightly pointed and very white teeth, and rose from his large cornflower blue cushion in one fluid motion. The Faë he'd been talking to—a muscle-bound Sidhe about my height with shoulder-length, dark brown hair—stood as well. A pair of ridged ram horns curled back from his forehead and spiraled next to his skull. I reckoned he must have been the local Faë head-butting champion. His inhuman, horse-brown eyes with large horizontal pupils gave me the impression he was sizing me up.

"Mr. Hakala, so kind of you to join us," the Faë leader said with an insincere smile. "I'd like to apologize for the accommodations and your various contusions, but you did anger me by slaying poor Geógh. He had been with the family for centuries and púcas are so hard to replace."

I kept my silence.

That insincere smile didn't waver a fraction. "Mr. Hakala?"

"You would like to apologize," I began slowly. "Riiiiight."

A touch of frost reached his yellow eyes. "Quite. My actions, however regrettable, were justified." He inhaled deeply, as though taking in my scent, and the chill left his features. "My name is Ephelor. Prince Ephelor of the Unseelie Court."

Cold pricklies crept down my back, but I did my darndest not to reveal my surprise. I had totally forgotten about the Seelie and the Unseelie courts. I was feeling like a prize idiot.

I prayed that I'd live long enough to keep on feeling foolish.

According to legend, the Sidhe were divided up into two kingdoms, or Courts. The Seelie and The Unseelie. The Seelie (or Blessed) Court was composed of those Faë who were kindly disposed towards humans. My Brownie friends, for instance. I think you can guess what kind of Faë belonged to the Unseelie Court—the kind who would do anything and everything to destroy mankind. If Ephelor was a prince, then there must be a far more powerful king or queen waiting in the wings.

Wonderful.

Chapter Seventeen
Proving Ground

Ephelor continued as if the walls of my reality weren't crashing down around my ears. "I see you have met my cousin, Uloeth." He gestured toward the woman who had escorted us. "Let me welcome you to our gathering here, a copy of the Blessing Vale, lost to us for many centuries."

My brain finally started to reboot. "So, where are we really?"

The prince gestured for us to take a seat on the soft grass in front of his cushion. He waited for us to hunker down cross-legged before he himself reclined. I snagged a tuft of grass, brought it to my nose and inhaled. It smelled like summer, the same scent that had clung to my sister Leena when we were kids. Clumps of moist dirt at the roots felt real, slightly damp and rich.

Canton and Winch were looking around in wonder, sitting very close together in mutual support and again I felt a stab a longing for Jeanie. Glad she wasn't with us, though.

A short Faë—perhaps two feet tall, but perfectly proportioned and covered head to toe in shiny black fur—set green glass plates of sliced meat and fruit in front of us while another, whiskered like a cat, brought us pink-glass goblets.

"It is safe for you to eat and drink here, Mr. Hakala," Ephelor said, taking a long swig from his own goblet. His smile was chock full of arrogant amusement. "It is ordinary, Earthly food, not from Faërie."

I held up a sliver of meat and sniffed. Pork. My stomach made rumbly sounds, so I shoveled it in. Cooked perfectly and seasoned with salt and pepper. "We aren't in the World Under, then?" I asked, licking my lips. My other two team members, seeing that I wasn't dying of some horrible poison, dug in.

Ephelor laughed and the other Faë joined in, the whole meadow ringing with silvery peals of Sidhe mirth. "Oh, dear me, no! We are still firmly rooted in the human world, our former home. You and your companions would not last long in Faërie. Had you crossed into *my* world, agent Hakala, the Interdiction placed in your mind by the Bureau would no longer exist."

A few months ago I had discovered that—whether you travel to a distant world or travel in time—any spell that happens to be on you will disappear. It had been quite a relief when the octopus presence of the Interdiction—which prevented us from telling any outsiders about the Bureau's existence—had vanished, and those tentacles of magic were no longer winding through my brain. Of course BB had made sure that as soon as I returned to the Bureau's tender embrace the Interdiction was once again nestled firmly in my mind.

When the prince's words registered, I had a major crap-attack.

The Bureau ... He knew. I wanted to ask how, but the Interdiction squeezed my brain and the words died in my throat. From the look on his face, he knew exactly what I was thinking. I exchanged glances with Canton and Winch, their faces twitching in strain as their own spells held them fast.

It dawned on us simultaneously how the prince could have known about the Bureau, and the horror of it filled me to the brim. Ephelor must have seen the revelation on our faces.

"Your former associate, Thomas Mace, was once a guest of ours, *Agent* Hakala, and during his time here, I extracted all his knowledge of the Bureau of Supernatural Investigation."

Hate. Lots and lots of hate. Bucketsful, barrels of smoldering hot hate. First Mace, then Wilkes and lastly Ilena. Prince Ephelor had much to answer for and I didn't bother to keep that resolve from my face. It only served to amuse him.

"He was a nature lover, you know." Ephelor took a sip from his glass goblet. "Or perhaps you did not. It seems that you Bureau types do not care to share personal experiences. When Mr. Mace approached the island a couple of months ago to view the seals, he attempted to converse with the researchers. Once humans are under Sidhe control, they are no longer … normal. That, of course, aroused his suspicion."

The entire circle of some fifty Faë had stopped their chatter, hanging on the prince's every word. Even the dwarfish servants had stopped their circling of the guests, leaving goblets and plates empty.

"We had begun the final stage of our plan here on the Farallons and were 'circling the wagons' as you humans like to say. Perhaps we acted too hastily, but we could not afford any interference with our efforts.

"Mr. Mace may well have suspected what you call 'Supernatural' involvement. Perhaps if we were better versed in the control of you modern humans he would not have grown suspicious. It does not matter; he came to the island in the dead of night to investigate and was captured. Quite easily, as a matter of fact. After that, it was simplicity itself to … download his mind, as you modern humans would say." The prince's smile was pure, liquid mean.

Canton almost made it to his feet, but I snagged his forearm before he could complete the motion. Instantly a dozen red sword points appeared at the Apache's neck, a hair's breadth from piercing his skin. Our black-glass knights had joined us and we hadn't even heard them move. The Apache subsided and sat down again, but the swords never left his throat. He was trapped by a hedge of red death.

Ephelor grinned as if the incident was the best entertainment he'd had in quite a while. Perhaps it was. "Mr. Mace managed to escape our august company, despite the anguish he must have felt from our mental ministrations," he continued, the slightest hint of annoyance in his melodic voice. "I sent one of my púcas after him as well as a gargoyle and Black Shuck, but I see that his death was unusual enough to bring your team here." He nodded to the ram-headed Faë. "Toruim here thought that Mace's death would be the end of the matter." The other Faë narrowed his horse-eyes at the prince, but kept his mouth shut. "However, it was easy to anticipate your arrival and keep an eye on you. I was not surprised when your team killed my wasp." The prince leaned forward, yellow eyes ablaze. "But imagine my surprise when you killed my púca and defeated my gargoyle. You are deserving of the admiration Mr. Mace felt for you."

If Mace ever admired me, he sure kept it to himself, but that wasn't unusual. Emotional attachment was a luxury we couldn't afford. You never knew when the person you were fighting with would die a horrible, messy death. Case in point, Ilena.

The constant threat of imminent death made friendships like the one I shared with Canton more precious and wonderful. And their loss all the more painful. Once again I thought of Jeanie and my stomach clenched at the thought of her dying a gruesome death. Turns out that despite years of practice avoiding emotional entanglements, I done got myself wrapped up in one pretty well.

Boy, was I screwed.

I took a sip from my goblet. Some sort of fruit juice, sweet and tangy. "So what now?"

"You and your friends will be our … guests for a time," he purred. "Then, when the time is right, I will let you free."

"I meant, what is your plan now that you have caught us? You have something in mind for San Francisco."

His laugh was the tinkling of bells mixed with the rending of flesh. "Oh, that 'what now'! Agent Hakala, may I call you Kalevi?" He didn't wait for an answer. "Those plans are for me to know and you to never find out." His eyes lit up. "Unless you want to challenge for the knowledge?"

Out of the corner of my eye, I saw Uloeth stiffen, the muscles at the corners of her jaws tightening. Yeah, I could challenge, but I had the feeling that doing so would definitely shorten my lifespan considerably.

"No thank you, Ephelor," I drawled, watching his face become flat and unreadable at my familiarity. More pork found its way into my gullet. "Not today."

Something like respect crept onto the prince's face. "Very well." He considered his goblet for a moment, as if divining answers from its depths. "What have you told your Bureau?" he asked suddenly.

For a split second I nearly ruined everything by talking. The prince's eyes burned into mine, and I felt the pull of his indomitable will. My mouth parted and my tongue began to betray me, but the sudden memory of the púca's psychic attack forced my lips shut. Anger started to boil in my gut and I felt the prince's grip on my psyche weakening. Pressing my advantage, I gathered my wits and *pushed* back, temples throbbing and pulse pounding. I caught Uloeth's eye, and she offered me a slight smile.

"Sorry, Ephie," I grated, keeping an eye on the prince's cousin. "But if *you* want information, *you'll* have to offer challenge." Uloeth's lips curled upward but the little smile was gone so quickly I almost believed I hadn't seen it.

Hmmm. I got the feeling that calling out a challenge was a dangerous prospect indeed.

"Show the prince his due and proper respect, human!" snarled Toruim, the ram-horned Faë.

Canton swung in with as much contempt as he could muster, which was sizable. "You better untwist your horns a bit there, hoss. He ain't *our prince.*" By the set of his shoulders, my friend was ready to go in for the kill, swords at his throat be damned.

Toruim jumped to his feet, fists clenched and head lowered as if he intended to ram my friend in the face. Anticipating his reaction, I was there to intercept him.

My right hand grabbed one of his horns and I twisted my torso and pulled, throwing the startled Faë over my right hip. He landed with a loud *thud* on the grass. His yellow and blue tunic flared briefly, then became dull fiber. Go figure that the Faë would use illusions on their clothing.

"You got a problem with one of my team," I panted. Adrenaline kicked in hard, heightening my senses. "Then you got a problem with me, buster."

Just as sheep-boy sprang to his feet and a half-dozen black knights drew close, swords raised, the prince intervened.

"Stop!" he shouted, his voice a trumpet. The black knights took a step back while Toruim stood his ground, glaring daggers my way.

"That's enough of that! We are adults here." Ephelor hadn't even moved from his cushion, but ire dripped from his amber eyes.

"Then I cry challenge on both of them," said Toruim, shaking his massive head. He pointed to Canton. "He has insulted me!" That finger came round to point between my eyes. "And *he* has touched me!"

"Then the human has the right to choose his weapons," Uloeth barked, a smile in her voice.

"Cousin!" warned the prince, pale cheeks flushed. "Do not interfere!"

"It is his right."

Oh-ho! So that was the rusty nail in the breakfast cereal. I felt a big crap-eating smile stretch my face. Just when I was about to say "Pistols," Uloeth rained on my parade.

"Hand-to-hand weapons only," she said softly, as if reading my mind.

Crap.

Oh, well, go for the gusto. "I choose as my weapon my Bowie knife."

"Me, too," Canton said, slowly rising to his feet, a smile on his broad face.

Toruim blanched, so pale I thought he'd go transparent. "My lord!" he cried.

Ephelor stood, every muscle taut and quivering his rage. "You fool," he spat. "Challenge was issued by you, and by our laws ..." He sighed. "They have the choice of weapons."

Heck yeah! My elation lasted about as long as a Klansman in Harlem as a beagle-faced gnome staggered in from God-knows-where. He was bent almost in half under a large wooden chest with silver clasps and hinges. After carefully placing his burden on the ground (and nearly getting squished in the process), the little guy wobbled off.

Torium opened the container. Armor, green as grass, green as jade and emeralds and everything springtime, was removed and set to one side. A bevy of tiny servants, each one bearing their own animal-like feature—from bat ears to chicken beaks—dressed the Faë for battle.

Canton tapped me on the shoulder. "Uh, Kal?"

"Yeah, buddy?"

"We don't get any armor, do we?"

"I don't thinks so."

"How do I get out of this chicken-squat outfit?"

Toruim's angry horse gaze met my baby blues and I could feel the hate boiling off of his skin. "Only way out is through him, I think."

"Great, Kal," Winch muttered. "What's next? Sodomy and mutilation?"

God, I hoped not.

"You were wise to have him challenge you," Uloeth said from behind, startling me. I didn't jump. Much. "However it would have been better if you did not fight at all. Toruim is my cousin's Champion and as good with a knife as he is with a sword."

I took a deep breath. "Don't worry, I have … an angle."

"Oh, God," moaned Winch.

Uloeth looked puzzled. "What? What's wrong?"

Winch gave me a good hard squint. "Whenever he says that, something bad is about to happen."

"Is this true?"

I shrugged. "Sometimes."

"Cousin!" barked the prince. "You have interfered enough. Stand aside."

Uloeth's face shut down hard. "No."

The circle went silent. Even the dwarfish helpers stopped what they were doing to watch what would happen next.

"Cousin," Ephelor said with menace.

"No, *cousin*." Uloeth's voice was pure poison and her midnight hair began to rise until it floated around her head on some unseen current. Her purple eyes grew dark; even the whites were black as pitch. "I am a princess of the Sidhe, though a hostage for the good behavior of my family, and I will be treated with the respect I deserve." Two spots of crimson appeared on the prince's cheeks. He was about to make a retort, but she cut him off. "Never forget that I am your equal in all things. I will inform this human of what is his due in this contest, as dictated by law, and you may *not* gainsay me!"

The hair on my neck bristled from their magic, which traveled along my skin like an electric current, and I felt Leena stir in her sleep like a tickle in the back of my mind. Everyone, including us human-types, took a step away from the two. I prayed that the confrontation wouldn't go nuclear.

The moment stretched and I felt a familiar itch in my palms—the desire to grab a weapon and go to work—but I held back. I expected an imminent Faë throw-down.

The moment passed. "Very well, cousin," Ephelor conceded with ill grace. "But remember, you only represent the Seelie Court as a hostage, not as a policy maker."

Frost could have formed on Uloeth's lashes. "And you might do well to remember, cousin, that your brother is the next King of the Unseelie Court, not you."

Exactly the thing to say if you wanted to piss off a princeling. I almost applauded as Ephelor hid his face behind his goblet, only a slight trembling in his hands betraying his agitation.

Uloeth inclined her head toward me. "You'd better be worth it, Kalevi Hakala," she whispered urgently. "For I have made an enemy dire."

"Don't worry," I muttered, watching a female dwarf draw close. She had iridescent scales at her throat, but otherwise looked like a perfectly normal person, albeit two feet tall. In her small hands she carried a wicker basket, which she handed to me. Another servant sporting a long pink tail like a rat's handed an identical basket to Canton. I began to smile as we opened the lids.

Our Bowies. Life had just gotten a whole lot better. And no

wonder the little servants were handling them with kid gloves; one good scratch and it's bye-bye tiny Faë. As for the rest, they all sucked in their breath when we drew our blades, the edges shiny and sharp. I spared them a humorless grin; it was so easy to imagine what I could do with that knife.

"You will each fight an opponent," the prince said, amber eyes fixed on the Bowies. A brace of black knights stood between us, ready to die to protect their royal leaders. "The native will fight first."

Canton laughed, hardly a spontaneous outburst of joy. "To the death, right?"

One long eyebrow lifted. "Of course."

"Good. Thought so. Do I get the bozo with the horns or a real opponent?"

"Toruim is my greatest warrior and shall face your Bureau's finest. You shall fight Olludir, a worthy rival, you shall find." The knight who stepped forward wore an open-faced helmet with a crown of spikes, revealing cruel, green eyes. His armor glowed harsh silver with looping and whirling runes that seemed to shift the longer you stared. Olludir handed his scabbarded sword to his fellow knight and drew a rose-colored double-edged dagger at least ten inches long.

"He gets armor?" asked the Apache.

"You use deadly iron, native. It is only right he wears armor."

Canton nodded and stepped to the middle of the circle and smiled. It wasn't pleasant.

"Agent Hakala, I trust that I have your vow of non-violence until your match."

I nodded. "You have it." As soon as the words fell from my lips I felt a tingle at the back of my neck. I glanced at Uloeth.

"A promise made in the Blessing Vale, even a poor copy such as this, carries the weight of a dire oath," she said tonelessly. "Should you break that oath, bad things will happen."

Right. Bad things. Got it, but the prospect of a gruesome death didn't stop me from snarling at the nearest Faë as Winch and I took our places at the edge of the circle. I was a little surprised when Uloeth joined us. Perhaps her fate was tied to ours.

"You wouldn't happen to know what time it is?" I asked the Sidhe princess.

"What?"

"The time. Pacific Standard time in the really real world."

She shook her head in confusion.

Winch grabbed my arm. "What is it, boss? What do you have working?"

I grinned. "Something wonderful."

She gave me a skeptical yet vaguely hopeful look. I could tell she wanted to ask for details, but there was too much risk of being overheard by pointed ears.

Olludir stepped into the circle, rose-colored dagger in hand. Canton bared his teeth in a primal show of aggression and lifted his Bowie.

"A challenge has been issued by Toruim and supported by Olludir against the two human men, who have accepted and chosen knives of cold iron," Ephelor began. "The fight is to the death. The human is Canton Alsate, from the Apache tribe, a formidable opponent. For a human. However, as you know, Olludir has never lost a challenge and is considered one of the greatest warriors among the Sidhe. This should be … entertaining." There was a smattering of silvery laughter.

"Begin," thundered the prince.

Canton leapt.

Chapter Eighteen
The Deal

Canton had always been fast. The fastest I'd ever seen—able to strike and recover before his opponent had a chance to bleed. He must have been counting on his phenomenal speed to carry the day.

He wasn't fast enough.

Olludir was just as swift, his obsidian armor proving no hindrance to his snake-quick reflexes. Canton's rush carried him close, but the Faë avoided his first strike easily, and the counter nearly gave the Apache another mouth to breathe from. Instead of opening his throat, the scarlet dagger swept down without losing speed and sliced off Canton's pinkie finger. The digit fell to the grass, followed by a spurt of blood.

Winch moaned—a deep, jagged sound.

The crowd pealed their savage approval as the blood flowed. Canton didn't even bother to look at the damage; he kept his eyes on the circling Olludir, who moved as if his runed armor was made of nothing but silk. The Faë sought to press his advantage and paid for his eagerness with a slash to the chest. One of the swirling runes flared briefly before winking out.

The two circled more carefully after that, Canton with his left arm held out to the side for balance, blood from his pinkie stump trickling onto the grass. Olludir wove the rose-colored dagger in front of my friend like a swaying snake.

Almost faster than thought, the two rushed together, testing, probing and feinting, before jumping back and circling again. It was an elaborate dance where one misstep could lead to death.

More feinting ... Canton striking toward the open face of the helmet, the Faë aiming for the Apache's tender midsection, both whirling away from each other.

"How good is he?" Uloeth asked, jaw and fists clenched.

"He's the best that's ever been, or ever will be," Winch replied absently, eyes locked on the scene.

It was true; I'd never seen better. Fast as a blink, graceful as a ballet dancer and one of the smartest men I'd ever known, he redefined the word *lethal*.

But Olludir looked to be every bit as good.

"What you don't realize," Uloeth said, stony-voiced, "is that Faë warriors have centuries to practice the art of killing." Her violet eyes bored into mine. "In the case of Toruim, millennia."

"Why so chatty?"

Her lavender eyes crinkled slightly. "I have no love for my cousins of the Unseelie Court. They have terrible, monstrous plans, plans that run counter to the wishes of the Seelie Court. I would use you and your team to upset those plans."

"That's pretty risky for you, being a hostage and all."

"I have ceased to care for my welfare." She sounded cool and detached, but with an undercurrent of sorrow.

Canton aimed a strike at his opponent's throat and was blocked by an armored forearm. The Bowie skittered across the black glass and another rune flared and died. Olludir's dagger plunged upward, only to be stopped by *both* of Canton's hands as he gripped the Sidhe's forearm. The Bowie fell to the grass.

The rosy dagger hovered between then, a couple inches from Canton's throat, but the black knight couldn't gain the upper hand. Canton grinned and twisted his torso to the side, pulling on his opponent's arm to throw him off balance. A well-placed foot tripped the knight and sent him crashing to the ground.

Silvery cries of alarm echoed through the vale as Canton grabbed his fallen knife and leapt on the knight, the Bowie blurring toward tender flesh. Bucking wildly, Olludir slammed his spiky helmet into the Apache's midsection.

Winch screamed in denial.

The crowd roared, no longer a silver pealing, but an animalistic bellowing of bloodlust.

Canton fell backward, face a mask of pain, blood staining his tunic, gasping for air. His body twitched, and his eyes were glazed with agony.

Tears stained Winch's cheeks as she watched her boyfriend's life blood pour out onto the lush grass.

Olludir rose to his feet and stood over the fallen man, rosy dagger clenched hard in one gauntleted hand. He lowered himself to one knee and prepared to thrust the dagger into Canton's heaving chest.

It was over in an instant.

Before the dagger could plunge into Canton's heart, the Apache blurred into motion, fist filled with Bowie, and stabbed. The fourteen-inch blade struck the knight in the breastplate on the exact spot where the silvery runes had died and *crunched* through the glass, sending obsidian splinters flying.

Canton, face slick with sweat, lips parted in a snarl, twisted the blade savagely and a gout of black blood gushed from the knight's chest. Olludir shuddered violently, dropped the rose-colored dagger, and died.

The Apache lowered the fallen warrior to the grass and stood, legs trembling. He let out a victory whoop, bloody knife held high. Winch joined in with her own cry of relief as she ran into her lover's arms.

Silence greeted the couple, the Faë staring thunderstruck at their fallen champion. I noticed a tic begin to tease the corner of Ephelor's left eye; otherwise his expression was impassive.

He was one pissed puppy.

"*That* is why he is the best," I uttered gravely.

Uloeth's face was tight. "What he did, feigning grave injury, is considered poor form."

"Is it against the rules?"

She considered a moment. "No."

"Then screw it. Winning is what counts."

"Ephelor will consider it an act of barbarism."

I sighed. "He ain't seen nothing yet." With that, I walked to the happy couple and hugged them hard.

"You had me worried, buddy." Hay fever thickened my voice. Yeah, that's it. Hay fever.

Canton rested his forehead against mine, with Winch sandwiched between us. "He was the best I ever faced, white boy. I had to do me some strategizing. Figured that when the steel took out those runes, the armor underneath would be useless. Glad I was right."

" 'Bout gave me a heart-attack, you big knucklehead," Winch whispered.

He gripped my shoulder. "Listen Kal, I don't think you can beat that sheep-headed guy. You're good, but he'll be better." I felt the bottom drop out of my stomach. If Canton believed Toruim was better, then he was. That boded ill for Mama Hakala's blue-eyed boy. "But listen: they are strong, but I think we are stronger. I could feel it when I fought that guy. When I tried to throw him, he countered, but he couldn't counter my strength. You gotta grapple with him." Canton's deep eyes held a wealth of concern.

"Don't worry, buddy, I've got … an angle."

"Jesus …" he snorted.

"Congratulations, Agent Alsate," the prince said, voice seething with venom. "You are the winner, although by distasteful, barbaric means." The gathered Faë murmured their agreement.

"I cry the right to heal the victor," Uloeth shouted, drowning out the crowd. "It is only proper."

Ephelor conceded with ill grace and Uloeth pried the happy couple apart, laying a hand on Canton's gouged midsection. "It looks worse than it is," Canton said, "maybe only a couple inches deep."

"Shh," came her reply. Eyes closed, she concentrated for a moment then stepped away, leaving the Apache to stare in amazement at his healed torso. Smiling, he also held up his hand. The pinkie was gone, but otherwise the skin was fully healed.

"Damn, that was *fast*," Winch breathed.

Was that a smile on Uloeth's face? *Showoff.*

"Agent Hakala." Ephelor no longer sounded amused.

"Yes?"

"I trust you will not resort to such trickery in your match?"

I glanced at Toruim, who was giving me his best Glare-o-Death. Somehow I didn't think he'd fall for such a ploy. The prince's mouth quirked in a small grin that said he didn't think so, either.

"Not a problem." As I stood there, staring at the horned Faë who was trying to bore a hole into me with his eyes, I had a burst of inspiration. "Say, Ephelor, care to make things really interesting?"

One perfect eyebrow lifted and nearly disappeared beneath his pale hair. "A wager, Agent Hakala? What do you have in mind?"

"Ever thought of getting a white Persian cat you could pet while monologuing on your evil plans?"

Bright and slightly sharp teeth became visible. "Very amusing. A Blofeld reference. How droll, Mr. Hakala."

"You know Bond?"

"We have cable. Premium package."

Weirdest conversation. *Ever.*

"Simple bet. I win, you tell me what the hell your big plan is, the whole enchilada."

Ephelor's smile turned feral. "I am not sure you have anything to offer me, Agent Hakala."

My answering grin was every bit as wild. "How about the Bureau's contingency plan should I fail to make contact?"

And there went his smile. "Deal."

"My lord," Toruim began, fair face becoming flushed. "You cannot trust this human! We can take the information from his mind."

"Can you?" I asked the ram-horned warrior archly. "Is it really that simple, or does it take a while? I have a funny feeling that ol' Ephie can't get the information quick enough to do any good."

"My lord—"

"Hush." The prince's voice was soft but firm, and the knight's mouth snapped shut. "You will give your oath that your agents have the information I want."

"My word on it." Again that strange tingle on the back of my neck.

"And their promise to divulge that information."

"Done."

"Very well, Agent Hakala, do you need more time or may we continue with the challenge?"

"One minute, if you will."

"Granted. Oh, and by the way, you may not employ that famous Rage of yours. This is challenge of skill at arms, not magic."

Wonderful.

Canton and Winch stood calmly at the edge of the circle, Uloeth at their side. The Apache regarded his mutilated hand with a slight frown, as if it were a minor inconvenience. His Bowie was nowhere in sight, having been scooped up by one of the tiny servants. The Faë had moved to give them room, as if they were plague carriers.

"You two, if I lose, don't tell that bastard a thing," I whispered, "not for a few hours at least."

"You swore an oath!" hissed the princess.

"And they will keep it, but only after a certain amount of time has passed."

Understanding dawned on her flawless features. "You bargain like a Sidhe," she said.

"Let's not be nasty."

"If he wants the intel, Kal," Winch shot back, "can't he just pluck it out of our heads?"

Canton snorted. "It must have taken Ephelor a good while to break Mace, or he wouldn't have asked for it in the first place. That means that whatever he's up to, it's happening soon."

I considered my friends for a moment. "Canton, remember that Williamsburg incident where we fought the hydra?"

He nodded slowly.

Near ten years ago, before Canton left the Bureau, we battled the closest thing to a dragon I'd ever seen. How we took it out … well, let's just say it was as effective as it was inelegant. "That's what's going to happen if I don't check in with BB. It's all set."

His dark eyes grew wide. "Damn, that's pretty extreme." Slowly, his lips stretched wide in savage smile. "I love it."

My answering smile was just as viscious. Now he had the information, and if I died, he could hopefully resist the Prince's Vulcan Mind Probe for a goodly while. At least until sunup.

Uloeth nodded to the Prince. "If he were to take you by surprise, he could pluck the information in a manner of seconds, but a prepared person can resist for quite a while. It took him almost a month to wear Thomas Mace down." She took a deep breath. "I must go lest I arouse more suspicion. I must not give my cousin the impression I still fear him." With inhuman grace, she glided over to Ephelor and took a seat to his right, face set in stone and hoarfrost.

Toruim was almost fully encased in his green-glass armor. I noticed ridges running along the greaves, breastplate and vambraces—ridges that were bladed and winking at me in the sunlight.

Those ridges were sharp enough to cut an idea.

Note to self: no grappling.

The knight caught me looking and grinned. Spiders must grin like that before pouncing.

He knelt, allowing the tiny servants to place an open-faced helmet on his head, designed to accommodate the enormous, curling horns. When he rose to his full height and squared his shoulders, he appeared at least six inches taller than my own six-foot four.

Wonderful. I was in a death-match with the Jolly Green Giant.

A tiny servant handed him a sheathed dagger, which he drew and held up to the light. Its edge sparked rainbows, as if the blade could cut light to shreds. I heard a hiss as the crowd drew in a collective breath.

"Foul," Uloeth cried, quivering with indignation. "Bane weapons are not allowed in a challenge."

Ephelor shook his head. "That is untrue. They are frowned upon, but not forbidden, and since there was no stipulation against them, my champion may use one."

Uloeth stared hard at her cousin, but he merely smiled slightly and drank from his goblet. "Then I shall inform the mortal warrior of what he faces, as is proper."

"Very well," the prince sighed, as if the matter was beneath him. "You may."

"What is a Bane weapon?" I asked as she drew close.

Surely that wasn't fear in her eyes? "There are only five Bane weapons in all of Faërie, created by the master weapon crafter Owwin. No other Sidhe could make such dread devices."

She was making my head hurt. "Skip to the good part."

"Whoever is struck by a Bane weapon dies in a particularly terrible manner. Each death is different; each inflicts the worst pain imaginable. All Toruim needs is one small prick."

Too easy, I had to let that one slide. "Worst death imaginable. No problem. Thank you."

She stared into my face for a long moment. "Do you not care that he wields one of the most potent Sidhe weapons in all of Faërie? Are you truly fearless?"

Hmph. If she only knew. I was a second and a half away from losing twenty pounds. All brown. "I don't have time to be scared. Unless you offer any hints as to horn-head's weaknesses, like a glass jaw or kryptonite, you better hop back to your cousin so I can get to work."

Uloeth frowned in worry, the first truly human look I'd seen her give. It transformed her from a Sidhe Ice Princess to a vulnerable, caring woman.

"Toruim is the greatest champion among my cousin's cohorts. He is fiercely strong, though he does not possess the speed of the unlamented Olludir. He is better with any weapon you care to name save for those modern devices you call 'guns.' "

"So what you're saying is that he is pretty much unbeatable."

She nodded.

Wonderful.

As she took her place next to her cousin once more, I faced my opponent. "Don't suppose you'd care to concede?"

He snarled.

"Call it a draw, then?"

More snarling. No sense of humor. Must be a Sidhe trait.

"Last chance," I offered, holding the Bowie low along my thigh. "Best offer you're gonna get."

"I see your fear, human," thundered the massive Faë. The crowd became hushed, expectant. "I, who have lived for millennia, who have hunted your kind and have dragged them squealing from their caves. They worshipped the Sidhe as gods and feared us as such. My kind knows more about killing than you can ever hope to know."

Blah, blah, blah. He sounded like Charlie Brown's teacher. "Yes, but I have been specially trained in knives, horn-head. What do you know?"

He began to spin the blood-colored dagger, flipping it over the back of his hand and through his gauntleted fingers in a display of amazing dexterity. It was beautiful, almost hypnotic.

I threw my Bowie.

The knife flew end over end and the knight attempted to dodge, but it was too late. With a solid *thunk* the wooden handle hit the massive Faë between the eyes causing him to drop the Bane dagger. It landed point first into the soft sod.

Before he could recover, I was on him, grabbing a horn and throwing him to the ground. No razored ridges on his back plate, so I straddled his writhing body, crossed my arms, took a huge horn in each hand, set my shoulders and began to *twist*.

Toruim was thrashing and bucking in earnest, but I held the big Faë down and kept on wrenching at his head. Slowly, every muscle in his neck straining with effort and fueled by the strength of panic, the Faë's head began to turn.

My mouth was stretched in a snarl of hatred and rage, not the berserker rage that was Leena, but good, old-fashioned human fury. I used the full strength of my limbs, my torso, to rotate that head. It had become my universe, my whole reason for being. The thrashing between my legs and under my butt disappeared and the silvery, discordant roar of the crowd and cries of dismay no longer registered. They were ghost things, pale and unshapely, not fit for my consciousness. My only focus was my enemy's skull, my only sensation the feel of his horns. The rest of the world was nothing but shadows and dust.

A gauntleted hand grabbed my forearm, squeezing hard enough that my bones protested. I closed my eyes to my pain and continued to heave, setting my shoulders to the task. The pain in my forearm began to build, but it was nothing compared to my need to twist, to pull, to *heave*. There suddenly came a sound like the tearing of cardboard and warm wetness splashed my forearms.

Eventually I came to notice the silence.

And my breathing. I was gulping air as if I'd run a marathon. My arms shook and my fists were locked shut. I couldn't feel my fingers.

Slowly I cracked my eyes open. Toruim stared at me with shock-wide eyes, his mouth agape. His nose was a mere five inches from mine. The pulse of my blood through my veins accompanied the sight of my hands locked on his horns.

Patter, pat, pat. The slow drip of blood and a wetness on my thighs. I looked down to see the ragged, pink stump of the Faë's head dripping blood onto my legs.

I had ripped my opponent's head off.

Tearing my eyes away from the grotesque scene was one of the hardest things I'd ever done. I met the prince's astonished gaze, his yellow eyes glazed in horror. One of his many black-glass knights had a hold of my forearm, but when he met my burning gaze he hurriedly let go.

Muscles protesting with every slight movement, I stood, heaving and shuddering, and slowly staggered toward the stunned Ephelor. Bending slowly, I set the dripping head on his fine blue pillow. It took a concerted effort to unlock my fingers from their death grip.

"He may have been a champion," I panted. "But I'm Bureau, jack, and that's how we get things done."

Chapter Nineteen

The Iron Plan

"Come with me," commanded the prince, his face a study of neutrality. To Uloeth, "Cousin, you stay here. We shall speak again soon." His words were mild, but his tone promised darker things.

Ephelor led us up the vale in the opposite direction of our entrance. Before we reached the top of the shallow bowl, we found ourselves once again in a hallway—no transition whatsoever. I glanced behind me, but my eyes met only blackness so dark it drank the harsh light from the crystals overhead. The sheer scale of the Faë's illusory power staggered me. As we walked, I heard the slightest scuffing of feet from behind and knew that black-glass knights followed *us*, on the alert in case we decided to attack the prince. I reckoned Ephelor was a lot tougher than he looked and any attempts on his life would result in the attacker's very messy death.

"So tell me," I said to the prince's stiff back. "What are you going to do with us?"

"I have not decided. Yet," came the frosty reply.

"I think someone's still pissed, white boy."

Winch snorted. "I think he needs more fiber."

We were poking the bear, but at that point I didn't care much.

Precious time was ticking away, but I needed more intel.

The hallway continued for another hundred steps before opening into a spacious, square room. Its black granite walls had been planed smooth and lit by more crystals; the effect was even harsher than in the hallway. Along the opposite wall at eyeball height was a thin rectangular window running horizontally for five feet and inset with thick glass.

What surprised me most was how much the room looked like a subterranean lounge, a place for office workers to gather at lunchtime. Along one granite wall was a kitchenette, complete with a microwave and an Amana side-by-side stainless steel refrigerator. The opposite wall had an enormous flat-screen television with a satellite hook-up. In the center of the room stood an oak table roughly six feet long with two plush office chairs on each end in front of identical Apple laptops. The power cords to each laptop ran across the table and met in the middle, where they plugged into a black, rectangular box. Scattered all over the table were empty soda cans and potato chip bags as well as rainbow remnants of peanut M&Ms.

A tall, thin man—young, perhaps twenty-five—sat at the laptop farthest from us, eyes glued to the screen. A *man*, not a Faë. Long, wavy, black hair fell to his shoulders and was gelled carefully into place; it was obviously a point of pride. Dressed in a black Oxford button down, black jeans and black biker boots, the guy was aiming for either Goth or rock star.

The prince strode to the opposite end of the table and waited for the man to notice him. A minute passed. Then two. No good; the thin man was too absorbed, too focused on the computer.

"David," the prince said quietly.

The thin man, David, practically flew out of his seat. "Sir, so good to see you!"

"David, this is Agent Hakala, Agent Alsate, and Agent Pennington of the Bureau of Supernatural Investigation." The prince gestured for us to come forward. "Agents, this is David Alexander, one of the linchpins of my plan."

David's face lit up like a lantern. "Awesome!" He raced around the table to shake our hands. When we didn't grasp his, it didn't faze him one bit. "Great to meet you guys. Mr. Ephelor told me all about you. Wicked stuff, dudes!"

I saw Canton's hands clench and knew he wanted to shove his fists down the thin man's throat. He was clearly a willing participant in whatever the prince had cooked up. That made him a traitor to humankind. My own hands were itching to pull his spine out through his nose.

Ephelor gestured languidly. "David, please show these good people the project we are working on."

I didn't think it was possible, but David's smile grew even wider. "Yessir. That would be totally wicked awesome! Come this way, folks." Without further ado, he led us to the strange, narrow window on the other side of the room. Peering through, we saw a cavern the size of an airplane hangar lit by more crystals, rough-hewn and craggy. A silvery cauldron that could have cooked a horse sat in the center, under a brass hood leading to a stovepipe chimney that extended into the ceiling. A mind-warping Celtic knot ran around the exterior of the cauldron in a spiral. The cauldron was filled with a gray, powdery substance that roiled and swirled under its own power.

"That is the heart of the matter," David exclaimed with pride.

"I take it that isn't dust," Winch drawled.

The thin man let out a short bark of laughter. "No, the cauldron contains nanites."

Ladies and gentleman, prepare for an emergency landing.

"What do you mean?" I blurted, alarmed.

"Well, white boy, I think he's telling us that the big pot over there is chock full of micromachines ready to do nasty business."

Wonderful. All my fears, confirmed.

David beamed. "Exactly, Mr. Alsate."

"They work?"

"Perfectly."

"How?"

"Let me show you," David said, practically wringing his hands with glee. Striding over to his laptop, he tapped a few keys and an image appeared on the screen. It looked like the spiderbot, but with gossamer wings like a dragonfly's. "This is it, the Alexandrian mite."

Was that a little bit of puke at the back of my throat?

I'd spaced out for a second, taken aback by the reality of the situation. I'd expected something a little more ... obvious. The Great Hunt, or a tornado of magic sweeping the land, not a mechanical bug the size of a red blood cell. Nanites were machines designed to perform simple tasks, like theoretically breaking down oil into its component hydrogen and carbon atoms to clean up oil spills. What would the Sidhe need to break down?

Oh, crap.

"Iron," Canton growled. "You're going to use them to tear apart iron."

"Yes, Agent Alsate," David said with pride. "They were created to render iron into dust."

"How is that possible?" asked Winch. "Not even the Bureau is close to creating something like *this*!"

Canton rubbed his face. "Magic, hon. That's the Sidhe contribution. This couldn't work without magic. We are *at least* a good thirty years from even coming close to 'something like this.' No, David here, he wanted to make nanites and the Sidhe needed someone to create them, so it was a deal made in hell."

"Now, Agent Alsate—" the thin man began.

"*Shut up!*" the Apache hissed, fists clenched in fury. "Not another goddamned word."

Ephelor strode forward before my friend could twist David inside out. "Enough of that," he commanded, power radiating from his voice. The thin scientist backed up and stood slightly behind the prince, using him as a shield.

"Easy, buddy," I soothed, clapping a hand on Canton's shoulder. "The real question is, how the heck would the Sidhe even *know* about nanites and find someone capable of creating one."

"We have been in this, our former world, for a little over two years now, Kalevi Hakala," said the prince. "Thanks to your Internet and a few humans we drained of knowledge, I was able to conceive of this plan and bring it to fruition." He spoke with the certainty of inevitability.

Wonderful.

"Although Mr. Ephelor and his people set this place up and provided me with every luxury," David interjected, "it was human science, not just Sidhe, that allowed me to create the nanites. Sidhe magic is powerful, but we needed a softer, human touch to complete the fabrication process and power issues. No offense, sir."

The prince smiled at the scientist as if he were an amusing yet mentally deficient house pet. "None taken, David."

Moving to the laptop while keeping a wary eye on Canton, the thin scientist pointed to some readouts next to the image of the nano. "You see here, that's human science that created the bugs, but we had a powering problem—how to keep the little suckers going for an extended period of time. Thanks to Mr. Ephelor and Sidhe magic, a spell was devised that allowed the nanos to become solar-powered. The spell itself is solar-powered as well. You see here and here." His finger traced two legs, one on either side of the crystalline abdomen. "These legs are actually micro-diamond composite magically manufactured by the Sidhe en masse. See the fanciful micro-etching? Those are the spell Shapes that power and guide the nano-machines. As long as the critters stay in sunlight, they can run forever."

Toward the end of his explanation, David had started to become more and more excited, forgetting that we agents wanted to do him some serious dirt. Had he looked up and seen our faces, he would have run screaming from the room. Ephelor, however, was watching us with a small smile curling his lips, radiating amusement.

"How many nanites are you planning to release?" I asked, dreading the answer.

"The final phase of testing has already been carried out," David answered, eyes glued to the laptop. "When the time is right, the hood above the cauldron will be activated, pulling the nanites up the chimney pipe and ejecting them into the atmosphere from the top of the lighthouse. The cauldron will then reproduce the nanites within a matter of minutes. That is yet another valuable Sidhe contribution—

an ancient artifact that can reproduce any non-organic material. We can, in a matter of a few hours, replicate enough nanites to completely render to dust all the iron and steel on the face of the planet. That process will be completed in an estimated two weeks."

Two weeks? My imagination went into overdrive as I pictured cars falling apart into so much fine powder, buildings crashing to the ground, starting fires that firefighters couldn't control because their trucks were just so much powder. Power plants collapsing, nuclear plants melting down, a series of radioactive disasters annihilating millions. Whole cities would become manifestations of hell as firestorms raged uncontrolled, spewing poisonous smoke into the sky, and millions more died from the lack of food, rioting and plain old savage mob mentality. I saw visions of wandering bands of marauders scouring the countryside, using whatever aluminum or wooden weapons were available to them because modern weaponry had disappeared, falling into drifts of metallic snow. There would be cannibalism and old rivalries and grudges would erupt into wars because no civil authority would be around to stave off the violence. Warlords, holding power with the sheer force of will and charisma, would rise like weeds from the rubble of civilization and use cruel and harsh methods to secure power, hoarding what food they could grow and scrounge. Winter would come with fingers of burning ice as poison snow killed what frigid cold did not. Plagues would kill millions more, along with sickness from malnutrition and poor sanitary conditions—cholera, typhus ...

Those visions of horror and madness tumbled across the vista of my mind and I knew deep in my bones that those scenes didn't approach the horror of what would come. Everything I had fought for, everything legions of agents had died for, would come to an end. The Supernaturals would inherit the earth, because there would be no Bureau with ultra-modern weapons to combat them and magic would not be enough.

Something the evil scientist geek said brought me back to the present. "You said 'final phase of testing'? Those ships that went missing in L.A. Harbor—that was you, wasn't it."

The thin man nodded, looking up from the laptop and smiling happily. "Yes, Agent Hakala. One cauldron full of nanites destroyed them in less than fifteen minutes."

Holy crap!

David must have seen the bloody murder in my eyes because he hightailed it behind his boss, his face a mask of fear. I almost decided to go for the man, but then I noticed the black knights who had apparently followed us into the room and until then lurked unseen in the shadows. A dozen red-crystal swords hovered in the air less than two feet away from our tender bods. The scene remained frozen like that for a long, fear-drenched moment.

"Am I interrupting?"

I nearly jumped out of my skin, but those crystal swords didn't waver a millimeter. Maybe the Sidhe were immune to surprise. The question had come from a medium-sized, slightly portly man with thinning blond hair and bright blue eyes. He stood next to what had been a concealed door next to the fridge, smiling benignly at us and dressed in a dove gray suit—Armani, I guessed.

My jaw hit my chest and bounced back. I knew that man, had seen his picture a hundred times on magazines and in television. He'd shaken hands with Presidents and captains of industry and bedded starlets by the dozen. The last time I read about him was in an obituary.

"You're supposed to be dead," I breathed.

The pudgy man smiled even wider and I wanted to rip that hateful grin out by the roots. "And you are still alive, Agent Hakala of the Bureau of Supernatural Investigation." He laughed at my surprised look. "Oh yes, I know who you are. My glorious Sidhe benefactors have supplied me with all the intelligence of your recent activities. You have been under surveillance for a long, long time now."

"White boy, is that who I think it is?" Canton sounded as if he were talking through a throat full of vomit. Apparently he recognized the man as well.

"It all makes sense now," I said tonelessly.

Winch wasn't in the mood to wait for us to reveal the mystery. She gave us each a hard poke and said, "Spill, you two."

My mouth felt full of sand. "Bruno Jeppeson, formerly the third wealthiest man in America and founder of Jeppeson Avionics, Jeppeson Cybernetic Systems, etc, etc."

From her harsh, indrawn breath, she recognized the name, if not the face. Not surprising, considering that much of the computer tech the Bureau used was from Jeppeson Labs.

As a young man in 1975, Bruno Jeppeson invested in a little known company with friends Paul Allen and William Gates. That company later became Microsoft. After splitting with the company in the early '80s, he used his newly accumulated wealth to form Jeppeson Computer Systems, purportedly stealing many of Gate's and Allen's ideas. His wealth exploded exponentially from there.

A little less than two years ago his private jet had disappeared off the coast of Florida. The wreckage was never found.

"I thought you had died."

His flat blue eyes were devoid of humanity. "I read that somewhere."

There it was, underneath his perfect diction—the cold, remorseless tones of a soulless killer. I wanted to leap, to tear and rend and bite and claw until he was reduced to a few chunks of quivering red flesh.

But first things first.

"So let me guess ... you were contacted by the Sidhe and they showed you a world of magic you never dreamed of and the possibility for even greater power and wealth? It was you who hooked them up with this skinny skink here. One of your employees, perhaps? A genius you hired for your computer company, someone gullible enough and self-centered enough to do the job. What did the Sidhe offer you that you didn't already have, Jeppeson? You're richer than Saudi Arabia and more influential than the President. What did they offer you to betray your species?"

Ephelor's silvery peals of amusement spent echoed off the walls.

Bastard.

"His species," the prince sneered. "What a pathetic little joke. Thanks to the pervasiveness of the media, finding a possible accomplice was quite simple. Imagine my surprise when I approached him and found out that he was dying of prostate cancer with only months left to live. There was nothing 'his species' could do to aid him. Healing him took only one spell and with that, he was *mine*. With his help I secured the specialists I needed to complete the nanite fabrication process. Thanks to his vast wealth, we have had all the resources we needed to implement my plan.

"I have been the spider hidden in the web," he droned on, "the puppet master behind the scenes, manipulating events, controlling the humans on this island and the surrounding beasts. It was sheer good fortune that you stumbled onto this plan and thus became my prisoner. Your capture and death will increase my standing in the Unseelie Court tenfold."

At my look of surprise, the Faë prince's smile grew wider and he approached, his piss-yellow eyes appearing to grow to twice their size. I felt his will caress mine, causing Leena to stir like a beast in restless slumber. "Yes, Agent Hakala, you are known to the Sidhe. You are the boogeyman every creature you call a Supernatural fears. Faë children are told that if they do not mind their manners, the dreaded, evil human called Hakala will come for them."

His voice dropped to a whisper. "Faërie, Tír na nóg, Mag Mell, the World Under, or whatever name you wish to give it, is our home now. The Unseelie Court rules the Winter Gardens while the Seelie Court reigns over the Summer Hills, but know this, Kalevi Hakala … *we* were here first and we shall come to rule this place once again."

"You'll inherit a burned and tattered place with poisonous air. You will rule over a graveyard." I layered on the contempt and anger. "But was it worth it? Trading health for the good of mankind? You sold your soul to the devil."

Jeppeson smiled like a shark spotting a plump little seal. "Yes, I sold my soul and I will rule what humans are left and have a seat at the Sidhe table. Yes, Agent Hakala, it was worth it." He gazed with adoring eyes at the Prince, who indulged him with a patronizing smile.

"Of course you will, Bruno," he said. To me, "Humans are limited by time and weak magic. While the world will suffer, it will not die.

We have time enough to make the world a paradise again."

"It's going to happen in the morning, isn't it? As soon as the sun clears the horizon." Canton sounded like I felt, stretched to the snapping point.

"Ah, the native speaks."

"Answer the damn question!"

"Yes, Alsate, when the sun clears the horizon."

The thread of the conversation was beyond me. I was too busy dealing with the enormity, the complexity, of the Sidhe plan, to form the necessary mental connections. For the first time in a long while, I was lost while others steadily navigated.

Canton, of course, read all that in my face. "The nanites, Kal. They are going to be released as soon as the sun comes up to power them. They start the final phase of their plan in the morning. That's why he was willing to host this charade. He'd already won."

My eyes met Winch's. If my guess was right, Canton was correct: Ephelor had won. Unless we could do something drastic and do it soon.

Mouth dry, I looked the prince dead in the eye and said, "I'd like to go back to my hole now."

Chapter Twenty

With Friends Like These ...

We were once again in the oubliette, escorted there by black-glass knights whose faces were like alabaster—pale and hard, devoid of human emotion.

In that hole lit by an azure crystal, I pulled up my t-shirt, revealing a square of gauze running vertically up my waist. Peeling it back, I revealed a two-inch incision closed with stitches. The wound was dry and scabby, clear of infection.

"What did you do, Kal?" Canton's eyes were wide.

I tugged on one of the knots. The flesh pulled outward before the knot gave way as it was designed to do and the thread came free. One down, eight more to go. I was sure glad that the beating I'd taken earlier hadn't popped the stitches. Maybe things were going my way for once.

"Insurance plan. Gimme a hand, please?"

Winch gently pushed her boyfriend out of the way. "Allow me." She knelt at my side and began to unknot the stitches, one by one. It hurt more than expected; the dried blood was almost as tenacious as Super Glue.

"What kind of insurance plan?"

"I had Ilena plant something inside me just in case. Ow!"

"Baby," Winch muttered.

The Apache stared, fascinated, as the seventh stitch was removed. Soon nine pieces of pale thread lay discarded on the floor and I placed a hand to either side of the cut. "Okay, Winch, when I hold the flesh apart, reach in and pull out what's inside. Should be easy to find." It struck me that this was the second time in as many hours that I was having one of the weirdest conversations of my life.

One breath, then two ... pull!

A ripping sound as the scab broke and blood flowed. It hurt a hell of a lot more than I thought it would—sharp and hot, a deep fiery blade of pain that brought vomit to my throat.

From its sheath of subcutaneous fat, the end of a small cylinder popped out, bloody and slick. Winch plucked it free and held it up to the light. Black plastic, about two and a half inches long.

"You realize you could have tied thread to that and then swallowed it," Canton remarked, eyes wide. "Then tied the thread around a molar. That way you could of pulled it up at any time."

"I thought of that, but it was too gross."

"*That* was too gross?"

I nodded.

"So you pulled a Bourne Identity and had Ilena cut into your side, put that in and stitch you back up?"

"Yeah."

"And that ain't gross?"

"No, not really."

Canton turned his back, muttering about fools and just desserts.

"You gonna use that now, boss?" Winch asked.

I shook my head. "Too early. We need to get out of here first, delay Ephie's plans."

"And how do we get out of here?"

"I'm working on it."

I continued to work on it for the next couple of hours, racking my brain until the harsh blue light that painted us in corpse colors moved, then disappeared as the trap door was opened. "Why is it I have the feeling I am expected?" a woman's voice asked.

Uloeth.

I could have kissed her, but I knew that if I did, Jeanie—wherever she happened to be—would somehow psychically know; then, if I survived, she would kill me. Slowly. Magicians make scary girlfriends.

My grin was wide enough to hurt. "I was hoping, but wasn't sure."

"Can you stop my cousin?" the princess asked, giving me a long, impassive look.

I shook my head. "Not alone."

"Then why should I let you out?"

She refused to be melted by my hundred-watt smile. I was going to have to practice more. "Because I'm not alone."

"And he has an … angle," Winch said dryly. "He always does."

Uloeth looked less than impressed. "This … angle, will it work?"

"If we can get out of this hole … probably."

"Dangerous?"

"We'll all probably die."

She smiled, and on a Faë woman, a smile is a glorious thing. "Then I should assist you." As quickly as it appeared, the smile vanished. "All of you look into my eyes."

I nodded. At that point, we had no choice but to trust her; our options were limited.

Uloeth's purple eyes grew large and I felt a gentle pressure like passing through dry air into humid—a push that radiated along all the surface of my skin. For a brief moment, my eyes stung as if grit had slapped my corneas; then my vision cleared.

Whoa.

We stood in a cavern hewn roughly into granite. No oubliette, no trap door with an inset blue light crystal. In front of us stood Uloeth and she looked … different. Her clothes, while still fine, no long shone as if lit from within. While her features were still Sidhe perfection, they had an alien symmetry that spoke to my primitive hindbrain, whispering dark and terrible things. It wasn't that she looked evil or dangerous; she just looked *wrong*. Her cheekbones were high and protruding, leaving hollows, and her eyes, while still the purple of twilight, had cat-like slits for pupils and the whites were lightly tinged with blue. On her hands were creamy leather gloves.

Four black-glass knights stood behind her, red swords sheathed. All were just as perfect but subtly alien, exemplifying the same wrongness that put my teeth on edge. Their armor no longer bore spikes or blades or mind-bending whorls and loops, only softly glowing runes.

"This ain't real, is it, Kal?" The Apache sounded as freaked out as I felt.

"All you have beheld has been illusion," Uloeth said quietly, her gentle smile revealing stark-white, pointed teeth. "We Sidhe are masters of trickery and have been using such methods since we first encountered mankind millennia ago."

I tried to keep my head from spinning off my shoulders. "Damn, this explains a lot."

"Indeed, Kalevi Hakala." From under her toga-like wrap, she drew out Winch's Sig, an incongruous sight in her small hands. "I have seen these on your television shows. They hurl lead projectiles, but we Sidhe heal quickly from such things, even if shot in the head. I hope you have brought more puissant devices."

"They don't shoot lead," I replied with a smile. "The bullets are iron."

Her finely arched eyebrows tried to make the acquaintance with the back of her head as she spun around.

Pffft, pffft, pffft. Three shots from the silenced weapon, center mass on the black knight on the left. His breastplate shattered into a thousand pieces, which hit the floor the same time his body did. He died without a sound.

"That one was *not* one of mine," she said grimly, holding the weapon out to us. Winch took it carefully. "He was sent here by my cousin as a watchdog of sorts."

If the other black knights were nonplussed at the act, they gave no sign. The Sidhe warriors remained still and inexpressive as statues.

"Xaralor, the packages." The princess gestured toward the entrance to the cavern. One of the black knights trotted out and returned with two leather sacks, which he placed at our feet.

"These may be of assistance," the princess said, not quite hiding a smile.

She didn't have to tell me twice. I broke the bindings to the mouth of one of the sacks and found our equipment, including armor.

"Oh, sweet Jesus," breathed Canton in relief. "Now we can show these mothers how we do things downtown!"

Winch gave him a fond look. "That's what I love about you, hon, your eloquence."

He tossed her a lascivious grin. "I thought you loved my—"

"Finish that sentence," I cut in. "And I will kill you."

Their joy in each other was silent but eloquent. I, too, smiled as I strapped on my armor.

"From all that Ephelor learned of the Bureau, including the information gleaned from Agent Mace's mind, it was assumed that it had no clue as to what is occurring here. You three have discovered much in a short period of time." Uloeth might have been an anthropologist discussing tribal customs. For all I knew, she was. Her subject: The Human Tribe.

"We ain't your normal agents." Canton's face did not register any humor now that armor covered him once more. He was fortifying his resolve, bringing his game face out for the big show. "We survived some weird stuff, lady, been through the grinder and made it out whole." He held up his hand with the missing finger and grinned. "Well, almost." He added, "We ain't just agents anymore—"

"We're family," Winch finished.

Hmm. Never thought of it that way, but now that she said it, I knew she was right. It *felt* right. And of course, that scared the bejesus out of me. For over ten years I had steeled myself against sentiment. Sure, I felt camaraderie, fellowship and a sort of casual friendship, but nothing deeper. There could be nothing deeper because that would invite caring, and caring would lead to weakness, the kind of weakness that would place others before The Mission. For me, The Mission eclipsed all; it ruled my life with razor hands and bitter wisdom. The Mission: to kill every Supernatural that threatened mankind until I found a way to destroy Iku-Turso and avenge my sister.

The Mission had ended with Iku-Turso banished to the World Under, where other things—terrible, mightier things—waited for it, waited for a vengeance long overdue. I was fairly certain Iku-Turso was not enjoying his homecoming and that was just fine with me.

I had been wrestling with the question of what to do with my life. I could stay in the Bureau or join the Straights. Perhaps Jeanie and I were truly meant to be a couple. A normal couple. Who knows? We could have kids and watch them grow, become old and gray together, feel the crystal touch of arthritis steal into much abused joints. Then I'd tell tall tales to my grandkids and watch them grow as well before dying in my bed surrounded by descendants.

Or I renew my contract with the Bureau until I met the Supernatural that finally punched my ticket. Perhaps survive long enough that they cashiered me out of active duty once I could no longer keep up with the next generation of agents. Become a recruiter, perhaps? Agent Emeritus who provided fresh meat for the grinder that was the never-ending war against the Supernatural world.

Holstering my .45, I pondered that word Winch had used: *family*. Against my better judgment, I had made those connections, had let others deeper into my heart than mere camaraderie allowed. Canton had become my best friend—a brother in arms as well as a brother of my heart. Winch had snuck in and had taken residence in the void left by my sister, that cold spot where nothing had dwelled for twenty years. While in some ways they made me stronger, I also knew that if push came to shove, they would weaken me as well.

But then it came to me that I didn't care about weakness, about guarding my heart and soul against others. I felt better than I had in a long, long time. I finally had something besides killing Supernaturals to look forward to.

"Yeah," I agreed as I checked the contents of my Bat Belt. "We're family."

Uloeth nodded absently as if processing a relevant bit of data for her cross-cultural files.

From my Bat Belt, I handed a pair of small black cubes the size of Vegas dice to both Winch and Canton. "Take these."

The Apache studied the matte-black cubes. "Missile beacons?"

"Three Harvester drones are on the way, each with a pair of Burrowers."

His smile brightened the cavern. "Just like at Williamsburg when we called in the air strike on the hydra."

"Right." A hydra had been squatting in Cobham Bay and had been coming ashore to snack on vacationers at the Queensmill Resort, ruining several peoples' party plans. Think of a big, flightless dragon with multiple heads. Every time you chopped one off, two grew back. Its natural armor could stop RPG fire cold. Six AGM-65 Maverick L missles had been required to turn it into hydra cutlets. It was one of the few times on an op when we were able to sit back and relax, call in an airstrike and let the Air Force do all the heavy lifting. My kind of mission. "Those drones will be here an hour after sunrise."

And there went the smile. "Oh, crap."

"Yeah, 'oh crap' is right." The missiles would arrive too late to destroy the first release of nanites into the atmosphere.

Back in 2002, POTUS had requested from the Bureau the manufacture of a new kind of missile that would be more effective than the standard Bunker Buster. This *request*, of course, was in direct violation of the Nuremburg Treaty (secret talks held during the Nuremburg Trials to prevent the use of magic to prosecute a war), but what POTUS wants, POTUS gets. The result: six lightweight missiles that could phase out of reality when approaching solid matter. Once they phased, a secondary protocol was enabled. That protocol would allow the missile to re-phase into our reality once a large enough open space was detected and then detonate. If no space was found in a period of fifteen seconds, the missile would deactivate and stay phased so there would be no reintegration with our normal space-time. If for some reason the missile did reintegrate inside solid rock or water ... well, let's just say the resultant release of energy from two sets of matter trying to occupy the same space at the same time would be more than a little intense.

Think Hiroshima. Only worse … much worse. In the end, POTUS had his missiles, but the cost in diamonds and production was almost prohibitively high and before they could be used in the Middle East, the Chinese got wind of the project and quietly raised a fuss. They claimed that what was good for the goose was good for the Peking Duck and threatened to develop and stockpile their own arsenal of magical weapons. Soon after, Israel, Egypt and North Korea were in the mix. The cat was out of the bag and the entire project was scrapped. The U.S. paid some major reparations for their part in breaking the treaty.

No one knows who leaked the information, or if the Chinese managed to break Bureau or NSA encryption. I have my suspicions, but, for the sake of fairness, I will keep my trap shut.

"So, white boy, we have to delay the release of the nanites for at least an hour."

Uloeth stepped forward. "You must do more than that. Your missiles will not be able to destroy the Cauldron of Cian. Only magic may do it harm."

I fingered the tube that had been buried in my side. "Well then, let's go back to the Cauldron room and see what we can do about that."

"Do not wear those coats of yours," the princess said, frowning as I was readying my Faraday coat. "I understand the efficacy of silver, but if Ephelor were to use the Wand of Lugh against us, it would destroy you as it did your magician."

We dropped our coats.

"How can a wand do so much?" Winch asked, double-checking her gear.

For the first time the princess looked troubled. "It takes a Sidhe Master Artificer five hundred of your years to make such an item and they are greatly prized by my people. However, they are scarce, for the only creatures who are able to repeatedly channel that much magic are the púca, and the Sidhe envy their power. That does not mean a Sidhe *cannot* use it; it simply means there are drastic consequences if it is used by anyone other than a púca."

Winch nodded. "If he does use it?"

"Then we are dead. The wands are, as you would say, magical batteries of the highest order. If he does not, I may be able to use some small magics to aid us."

"Damned if we do, damned if we don't. How do you know about batteries?"

Uloeth smiled. "The Learning Channel. We Sidhe are fascinated by human theater. I hope someday to learn if Stephan and Elena manage to overcome their troubles and live together happily and in peace."

"You watch *The Vampire Diaries*?"

"Yes, it is my favorite television show."

Okay, *third* weirdest conversation. *Ever.*

"I will lead you out," the princess continued. "You have seen only illusion and would never find your way."

I nodded and we followed, the three remaining black glass knights trailing behind. The dressed stone hallways were nothing but irregularly carved tunnels some seven feet high. So much for Ephelor's efforts to cow us with the majesty of Faë craftsmanship.

"Is this what you see all the time?" I whispered.

"No," she replied. "We see both the reality that is and the reality we wish were there."

Interesting.

Eventually we came to a circular cavern the size of a football field, better crafted than the hallway. The ceiling vaulted above our heads and the smooth floor sloped gently down to form a bowl, where multi-colored cushions were spread in a circle. Dotting the walls were tunnels, both large and small. I figured that the smaller tunnels were for the misshapen servants—the little people of the Faë—while the larger were for the Sidhe.

"Where are all the guards?" Canton whispered.

Good question. I waited for the princess to answer.

"There are not many. When you were first captured, my cousin had the whole of his troops with him. I do not know where the guards are at this moment. As for the rest of the Unseelie Court that traveled here with Ephelor, they are asleep."

As we passed the cushions, I pulled out one of the tracking cubes and twisted. The two halves rotated in opposite directions until there was a soft *click*. It was activated. I placed it under a cushion.

"What will that do?" Uloeth asked.

I gave her a twisted smile. "Guide a missile here. Nice open space for it to appear."

"How large are these weapons?"

"Rather small for missiles, only five feet long and ten inches wide."

"That doesn't sound dangerous."

Canton suppressed a laugh. "It may be small, but it packs a mean punch. You don't want to be in the same city when these suckers pop off."

Uloeth smiled grimly and soldiered on.

From the big cavern she chose the middle of three large tunnels opposite from where we had entered.

"I have never traveled this hallway," Uloeth said. "It is forbidden."

"What about the other hallways?" asked Winch, shoulder to shoulder with the Faë princess. The two seemed to have formed a bond, perhaps as the only female opponents to Ephelor's plans.

"Bedrooms, dining halls and common rooms where we entertain and watch television."

"Really? You folks watch way too much TV."

"Yes, but it is certain I will be forced to return to Faërie and I will miss Alec Baldwin hosting *Saturday Night Live*."

The rest of this bizarre conversation would have to wait. The archway to the computer room had come into view, allowing us to see for ourselves what had happened to the guards.

A dozen black-glass knights with swords drawn stood in the center of the room, occupying the space where the table and laptops had been. From behind Uloeth's knights, we heard the tramp of boots. We were surrounded.

"Give up, Kalevi Hakala, and I will not harm you."

Although I couldn't see the prince, I heard his hateful voice.

Oh crap.

Chapter Twenty-One

...Who Needs Enemies?

"I don't think so, Ephie; you'd just kill my friends." My tone was light, carefree, but my guts were boiling with acid.

"You know what they say about eggs and omelets."

That line always pissed me off. "How about we try something new?" I pulled my silver Zippo lighter from the Bat Belt.

"What would that be, Kalevi Hakala?" He sounded genuinely curious.

I drew forth the tube that had been implanted in my side. "How 'bout *you* give up and we call it a day?"

"What do you have in your hand, Hakala?"

Damn. I flicked the wheel on the lighter. A few sparks, but no flame. Sweat broke out on my brow. "Need me a cigarette, Ephie. I always smoke when I negotiate a surrender."

There came a shuffling as the prince pushed through his cadre of black-glass knights. He was dressed in his own set of armor, dark, blood-red with glowing crimson runes. His eyes were a brilliant yellow that shone against the pale flesh of his face. Now that the illusion that softened his features was gone, he looked crueler, more malicious than before. "I smell ... old magic, *wild* magic." His carious eyes burned with liquid malice. "Stop what you are doing."

"Canton, Winch, do it," I urged. *Flick.* More sparks, no flame. Without hesitation, the two lovers fired.

Click. Click.

Wonderful.

"Uh, so how about you go your way and we go ours?" *Flick.* Sparks and no flame. I was starting to wonder if the damn thing was out of fluid. Then the light bulb flashed above my head and I felt like three kinds of quality idiot. Whatever spell Ephelor had used to disable our weapons also worked on the lighter. I had seen something like this before in 1943, a spell gem given to me by a magician named Solange.

The grin on the prince's face confirmed my suspicions.

"Canton," I whispered.

"Yeah, Kal?"

"Give me your half of the acid."

Without looking, the Apache reached into his belt and handed me a cylinder.

Ephelor wasn't waiting around to see what I had in mind. "Kill them," he snarled to his knights.

"I need time!"

Canton and Winch drew their knives and stamped hard on their heels. Two-and-a-half inch steel blades sprang from the toes of their boots. It was an old KGB hidden-weapons trick made famous in *From Russia With Love.* I had been amazed when Special Branch had been able to cobble the contraptions together so quickly. You pay the most, you get the best.

The rending crystal clash of red swords filled the tunnel behind us as Uloeth's knights engaged their counterparts while my teammates reached to their belt buckles and pulled out what had been magnetically attached there.

Two razor steel shuriken flew through the air to hit two of the charging black knights in their faces, dropping them instantly in a spray of blood. Their quick deaths temporarily halted the rush of knights as two more shuriken flew through the air. Runes flashed as the guards' vambraces deflected the missiles. Two more shuriken produced identically disappointing results.

Canton smiled as he considered his Bowie and Winch brandished her two Recon Tantos combat knives. "Ready, love?" he asked.

Her smile was achingly beautiful. "Let's do this."

"Wait!" I cried.

The two held themselves in check, awaiting further commands, as the black-glass knights regrouped. I looked to the princess. "Can you help?"

Uloeth spared a glance from where her knights were tangling ass and bared her teeth, lavender eyes narrowing in concentration. Next to me, Canton and Winch stiffened, muscles bunching and writhing like snakes beneath their skins. Sweat ran down their faces and necks in rivulets. As they began to tremble, they grinned at each other in amazement.

"Go!" commanded the princess. "The spell will not last long."

Roaring, they flew toward the knights in graceful arcs, arms flashing with razor-edged death.

Over the din of combat I heard, and felt, the hum of a powerful engine. I swore under my breath as I realized that the sun must have risen. I was almost out of time. The blower was starting up, ready to fling a deadly payload into the atmosphere.

Dropping the small cylinder that Winch had removed from my side, I popped the caps on the binary acid containers and poured a small dose of liquid from each on the little cylinder. The mixture reacted in an instant and the thin polymer dissolved, exposing and eating the yellowish paper within.

"Joshua," I began, "your people, your city, are in need."

I prayed fervently that the good people of San Francisco had been paying attention to the morning news.

Canton spun and ducked with inhuman grace. Wherever his Bowie landed, runes flashed out of existence and Sidhe warriors died. He seemed to know where the knights would strike and dodged each blow with ease. His foot flashed forward and buried a small toe-blade into an unprotected knee. The Sidhe warrior bellowed mournfully as he died.

Meanwhile, Winch was a creature made of fluid, moving so quickly that the naked eye had trouble tracking her as she slid between her opponents' swords, slashing and stabbing at unprotected flesh that turned black and necrotic in an instant.

The hum of the blower grew louder. *Damn.*

Suddenly, it was far too cold in the tunnel. I watched my breath plume in the air and sighed with relief.

"Hakala." The voice resonated dread power. "What is your wish?"

Looming over me was Joshua Norton, eyes sparking with grim hatred and fury.

The witches had done their job.

I had given Trisol and her cadre of half-trained magicians she'd recruited the spell Shape Ilena had drawn, one that had contained a very specific, albeit low-power spell: illusion. The spell created a vision of Joshua Norton in all his regalia. The illusory ghost could appear to walk, jump, skip or hop, and most importantly … speak.

The previous evening, just before the sun touched the Pacific, at four different locations around the city in front of crowds of people, the witches cast their spells. A translucent image of Joshua Norton, Emperor of the United States and Defender of Mexico, burst forth in a shower of sparks and held its arms high—a figure both ridiculous and majestic.

"Citizens of my mighty empire," roared the illusory monarch, "know that in these troubled times, I, Joshua Abraham Norton the First, your right and true liege, have come to you with a message. In this dark age, where rich financiers and captains of industry take advantage of common citizenry, know that I, your Emperor, am here to safeguard your welfare. I have continually watched over this city I love so much with the utmost fabric of my being, this city which has sheltered and loved me in turn and I will NOT let the evils of greedy men consume its soul.

"I am here, good and loving citizens, to inform you that you are cared for and will be protected. Even though the battle takes me to the heights of Heaven or the fabled depths of Perdition, I shall be the shield that protects this city.

"So say I, Joshua Abraham Norton the First, your true and rightful liege. Farewell."

At all locations the image of Joshua Norton faded away. Every person with a cellphone camera had to be taking pictures and recording the events.

Of course the various videos went viral, causing a YouTube overload. As early as they could manage, radio, television, and newspapers hammered the populace with taglines such as "Mad Monarch Materializes," and called every psychic and psychic wannabe in the United States for their read on the event.

Best guess … the whole city, if not the country, was in an uproar.

And Joshua Norton became powerful again. The ghost himself had given me the idea when I had summoned him in the graveyard: "I, who am the Guardian, do not have the power to face this thing that comes. My people no longer believe in me; they do not remember and so I am diminished."

Belief and memory. Such simple concepts, but they were the key to Joshua's power, to his ability to act as Guardian of San Francisco. So I provided him with the sustenance he needed most: millions of media-addicted people who were willing, who needed, to believe in a power greater than themselves.

Joshua said we couldn't face this peril alone and the Bureau wouldn't help. Good thing I had him. And Uloeth. The first I managed to manufacture out of whole cloth; the second was plain old dumb luck.

Better lucky than good.

What hovered before me was the real deal. Joshua Norton's ghost, its full powers restored by the citizens of San Francisco and their cellphone cameras. Hardly able to meet his burning gaze, I pointed past the combatants, toward the viewing window. "In that cavern is a cauldron and chimney connected to a blower. Destroy them."

"I will grant you only one boon, Hakala, though it pains me to do so much for one who has failed me as you have. One boon: cauldron or chimney."

Screaming until my face went numb didn't seem like the

appropriate response, but I sure was tempted. I had to content myself with quick thinking. "The blower. Tear it apart."

Joshua Norton inclined his head and vanished.

Less than a second later the grinding shriek of tearing metal reverberated throughout the room, drowning out the chiming clash of battle. Ephelor screamed in rage while I drew my Bowie.

Time to play.

As I entered the melee, I saw Winch bury a knife in the eye of an unlucky black-glass knight, who screamed horribly as his skull slid off the blade. Canton blocked a slash with a NewTanium sheathed forearm and pounded his Bowie into a rune-less breastplate that gave way under the blow. Another knight gone; only three left. Canton's armor was tattered nearly to pieces, while Winch's seemed untouched.

Ephelor drew his sword and came straight for me, which didn't hurt my feelings none. Growling deep in my throat, I charged as well, ready to carve me up some Sidhe steaks.

He lunged … I felt a slight sting as the edge of his sword grazed my ear. I brushed it aside with an armored forearm and countered with a thrust, which he dodged easily.

I leaped back to regroup. Damn, he was *fast*! Faster than me, faster than Canton, faster than a body had a right to be and I knew then I couldn't beat him. He would carve me up into Kal chops.

Canton and Winch were still locking horns with what was left of the black-glass knights, so no help there. In fact, Winch seemed be moving at normal speeds and Canton's unearthly grace had vanished. Now they were merely deadly rather than liquid murder. They would have their hands full for the next few minutes.

The air filled with Ephelor's silvery peals of laughter as he whipped his sword from side to side in a display of casual arrogance. The rat bastard knew he had me. Served me right for bringing a knife to a swordfight.

"I shall enjoy slicing you into ribbons, agent Hakala. I no longer treasure you. Indeed, I would have brought you with me to Faërie as a favored pet, much like a lion on a leash. Alas, you no longer amuse me."

Alas? Who talked like that? While he graced me with his Faë wit and charm, I sheathed the Bowie and drew out a pair of cylinders from the Bat Belt. Just as he finished a bit of monologuing, I squirted two small streams of fluid.

Have to give him credit; Ephelor's reflexes were dead on. Almost all the fluid missed … except for a couple of small splatters, one on his sword hand and one on his chest. Both gauntlet and breastplate began to smoke. There came the sizzling sound of frying bacon. Ephelor shrieked and he dropped his sword, flinging the smoking gauntlet to the floor.

My turn.

The Bowie in one hand and the acid cylinders in the other, I rushed the prince, a fierce snarl on my face and cold fury in my heart. As I neared, Ephelor flung a small, dark object at me, which I batted aside without thinking.

The prince evaded my first lunge with ease, despite the pain from the smoking ruin of his right hand, and ran backwards until his back hit the fridge. Then he began to cackle as he used his good hand to rip away his ruined breastplate.

A low growl, just behind me.

Oh crap.

I turned as the beast lunged. A dog, a monstrous black dog the size of horse with dagger-long fangs came at me with the inevitability of sunrise, the bringer of very messy death. My Bowie rose, too slow … my whole body seemed to be encased in treacle that hampered movement. I stared into its dull red eyes and prepared to meet those agents I'd watched die over many long years. Black Shuck was coming for me.

A body encased in Kevlar and NewTanium flew into the beast's path, twin knives flashing. Almost casually, Shuck snapped Winch from the floor with one bite of its enormous jaws as she plunged both knives into its muzzle. It shook her like a terrier would a rat and flung her against the far wall with bone-shattering force.

Canton's howl was broken glass and aching denial that almost matched mine for sheer heartbreak. With a kind of absentminded contempt, the Apache ran his Bowie through his opponent's mouth and savagely yanked the blade free in a welter of blood. The black-glass knight, the last one left, fell in a clatter of obsidian.

Roaring, Canton leapt on the monster, plunging his Bowie deep, deep into the space between the black dog's shoulder blades. With a tortured-metal howl, Shuck shook his massive body, trying to fling the furious Native American off his back, but Canton held on, both hands wrapped around the hilt of his knife, legs clamped around its torso. The beast tried to snap at the man who caused it such pain, but Canton avoided each snap of those powerful jaws.

Tears streaming from my eyes, I sprang at the dog, throat closed tight against screams begging for release. Shuck's greasy red eyes focused on my approaching form, and it attacked.

Jaws bigger than a shark's closed around my waist, teeth momentarily blunted by my NewTanium armor; then my world was compressed into a belt of agony as the monster began to bite down *hard.*

Stomach, kidneys, and liver were shuffled around like so many playing cards in a visceral game of Three-card Monte as agonizing *pressure* from Shuck's jaws tried to squirt my insides out through my nose. The intense pressure drove the wind from my lungs and set black spots dancing before my eyes. I had maybe less than two seconds before something gave way and my guts filled with blood.

No breath to scream, none even to grunt, I aimed what was in my left hand at a glowing red eye and *squeezed.* Twin streams of fluid hit the baseball-sized orb, coating it thoroughly, then moved to the other.

When Shuck had held Winch in its grasp, I knew it was too late for her. Aware that the Bowie wouldn't be enough to kill the beast, I had readied the cylinders and waited for my shot. I just wished it hadn't been from inside the damn thing's mouth.

It took only a couple of drops from each cylinder to eat a softball-sized hole in wood and burn through two inches of brass. I had nearly emptied both, soaking the monster's head from eyeball to eyeball.

Shuck opened its mouth wide to bellow its agony and I fell out, hitting the ground gracelessly, shocking my lungs. While I writhed, Canton pulled the Bowie free and plunged it into the monster's side over and over between the ribs.

Most dogs would have run for the hills, yelping in agony, but not Shuck. It stood with front legs splayed wide, shaking its massive head. Acrid smoke billowed from its flesh, emitting sickening popping and sizzling sounds. Its shriek started as a subsonic thrum that vibrated the fillings in my teeth and grew to a bass roar that seemed to tear bloody chunks from my ears.

Canton's arm was a blur as he stabbed over and over again, pulping flesh, seeking the tough, fibrous muscle of the monster's heart while the acid ate through hair, dug into skin and destroyed bone, spitting drops of melted tissue. Shuck's roar became a mournful howl of animal despair as both eyeballs burned away, leaving fluid to gush forth as acid enlarged the cavities beneath.

How my friend held on while Shuck flung its head from side to side was anyone's guess, but held on he did, continuing to stab, stab, stab, the battered armor of his arm covered in monstrous gore. An almost inhuman rictus of hate was carved onto his normally inscrutable face.

Shuck stopped shuddering and stood there, head between its front legs, dripping foul fluid onto the floor where it sizzled, eating pits into the granite. A low moan that sounded of despair issued from its massive chest while Canton continued to stab and stab, searching for its heart. With a ragged cough, the beast finally collapsed, hitting the rock hard enough to send small shock waves my way.

From his perch atop the monster's back, Canton continued to thrust with his Bowie until Shuck began to dissipate, its form blurring into black smoke. All that was left was an onyx figurine of a dog lying cracked and broken on cold stone, the dark object Ephelor had thrown. Black Shuck had been magical artifact, not a true flesh and bone Supernatural.

I looked up to see the desolation in my friend's face while black blood slowly dripped from his Bowie.

We had won. But at what price?

Chapter Twenty-Two

Hard Won Truths

I spun, trusting Canton to take care of Winch, because my focus was on stopping the prince once and for all. When I leapt to my feet, my insides contracted so painfully that I immediately kissed the floor, writhing in pain.

In that brief moment, I had caught a glimpse of Ephelor. He lay propped against the stainless-steel fridge, hardly moving, his bare torso (the breastplate lay several feet away, a smoking ruin) a mass of liquid looking burns that steamed softly and leaked a clear, thick fluid. His eyes were slitted in pain and his breath came shallow and fast, almost as if he were panting.

I crawled toward him, clawing at the floor, while my guts rebelled, a tearing pain as if the tissues inside me had parted and snapped. Every inch I traveled was a lesson in agony, but I refused to be daunted. The prince lay so close. No way was I going to let him escape.

"More … resourceful … than I thought … Agent … Hakala," he panted, spit running from his lower lip.

"Should have … used that dog … earlier," I gritted through clenched teeth, sweat stinging my eyes. "You might … have won."

His laughter was a broken thing. "Last resort … hard to control … listens only to … the púca. And thanks to you … they are all … dead."

Almost there. My hand found the handle of my Bowie and drew it forth. He was mine.

"Stop." Uloeth stood above us both, glaring down with a haughty purple gaze.

"I've got to put an end to this," I moaned.

God, it hurt so much to breathe.

It came to me that I was slowly dying. Snarling, I cleared a few more inches, damned if my revenge would be thwarted.

She shook her head and placed a boot on my knife hand. I had no choice but to drop the Bowie. "It is ended. I will take him back to the Summer Hills where his fate will lie in the hands of my mother, the Queen." Her gaze softened and she knelt. "But I owe you this, Kalevi Hakala." A soft hand rested on my brow and a soothing wave of heat flushed through my body, eventually centering upon my torso. The pain faded, replaced by a delicious ecstasy.

"Thanks," I breathed, my muscles relaxing in relief.

"Sorry, princess, but that there boy is mine." Sand sliding along delicate gears, fingernails along a chalkboard. Canton's voice throbbed with equal parts misery and hate.

My eyes sprang open to see him looming above the three of us, bloody great knife held tight in one strong fist. I knew then that Winch was dead.

Throat tight, I tried to find the words. "Oh, damn man … I—"

"Not now, white boy." His dead, dark eyes were focused on the prince. *Talk to the hand, Kal.*

Uloeth shook her head violently enough to send her hair flying. "I cannot let you kill him, for he is now a captive of the Seelie Court." There was a soft footfall and the princess's last surviving knight halted to stand above the prince—sword drawn, but pointed at the ceiling. Not a threat, just a statement of how things stood.

Her face crumpled at the edges. "My grief is an echo of yours, brave Canton Alsate, but Ephelor must answer to Queen Miluwyn, my mother, for his crimes." Uloeth's violet eyes grew stormy. "And, good sir, the answer for such crimes will be dread."

Canton spat on the floor. "Why didn't he bring that wand battery thing? Coulda taken all of us on singlehandedly."

The answer came to me before Uloeth could reply. "Too arrogant," I said. "He was sure he had us with his knights and the spell neutralizing our firearms. Never thought he'd have to use it."

The prince gagged, a rattly, chuffing sound that evolved into bitter mirth that hurt to look at. More of that pale, thick fluid oozed from his chest. "Yes, my arrogance, Hakala, and it cost me dear. However, because of my stature in the Unseelie Court, I shall live in the Summer Hills rather than face a death of iron."

A slender hand landed flat on the center of the liquid mass of his chest, and his shriek bounced off the walls for a good fifteen seconds.

"Silence, vermin!" The princess snarled. "The Summer Hills are not for you! The Jade Grove will be your prison."

I sure the heck didn't know what the Jade Grove was, but from Ephelor's spasm of fear, it must have been nasty on a stick. As he began babbling, begging for mercy, my friend knelt and punched him one, two, three times in the face until he lay limp and bloody, features misshapen, shattered. A look from Uloeth kept her last black-glass knight from interfering.

"It is his right," she said, staring at the trembling Apache. "Poor recompense for the death of his love." Standing, Uloeth placed a slim hand on Canton's cheek. I could almost see the healing wave emanate from her body. The Apache sighed, a low, mournful sound of desolation that cut at my heart with daggers of sorrow.

"Inim, take the prince to the exit," Uloeth commanded the lone knight. "Anyone you see, instruct them, from me, to evacuate. I will assemble the rest."

We watched the knight gather up the battered prince in his arms and stride away. "What now, white boy?"

I checked my watch. "We have a little less than an hour."

"It falls on me to remove my people from this world," Uloeth stated flatly. "The portal to this world is far below, held open by potent magics. Are your missiles capable of destroying it?"

The smile that came to my lips almost hurt. I withdrew a cube and twisted. Handing it to her, I said, "Place this at the entrance." She nodded.

Meanwhile, Canton held Winch in his arms and stood in the center of the room, his eyes caressing her face. She looked … peaceful.

Uloeth stroked Winch's night-black hair. "I knew her but a short while, yet she was a woman I admired. Such courage, loyalty and faith." Her hard, alien face contorted with some unreadable emotion. "If you wish, I will take her to the Summer Hills, to the Grotto of the Fallen, where she will be laid to rest with the greatest of our heroes. She deserves no less."

Canton's voice was a tattered thing. "She would like that." New tears stung my eyes as he tenderly surrendered his precious burden to her. "You take care of her. She's the most important person in the world to me," he husked, eyes streaming.

Uloeth's eyes glistened with tears of her own.

"Find a way to destroy the Cauldron, or bury it forever. Ephelor's father, the King, will stop at nothing to retrieve such a valuable artifact." With that she left, leaving us to hold bitter things to our chests.

"That artifact is going nowhere," I growled, the harsh sting of grief giving away to a cold, implacable fury. Staring at the long slit of window, I had a hunch and drew my .45, unloading two rounds into the bulletproof glass. So I was right; when the prince left, his spell had left with him, rendering our pistols operable once again.

The two rounds, imbedded deep in the glass, were joined by the rest of clip, then four more after a reload. Bulletproof glass is a misnomer; it is actually bullet *resistant*. Canton unlimbered his weapon and joined me. We had soon drilled a respectable hole in the thick glass, the edges jagged and starred.

Voices emerged, tinny and frantic, though the four-inch hole. I peered in to see David and Jeppeson, both with their laptops, peering over the top of the cauldron. When David caught sight of me his eyes grew wide in fear.

"David, David!"

"Yes, Agent Hakala?" He made damn sure not to come out from behind the cauldron.

"I'm not going to hurt you. I just want to ask a few questions."

"What do you want?"

"How did you find out about the sensors? The ones on the cell towers."

"The P-prince," he stammered. "Apparently he got all the info from Agent Mace."

Damn, should have figured that one out for myself. Must have been getting slow in my old age.

"Shut up, you fool!" hissed Jeppeson.

I had an idea. "David, why don't you come on out and join us? We can use a programmer with your mad skills."

"No! I'm staying right here! Mr. Ephelor said he would come back for us."

Poor David. He was going to be waiting for the rest of his life. Which was only going to last another half hour.

"Tell you what, David. I am going to put a tracking cube in there. If old Ephie doesn't come, my people will. Then we can talk." I twisted another cube and dropped it through the glass.

"What about me?" asked Jeppeson, voice quavering. I guess his nerve had finally snapped.

"Sure, you, too. I know my boss will want to debrief you as well. Arrangements can be made."

"Sure, sure. Arrangements. All the same, I will wait with David here to see who shows up, your Bureau or the prince."

There was one more piece of the puzzle I needed. "Tell me, Jeppeson, where were the nanites fabricated? I don't see anything in that big room except the cauldron."

Silence and more silence.

I'd had enough. My patience for uncooperative assbags had reached an all-time low and I had no time to search for the entrance into that cavern. "Fine, how about I shove a couple dozen pounds of C4 through this little window and see what the pressure wave does to people in a confined space?" An empty threat, but they didn't know that.

"Jeppeson Labs in Seattle!" screamed David. "The boss there, Wykorski, is part of all this."

"Shut up!" Jeppeson yelled.

"Last chance to come on out, boys," I called, cutting off the enraged businessman before he could launch into a monumental tirade against the terrified David.

"Screw you. I'll wait for your boss to come to me." Jeppeson sounded slightly out of touch with reality. And by that, I mean he sounded like his mind had taken a walk off the map.

"Fine with me," I said, adding under my breath, "It's your funeral." Louder. "Okay, boys, stay put, no skin off my nose. Either the Bureau or the prince will be along shortly." Canton and I exchanged a glance and then boogied.

As we entered the room that served as the Vale, I realized I had no clue where I was going and that time was swiftly running out. We had a little less than half an hour.

"Don't worry, white boy," Canton said, voice hard enough to powder diamonds. "Uloeth downloaded a map into my head when she healed me."

Really? "Nice trick."

He took point, unerringly leading the way toward one of the tunnels. "Yeah, swell."

By the time we reached the top of the ladder to the lighthouse, we had two minutes left. I couldn't see the Harvester drones coming, but I knew they were out there, on their way with the most expensive payload since Fatman and Littleboy, the two A-bombs developed by the Manhattan Project. As we opened the lighthouse door, the sun stabbed our eyes, causing them to water.

One minute to go ... We had the gliders open and the cloth removed from both of the cylinders. They were low–heat, high-thrust (LHHT) engines created to add speed and distance for the gliders. With fifteen minutes of thrust, they just might see us to San Fran.

Thirty seconds left ... We ran and hit the drop-off over jagged rocks and turbulent waters, our gliders biting the air. We both reached up and pulled a weighted cord above our heads. The LHHT engines thrummed to life and we pushed our steering bars forward, climbing, climbing fast but would it be fast enough? Wind tore at my face, cold, severe. From above, six trails of smoke dropped down out of the sky, moving so fast I almost couldn't see the sleek, dark darts at their heads. They passed a few hundred yards overhead, but I fancied I could feel the glider buck and thrum from the turbulence. The smoke trails ended just above the ground near the lighthouse and I held my breath, wondering if the missiles would work as advertised.

Behind us Lighthouse Hill trembled, and daggers of rock were sheared from its shuddering flanks. We gained more altitude as the hill seemed to contract in on itself, shrinking before a large plume of dust and flame tore the lighthouse from the summit. Wood and concrete flew outward in an expanding wave of debris that clouded the island.

As we flew, rising higher and higher for the trek to the city, I sent a prayer for Winch's soul. I also prayed that this whole sorry mess was finally over.

But I had an odd feeling.

"Are you okay, Kal?" BB asked while cutting into a gorgeous New York Strip.

I downed my shot of chilled Van Gogh Wild Appel vodka. A little harsh, but the flavoring was nice. Every second of the burn was pleasant pain. "No, no I'm not, and Canton's worse."

We had reached San Francisco safely. BB had arrived, leading the cavalry, and met us in the park where we landed. The Golden Gate Heights Park, to be precise. Fate, it turned out, was not without a sense of irony. Every team not already tackling Supernatural menaces had arrived to save our bacon or avenge our deaths. Fortunately, neither task was required.

Winter daylight had streamed through the windows of the suite I shared with Canton, courtesy of the Bureau. I let the light caress my face as tears trickled down my cheeks. A time of mourning had come as I stood at the large plate glass window overlooking the city. I was dressed only in my jeans. On the ride in the black van to the hotel, the Bureau had confiscated my armor.

Canton entered the living room, bare feet swishing through thick pile carpeting. "What are you doing, white boy?" he asked, sounding almost normal. He held a monogrammed hand towel and was dressed in nothing but a bathrobe, his skin and hair still damp from the shower.

The city in winter looked almost peaceful, content. I felt glad that the Straights would never know about the danger that had loomed over the world. They had enough to worry about with the economy, greedy and incompetent politicians, and the job market. Supernatural threats could unhinge even the most stable of minds.

"Buddy, I wanted to tell you something."

He stood next to me, staring out the window and drying his short, black hair with the towel. "What is it?"

"Wanted to tell you I'm sorry about Winch. It was my fault she died. Shuck was coming for me—"

I didn't see the blow coming—he was *that* fast—but I sure as hell *felt* it. One second I was looking out over the city, the next a ball of fire exploded against my cheek and I went flying. Fortunately, the hardwood floor of the dining room broke my fall.

Blood filled my mouth and I swallowed reflexively, the coppery fluid sliding down my throat. Canton stood over me in a white, fluffy bathrobe, a menacing sight in spite of the cottony garb.

"I ain't gonna tell you more than once, white boy," he thundered, shaking with rage. "She done exactly what she wanted to do. No one could ever make her do different. Not you, not me, *no one*. You ain't the one who killed her, you ain't the one who made the decision to face down that damn dog. It was her, all her, and to try to take that away from her, to make her actions your responsibility, cheapens her sacrifice."

His voice melted and his shoulders slumped. "Don't you get it, Kal?" Face crumpling, he lowered himself to his haunches. "She was happy to die for you, just like I would be, because everyone knows, and I mean *everyone* at the Bureau knows, that you would lay down your life for any one of us. We *know* that like we know our own names. That's why she did it, Kal, because you're *that* guy. So don't blame yourself, don't take her decisions, her sacrifice away from her." Tears started at the corners of his eyes. "Don't do that."

I lay there, swallowing blood, listening to the gush of words, which were like dominoes in my mind, tumbling into each other one after the other, colliding with my self-recrimination, which I now realized was a kind of arrogance. Not one thought had I spared for Winch's sacrifice—the choice she had made to endanger herself on my behalf. Not once had I winged a prayer of thanks to her soul. Canton was right; it was not for me to debate her decisions, for they were hers alone to make and it was the utmost hubris that led me to lay the responsibility for that act upon myself.

What an asshat I had been to attempt to shoulder the burden of blame. Hell, *I* would have punched me.

"I'm sorry, buddy, I didn't think." Slivers of glass clogged my throat.

"Aw hell, white boy. There's your problem … you always think you can do something about things you ain't got no control over." He cleared his throat. "Damn, it's down to the two of us. That's all that's left of the old guard, not including BB." His sigh was melancholy. "You and me, white boy, we are the rocks others break against."

That was the loneliest, saddest thing I'd ever heard.

We must have stared at each other for a full minute before he held out a hand. The calluses on his palm were as thick as mine. I stood, holding his hand and staring into his obsidian eyes, and wondered at my pure dumb luck at having him as a friend. For having the Bureau.

With a start, I realized I'd made my decision as to whether I would stay with the BSI. And Jeanie. That thought was enough to melt the ice coating my heart right quick.

What was out there waiting for me in the wide world? I had plenty of cash, more than I could reasonably spend in my lifetime, but would I fit in? It seemed like it would be nearly impossible to fit a Kal shaped peg into the round hole of the world. For better or worse, the Bureau was my identity, my home, and the agents my family.

What the hell else would I do?

"Hate to say it, but I am sorry, buddy."

The Apache's small smile was heartbreaking. "No problem, white boy. That's why I'm here—to keep your ass on the straight and narrow. No one else wants the job." He punched my shoulder affectionately. "You wanna get drunk? Your treat."

"I would, but I have to meet BB for dinner."

"Your loss."

Later, I took the brunt of the debriefing; Canton was in no shape to endure prolonged questioning and filling out annoying forms. His contribution was limited to a terse report typed up on a RediPad.

My debriefing took hours, but in the end my report was magically verified, transcribed and sealed. My brain felt wrung out and hammered flat; even sorrow seemed leeched from my bones. Afterwards, BB took me to a fine restaurant where, I supposed, he could evaluate my mental condition. In truth, I didn't give a damn. I was hungry.

"Good work, Kal," he said around a large bite of steak. "Can't think of anything you could have done differently."

"Could have brought my entire team back alive." I wouldn't have felt so hollow, as if my insides had been removed with an ice cream scoop, leaving a raw, empty wound.

BB took another bite of his strip, then a drink of Courvoisier. "I've seen some nasty stuff, son. Some very grim encounters. Detroit 1998, that vampire mess in Texas, and our recent troubles. Believe me, Kal, I'm happy we only lost three agents."

For a brief moment, I felt the need to reach over the table and take his neck between my large hands, but it passed quickly. Even in his forties, BB was plenty good enough to put a serious hurting on me. "Only three, boss?"

He carefully set his knife and fork down and dabbed his lips with a napkin. "Listen carefully, because I do not wish to repeat myself." BB wagged a finger. "You led a single team into one of the biggest threats the Bureau has faced in its entire history, knowing that you couldn't rely on the BSI to back you up. Your team faced overwhelming numbers, superior magic, and almost certain failure—according to Joshua's prophesy. Despite all that, you prevailed. You twisted the prophesy to your advantage and conned an entire nation into believing in Joshua Norton."

At my startled look, he smiled wide, an event so rare that I was surprised pigs weren't soaring overhead. "Yes, your little stunt went viral and made the national news. Millions of people now believe in Joshua Norton, and San Francisco's protector is more powerful than ever. If the Sidhe do return to the area, they will have to face a terrible foe.

"So, with all that, plus a couple of duels to the death, your team tugged victory from the jaws of defeat. Yes, only three losses and I am sure you will find that your legend has grown yet again, as well as Mr. Alsate's."

Was I really that dense that people felt the need to lecture me?

Didn't matter. "I appreciate all that, BB, but it doesn't make me feel any better."

"Not supposed to, Kal."

For a while we ate in silence, enjoying fine food and even finer booze. When the corners of my stomach had been filled, I asked, "Who were those people at the Farallons, and what happened to them?" Somehow I didn't think I was going to like the answer.

And I was right. "All of them are dead," he said softly into his brandy. "Preliminary examination shows massive CVAs, as if all the major vessels in their brains exploded at once. Fortunately, their deaths were quick and virtually painless. Most likely the result of the Sidhe leaving this world."

"Damn. Poor bastards. Any IDs?"

BB nodded, a slight frown creasing his face. "Yes, on virtually all of them. Missing persons dating back roughly two years ... engineers, historians, and such. People Ephelor would have needed to mind-drain to understand the modern world. Not to mention the members of the PRBO."

The food in my stomach curdled a bit. "Any idea when and where the Faë arrived on our world?"

"After your debrief, I had Ghost check the records, searching for incursions two years ago, or unexplained phenomena we hadn't been able to account for."

A minute passed. "I'm not guessing, no matter how long you wait for it, boss."

He snorted. "We didn't find a damn thing. Plenty of floods, earthquakes, disasters, but no unexplained incursions. The Sidhe must have slipped into our world without a trace. Or the trace is so miniscule not even Ghost can find it.

"As for Seattle, we raided Jeppeson Labs and arrested the boss Wykorski on charges of espionage as well as confiscated all their nano-fabrication equipment. Safe to say that Mr. Wykorski will be safely esconced in the ADX Florence supermax prison in Colorado." He paused. "We also took out what we suppose was a member of the Unseelie Court dressed in a three-thousand-dollar Saville Row suit. Fortunately we were equipped with iron ammunition."

Just when I thought it was safe to go back into the water ...

"Do you think the Cauldron is really destroyed?" BB asked. I have to admit; he almost made the comment seem nonchalant.

"Uloeth said our missiles wouldn't work," I replied after a sip of Van Gogh. "But she was thinking chemical explosives. Burrowers use magic to fuel their explosions, so I doubt the Cauldron survived with all that destructive magical energy happening. If not, it's buried under a hundred million tons of rock."

BB gave a small grin. "Good." He took a long drink from his snifter of cognac and reached into a satchel he had placed next to his chair, bringing forth a RediPad, which he handed to me.

I scanned the contents. "A contract?"

"Yes. I thought we would take care of business tonight. It's a standard four-year number."

"What makes you think I will sign up again?"

"Kal, I know you better than you know yourself."

"You know I will sign up again?"

"I know everything. I even know the temperature of your ass in that seat."

Gross. Of course he had me dead to rights. "You bugged my suite, didn't you?"

"Of course."

My admiration for the boss rose a few notches. I placed my thumb on the signature line of the contract and the RediPad transferred my print to the document. It was done; another four years in the trenches.

"And I thought I was a sneaky sonofabitch."

BB shook his head as he sent the contract to the Bureau records department. "It's my job to outthink my agents, Kal. That's why I get paid the big bucks." He placed the tablet back in the satchel. "Can you leave for D.C. tonight?"

I shook my head sadly. "No can do, boss. There's a promise I need to keep."

Chapter Twenty-Three

San Francisco Story Concluded

Wilkes still looked dead. Nothing had changed, even though it felt like years since I last visited. I set the sonic scrambler next to his head.

"Hey, Wilkes. Me again. We completed the mission." I gave him a brief account of events. "If you see Ilena, give her my thanks. She was a brave agent. And tell Winch I'll take care of Canton for her."

I softly stroked his forehead, the cool flesh beneath my fingertips a reminder of failure where none can be tolerated. "Oh man, I hear you now: 'Stop dicking around and get on with the story, bonehead.' Right you are, chum. Time to get my clever on and conclude this stunning tale of bravery and horror."

With a heavy heart, I began to speak.

The decision had been made to summon Joshua Norton from his troubled slumber, and we went there that very night, using our FBI badges to force the night-shift caretaker to let us in. Ever been to a cemetery at night? Not like the movies, not even a little bit … no low-lying fog or half-dead trees looming over tilted and broken gravestones. No sonorous hoots of owls or slinking rats, but when I entered that dark and lonely place, I was struck by such an absence of soul, of vitality that it felt as if the very ground was sucking the life from me through my boots. Despite the streetlamps placed at odd intervals, their illumination was weak, as if the light itself was afraid to leave its source.

Mace knelt at Joshua Norton's headstone and burned one of the Emperor's bills, the fire flickering fitfully in the soft breeze. "Joshua Norton," he called out softly. "Your city, your people have need of you."

And there he was, a mournful ghost in ridiculous raiment, pale and transparent, and I felt the small hairs on the back of my neck prickle in response.

"Why have you summoned me from my slumber? The pain of this world tears at me with claws of misery and licentiousness."

Mace stared unblinking at the specter. "Sir, my name is Thomas Mace. I am an agent for the Bureau of Supernatural Investigation and I require your aid."

"I have been woken in the past by your fellows. They have always implied a great need, yet I am but a shade. How can I be of aid?" The ghost examined each of us in turn and when his eyes met mine, I felt an electric tingle along my spine.

"Who is this one?" he asked, pointing at me. "I sense a power within him, yet his future is a window through which I cannot peer."

"My name is Kalevi Hakala, sir," I uttered boldly, trying to hide the fact that Joshua was creeping me out something fierce.

"The music of your name marks you as one of the Finns, Kalevi Hakala. Why is it that I, who bear the curse of prophesy, cannot pierce the veil of your future?"

"I dunno, sir. Not my department."

Mace stepped between us. "Sir, agent Hakala is an interesting specimen, but we face a danger to the young women of your city that could escalate out of our control. There is a man out there, a murderer, who defiles women and kills them with magic. We need to catch him."

The ghost seemed to pale further. "So you seek me out for my vision, my prophesy."

"Yes, sir. If you would."

Joshua Norton, looking forlorn and weary, stared off to the north as if searching for a sign. One minute, then two … finally he let out a low, heartrending moan. Joshua fell to his insubstantial knees and placed his head in his hands.

"No … no-no-no-no-no! This cannot be!"

Mace's eyes were wide with alarm. "What is it, sir?"

"This evil man will slay her! He will … and I cannot stop him; I have not the power!"

"Who, sir?"

"My descendant," sobbed the spectral Emperor. "She will be killed by this man you seek and I cannot aid her. Oh, my heart, I cannot bear it."

Cold little mousy feet traveled up and down my spine. This was my first experience with Joshua Norton's prophetic visions and the raw emotion in his voice slid across my nerves like acid, removing any doubts I might have had.

Canton's voice was cold with disbelief. "I thought he died childless."

The spectral head turned and speared the Apache with a venomous regard. "Not that it is any concern of yours, savage, but during my time of madness, a kindly lady took me in and loved me. She bore me a child, though I did not know it, so lost was I to the madness that consumed me. Alice made arrangements with a priest at the local church to see that the lad was adopted. He grew to be a man of noble stature and keen intellect, a man of heroic proportions. His name was William."

Joshua Norton rose to his full height, ghostly eyes blazing. "And so began the line of Sanfield, goodly folk who prospered greatly, though stricken heavily by the evils that plague this world. World War I, World War II, Korea, Viet Nam, all these conflicts took their toll on the family and now only one remains. Her name is Jessica."

The Emperor of the United States and Defender of Mexico suddenly focused on me and, before I could even blink, was only inches away. Up close I caught a faint odor of dead soil and grave mold. "I sense in you, Hakala, the power to save my sweet descendant. Do so and you will have my undying gratitude and service. Fail, and I forbid you to ever again tread on this hallowed ground."

Wonderful.

Looking into those transparent, dead eyes, I felt the force of his will. "I will try, sir."

"Do not *try*!" Joshua screamed with such intensity it forced me to my knees, clasping my hands over my ears. "Just do it!"

"Sir!" Mace thundered. "Stop it, please! Just tell us where and when we can save her."

Joshua stared off into the night. "North. I see her north of here, in a park on a high hill surrounded by trees and overlooking the city."

Oh crap. "Boss, that sounds like ..."

"Where we just were," finished Canton. "That sonofabitch never left the park."

Mouth beat feet toward our two Vics. "Well, what the [CENSORED] are you waiting for?" she yelled. "Applause?"

No applause necessary. We made tracks toward the gate; however, as I entered the passenger side, Norton appeared, scaring the bejesus out of me.

"Do not fail, Hakala," he said. "If you do, my ire will be ceaseless."

What could I say? "Right, ceaseless ire. Got it." I closed the door in his dead face and we sped out of the cemetery, poised to kill a magician and save the last descendent of the Emperor of the United States.

Dead of night is not how I wanted to re-enter the park on the hunt for a rogue magician, but I had to screw my courage to the sticking point and get the job done. Besides, I had Canton at my side.

The trees swallowed us up with the faint crunch of rotting leaves and the smell of pine thick in the cool air. Cold sweat ran down the flat plane of my stomach, the Faraday coat a stifling reminder that something more dangerous than I was roaming the park.

"Keep your eyes peeled, agents," Mace sent. He, Winch and Mouth were a few hundred yards away, searching the far side for the villain in this story.

"Check, boss," Canton answered.

I was far more on edge that second time around, knowing that the survival of a young woman rested on my shoulders. How do you wrap your brain around that? It was enough to drive a person to drink. Right then, I'd have sold my Lahti for bottle of Finlandia vodka.

"Easy, white boy," the Apache sent. *"I can smell your tension from a mile away."*

Wonderful. What a thought. The Agent of Aroma, the Operative of Odor ... not quite cool enough for a major motion picture. Hell, not even a movie-of-the-week or direct to DVD. Well, maybe direct to DVD, starring Bruce Campbell.

Canton held up a hand. *"Shhh ... hear that?"*

I closed my eyes and focused. A few short seconds passed, then ... there! Muffled, a sound almost like a half-grunt, half-sob, abruptly cut off.

"To the left," I said.

Canton nodded. *"Mace, I hear something to my nine. Keep your ears on; we're checking it out."*

"Check," the big man sent. *"Careful. Squawk if you need us."*

"Check that, boss." Taking point, the Apache led me though the darkness, moving cat-quiet through the trees, our nightvision glasses rendering the heart of the night visible.

My heart hammered in my chest and an insane amount of pressure pulsed through my veins. The world blended into a monochrome blur as fear momentarily robbed me of my senses. I had faced a bug the size of a Greyhound bus and a whole passel of vampires, but the fate of one woman threatened to turn me into a lump of quivering Jell-O. If I hadn't been so terrified, I would have laughed. It wasn't the magician that frightened me, it was the thought of not arriving on *time.*

An angry roar came from ahead and to the right and we abandoned all pretense at stealth, running full out and dodging trees until we came to a clearing. A perfectly round circle of blanched earth told me we had returned to the scene of the crime, but this time there was an extra player on stage. Actually, two of them.

A plump young girl, maybe fifteen, was locked in the fierce embrace of a youngish man, who crouched behind her, using her as a living shield. Blood, quite black in my nightvision, stained her slashed and torn blouse, the only stitch of clothing she had on.

I felt a familiar heat at the back of my eyeballs as the first stirring of rage threaded through me, but I savagely quashed the feeling. I needed to be cold … cold as ice, cold as murder.

The rapist's night-black hair was a long, snarly mess that blended with his victim's. He had a lean face dominated by a beak of a nose, and he snarled at us as we raised our weapons. Before we could shoot, his dark eyes swam with liquid power and the air rent between us, a smoking black hole with jagged edges like torn paper. Through the rip came a stench like rotten eggs and feces with an undertone of burning rubber that made our eyes water and itch. The contents of my stomach tried to make a break for freedom as the blackness roiled with awful violence.

What had waited in the blackness exploded out into the night, an offense to the very fabric of reality. Ten feet tall, the creature was hard to see, because light seemed to be sucked into it, leaving a nightmare silhouette with glowing green eyes. Waves of dark energy boiled from it, spreading hoarfrost across my skin.

Roaring, revealing an impressive array of incandescent fangs— like tenpenny nails in an ape-like maw—it lowered its massive head and charged. Twin spike-like horns jutted from a broad forehead, aimed straight at Canton's tender giblets.

Demon! my mind gibbered even as I fired with the Lahti while Canton emptied his weapon into the onrushing monster.

"Need back-up!" Canton subvocaled as he dodged the monster, ducking under a plate-sized black paw. *"White boy, get the girl!"* A switchblade appeared as if by magic in his hand.

"But—"

He ducked another swing that would've torn his head off. *"Finish the damn mission!"* he roared.

Right, the mission. Cursing inwardly, I scanned the clearing and saw the magician and his victim on the opposite side, only a few feet from the trees.

I ran, hell-bent-for-leather, but before I could get within fifteen feet, the rapist spun toward me, once again using Jessica as a shield between him and the Lahti. Only small patch of his skull was showing from behind the girl.

"Let her go!" I hollered.

The rapist's voice was shrill. "No! You let us go, and I promise to let her live."

"*Canton, you okay, buddy?*" I sent, praying that his head was still attached to the rest of him.

"*Can't … talk … right now.*"

"*Kal, we got his six. What's going on?*" Mace sounded as if we were discussing nifty ways to dismember ghouls.

"*Our boy has a hostage. I don't have the shot.*"

"*Understood. Take the shot.*"

"Did you hear me?" screamed the magician in a shrill voice. "Let us go!"

"I heard you, kid." Take the shot? In my gut I knew Mace was right. The magician had to be put down like Old Yeller and I was the only one around who could do it. You don't negotiate with terrorists or out-of-their-damn-mind magicians. Ever. Period and end of story.

But the girl … so young, terrified and hurt, tears running down her face, lower lip trembling …

"*Take the shot, Kal.*"

"*Mace …*" I could barely get the words out.

"*Understood. Take the shot.*"

A rush of heat flowed over my body, a prickly warmth that dissipated as quickly has it had arrived and I immediately knew what had happened. The kid had tried to cast a spell on me. I thanked God for the Faraday coat and steadied my aim.

"*Take the shot!*"

Little raping, rat-bastard sonofabitch …

"*Take the shot!*"

The kid's voice broke as he yelled again. "Leave me alone!"

"Take the shot, Kal, goddammit!"

"I'll kill her, goddammit! I will!"

"Take the damn shot!"

God help me, I took the shot.

The 9mm round left the Lahti at over 1,200 feet-per-second and penetrated Jessica's right shoulder in a spray of blood and tissue. In the movies and on television, the hero always manages to catch a bullet in the shoulder and soldier on in spite of crippling pain. In real life, there is far too much going on in the human shoulder to allow that to happen.

Take, for example, the Brachial Plexus, a network of nerves that travels from the spine, under the clavicle and through the armpit and into the arm itself. Sever that and all you have attached to your shoulder is ten pounds of dead meat and bone.

Jessica wasn't so fortunate. The slug missed bone and traveled straight through what's called the Brachial Artery, severing it nicely before exiting in a shower of thick blood and pulverized flesh before punching into the rapist's jaw. By that time it was traveling at less than half speed, but still retained enough kinetic energy to shatter a thin bone like the mandible, sending teeth down the magician's throat.

Screaming, the kid dropped Jessica and fell in a heap, clawing at his face. Blood streamed from his bullet wound. My second round managed to miss his ribs and puncture his lung. I didn't have time for a third shot.

With a flash like the world's biggest strobe light, the kid disappeared, leaving behind the sound of thunder and wildly waving grass.

I examined the girl, but it was was too late. I caught a flicker of eyelids and a soft moan before her last breath brushed my cheek.

I had killed her.

As I sat at her side, holding her to my chest, heedless of the blood soaking my armor, I heard a distant howl, the mournful cry of a lost soul in unthinkable agony. That sad, lonely cry ripped at my heart and added to the crushing burden of guilt that pressed the air from my lungs.

From behind, I heard the muted *thup, thup, thup* of rapid gunfire and the roar of a demon. Its black chill beat against my back and crystallized my breath as it left my body. The cold also began to freeze the tears on my cheeks.

"In the name of the Lord, I banish thee!" came Mouth's shout, harsh and strident with fear. "I tell thee, demon, BEGONE!"

I heard an earth-shattering roar accompanied by more suppressed gunfire, then another wash of cold along my back that brought frost to my armor and a sting to the back of my neck. Sighing, I rose unsteadily to my feet as footfalls approached.

"You get him, white boy?"

I stared into the starry sky, trying to find Ursa Minor … the one constellation I always had trouble spotting. "Yeah. One in the chest, one in the jaw."

Mace knelt to examine the girl. "What happened to our guy?"

"Flash of light, then he disappeared."

"What the [CENSORED] do you mean 'disappeared'?"

That Mouth sure had a way with words.

"Like I said, he vanished with a clap of thunder." I rattled off the answers in a straight monotone, too heartsick, too tired, for anything else.

"Teleport … damn." Mace shook his head. "Serves the little bastard right."

I scratched my jaw. "What do you mean?"

Winch stepped up and placed a hand on my shoulder. "It's possible to use magic to teleport, but no one has ever found a spell Shape that could teleport a body *safely*. What appears at the other end of a teleport usually doesn't look … human. It's why the Bureau doesn't look into teleportation anymore. The results are unpredictable and always fatal. Always." He stared at the girl. "What happened, Kal?"

"I took the shot."

Mace nodded, clapped a ham-sized hand on my back and walked away. The ladies began to follow, while Canton stayed at my side.

"What about the girl?" I whispered.

"She has to stay here, white boy. Someone will find her in the morning—the last victim of the serial rapist."

"So we just leave her here?"

The Apache's voice became soft with compassion. "We can't do anything else for her, Kal, can we?"

"What about our rapist?"

"The way that bastard was devolving, if he somehow survived the teleport, then he won't stop killing and we'll find out pretty damn soon. Until then, we stay in town and wait for the second Supernatural event to occur."

A single tear trailed down my cheek and fell into the spring grass. "You know what, buddy? I need a friggin' drink."

Of course I went to the cemetery to apologize to Joshua. A duty I had no real stomach for, but it had to be done.

No funny money had to be burned; the Emperor was waiting for us.

"You killed her," were his first words to me as I approached. His spectral eyes radiated hatred and sorrow.

"I am sorry, Joshua. That wasn't my intention." My throat was dry as paper.

"He was ordered to take the shot, sir." Mace stood with arms akimbo, as if daring the ghost to gainsay him.

Joshua's gaze was icy misery. "It matters not what orders were given. The issue is the following of them. He took the life of my kin, the last of my line."

I cleared my throat. "Sir, you know I did everything—"

"I KNOW NO SUCH THING!" shrieked the spirit, suddenly in front of me, teeth bared, his razor-sharp voice slicing my eardrums. "You slew my kin! I shall have no part of you. You are dead to me."

"Sir," Mace said reasonably, as if irritated haunts were commonplace. Come to think of it, in the BSI … they are. "If agent Hakala were to come to San Francisco in search of aid, you are obliged to give it, even though you may bear him no small amount of ill will."

Joshua kept his icy gaze on me. "You quibble like a lawyer, Thomas Mace, but correctly so. Yes, I will come if he summons me, but only the barest aid will I render. Enough to turn the tide should he be wise, but no more."

Mace crossed his arms over his massive chest. "Sir—"

"I have spoken!"

My eyes brimmed with tears that would not come. "Sir, I just wanted to come and face you man-to-man and give my sincerest apologies."

The Emperor closed his eyes and took a spectral breath. He held that pose for a full two minutes while we stood still as statues. Eventually he opened his eyes. They were bone white, cold, and filled with terrible knowledge.

"What little of your life I do see will be full of strife, Kalevi Hakala of the Finns," Joshua intoned, his voice full of terrible malice. "If you choose wisely the course of your life, then a fine one it will be, but the road is not certain. Missteps abound and you may yet die a sloppy, ignoble death devoid of honor. I pray the latter will come true."

The ghost faded, but his white eyes never wavered from mine and I felt pierced to the soul.

Oddly enough, I was comforted rather than daunted by the foretelling. As long as Iku-Turso remained at large, I knew my choices would be wise. There was plenty of time for ignoble, sloppy deaths thereafter.

I had a promise to keep.

"So that's it, the last bit of the tale." Once again my throat was dust dry from the telling, but I felt lighter, as if a burden had been lifted. I stroked the big man's forehead. "Thanks for being a good listener."

I picked up the scrambler and was about to turn it off when a thought struck me. "You remember the part where the others fought the demon while I faced down the magician? All that 'Begone' and such from Mouth?" I smiled. "Turns out, she was an ordained minister. All teams are required to have at least one, in case an exorcism is needed. Between her and the silver bullets Mace carried around for emergencies, the demon didn't have a chance."

My laughter shook the morgue. "It takes faith to banish a demon, so imagine the most foul-mouthed lady you ever met with faith enough for the world. Ain't that something?"

No answer. I guessed he was taking his opinions to the hereafter.

I gently zipped the body up and slid the drawer back into the wall. Time to go, time to rest while another team worried about a second Supernatural occurrence. Putting the scrambler in the pocket of my jeans, I exited through the swinging double doors, happy to leave behind that hideous neutral smell and the eerie quiet.

Before I took three steps into the corridor, I felt a sharp, stinging pain in my ass. What had to be 50,000 volts of electricity hit me like a runaway freight train. My muscles performed the Macarena without any guidance from my brain and I hit the floor in a convulsing heap.

I shuddered and shook, my mind a scrambly mess as my higher functions went sayonara, leaving me with just enough mental capacity to feel pain. And plenty of it. From my vantage point up close and personal with the linoleum, I saw a pair of shiny, rubber-soled loafers. One of those shoes drew back, then came forward with shocking speed.

More pain.

Out.

Chapter Twenty-Four

The Plot Moistens

The humming woke me, a constant thrum punctuated by a high-pitched squeal every few minutes. The air was stuffy and close and I couldn't see a damn thing, thanks to a flexible stickiness that covered my eyes and wrapped around my head. My hands were bound behind my back with a thin strip of plastic—one of those restraints sometimes used instead of handcuffs. My ankles were trussed with equal efficiency. Wherever I was, there wasn't enough room to twist around. They must have looped duct tape around my skull; I knew by the raspy feet of it and the way my skin stung.

Oil, exhaust and dust … it smelled like a garage. Then it hit me: *I'm in the trunk of a car!*

Wonderful.

Okay, no problem, I had been in tighter spots, meaner situations. This wasn't so bad because despite the aching flow across my muscles and skull, I was still in pretty good shape. No broken bones, torn muscles or fresh burns. However, being hogtied sure had its disadvantages.

A low heat throbbed around my left eye, a dull ache that flowed through the bones of my skull and set up shop at the base of my neck. I remembered the rubber-soled leather shoes and realized I had been kicked unconscious, an act that could have broken my neck or put out an eye. Whoever owned those shoes wasn't particularly worried about the consequences and that led to only one conclusion: I hadn't been kidnapped for interrogation.

This was the first move in my murder.

Wonderful.

Instead of riding the whole thing out in hopes of a rescue, it looked like I would have to rescue myself. It's always something.

After a while the car came to a stop and I heard the sound of the trunk latch springing open. Playing 'possum seemed to be my only option. Footsteps, then the creaking of the trunk lid. A long pause … a sloshing of liquid. Then a soft cloth over my nose and mouth.

Chloroform.

The thick medicinal odor of the chemical clogged my nose and coated my tongue in a pungent film. I bucked, but a hand grabbed a hank of hair and forced my head back while I tried not to breathe in the harsh vapors. The stuff was like camphor squared and it hurt my lungs. I shook my head but the fist holding my hair wouldn't let go and it hurt and God my lungs were on fire ... I wanted to cough and thrash but my movements were becoming sluggish and everything had begun to fade at the edges.

A long, ragged breath … awake. I was awake and the headache that had plagued me before had turned into a big brass band complete with kettledrums.

A groan escaped my lips, whether from the just-awake groggies or the headache, it didn't matter; the sound elicited a response.

"Good, you're awake."

My heart went some hundred miles south of the equator. I knew that voice and a few pieces of the San Francisco puzzle began clicking into place.

Sarkasian.

I opened my eyes. Well, at least the duct tape was gone, but its removal had taken a few good-sized chunks of blond hair with it and probably a few eyelashes. Damn, I'd paid twenty bucks for that hairdo. Now it was a hairdon't.

"So it's you," I rasped, licking dry lips and staring at my lap. My neck muscles didn't want to cooperate. Must have been the effect of the Taser.

Rat bastard.

"Good to know I can get one-up on you, Dumont." Those rubber-soled shoes came into view. Of course, cop shoes. Dammit, getting slow in my old age.

Made the effort and was rewarded; I managed to lift my head, although it weighed several hundred pounds. Yep, there he was in his cheap black suit, head shining in the halogen light of what looked to be a warehouse. An old, abandoned warehouse that smelled of dust, oil and cat piss. And human waste … lots of it.

"Do you know how long I've been waiting for this?" he asked with a nasty grin, crouching in front of me.

I would have loved to kick his teeth in, but my legs and arms had been duct-taped to an old office chair. The black leather had long since rotted away and hung in strips while the foam underlayer lay brittle and crumbly on the metal bones.

"You missed me the first time, dickweed."

He casually backhanded me and it hurt a hell of a lot more than I thought it would. Blood sprayed from a cut lip caused by large, gold ring.

"Watch your mouth," he said calmly.

I spat a stream of bloody saliva at his shiny shoes. "Or what? You'll kill me twice?"

If anything, his smile became even nastier. "No, I don't have that kind of power. What I can promise you is a long and painful death."

True, that made perfect sense. "Okay, Sarkasian, I'll behave." Deep breath to clear my lungs of the chloroform taint. "What's this all about? You suddenly get a goddamn hard-on for us Fed types? Or are you just [CENSORED] [CENSORED] out of your [CENSORED] mind?" So I wasn't feeling very sensible.

Whap! Whap! Whappity-thwap!

His hand flashed almost faster than I could see while the Looney-Tunes sound effects marked a new high in lows for me, and his big gold ring sliced me up a treat. After a while the pain morphed into a strange kind of pleasure. I gave the furious Sarkasian a bloody grin and laughed in his flushed face.

"What is wrong with you!" he yelled, my blood decoratively splattered across his cheeks and hand.

"You think this hurts, you freaking moron?" I burbled through quickly thickening lips. "I've been hurt in ways you wouldn't *believe*! What are you going to use? Nails? Electricity? Glass? Rats?" Oh yeah, my mind was starting to take a ride toward the horizon and my rage refused my call. Leena still slumbered, the beast once willing was now reluctant. "Do you what you want, but don't expect me to comply with your notions of propriety … I don't take advice from those who are trying to kill me."

The detective laughed in my face. "Damn, boy, you got some spirit." He stood, producing a handkerchief from a pocket and wiped his face and hands. "It's going to be fun breaking you."

"You'll fail, just as you failed on that sniping fiasco."

He grinned. "I hadn't picked up a rifle in decades, not since 'Nam. I was rusty. Had I been in my prime, I would have nailed you and that Indian friend of yours."

My head felt heavy and I let it droop. Dark blood from my smashed lips pooled into my lap and I didn't bother to grace Sarkasian's ears with a reply, which seemed to suit his disposition. There came a click and a knife came into view, cutting my favorite flannel shirt from my body.

Glad I was paid so well, the way I went through clothes in this job.

As the last strips of red and black flannel came free, Sarkasian whistled. "Damn. You weren't kidding about pain, were you? Look at them scars! How did that happen?"

Neck muscles protesting, I raised my head enough to look him in the eye. "A red-headed psychotic bitch from hell. You two would have gotten along famously."

The detective chuckled. "You've got balls, Dumont, I gotta give you that. What happened to this psychotic bitch that hurt you so?"

My Interdiction tightened its octopus tentacles around my brain, but I still provided an answer. "I blew her damn head off with a shotgun. Her brains fit right in with her ugly wallpaper."

A hard hand gripped my jaw and I missed the opportunity to lay on a good bite. Don't bite the hand that bleeds you, right? I did release a little drool on his shirt cuff ... It was the small victories that kept me sane.

"You got a smart mouth, Dumont. I'm going to enjoy hearing it scream."

Wonderful.

"Before you get to the hot pinchers and the drills," I managed around the iron vise of his fingers. "Do you mind telling me how I pissed in your Wheaties? Or do you just hate Feds in general?"

The hard hand left my jaw and Sarkasian stood, rubbing his forehead. "Of course you don't know. How could you?" In his soft brown eyes I saw the ravages of painful memories and something else. Madness. The man's mind had gone bye-bye. Probably left without a forwarding address. "It happened so long ago ... what you did. I have been waiting ten long years to run into you and I had given up hope of ever finding you. I had a son." His eyes fixed on mine with manic intensity. "His name was Noah."

Sarkasian began to pace. "When I got back from 'Nam I became a cop. Seemed like the right thing to do. I didn't fit into normal civilian life anymore; it was too strange and chaotic compared to the military.

"Soon after I met Trish, my wife. We were meant for each other, I truly believe that, because there has never been another woman for me, no matter how beautiful or seductive. I only wanted to be with Trish. So I married her and in 1980, and we had our boy, Noah.

"Trish died of the female cancer and I raised Noah by myself. I was content with that because he was such a perfect little boy. So handsome, so smart. He grew into a young man I was immensely proud of."

The final pieces of the puzzle clattered into place and I began to belt out a raspy, hacking laugh that hurt all the way to my toes. "You bastard." Oh damn, something deep down was broken. "That rapist, the serial rapist and murderer I shot ten years ago … that was your *son!*"

"He was disturbed! All he needed was some help!" Spit hit me in the face as Sarkasian screamed at the top of his lungs. "You could have helped him!"

"The only thing I could have done was help him into the grave where he belonged." The moment the words left my mouth, I knew it was the exact wrong thing to say. The detective's fist flew and cracked against my jaw, sending a flare up through the top of my skull.

Over and over again that fist came, pulping my lips. My left cheekbone gave with a dull *crunch*, spiking agony into my brain. I blacked out for a moment. Fortunately, another punch to the same broken cheek woke me smooth the hell up.

Eventually my face tired him out. Good thing, too … I was just building up the manic strength to bleed all over him.

Sarkasian panted heavily and I was proud to see that he favored his right hand. I'd broken it with my face. We Finns are a tough lot, although I had trouble focusing now that one eye was rapidly swelling shut. My flesh and skull felt burned and twisted, throbbing with the beat of my heart.

"You got some sand, boy," he grunted painfully.

"Mdlpt."

"Yeah," he said, "hard to talk with broken teeth and smashed lips, I'll give you that."

"Puhk 'oo!"

"You know what happened, that last night in the park? I was sitting in my living room—in my recliner reading *The Grapes of Wrath* because a buddy of mine at the station told me it was a great book. I was doing my best to wade through all the human misery Steinbeck was heaping on, when Noah appeared out of thin air and crashed into the coffee table, smashing it to smithereens."

Pure wretchedness and desolation colored the detective's voice. "Do you know what had happened to him, Dumont? He was almost fully *inside out!* He was laying in a puddle of his own guts while his heart pumped on the outside of his chest!" Sarkasian came closer, face a broken mass of grief, snot dripping from his nose. "My boy, my beautiful baby boy was dying, and the only undamaged parts were his eyes. They looked *into* me, into my soul, and at that moment, that split second before his heart stopped, he poured all his knowledge into me."

With a shuddering breath, Sarkasian stood and began to meticulously straighten his rumpled and stained suit. "I learned about the magic, about the tramps who tempted him, *lured* him into sexual congress. I learned about *you*!" He tapped his forehead with the fingers of his good hand. "Every day, every night, every moment I see your face with those *Matrix*-style sunglasses and shiny black coats and I *see* you shoot him before he can punish that girl for tempting him."

I stared at him with my one good eye and felt pity. Strange thing to say, huh? Me, all beat to hell and back, pitying the man who was about to steal my life, but it was true. No parent should outlive their child and no parent should have to deal with the fact that their child is a sociopath, a serial rapist-murderer. Especially if that parent is in law-enforcement. No wonder Sarkasian was a few fries short of a Happy Meal.

"I buried my boy at sea. He always loved the water. We used to go fishing out in the open ocean and he had told me many times that the water comforted him. So I wrapped him in his mother's best tablecloth and weighted him down. Ten miles out, almost halfway to the Farallons, I set my baby boy to rest. Two days later I reported him missing. I was quite touched at the support I received from my fellow officers.

"Now I am all alone, but soon I'll feel much better." His glazed eyes stared through me. "Now my son will have his revenge, but there are things I must understand.

"What I want to know, Dumont, is what kind of Fed are you? You're not FBI. They don't act like you, sleep in the same loft or wear those interesting coats with full body armor underneath." I couldn't help a start of surprise. Had I been less injured, my control would have prevented that. "Yeah, I saw your fancy body armor, and that giant bat-thing you fought in your loft downtown. What the hell was that?"

I would have spat more blood at him, but my lips had decided to take a vacation and my tongue was cut to ribbons by the ragged stumps of my teeth.

Sarkasian walked out of view and came back a moment later with a battery operated drill, a three-eighths bit chocked tight and ready to do some damage. He tested the tool, spinning the steel bit with a harsh buzz.

"You probably won't tell me what agency you're from, no matter what kind of torture I inflict, I can see that now. You are far too tough, too stubborn to betray your friends. It's okay, I understand."

The bit came to rest on my knee. "Don't worry, Dumont, this will only hurt … a lot."

It did.

Somewhere in the middle of watching flakes of bone run up the drill bit runnels, along with a crapload of blood, I passed out.

Thank God.

A thick, honey warmth encased me, buoying me in the velvety blackness I found myself in. Womb-like, the warmth penetrated my skin, my organs and my bones, infusing me with a quiet lassitude that filled me with the comfort of a homecoming. My mind slowly uncurled, flexing against the warm cocoon, taking stock of the backlog of memories I needed to process.

Torture. The tearing pain of a drill bit shredding bone and cartilage, the warm wetness of my blood soaking my pants. I'm pretty sure I screamed more than once. Sarkasian's laugh as I writhed against my bonds.

Where had my rage been? Where was Leena?

The scent of fresh-cut grass. *Right here, Kal.*

Leena?

Yes. Tinkling laughter.

What's going on?

You are in another place, where I live. I wanted to talk to you.

I miss you, sis. I love you.

I love you, bro. Always, but that's not what we need to talk about.

What then?

My interference in your life.

What do you mean?

The rage, the power I give you. The magic I inherited from Mom … *you've been using it far too often.*

But I need it! That … you … it's why I'm still alive.

I'm not so sure. Do you realize that you succeeded in the mission against the Sidhe without once calling on me? That is proof you need me much less than you think. It has come to my attention that I have become your crutch.

You've never objected before.

I was asleep before, lending you the magic you needed to be strong and fast, but since that time in San Diego when we banished Iku-Turso back to the World Under, I have been more … awake and involved with our … surroundings. It has been wonderful, observing the wide world through your eyes.

Leena's musical voice grew a touch melancholy.

I have felt what you felt, every sensation and it hasn't all been pleasant. Also, I have been remembering your life since you joined the Bureau, down to the last detail.

Ugh. Not something I wanted my little sister to experience.

It's been like watching a really good TV show you can feel, Kal. But the one thing I noticed, the one thing you've been hiding from yourself, is your loneliness.

Me? Nah, I got lots of friends.

But very little intimacy, bro. You've hardened yourself too much and I'm afraid you'll break soon.

Fat chance, sis.

A very good chance, I'm afraid. That's why I am so happy you have Jeanie. Don't screw that up.

Hmph. You're hardly the one to give me relationship advice.

I'm exactly the one to give you relationship advice, bonehead. Who knows you better than me?

Her voice had become enough like Mom's to scare me a little.

Okay, okay … settle down, sis. I promise. I'll do my best. Really.

Good. Now, about the rage … You have been using it far too much … That can't continue.

Why not? It's been working well for the last ten years.

Because your body is beginning to burn out with all the strain. I have been trying my best to heal you from all the stress, but you are accumulating too much damage. If you don't rely on me less and start trusting your own abilities, you will become too damaged—mentally and physically—to continue. You will die.

Crap. Well, that sucks. So, I can't rely on your … assistance anymore?

I didn't say that. You can always call on me, but do so less frequently, only in times of great need. As a last resort.

How about on weekends for a chat, maybe a game of scrabble?

A crystalline sigh.

No, I wish, bro. My abilities are … limited. We're talking now only because of how close you've come to dying. Only in this place between life and death can we talk.

Could have used you in the warehouse while Sarkasian was drilling into my kneecap.

I knew you would be okay, big brother, because BB had you lojacked all those years ago.

That's right, the micro-locater injected into my left butt cheek during a physical.

Yes. Canton and others had arrived. After the detective had drilled the second hole, the Bureau apprehended him. You are now back at Warehouse being worked on by Alex and Jeanie, putting Humpty Hakala back together again. Since they cannot regenerate teeth, you have a full set of NewTanium and porcelain replacements. Your kneecap and the bones of your face have been healed. Six diamonds full of magic have been used to stitch you together.

So that's it then? I have to rely on … me?

Don't sell yourself short, bro. The Bureau doesn't have any spare borderline crazy geniuses these days. They'll even settle for big dorky ones like you. Now, get ready, they are about to wake you up.

What about you? I want to stay here for a while and talk to you!

Joyful laughter.

Don't worry, silly. I'm not going anywhere.

"Kal honey? It's me, it's Jeanie."

Her face was a dark smear above my own. It took several seconds for her to come into focus. There she was … lovely Jeanie with the big brown eyes. I smiled at that beautiful face, vastly relieved.

"Hey there, gorgeous," I croaked.

Her relief flooded over me as tears lit the corners of her eyes. "Hey yourself, handsome."

I raised a hand and felt my face. All there. My teeth felt odd, but I knew I'd get used to them. "You and Alex did a great job."

A crinkly line of puzzlement crossed her brow. "How did—"

My fingers traced her jawline. "A little birdie told me."

Born in Helsinki, Finland, **Mark Everett Stone** arrived in the U.S. at a young age and promptly dove into the world of the fantastic. Starting at age seven with the *Iliad* and the *Odyssey*, he went on to consume every scrap of Norse Mythology he could get his grubby little paws on. At age thirteen he graduated to Tolkien and Heinlein, building up a book collection that soon rivaled the local public library's. In college Mark majored in Journalism and minored in English. Mark has published three other books with Camel Press: *Things to Do in Denver When You're Un-Dead*, *What Happens in Vegas Dies in Vegas* (Books 1 and 2 of the From the Files of the BSI series) as well as a standalone novel, *The Judas Line*.

Mark lives in Denver with his amazingly patient wife, Brandie, and their two sons, Aeden and Gabriel. You can find Mark on the Web at www.markeverettstone.com.